Joy's Summer Love Playlist

DELUXE

PIPER BEE

First paperback edition July 2021

Book cover art by Amelia Buff

ISBN 978-1-7349492-2-3 (paperback)
ISBN 978-1-7349492-3-0 (hardcover)

PIPERBEEAUTHOR.COM

Sensitive content warning:

Very brief, non-graphic descriptions of sexual assault are contained in this book.

The first was for Jimmy,

The second was for you,

This last one feels like it was a gift to me, so I can finally say goodbye.

Joy's Summer Love Playlist

Playlist

TRACK 01 -
CAN'T BLAME
A GIRL FOR
TRYING

June 5th

BEFORE I HIT THIRTEEN, my arms were perpetually sticky with watermelon juice for the month of July. That subtle sweetness dripping from firm, pink flesh was like a bite of summer. I always kind of wanted to be like a watermelon: shiny and tough on the outside, but mostly soft and sweet in substance. It's funny how freely we dream when we're kids.

That childlike freedom eludes me now that I'm an 18-year-old glorified mascot for my big brother's baseball schedule. And since there is no replacement for the "lucky" baseball tee he gifted to me (which must be worn at *every* game), sticky watermelon-juice arms are a no-go. Any remnant of a stain somehow makes it "unlucky."

I'd say my brother's sports superstition is strong, but he's actually just controlling.

"Shoot!" I thumb the brown patch of mud that materialized on my shirt. I don't know why I decided to put it on two hours before his game.

"What?" Lena asks, perching herself up on her elbows. We're sitting on this fallen tree that's in a secluded clearing near my suburban neighborhood. Her raven hair tickles the bark. No one at school would guess that cheer captain Lena Garcia would drape herself over a log to get a tan.

No one but me, I guess.

"I have to go home and wash this before the game," I tell her. "Carson will flip if it's dirty."

She scoffs. "My dad says you're never supposed to wash a lucky shirt."

Explaining this quirk has gotten a bit old. "Yeah, well, even Carson's superstitions are particular, I guess."

"Screw your brother, Joy!" She rolls her pear-colored eyes. "It's just a stupid shirt."

I'm glad Lena seems immune to Carson. He's a dangerous kind of handsome, but she always brushes him off. Given that she's dated like eight guys since I moved here last year—due in no small part to her supermodel Greek/Latin genes—it's basically a miracle they never happened.

I swing my leg over so both my feet dangle off one side of the tree. *Deep breath.* There's a sparkle of fuzz dancing in the air, glowing from the sun. Sometimes I wish I could float away like that, drifting in the summer breeze. But even once I've graduated from the demands of high school, it won't be that way. I'll be glued to a stadium seat all summer.

Impromptu log-lounging with Lena is as free as I'm gonna get.

I brush the spot with my knuckle. "I can probably spot clean it."

"Wait, isn't it glee's karaoke night? I saw Cale put like ten posters on your locker."

"I told him I wasn't going."

Lena sits up and gapes at me. "But you *want* to go, right?"

I don't answer. Of course I want to, I just can't.

She flops back and continues her unnecessary tan. Her even, medium skin is beautiful enough without sun. My freckles get darker, but that's it.

"You break your back for your brother, Joy," she sighs. "The world doesn't freaking revolve around him."

But mine does. It has to. Otherwise he might break again.

Lena doesn't know that. We've only been friends since the start of senior year, but I still worry every day she'll figure out what happened in our old town last year. No one has yet, thank God.

I hop off the tree, my Converse squishing in the soft ground.

Lena shades her eyes. "Don't go yet! I want to soak this up a little longer."

"You know the sun is supposed to age you."

"Oh my god, I had no idea," she says monotone, then she closes her eyes to bask in it.

This is her favorite spot. When she found out that I lived in the neighborhood across the street, she freaked out in a good way. Her mansion is up in the hills, with an incredible view of the countryside, yet she brings me to this decaying log time and time again.

There's a gleam in her eyes whenever she talks about the guy that brought her here.

"Jin's coming home soon," she says. "Finally."

Jin Park is Lena's neighbor and childhood bestie. She's kept her love for him a secret for years, I guess. All her other friends knew him when he went to our high school, but I've yet to lay eyes on this Korean God of Handsome.

"Do I get to meet him this time?" I ask, hoisting myself up on the log again.

"Only if you promise not to fall in love with him like everyone else does."

"I've kinda sworn off boys for the time being." It's easy to say, but kinda hard to face.

She props herself up to squint at me. "Why *is* that? Are you sure you swing that way?"

"Oh yeah, I like guys." There's no doubt about that, it's just... they've gotten me in trouble. Hence the reason we got the hell out of Salem a year ago. But I can't tell Lena that. "I'm just busy. Carson's baseball schedule is super demanding, and it was brutal catching up to Willow Haven's grad requirements. I don't anticipate my first year of college will be easier."

"I know mine will be," she says, closing her eyes under sunbeams again.

I laugh. "How could you know that?"

"Because Jin will be there." Her soft, full lips roll out a pleased smile. God help this Jin guy.

Lena and I cross the field heading back to my house, jay-walking across the street and passing the very suburban sign that reads "Oak Meadows" in chipped navy paint. Each house in my neighborhood has one of seven faces and one of nine neutral paint jobs. Mine is the color of oatmeal. The only thing that makes it distinct is Dad's random Seahawks gnome.

And sometimes, Carson's red Dodge Dakota parked out front.

I walk into the entryway and peel my mud-covered shoes off my feet with my toes. Guess I'll have to wash those, too. Lena closes the front door after me, shutting out the crisp summer afternoon. I see straight into the galley kitchen, the beige ceramic tile reflecting the sunlight onto my brother making himself a sandwich.

Shirtless.

Ugh. Why couldn't he just wear a shirt?

Wet, copper curls dangle over his sharp jaw, dripping onto his baseball muscles. He glances over at me, his mouth half full. He frowns when he sees my tee. "You're gonna wash that, right?"

I walk up to him. "When you put a shirt on, you can complain about mine."

His eyes focus past me and onto Lena. He swallows and stretches his lips into one of his charming smiles, as if I'm not right in front of him. "Hey, Lena."

"Hi, Carson." Lena cocks her head with a sardonic smile, giving Carson the eyes she reserves for all the boys that have no chance with her.

She folds her arms. "Joy can't go to your game, 'kay?"

I whip my head around, my chest pounding. "Lena!"

"What? He knows you have the glee thing, right?"

Deep breath. I turn to Carson, ready to diffuse. "I never said I was going to that."

His brow tenses. "What, you don't want to come to my game?"

"I'm coming to the game," I assure him.

"That's not what I asked. Do you *want* to?" There's a subtle sparkle of sadness in his honey eyes when I don't answer right away.

"I mean... I wanted to do karaoke, too," I finally say.

A muscle in his jaw pops, but he nods. "Yeah. I get it." Then he softens. "It's a lot of games."

The calm way he takes a bite of his sandwich unsettles me. What... happened to my brother?

I pinch my shirt. "I'm gonna go put this in the wash," I say, my wide eyes watching him. There's no way he'd release me just like that. I'm at every game. We nod at each other before his first pitch every game. I wear this stupid shirt to *every game.*

"No, you should do the singing thing," he says. "Do what you really want."

I shift toward the hall, but look back at him. I'm so confused. But if he's okay with it, maybe I should. "I'll go get changed then. Be right back."

Carson sets the plate on the counter. "I actually gotta get dressed too. Later, Lena." He winks at her. *Barf.*

She rolls her eyes with no hint of a smile. Pretty sure there's no danger of them getting romantic.

In the hall, Carson leans over my shoulder and whispers, "She's into me."

"No, but it's cute you think so," I whisper back.

We pass the gallery wall of mixed childhood photos and kid-mindscapes scrawled in crayon. Coordinated Halloween costumes, Carson's first Little League portrait, my over-painted face grinning post-dance recital, and various sibling side hugs and missing tooth grins. It's evidence that we're attached, but it's also a bit of a facade. Something broke before our teen years, and none of us really know what.

Carson stops at his open bedroom door. His room is shades of blue with clothes scattered like paint splatters.

I put my hand on my door frame, looking over at him. We end up here a lot, on opposite sides of the hall, glancing at each other before we enter our own spaces. He'll always be my barely older brother.

"I'll miss you at the game," he says, almost wistful, but not quite. He's never been good at emotions outside of thrill and anger.

"I'll miss you, too."

I head into my room, the sound of his door closing off-set from mine.

The truth is, I'm a little lost without Carson. We take care of each other. That's why I'm going to his school, Frederick University. That's why I show up at all of his games. I traded my life in Salem so he could have a real future. Even if he's not the most thoughtful brother on the planet, I'm loyal to him.

But I'll be damned if I'm not excited for some actual fun.

I pull my phone from my back pocket and text my only other friend, fellow glee member and textbook class clown, Cale Thomas.

Joy: Guess what?? I can make it tonight! Pick me up?

It takes two seconds for him to reply.

Cale: YASSSSS!!!!! I'm sobbing Becker

Cale: SOBBING
Cale: Gonna be LIT with you there!
Cale: See you at 7 sharp Almond Joy

I giggle at the rapid succession of quips. Typical Cale.

Joy: Sure thing Cale Salad :)

I'm buzzing with good nerves now. Cale's like an energy drink that hits you right up front and keeps you going as long as he's around.

I grin looking at my closet. No matter what I wear, I'll feel on top of the world tonight.

"Wait, you're not coming?" I bolt upright on my mom's floral couch, abandoning Instagram.

Lena sits criss-crossed next to me, scrolling through whatever feed is on her phone. "I'm not even in glee."

True. But I'm not really friends with anyone except Cale, who's friends with *everyone*. They'll all be vying for his attention, no doubt. I want to argue with her, but I'm terrible at conflict.

Guess I'll just suck it up and let the singing be enough. It usually is.

"I still have to pack for next week, anyway," she says.

"It only takes like a couple hours to pack for a week-long vacation."

She eyes me. "Maybe for *you*."

Lena's an odd mix of careless and high-maintenance. She constantly curates her outfits and perfects her makeup, but when she whines about wrinkles or chipped nails, she's completely joking. I'm the only one who gets her humor, I guess.

But maybe we're all an odd mix of careless and high-maintenance, for different things.

I have a well-organized closet with a few vintage pieces, my brother's sports-related hand-me-downs, and yoga leggings galore. When I try to look cute, I pick one piece to center my outfit around. Tonight, my favorite gold peplum top.

It's a special occasion, after all. The first night I've had to myself in forever.

My phone chimes on the coffee table. I grab it.

Cale: 5 mins

It's 6:55 PM. I thought "sharp" meant basically nothing these days, but I should never underestimate Cale. I've learned this.

When I pass the entryway mirror, I tug strands of my dirty blond hair to adjust my black and gold bow before going outside to wait for Cale.

"You're cute, okay? Stop being so fidgety!" Lena slaps my arms. I obey her and we walk out the door.

Cale's beige, unwashed Ford Escort that he affectionately calls "the beater" rolls up at the edge of my fresh-cut lawn. Seven *sharp*. The engine rattles in a concerning way. He turns it off and the sputtering sound makes it seem like the car is struggling to decide if it should shut off or not. It does.

Cale pops out of the car with both arms in the air. "The chariot arrives!" His dark brown skin gleams in the sunshine, but his open-mouth smile is brighter.

"I see I'm the only one who decided to dress up," I say, looking him up and down with fake smugness. He's in his usual pretends-he's-a-baller uniform: a crimson t-shirt that's two sizes too big, shiny grey basketball shorts, and pristine Nike high tops.

"Um, THANKS FOR NOTICING MY HAIRCUT," he chimes, rubbing his head. I crack up because there's no way his already close-cropped hair is more than a centimeter shorter.

"What's wrong with your car?" Lena asks, adopting a judgmental lilt.

He rubs the hood. "I think what you mean, Miss Garcia, is how did my lovely beast get such a unique purr?" Cale points his forehead at her and waggles his eyebrows.

Lena bursts out laughing. "Okay, *Mr. Thomas*."

"At least he *has* a car!" I'm a bit sore about the fact that Carson's 12-month seniority over me is the lone factor in his vehicular inheritance.

"You should really change that," Lena says.

I swing my mini backpack over my shoulder. "How? I have no money to get my own car."

"You could take the dog-sitting gig."

"Lena," I sigh. "Your house is way up in the hills. I have to use *a car* to get there. The need is cyclical." I draw a circle with my finger. She already offered to pay in advance, but the money wouldn't buy me a car with a working engine. The circle motion also represents the number of times we've gone around this conversation.

She shrugs and starts fishing her own car keys out of her fringe purse.

I head for Cale's passenger door. "Enjoy packing."

"Don't have too much fun," she says with a wicked grin. *As if.*

I try the handle but it doesn't open, so I look to Cale. "It's locked."

Cale reaches by me. "Nope. Nope. Just persnickety!" He pulls the handle up with both hands and lifts the door up just enough that it cracks open. "But I love her!"

I get in the car and Cale shuts the door for me. He rounds around the front and crashes into the driver's seat. Then he looks out the window and winks at Lena. She laughs at him.

It's significant how different her reaction to Cale's wink is. Cale's just goofy and genuine, giving the wink like it's a gift of comedy. Carson only winks when he thinks he'll get something.

Notable difference.

Cale starts up his crap car, grinning at me with his thick lips while it rumbles.

"And we are off, milady!" He puts the car in gear and the jolt forward sends my heart racing.

But it's not just the fact that I'm startled. I'm bubbling like a can of shaken up soda, ready to burst.

I was not expecting Garth of all people to pick such a cool place for karaoke. I mean, cracked wood bar with old-school stereo karaoke machines, sure, but this... it's modern, angsty, and refined. Really, the opposite of Garth. But I gotta be honest, that country boy is a lot more than he looks. He's a baritone with a taste for jazz *and* Selena Gomez, wrapped in a plaid button-down and blue jeans.

The Boxal has anime graffiti on the walls, ultra-sleek purple velvet furniture, and a chandelier made of silver tubes. And that's just the entry.

Cale grabs Garth on the back of his thick neck and shakes him like a maraca. "Ooooh! This place is BANGIN', G!"

I can't help but notice Cale's Nikes glow purple in the blacklight as he bounces between everyone like a pinball lighting up a machine. I tend to trail behind because, despite having impressed this group with my voice this past year, I only connected with one. The one who shook me out of my shell the first day of glee and continued chip away at what was left the rest of the year.

Cale hangs back and sticks to my side. Almost literally.

He elbows me over and over. "You ready? You ready? YOU READYYY?"

I squeeze my eyes shut and scream, "I'M READY!" My giggle dwindling, I add, "Thanks for picking me up."

A black-clad staff member with a myriad of carnival-themed tattoos ushers the front of our eight-person group down the hall, so we follow.

Cale shrugs. "I aim to please, Almond Joy. I aim to please."

"I owe you."

In response, he rushes ahead and turns to face me, walking backward. "Careful, Becker. You say that, you *might* just have to make good on it." He cocks his head and swivels around.

As he jogs ahead, I'm really, *really* curious if he means something by that.

Our private party room boasts a slick tangerine couch that curves in a U-shape around a giant screen flipping through ads. Cale weaves through the others and immediately grabs the tablet, fiddling with the karaoke program. On the table is a mirrored tray covered in sodas with various fruits decorating the glasses.

I'm eyeing the one with the watermelon wedge.

"Ooooh!" Cale laughs like a maniac with his face lit up by the tablet. "They got it! Semi-finals showstopper!"

Okay, now I'm excited. We killed it with that number last April.

Everyone squeezes themselves between the couch and the table to find a spot. Cale jumps over the back of the couch and plops right next to me.

"Duet?" he says, holding out a mic to me.

"DO IT!" Emma shouts, sort of echoing the word. She's our blonde, bubbly cheerleader. Not, like, an actual cheerleader, but the one who is pumping everyone up. Second only to Cale.

I grin, holding eye contact with Cale as I snatch the mic from him.

Cale starts "Somebody to Love" by Queen with his lone voice, and everyone else joins right after with the choir vocals as the karaoke machine pumps out the piano.

And Garth comes in with his deep command of the word "love."

Then it's me. I stand up where I am and grip the mic as my singing voice vibrates into the limited airspace, behaving beautifully through each up-and-down note. Then Cale stands up and takes the other part, rivaling Freddie Mercury with his smooth delivery. The rest of the group hits each verse with their choral expertise, sounding like an energetic church choir.

Pulling this song out is even better without judges or Mr. Allen Jr.

constantly tweaking our form. It's fun and vibrant, like the room widens when we come into the song together. Me and Cale harmonize like it's instinct, and Cale's expressions as he sings are over-the-top and authentic at once.

I get this sense of belonging when I cry out to the sky with my voice. I honestly don't feel separate from the song, the message, or the emotion of it. When I sing, it's in my veins. My hips and head and arms respond in rhythm. Everyone else claps or stomps to the beat, all moving as one.

We might've lost semi-finals, but being in-sync like this is its own victory.

Emma takes the final high note, channeling power like Aretha Franklin. Cale yelps when she hits it just right.

We're all a bit out of breath when it's over and the high lingers for a few seconds. I love this part, floating atop the finish as if it's still going. The camaraderie of crushing a performance is kinda unrivaled. I reach for the watermelon drink, giddy and so glad I came.

But what sucks about highs like this: they end.

I notice my phone buzzing on the table with my mom's picture. It turns a fraction with each vibration.

If Mom's calling me now, it can't be good.

Mom's voice is always frantic. Always. But I can't tell if it's normal frantic or seriously-wrong frantic. I step outside into the neon pink twilight to find out which.

Seriously-wrong frantic, for sure.

Carson threw out his shoulder.

I lean against the uneven bricks on the wall of The Boxal. *Of course* he would injure himself when I wasn't there. Maybe even *because* I wasn't there.

I should've gone to the game.

Every self-deprecating thought I'm thinking about myself is echoed by Mom's cracked voice on the other end of the phone. It's like throwing hot sand that gets blown back into your face. *I'm a terrible sister.* I shouldn't have skipped the second tournament game. Baseball is his career, singing is my hobby. Carson really needs my support.

"The medic said his season is most likely over!" she yells at me. She's definitely been sobbing.

"Mom..."

"What's he going to do now?" she questions, though it's less a question for me than for the universe.

Will he have another outburst? And at who? That's my question. Last time it was the mayor's kid.

The swell of the karaoke joint's music flows out when the door opens. Someone just walked out, but I don't bother to see who it was. I'm swimming in a thousand what-ifs. No. More like drowning.

"You ok, Joy?" It's Cale. I suddenly realize I'm crying.

Ugh. How embarrassing.

I pull the phone away from my ear and muffle Mom's cries on my shoulder. "My brother got hurt during his game."

"That sucks," he says. I just nod, afraid I'll cry more and turn into my mother if I keep talking.

Cale offers to give me a ride back home on the spot.

I plop my sad self into Cale's car. My gaze lands on the tape deck and I wonder for a second how many of those I've seen in real life. The old-school green numbers show the time. 8:09. I was out for a hair more than an hour.

Once we're on the road, Cale turns up the staticky radio and ukulele strums blare. He belts out the song, which is particularly ridiculous because it's Sabrina Carpenter's high and sweet voice singing about being a stupid girl in love. *Singing* about crying ironically pulls me out of my wallowing.

I'm actually shocked at how well Cale makes the song his own. He gets the high note like it's nothing. This song is definitely going on my summer playlist.

I'm in better spirits when the next track hits the speakers. I get a thrill of recognition.

"I love The Crux Constellation! I can't believe they're on the radio!"

They balance the synth, beat, and acoustic guitar so harmoniously. The singer croons about love as far off as another galaxy.

"Whoa, she sounds *just* like you," Cale says.

"Really?"

"Yeah, it's crazy close!"

I pay closer attention. He has a point. It's hard to unhear.

The incandescent street lights flicker on. Once the song is over, I'm hoping Carson's season actually is over.

"Sorry about your brother," Cale says, almost like he's reading my mind.

"It's okay." I backtrack. "I mean, it's not, but if he can't play, that actually means my summer frees up. I'm so used to his games that I didn't even make plans. Well, that and I don't have a car so..." I trail off.

"Speaking of that, I got an idea to run past ya." There's a sly smile on his plump lips.

"Go on."

"Ok, so you know Lena?" he starts. My eyes narrow.

"She was at my house, Cale. She's literally my only other friend."

He nods knowingly. Like a mental *duh!*

"Well, I don't think she really knows *me*," he says. He bites his thick lower lip.

I blink. Not Cale, too. Poor guy.

He stutters a bit. "I-I, just, I don't think she thinks of me *romantically*."

"Yeah, I got that. You know there's a support group, right?"

Cale throws his head back in a single laugh and then snaps back to the point. "Seriously, though. I'm hoping to maybe persuade her with a crazy plan. And it involves *you*, Almond Joy."

I point at myself and mouth "me?" He nods profusely.

"So if I wanna hang out with Lena... the best way is through you, right?"

"Right..."

"But if I hang around too much, she'll be kinda weirded out. So I thought you and me could *pretend* to date for part of the summer..."

I laugh like he's joking. He is joking, right?

"Why would that work on her?" I finally ask.

"You kidding? Lena's jealous of you, Becker!"

Of me? This petite, freckled, wears-her-brother's-old-clothes girl makes *Lena* jealous?

"No, she's not," I say with resolve.

"She definitely is. You're smart and got wicked pipes, girl!"

"But *Lena*--"

"Yes, she's fine as hell! She knows it. Obviously I know it. But you've got the girl next door thing working for you."

"Really? Is that why you picked me to be your fake girlfriend?"

Cale laughs generously. "I'm just sayin'... maybe she'll look my way if she can't have me. Don't underestimate the power of being off-limits." He flashes me a grin.

I nod, but only because I'm following. Not agreeing.

"So? It's good?" he asks, excitement registering on his shiny cheeks. My nodding abruptly changes to shaking my head.

"No." He silently pleads, I hesitate, and he's not looking at the road and I'm getting nervous and OKAY, I amend it! "I mean! I don't know! I'd have to think about it."

He grips the steering wheel, tensing his shoulders, then sighs. "What if I sweeten the deal?"

I size him up. "How so?"

"If you agree, you can be the proud new owner of this here vehicle." He gestures to the inside of his car. "I'm getting a Hyundai, manufactured

this century, as a graduation gift, so gotta do something with the beater."
He winks at me.

Despite that the night has turned to black, I know my wide eyes light up the interior of this piece of junk.

A piece of junk that could be mine.

June 10th

GRADUATION. The first day of the summer in between high school and college. Stepping out on the courtyard to meet my family after the ceremony, I squeeze my diploma.

Sweet, seedless summer, here I come!

I should think it's a shame that Carson can't play the season. I *should*. But my fantasies about what this summer is going to be like flood my brain. Lena's poolside, soaking up the direct sun with a sparkling strawberry lemonade and chill house playing. Binge-watching Netflix well into the A.M. Staying past dark at the state fair. Hitting outdoor concerts in the middle of the day. Day trips to the beach for a picnic. Never once worrying that watermelon juice or barbecue sauce won't come out of the lucky baseball tee, because my brother won't make me wear it.

At the moment, though, I still need him to drive me everywhere. So, in that way, I'm not free. But, there is Cale's little deal. I haven't accepted it yet because...

Fake boyfriend? I've never even had a *real* one. Does that make it better or worse?

It's not like I wasn't going to invite Cale to hang out with me and Lena, but I see his point about freaking her out. His plan is convoluted, but no other guy has tried it on her, so who's to say it wouldn't actually work?

And I'm getting sick of Carson bargaining rides for my small amount of freedom. He can never just drop me off or pick me up because he's a good brother. Also, since he threw out his shoulder, he took a job doing administrative and odd jobs at a Victoria Lake Resort, taking his sweet, sputtering truck with him.

When it comes to me, Carson always wins.

I scan the sea of navy robes and caps for my brother's capless curly halo. It's weird to think we were switched last year when he graduated.

It's a bobbing, apparently-recently-cut-his-hair head that I see first.

"Almond Joy!" Cale chants through the crowd. He scratches his neck with his cap in hand.

"Cale Salad!" I say.

His abrupt clap startles me. His face is all business. "Snag a seat next to me on the party bus. We gotta talk."

"Sure thing!" I say, despite my nervousness. He doesn't seem to notice. He's off greeting some of his many friends with high-beam energy.

I know I *need* a car. And a summer with a fake boyfriend who also happens to be a good friend should not be a bad trade-off.

But my insides twist around. I'm really not the best liar. Mostly because I don't want to lie.

Lena's visible through the crowd, all legs even in flappy navy graduation robes. I suddenly recall we were supposed to sit together on the party bus. I'd feel guilty if I didn't know without a doubt that there'd be twelve cheerleaders in line to take my spot.

Where is Carson? Crowds are a bit disorienting for me, even in the open-air courtyard. Unless I'm performing for them, I'm not really a crowd-person. Usually it's the other way around, but I embrace it.

A body barrels into me and nearly knocks me down, carrying the scent of rose-and-sugar perfume. Lena.

I'm immediately at ease. I remember when she was voted homecoming queen, I thought we'd never be friends. But I tutored her when we did physics homework, and later she told me that it was nice to have a friend who didn't think she would stay dumb. I didn't know what she meant until I witnessed her reputation for myself.

"I'm so glad that stupid ceremony is over! I thought people exaggerated when they said you could die of boredom." Her overly-disgusted face makes me grin. She's extra bouncy for a person in five-inch heels who hates dull social rituals. Her manicured hands grip my shoulders and square me to her.

"Five-thousand names," she says. "Five. Thousand."

"More like five hundred. Which really isn't that many," I tell her, and she raises a perfectly preened eyebrow at me. "But it felt like an eternity," I add.

"At least we have Grad Night!"

My heart leaps a bit even thinking about getting on the party bus and finding my seat next to Cale.

Am I really going to say "fake yes" to fake dating?

Lena's olive skin looks airbrushed. Her raven hair catches the wind perfectly, like a shampoo ad.

Then there's me, still pale after an hour of tanning, and covered in freckles, like a grainy image in comparison to Lena. No matter how many amazing photographers capture sad, freckled subjects, I'll never feel glamorous.

Cale's comment about me having a "girl next door" thing wasn't unwelcome, though. Still, it's easy to see why he'd go for Lena. I'm thinking he might need all the help he can get.

"Oh, by the way, any word on dog-sitting?" she says. I forgot they leave for Italy in a few days.

"Still no car," I say.

She rolls her eyes. "That's so unfair! Diamond loves you. I don't want to take him to the kennel. Can't you borrow Carson's truck?"

Speaking of Carson...

"She's here!" I hear him say. He and my parents have finally located me. Carson's field tan stands out in the harsh sun and navy-clad figures. My brother is the kind of handsome that makes him stand out like he's an actor slipping through curtains. Of course, I can only see my big brother.

"Congrats, you two!" he says with that charming grin that never works on Lena.

"Yeah, thanks. Why can't Joy have your truck?" She says it flat and like it's all one word.

I know he's catching ears with that charismatic laugh of his. Once people get a look at him, they're stuck like flies in honey.

"I need it for my job at Victoria Lake and all my physical therapy sessions. She's outta luck."

Ah, yes. Victoria Lake Resort. The big, fancy natural recreation community with giant grounds that attracts enthusiasts of Pacific Northwest nature. Willow Haven, my current unremarkable town, is only about an hour southeast, but technically that's from the resort entrance. It's enough to justify Carson staying on resort grounds while he tackles odd jobs and heals his shoulder.

He tries that cocked-head grin on Lena and she rolls her eyes.

Lena turns to me. "I'll be on bus four. Later!"

I wave as she walks back into the crowd.

I spot Mom's salon highlights and Dad's coke-bottle glasses. Mom hugs me. Her small-boned German arms have a lot of strength in them when I make her proud. Hugs like these are only offered on holidays or when we accomplish the Saturday cleaning.

"I'm so proud of you," she says. "It's too bad you weren't valedictorian, though."

There it is. Where I still lack full achievement.

My always-silent Dad offers me a side hug, and a forehead kiss since it's a special occasion, which makes my underachievement melt away.

Then, I face Carson. We might butt heads, but I still expect him to show me he's proud that I graduated and survived a hard year. He smiles. It's not big, not silly, not dreamy like a lot of his other smiles. It's the most genuine one in his repertoire.

"Congratulations, Joy Bear," he tells me.

I honestly couldn't be happier if I heard the jingling sound of the truck keys. "Thanks, Racecar."

Heavy bass and purple track lights deliver me from the high school's concrete courtyard and into the buzzing party bus. The atmosphere jolts me awake for the school-funded party like an espresso shot.

I see Cale's frantic waving above the seats. "Joy!"

Great. I've got to squeeze past over-excited teenagers to get to the back. I hold my breath, trying to maintain composure as I pass the rows of maroon and teal upholstered seats. This bus looks like it's from the '90s, but I can't tell if it's clean and old or ironic and new.

Lena's barricaded in the front by guys ready to change their relationship status, should the need arise, which is presumably why Cale chose to sit in the back. Doesn't seem like she even noticed that my seat is left open.

"Sit, sit!" Cale says as I get near.

As soon as my butt hits the seat, the bus shifts forward. The driver doesn't seem to care that half the students are still standing. People shout goodbyes and wave out of the windows, but I focus on Cale. He does a quick "coast is clear" check of the perimeter.

"So? What'd you decide?" he asks.

"It's just... what if I don't want to be off the market for a fake relationship?" My voice is a bit of a whisper on the last part.

"Wait wait wait. You eyeing someone, Becker?"

"Pfft! No, I just... you know, might... at some point," I say sheepishly.

He fake-wipes his brow. "You had me for a second there!"

Cale's comedy puts me at ease, but he still seems nervous. His knee bounces up and down. He bites his plump bottom lip and glances at the front of the bus.

Damn. I guess he really does like Lena.

And I *know* I really like the sound of a beat-up old car to call my own.

"Ok, fine!" I give in. "I'll be your girlfriend!" *Only for the summer*, I repeat in my head. My rapid heartbeat still doesn't seem to register this as a business deal.

Cale lights up, even though I was certain it wasn't possible for him to be... brighter.

"Girl!" he says, and suddenly his arms wrap around me, squeezing my shoulders. Just as quickly, Cale lets me go and stands up. Then he pounds the roof of the bus with his floppy hand.

"This girl," he starts loudly, and it's like I feel the flood of mortification before it hits me. Because the last thing I want is the attention of 50 seniors on me right now. "...has just agreed to be my girlfriend, y'all!"

When the entire party bus whoops, Lena's howl pierces the crowd. She grins wide and I cover my blushing face. Guess we'll see how good of a performer I really am.

June 11th

My throat is sore and dry from endless karaoke at the family fun park, but it was worth it. My first night as a fake girlfriend was actually pretty fun.

And pretty not different from just being friends. So that's nice.

I snagged a few hours of sleep after getting home from the all-nighter. I'm bleary-eyed when I get a text from Lena.

Lena: Jin is back from university and HOTTER THAN EVER

That's right. *Jin*. The ridiculously gorgeous Korean neighbor/childhood friend that Lena's in love with.

She sends me a gif of Santana from *Glee* fanning herself. If I wasn't so familiar with the show, I almost would have thought it was a gif of Lena herself.

Lena: This is our year …
Lena: I can feel it

I vividly remember when she slammed her soda can down on the cafeteria table the day she decided to tell me about Jin Park. She launched into a detailed history of their families and their world travels together. She's not high-energy very often, but that day, it was like she'd channeled Cale. It was the first day I realized we were friends.

It's why her romantic flames go out so fast, I think. Jin's always been out of reach for her. He's only two years older, but that's been enough to stunt romantic progression, so she says.

While I am Team CaLena, part of me is already convinced she'll get what she wants and end up with Jin. Since he's been away at the University of Washington for two years, he's been just beyond her sights.

I'm starting to think that him being back for summer could be problematic for Cale…

I have yet to meet Jin, but I have seen his ridiculous mansion in the mountains because it's right next to Lena's ridiculous mansion in the mountains. They basically share a driveway, complete with a lighted fountain sculpture. The one I'll have to be careful not to crash into with my new-to-me vehicle.

That reminds me. I text her that I can take the dog-sitting job.

The three dots blink as I await her reply. I wonder if she'll think I'm dating him for the car... even though I am.

Her message pops up.

Lena: No getting frisky w your bf in my house ;)

Oi. Good luck, Cale.

June 16th

WELL, THE BRAKES WORK. They hold up when I pound them at every stop. Accelerator works fine, too. I don't crash into the Garcias' fountain, even though I could.

I *really* could.

I should have never told my brother that Cale gave me the car. Carson had a raging fit over it because guys only want "one thing."

So yeah, the brakes work.

Zero concern is elicited when the screeches announce my arrival at the Garcia estate. I don't care that I'm driving through the automatic gate to the freaking palace of the gods. I'm peeved about Carson's reaction to my "boyfriend." Mostly because he, himself, is one of *those* guys he went on about. He's such a hypocrite, but I knew that.

At least Dad was there, armed with his extreme work ethic. "She has a job to get to. Shut your trap."

It was honestly the most affectionate thing he's ever said.

The stupid part is that shame still hangs over me. I'm not being taken advantage of. But I am taking advantage of Cale. I'm lying for a car. But if I told Carson the truth, he'd just hold it over me. Guess I choose shame.

Just until summer's over. Then I can take this beater car on my way, guilt-free. Maybe Cale's plan will have worked by then, who knows?

I get out of my car. It's 10 AM and already mid-seventies outside. The summer morning reminds me that good things still exist. There's a breeze like God's gentle breath, trickling fountain water, rustling leaves from manicured bushes and trees, and the blue, hazy hills out on the horizon. The mountain air is clear, like a glass of water for my thirsty lungs. It's a terrible day to spend cooped up in an airplane. But at least the Garcias and the Parks will be in Italy at the end of it.

A limo gleams in the driveway. Rich people. Of course they'd get a limo up to this mountainside. I almost don't notice the silver and black Harley Davidson past the shine of pristine luxury cars.

I wonder if Lena's dad rides motorcycles. He seems the type.

No one's out here, so I grab all of my things myself. I'm one of those people who opts for one hard trip instead of multiple easy ones. I don't care that I'm over-encumbered. I *will* get into the house in one go.

My arms are fluffed full of my preteen dream pillow and blanket, one hand on the handle of my suitcase, and my stuffed Justin Bieber canvas bag dangling from my other arm. I can't manage a knock. I can push the door open, though.

They know I'm coming. I let me and my overfull arms into the massive foyer.

The suitcase wheels get stuck on the threshold. *Great.* I yank the handle and it gives way too easily. I barrel down and crash into the sparkling tile floor.

My pillow and blanket exit my arms like they're spring-loaded. My bag swings upside down and all my things plop one by one to the ground.

Chapstick. Shampoo. Deodorant. Toothbrush. The YA romance novel slides across the floor.

My pitiful teenage existence is scattered around me as I lay on the floor, close my eyes, and question my life choices. I'll have a hip bruise to add to my summer edition of the "Joy is a Major Klutz" collection.

Sigh. This tile is nice and cool, at least. The beater is void of AC, and lugging my junk inside is way more exercise than I'm used to, so I'll just close my eyes and cool off for a sec--

"Uh..."

It's a male voice. I assume Fernando Garcia, the patriarch of this fine establishment. But when I peel my eyes open, I see a remarkably different male.

Whoa.

Like, *really* whoa.

His inquisitive face is the most good-looking thing I've seen, like, ever. An amused smile unfolds on perfect lips. "You okay?"

He offers his hand to me, so I take it. Was there a reason I was on the floor? The heat returns to me.

"I'm fine," I say after I'm upright. My word, this human is gorgeous. Smooth skin, long neck under a sharp jaw, black hair textured just enough to look effortless but not messy. His dark eyes squint slightly as he gives me a heart-melting smile. It's like a lipstick commercial, but in a masculine way.

This is definitely him.

"Jin Park," he says. I realize I had never let go of his hand. I take my hand back and laugh courteously. Or nervously. I'm not sure which.

"I know," I say. His eyebrows go up and I stammer. "I- I mean, I'm Lena's friend. I've heard of you. Joy!" I wince. "Joy is my *name*. Sorry."

His mid-range voice makes his laugh sound sultry and innocent at the same time. Is that even possible? "Don't be sorry. Nice to meet you, Joy."

I smile briefly before assessing the damage. Immediately, I gather my ridiculously embarrassing items. Jin bends down, but I tell him not to

worry about it. Instead of listening, he lifts my pillow and blanket from the floor and moves them to the stairs.

He touched my hot pink fuzzy Barbie blanket. And Lisa Frank pillow. The blanket is from my tween days, but the pillow is a recent acquisition. Not that it matters. They're both very unsexy.

"I see you met our dog-sitter!"

Now *that* Puerto Rican voice I know belongs to Fernando Garcia. And the aroma that suddenly hits me is unmistakably his chocolate chip cookies.

I whip around to confirm.

"Are those for me?" I ask in desperation. I can always be distracted by cookies.

"No, they're for TSA," he replies in his thick accent, with a smirk on his goatee. I chuck my chapstick at him and he barely dodges.

"Resorting to violence, Miss Joy?" Mr. Garcia's eyes are playfully wide. We're both grinning.

"I'll keep your dog alive while you're in Italy!" I offer in a sing-song manner.

Jin chuckles. I'd forgotten he was standing there.

"Were we supposed to pay her in cookies?" he asks, his question directed at Fernando.

We?

"Oh, you're here!" The voice above is Lena's. She leans over the rail. Their bright foyer is two stories tall, with a chandelier and a massive window as the main features. Yet, Lena seems to sparkle far more. She bounds down the curving staircase, which is presently decorated by my garish middle-school bedding.

Her high ponytail sways as she bounces down the steps. She's in a casual pink tee, yoga leggings, Nikes, and Ray-Bans that complete the glamorous traveler look I'm sure she was going for.

She reaches the bottom and immediately places her hand on Jin's arm.

"Can you go up and get my luggage for me? It's a little heavy." Her smile is almost sweeter than the smell of brown sugar and chocolate and butter coming from the kitchen.

"Sure," he says. It's neither eager nor fake. He looks at me. "Should I take your stuff upstairs, Joy?"

I blink. He said my name so easily.

"Um... okay." I internally facepalm. *Yes, please take my unsexy bedding up to Lena's immaculate bedroom, thanks!*

"I'm so glad he's back," Lena whispers to me as she breezes past, tossing her sunglasses on top of her head.

I follow her into the kitchen. Nearing the cookies grounds me. I can see them through the archway, still radiating on the sheet pan Fernando placed on the granite-top island.

Lena reaches for one, but Fernando swats his spatula at her and she jumps back. He's wearing a frilly apron. Classic Mr. Garcia.

"Dad!" she scolds.

"I made a deal with the devil!" he says with exaggerated intensity. My generous laugh echoes throughout their immaculately clean and immaculately designed kitchen. I hover over the fresh-baked goods. These cookies are life. The gooey chocolate, browned butter, sugar, sea salt... I know they'll melt in my mouth. They probably *could have* paid me in cookies.

A pudgy ball of orange creamsicle fur waddles into the room. Diamond is the chillest corgi known to man. People would pay to hang with him, but I managed to get them to pay me for it. Don't say I'm not an evil genius.

The sight of the dog reminds me.

"I'm curious why Jin said 'were we supposed to pay her in cookies?' What did he mean by 'we?'" I ask Lena, as she attempts to grab another one.

Lena's eyes open a little wider. "I didn't tell you?"

Fernando overhears and swats at Lena's hand. "This is now a bribe!

Hands off!"

She shoots him a mean look and drops the cookie back onto the pan. "I told the Parks you could watch their dog, too. I figured it wouldn't be that much more work for double the pay."

Double the pay? I'm already getting overpaid to spend the week in a pristine mansion, cuddle a fat corgi, marathon whatever I want on Starz, swim in their heated pool, and marvel at their view of the rolling hills and farmland during the best weather week in the Pacific Northwest.

Jin walks into the kitchen. "Are those—"

"They're a bribe!" Fernando says, attempting to look intimidating by pointing his spatula at Jin's surprised face.

"Oh, that reminds me," Jin says. He reaches into his back pocket, then holds out an envelope to me. "This is for watching Zany."

"Zany?" Interesting name for a dog...

"Joy didn't know she was watching two dogs," Lena informs him.

Slight disappointment manifests in his expression. "Oh."

"Oh no, no! It's fine!" I say, to ease any immediate worry. "You don't have to pay me. The cookie bribe is plenty."

Jin smiles and pushes the envelope forward again. "No, you saved us. Zany will be happier at home. And I can't bring this back to my mom." He whispers, "Take it."

Diamond bumps into my leg and I stumble forward, a little too close to Jin. Then, I pluck the envelope from him.

"Thanks," I say, backing away.

In the span of a few seconds, my earnings doubled and my workload barely got any heavier.

Cale's puppy love for Lena is really paying off.

Once I've waved farewell to the limo filled with glamorous rich people on their luxurious trip to Rome and Tuscany, I head up to Lena's room with a mouthful of cookie. She has a fluffy queen bed with an indigo velvet upholstered headboard that made me drool the first time I saw it. Diamond has a castle dog bed. Dog panting echoes in the empty house.

Even though I ate, like, four huge cookies, I'm still starving. Food may be the first order of business.

...after I relax in my solitude for a second.

I can't believe I just earned fourteen hundred dollars to vacation in a mountain mansion. Two of them!

Hopefully Zany is as easy going as Diamond. He is already snoring in his comical dog bed. I copy him and fall back onto Lena's velvety, queen-size comforter.

My horizontal orientation reminds me of my introduction to Jin Park.

He's the first person I've ever met while lying down. So that was interesting.

And no freakin' wonder Lena's taken with Jin Park. He's Korean dreamy, like a K-pop idol who has a thousand gifs of him smiling. He doesn't seem to know it. The sight of his bony shoulders under that plain white tee lingers in my mind. Do I have a thing for shoulders?

All I can say is Cale's getting a run for his money.

The subtle way she touched his arm, the way her eyes lit up when he entered the room, I mean... I've never seen her like that. And they're on a literal Roman-tic trip together, right this second.

I'd be jealous, but I can't even believe my current fantastic situation.

I trace the Park's house-key with my fingertip. I briefly greeted Jin's mom, Jan-di Park, before they took off. She said, in her adorable broken English, that the instructions for Zany's care would be in the envelope with the money. I open it up.

Hmm. Sure looks like it's just cash. Okay...

It's just a dog. I mean, I can handle a dog without the instructions. Even if I've never technically done that until right this second.

TRACK 04 -
ONE CALL
AWAY

Still June 16th

WELL. YEAH. I WAS WRONG. A few hours into this gig, and I'm already in way over my head.

Do black labs often growl? I'm too afraid to get close and find out why. When they joked that she got the name "Zany" for a reason, I was dumb enough to think they were teasing.

Nope. She's actually moody.

My butt's getting sore from sitting on this slate floor in the Parks' equally gorgeous kitchen. Their mansion is decked in different colors, with a contrastive palette of cream and mahogany. I think it's Korean influence with straight lines, solid wood and gold details. It's like an art exhibit or a lived-in antique shop.

Normally I like being alone, but massive immaculate mansions test the limits of my introverted nature. Maybe I'm more of an ambivert?

Zany yips from her kennel. My confidence in dog-sitting skills is dwindling. Fast.

I bite my lip. I could really use back-up. So I text Cale.

Joy: You don't know anything about dogs, do you?

I watch for the three dots. Zany won't come out to eat. If I so much as put my hand near her kennel, her vocals rumble at me. I even carried Diamond over here to spread his calming energy, to no avail.

Cale: Yeah. My mom's a dog trainer, why?

THANK THE GOOD LORD. I swiftly type out my message.

Joy: This dog I'm taking care of growls anytime I get close to her.

Cale: Hungry? Hurt?

Joy: Idk. I can't get close enough to her cage to figure it out. But she hasn't eaten in like a day.

Cale: Did she mess her kennel?

Joy: Don't think so

Cale: She's prolly scared

I peek at Zany through the crisscrossed grate. She's not showing teeth. No furrowed brow or snarling. I wish I could read dogs. Of humans and animals, Diamond is the only creature who makes sense to me.

Cale: I can come by if you want. Turn on my charms ;)

Joy: Do they ever turn off? lol

I hug my knees and set my phone on the floor. I *am* kinda craving human interaction. Lena's text about "getting frisky" echoes in my head and I blush. There's no chance of that, but still.

I send Cale the address and gate code, and I'm relieved already. Diamond snuggles up next to me and I pet the folds of his neck.

Twenty minutes go by, then the deep gong of the doorbell echoes into the high, crown-molded ceilings. Diamond skitters off my lap and beats me to the stained glass front door. I could not be more thankful for the bright, toothy grin that greets me when I open the door.

Cale's oversized t-shirt and basketball shorts are stark against the fanciful entry decor, which reminds me of those carved frames you see in museums. Basically, he looks like a gumball on fine china.

His whistle reverberates off the vaulted walls and the bronze chandelier that hovers over us. It's decorated with hummingbirds. The two-story wall opposite the entry is covered in a cherry blossom wallpaper with an apple red background.

Cale's Nikes squeak on the floor and I stop him. It's walnut and oat basket weave wood floor, far too shiny to lay a shoe on.

"You cannot wear those in here!" His surprise invites me to whisper, "They're *Korean.*"

His head snaps back. "Lena's Korean?"

I laugh. "No! I'll explain, just take your shoes off!"

As he unlaces his shoes, I think how strange it is to see my plastic-school-chairs, hamburgers-and-french-fries friend walk into this place. Then again, in my college sweatshirt, I probably look pretty foreign, too.

When I point to the kennel, Cale clicks his tongue repeatedly. Tip-toeing with his lanky fingers held out, she sniffs him. Zany growls.

"You scared, sweet girl?" says Cale, in a high pitch voice. He keeps his cool as she watches him swing the grate open slowly.

He's calmer than usual. I didn't know he could be so even-tempered.

I stand about ten feet away, with Diamond in my arms. His panting sends dog breath stinking up my personal bubble. Still, it's comforting.

"They got a fence outside?" Cale asks me.

I point to the door at the corner of the kitchen. "There's a dog run through there," I say. Cale nods.

With low energy like a gentle stream, he goes and opens the back door. Then he distances himself. There's a comforting smile on his face when he looks at me and I release a breath I'd been holding. Cale's usually bounding with puppy-like energy, which is something I like about him, but I had no idea he could come to my rescue. With calm.

Suddenly I hear the skittering sound of dog nails on the slate floor as Zany races out the door. She's a shiny black blur. Her kennel shifted back a foot in her speedy escape.

Cale steadily walks over and peeks out, confirming exactly what I hope he would. A report of abundant excrement and urine.

Then, he examines her bowl of food that I set out. He takes the time to *read the bag* and adds hot water like I should have done hours ago. He puts it right by the opening of the door and then takes a seat with me on the kitchen floor to observe.

Eventually, Zany sheepishly walks up and eats.

Cale gives me his cheesiest big smile.

Finally, I can relax. "I owe you one, Cale Salad."

"Nah! I'm happy to help." He scratches Diamond's ear. "But, uh, whose Korean?"

"Oh yeah. This house belongs to the Parks. Lena's is next door."

"Really?" He sounds intrigued.

"Yeah. They're super close, like one big family. They're on their trip to Italy together."

"Cool." His eyes wander as he places his lanky elbows on his knees.

Should I warn him about Jin? Or would that be pointless?

Cale turns his head to me. "So, what does a girl like you do with *two* huge mansions and a couple of mutts?"

"Excuse me, this is a purebred corgi."

Cale's deep, somewhat goofy laugh always puts me at ease.

"But, to answer your question," I continue, "I make full use of their pool and Starz subscription."

His laugh stops immediately and he startles me by getting up abruptly.

"Then let's go, girlfriend!" he says to me, and then stops in his tracks, turning around to give me a sly look, "Get it?"

"Ha, ha," I offer in consolation.

June 21st

Floating in the vaguely cold pool would be much nicer if I were totally alone and not worried about an impending cannonball. But here I am, periodically opening my eyes at every twitch of the water surface so I can dodge Cale's manufactured tsunamis.

I'm failing, obviously.

These past few days have been way nicer with him here to help with Zany, but while I am seriously grateful for his last-minute heroism, I didn't expect he'd be by in his new-to-him car every day. However... my offering to watch all the Harry Potter movies with him might've insinuated an invitation. As much as this muggle loves HP, I kinda wish I hadn't committed to the marathon. The average person doesn't get the chance to live in a secluded mansion and soak up 100% autonomy.

Splash!

Fat drops of water spray me. Now I'm soaked. The beating midday sun had just dried my front.

"Cale!" I scold when that sparkly brown head pops up.

He pretends to be oblivious. "What?"

I wipe my face with my hand. "You're ruining my spa vibe."

"What's the point of a pool if you can't cannonball?"

I roll my eyes, but he has a point. He's here to have fun. And I feel kinda selfish for wanting this place to myself.

I'm just gonna call it quits and dry off with a towel.

The pool water cascades down my body when I lift myself out of the pool. My black one-piece catches a drift and cools me off. I grab a towel and dab my face.

"I'm gonna order a pizza."

"How many movies we got left?" He pulls himself out of the water too.

"I think there are four left."

He grabs a towel, too. "But I thought there were only 7 books."

"They made the last book into two movies. Which I still can't believe you haven't seen!"

"Take it up with my mom!"

Cale's mom is very kind... and *very* formidable. "No thanks," I laugh.

"No, you're right. Bad idea!" The way his laugh dwindles reminds me of a young Will Smith, *Fresh Prince* era. He stands a little close to me, the faint cologne that's mixed with the chlorine burns my nose.

Lena's warning text rings in my head again. *No getting frisky.*

I swing my striped beach towel over my shoulders like a cape and cover up what's left of my exposed skin.

I hope I'm not blushing. IhopeImnotblushing.

Briskly I walk into the house without another word because, even though Cale is my *friend*, it feels like there's some line we've crossed. Faking a relationship. Being alone in a glamorous mansion. Standing inches away in our sopping wet bathing suits.

That friendly smile just felt a little heavier than I expected it to.

"Hey, Joy?" He glistens, framed by the back door and harsh sun. "You're not mad, are you?"

I try to sound cheery. "No! I'm not mad."

He smiles. "Okay, just checkin'."

I remind myself that Cale is interested in Lena. That's the whole reason I'm even standing in this place. He gave me his car, I'm faking a romance with him, and the rest of it, the reality part, is that we're friends. Though, if I'd known Cale was going to come by as often as he is, I probably could've cut him into the deal as my chauffeur instead of doing the fake dating thing.

Then maybe I wouldn't be feeling my heartbeat in my face when he smiles at me.

TRACK 05 -
NEVER BEEN
IN LOVE

June 24th

LIGHT-FILLED PICTURES OF MY FANTASY DREAMS pass under my thumb as I scroll. I'm finally back in my own room, lying on my white down blanket that is much homier than Lena's luxurious bedspread. I appreciate my naked walls and cotton sheets a lot more when I've been away from them for a week, even if I am daydreaming while searching AirBnBs on the Oregon Coast at nine in the morning.

It's easy to dream a bit more since I had an unexpected influx of dog-sitting cash. I offered some to Cale, but he said the intro to Harry Potter was more than payment enough. It doesn't seem fair since I probably couldn't have walked her by myself without his advice.

My house is super quiet now. Carson decided to stay at the Victoria Lake Resort so he could keep up with the appointments and injury-friendly resort jobs. I'm finally alone like I wanted. And bonus: the Cocoa

Puffs last a lot longer.

I don't know what is so appealing about getting away by myself. I want to hear the ocean waves, smell the salty air, feel tiny grains of sand massage my feet. I'll spend my money on something boring and useful if I don't force myself to book something.

Lena sent me a long string of vacation pictures over the course of her trip, but I haven't had the chance to ask her how things went. I switch to that text chain and get lost in the images of her heavenly Italian excursion. Warm gradient sunsets, handmade pasta and deep red wine, and most notably, sunny selfies with a certain Korean gentleman.

I saw lots of pictures of Jin around his house. A few in a neon-lit city in Korea at various ages. One of him riding a horse on a ranch, fishing in another, holding awards for piano competitions. My favorite was where he had a wide grin with surprised eyes, surrounded by Christmas wrapping paper like he'd opened some remarkable, long-awaited gift.

My new favorite is the one Lena sent me. He's super cute.

The phone buzzes, as if it's judging me. It's Lena complaining about jet lag.

I haven't forgotten about my sacred duty to Cale. I figure I can feel out where she's at if I ask how "things" went with Jin.

Lena: Nothing romantic :/
Lena: The mood never quite struck. Our parents were ALWAYS around.
Lena: But, it was still...

She sends me a gif of Heidi Klum saying "Perfection."

Joy: I'm glad you had a good time :)
Joy: Too bad about the lack of mood haha
Joy: You'll get another chance
...
Lena: True. It was fun to see Italy together.
Lena: ...even if I am burning to make-out!!

I wonder if the yearning gets stronger for someone who *has* actually made-out before. I have no qualms about my lack of experience, but I kinda want to know what it's like to have a *real* kiss. The kind that's mutual and fun and... *burning*.

Maybe I'm not the *burning* type.

I've never met a guy I really wanted to kiss. At least, not enough to put him through my brother. It's risky enough that Cale's my fake boyfriend. I'm totally fine remaining unkissed at the moment.

Thinking about Lena has me mindlessly scrolling through her Italy pictures again. Impressive limestone fountains with detailed scenes. Impossible architecture. Food that belongs on Zeus's table. I find one of their two families. Two golden only-children and four parents. Jin's dad sticks out in this picture for some reason. I saw younger pictures of him at the house, but here he looks oddly familiar. Then again, he looks a lot like Jin.

I swipe back to my favorite pic. Lena in a wide-open smile and Jin playfully raising an eyebrow at the camera.

How can he look *that* cool and *that* goofy in one facial expression? It's unfair.

I put my phone down. I can't develop even a minuscule crush on this guy. He's cute and all, but he is off-limits. Lena has history with him, and I've been through enough to know how much that matters. Until she notices Cale, I refuse to be one of those girls that Lena told me about.

I should probably give the plot a nudge, though. My plan included getting them both to the State Fair with me and letting Cale's sparkly personality do some legwork. I gear up to text her.

Staring at Lena's most recent message, it suddenly occurs to me: is she going to wonder if Cale and I never kiss?

My heart picks up pace as I rest my phone on my chest. She's *definitely* going to broach that territory.

So, either I give Cale my very first (fake) kiss, or I come up with a way to work around it. I don't *hate* the idea of kissing Cale. It might be kinda nice...

But I'm not sure I could go there for something that isn't real. No, I know I want genuine romance if I'm gonna kiss someone.

My phone buzzes. I flip it up and the soft light burns my tired eyes.

Lena: We still on for the fair this weekend?

That was an easy way to broach the subject.

Joy: Of course! You've never been! You NEED to

Lena: K! Looking forward to it :D
Lena: Be sure to bring your BF ;)

Joy: Will do

My mission is clear: capitalize on the fun/lovey-dovey nature of both the State Fair and Cale Thomas.

TRACK 06 -
HOLD MY
HAND

June 27th

I AM WAY TOO EXCITED to care about my blistering steering wheel or the hot tornado that whips through my car on the drive to the fairgrounds. I park in the dead grass field next to other dusty cars. Windblown stray hairs stick out from my blonde *Anne of Green Gables* braids. I'm kinda channeling Anne today, with my freckled skin, bright eyes, and high spirits. I'm pretty sure I was in a similar state when I first came as a kid, braids and all.

I spot Lena's pink wheeled VW Golf, but I still have to roll up all four of my windows manually before I can head over there.

Still glad it's mine.

The dried-out grass scratches the exposed skin on my ankles as I walk. Aromatic waves of greasy food hit my nose and the sound of wailing fair-goers tugs my thrill. The Washington State Fair was a few hours drive from my hometown, but it was supposedly better than Oregon's and at a better time in the year. When I was ten, I tenaciously convinced my folks to make the trip.

Even though it's lost some of its luster, there's another kind of magic in the nostalgia.

I'm within a few feet of her car when Lena spots me and rolls her automatic window down.

Oh. She's not alone. Jin's in the passenger seat.

He half-salutes, half-waves at me and I wave back.

Lena's wearing her hair the same way as me. A more Dorothy-esque look with her blue gingham top, but I know two things for sure: 1) Lena is particular about her hair, and 2) she does not like to match looks.

I make quick work of taking mine out. I mind far less than she does.

Jin emerges from the car into the beating sun. "Why take them out? They're cute."

Cute?! Whoo, I'm sweating already. Is the temperature really that high today?

"It would be weird for the veteran to play twins with the State Fair virgin," I say, averting my eyes from the way his stretching lifts the hem of his shirt.

Lena turns her car off and steps out. I'm not sure she heard what I just said, but Jin chuckles.

"Where's Cale?" Lena asks. She playfully stabs my side with her finger. "You invited your boyfriend, right?"

I swat her hand away and my heart races a little because Jin now knows I'm not single.

Even though technically I still am.

"He's driving himself." I pull my hair up into a ponytail.

Lena's *Wizard of Oz* Dorothy-themed outfit is almost comical. Almost. She could wear grocery bags sewn together with seaweed and look runway-ready.

She breathes deep and coughs. "Is that grease?" Disgust flickers on her face.

"Get used to it," says Cale, weaving through parked cars from behind. "That glorious fair food is going to turn in your stomach all night."

Lena scrunches her face, then takes a drink from her glittery water bottle.

Cale reaches an open hand across the hood of Lena's car.

"Hey, I'm Cale Thomas. Boyfriend extraordinaire."

I sputter a laugh.

Jin receives Cale's hand. "Jin Park. I... uh... can legally ride a motorcycle in all fifty states."

"Oh, I see," Cale says, his face serious. He pulls his hand back. "A one-upper."

"Let's get this over with," Lena says, but when she looks at me, there's a side smile on her glossy pink lips.

Cheap wristbands always stick to the little hairs on my arm, but the benefit of all-access to the fair activities is worth the few plucked hairs it costs me. It smells like dirt and fried fair food. Funnel cake, popcorn, french fries. The first layer of suntan sets in as people buzz around like bees, chomping shaved ice and corndogs. The Vegas plinking sounds from fair games and the creaking of rickety portable rides transport me to when I was tiny. Well, tinier.

I wore pigtails, not braids. Overall shorts and Carson's old t-shirt with the hole in the side. I lived in that outfit until the seams left indentations because I'd gotten so big.

But here I am, feeling like I'm in it all over again. I wish nostalgia wasn't so faintly soured by the reality of growing up.

"What should we do first? Games? Rides?" Cale asks, buzzing with excitement. "PETTING ZOO?!"

"Not before we eat, please," Lena says, her golden arms retreating close to her body.

Cale points at her. "Fair point, Ms. Garcia. More sanitary to eat first."

The crowd swerves around us. My feet are antsy to flow with them, but I don't know where I should end up. I spot an empty patch of dirt out of the stream and dash through fairgoers for it.

I expect the other three to follow, but I lost them. Scanning the crowd helps nothing.

Jin startles me by leaning in, his shirt brushing my shoulder. His scent is floral, but not feminine. Clean. Maybe peppery. I know this flower, but I can't name it.

"I should probably tell you I'm a State Fair virgin too," he says. His expression fakes embarrassment.

"Seriously? I have to teach *you* my ways too?" I say.

Jin shrugs with a grin on his face. I scratch my neck even though I don't itch. That smile was a lot like the first one he gave me. My nerves are jittery.

We're joined by Lena and Cale within a few seconds. I'm half-relieved that I'm no longer alone with Jin.

Why only half, I wonder?

What could a couple of State Fair pledges be compelled to do for initiation? My short stature makes my search difficult, but then I see the faded slate gray paint, rickety mechanisms, and depressing broken sign.

It's. Perfect.

"First, before we do anything else..." My sinister grin and pointed finger guide the helpless newbies. "Initiation."

It's still early, so the line to get into the Haunted House is short. Cale waggles his eyebrows and rubs his hands together to set the mood. Those who exit the attraction leave with expressions that clearly say "one-star review," but I don't care. If they hate it, it will have done its job.

"No open-toed shoes," the mid-teens polo-clad staff member tells Lena. She points to the sign and raises her brow. The famous Garcia look of irritation settles on Lena's face. The teenager says, "I don't make the rules." And then waves her away.

This isn't good. I don't want to lose so early in the day, but I have no idea how to get Cale and Lena in this broken-down attraction.

"I've got sneakers in my car, it's fine. Can you guys wait, like, ten minutes?" Lena says.

Jin nods and Cale nods and I nod because I could use the extra time to craft a better plan. I'm thinking: air shotgun range. Cale could show Lena how to point the gun. It's cute. But it'd be awkward if Jin and I are also there.

Lena heads back to the parking lot and the rest of us stand near the Haunted House attraction. And then, genius hits me.

"You're telling me, in your *twenty years of life*, you've never been to a fair?!" Cale says to Jin.

"I went to Carnival in Brazil a few years--"

I interrupt by ushering Cale the other direction. "Go! Cale, now, go go go! Take Lena to the air shotgun thing."

"What?" He gives minimal resistance to my shoving, and then it suddenly hits him that I'm trying to help him out. *You're welcome.*

"Just tell her it's her punishment for being an unprepared pledge," I say. "Go!"

"Okay, okay! I got it!" Cale puts his hands up in defense and then walks the same direction as Lena. But my mission is only partially accomplished.

I glance at Jin and gesture back toward the line to the Haunted House. "Let's go! Hurry!"

"Um, okay," he says, like a compliant little kid with a hint of wariness.

My toothy smile makes the staff member eye-roll as she waves us forward in line. I feel like I discovered mom's chocolate stash and got away with taking one for myself. It may only be a few minutes, but Lena and Cale are stuck together. I'm not completely useless after all.

"It's not too scary, right?" Jin says to me. I nearly forgot about him in the thrill of my victory.

I know he's joking. "If you can handle your own reflection, you should survive."

He furrows his brow. "Uh-oh. There are mirrors? That's not good."

I eye him. "Why not?"

He whispers to me, "I'm a vampire."

"Too bad I never got into the vampire hype," I say, but now I'm thinking he might think I'm into him, or not into him, and I don't know how I feel about either of those. I probably should've chosen giggle over quip.

He's a gracious laugher, which helps curb the overthinking.

If I had to get stuck with one of Lena's crushes, at least it isn't one who's drooling over her. He seems excited about this mediocre attraction, which might actually make it fun.

The sweat inside my shoes builds as we step forward in line.

"What was that about, pushing Cale to take Lena shooting?" Jin asks.

I whip my body to face him, my eyes wide. "Uh... well..." Shoot! I'm not sure what I should say. Despite my false relationship status, I'm bad at lying.

I guess I could try the truth.

"I'll tell you inside," I say and I can't help but grin. I might have discovered another way to help Cale.

We approach the archway coated in peeling paint, which doesn't seem like an intentional part of the decoration. A bad speaker at the front blares a scream repeatedly as a strobe light flashes. We lift our wristbands and the guy at the front waves us into the darkness. I can make out faint images of green and purple skeletons, but that's it.

This first part is cringe-central because we have to feel around to get through it. It's gross thinking about all the unwashed hands that have grazed these walls, but I feel around to get my bearings. My fingers bump into some cotton fabric with flesh underneath.

Jin.

I jump. "Sorry!"

"No worries," he says, but I can only barely make out the outline of his figure. My right hand hits the wall, thank goodness.

And my left runs into his body again.

"Ah, sorry!"

"It's fine, Joy," he says with a small laugh. "Here."

His hand wraps around my left wrist and he pulls me along. Lena sure missed her chance, opting for open-toed wedges. She could've been unapologetically hand-in-hand with Jin in this chamber of low-grade scares. But, now it's Jin's hand holding *my*... wrist.

Who am I hoping ends up with Lena anyway? Jin or Cale?

Ah! A cackling plastic witch head jolts at me. I flinch and squeal, my heartbeat pounding in my limbs.

Jin squeezes my wrist a little tighter. I try to shake all of my nerves off.

We round the corner and dark blue light flows in. The opening to the hall of mirrors boasts poor quality thunder sounds and rain effects. The neon light distorts everything but the perfect curves and angles of Jin's face. He drops my wrist, but his touch lingers, and he gestures for me to go ahead.

I head into the maze and it's easy to navigate at first, but after a couple turns I'm stopped by glass panes. Jin follows shortly behind.

I tap on a transparent frame that's between us. "So you're not a vampire after all!" I yell through the panes. He shrugs. Adorably.

Next is the shifting floor beside gruesome cartoon jailbirds that do anything but frighten. Fake arms reach through prison bars as Jin and I find balance on the track.

I'm wobbly as a pirate ship in a monsoon.

I look back. Jin's black Converse hit the moving track confidently. Tall people find their balance so much easier. I'm relieved when I've gotten past this obstacle.

I wonder how Cale and Lena are doing. Jin and I have hit the halfway mark and I'm guessing there hasn't been much headway.

"So, you gonna let me in on why you made your boyfriend go after Lena?" Jin asks when he joins me on solid ground.

"Yes, but you have to keep it a secret," I tell him.

His endearing wariness resurfaces. "Okay..."

I bounce up the split stairs that alternate up-and-down. This ride is desperate to make a show of my clumsiness, I swear. "I'm trying to pin Cale and Lena together as much as possible."

Solid platform. We have to cross a footbridge made of chains. I turn around and face Jin. The chains rattle and shake as I walk backward.

My eyes catch his for a brief moment. "Cale is really into Lena."

Jin looks at me with a furrowed brow. "And you're encouraging it?"

My foot finds the landing. "Well, that part's the secret."

We climb down the spiral staircase to the ground level, me before him. "Cale and I are faking it. He's actually trying to spend time with her, so I'm just playing along until... I don't know, she sees him in a different light."

We ignore the pitiful jump-scares as we talk.

His angular eyes narrow at me. "That's kinda weird."

"Yeah, but Cale thought a ridiculous ploy might get her attention. Nothing else does."

Jin laughs. "True. But, why are you letting me in on this?"

"Because I could use your help."

Jin thinks about it, his eyes wandering to nowhere in particular. I bite my lip in anticipation.

"Okay," he says. "Sure, I can play accomplice."

There's a sigh in me that I didn't know was there. "Thank you!"

We make for the exit. My face probably says "two-and-a-half stars," at least.

Jin leaves ahead of me, and I completely miss the slight step down.

I crash into his back and grip onto his shirt. Before I realize it, Jin's turned around and steadying me.

By grabbing my hand.

"You okay?" he asks.

I nod and pull myself together so I'm upright. Guess that haunted house made a fool of me after all. I pull my hand from his and dust myself off.

Now, Cale's chances may be better than I thought.

And maybe it's a tiny, itty bitty relief that I have one other person I don't have to pretend with.

Fair food is in a league of its own.

Our corn dogs don't last long. They're perfectly brown and crunchy on the outside, with a snap of salty pork flesh, lathered in corn-syrupy ketchup. Lena's prior disgust was clearly a facade. She inhales that thing.

After lunch, we head to the rodeo show and I finally get to ask Cale how it went at the shooting range.

He winks and says, "I let her win."

"I slaughtered him," she says as she leans over from Cale's other side. The show starts and Cale's focus becomes completely enraptured in rowdy cheering. One by one, the cowboys get flung into the dirt. Cale's ridiculous shrieking makes all of us laugh, but I think he's still nervous around Lena because he keeps asking *me* "did you see that?" or "wasn't that insane?"

I stealthily urge him the other direction. He hesitates but manages to get her attention a few times over the course of the show. His nerves are adorable.

Even though the fair food hits our stomachs like bricks, we ride a few rides before going to the petting zoo. Cale literally squeals at baby bunnies! Lena holds off, though. She's periodically staring at one flashing food cart, longing for the sugary sustenance of the Promised Land.

Funnel. Cake.

Oh, we sanitize! Lured by pictures of stacked pancake noodles topped with syrupy fruit and whipped cream, we buy ourselves some fried glory.

Funnel cake is always a bad idea. And I never regret it.

The sun is dipping low and the air finally feels bearable. Not bad weather for braving another grease-bomb. I dig in, but I'm already feeling my limits.

Jin gets his funnel cake and sniffs it.

He coughs, sending white powder out into the atmosphere like a dry firework. It peppers his arm and I have to turn from my plate as I laugh so I don't suffer the same fate.

Lena is in hysterics. Her cake slides off her floppy paper plate, jam-side down in the dirt.

Cale gasps. "The *humanity*!"

Jin wipes his face with a paper napkin and then offers his funnel cake to Lena. She lights up and accepts. He beams at her delight and I have two thoughts: a) either Jin enjoys being chivalrous more than eating funnel cake, or b) he likes making Lena happy.

Or both.

Cale holds a brief vigil for the poor, lost dessert. Despite how amusing that is, I can't take my attention off the electric Park-Garcia chemistry. They're so easy together. Like someone cast the two most beautiful people for this one scene at the fair to be best friends.

The lavender sky tells me sunset is fast approaching. The Ferris Wheel suddenly lights up like a beacon.

"We should go to the Ferris wheel right now," I tell them, with half my mouth full. "We'll get the sunset if we're lucky."

Lena nods, her pretty mouth dusted with powdered sugar and cheeks full of fried cake. I think we all feel that a few bites was enough, so we abandon our food in the trash. Lena and Jin walk ahead. The silhouette of them against the dotted lights of the wheel is like a movie poster.

Suddenly I feel a smooth palm slip into my hand. Cale's. I glance at him, but he keeps walking like it's nothing.

Without taking my hand away, I whisper, "What's this?"

"Keeping up the image," he says, his voice hushed.

How is he so natural at this? I hope I'm playing it cool. Holding his hand feels more than friendly, even in our context. I haven't built up the courage to talk about the limits of this "relationship," but I don't see a reason to object.

For a second, it feels real. And kind of sweet. Not the sickly sweet of sugary funnel cake. More like a summer blackberry, perfectly ripe. He squeezes my hand and grins, high on the fair atmosphere alone.

Keeping up the image. This is for show. For Lena. And that's fine. But it does make me wonder what it would feel like if it were real. I look up at him, and I can see him that way.

For Lena, I remind myself.

Cale and I catch up, approaching the line for the Ferris wheel. There are two side-by-side lines, separated by a rope. Lena is arguing with Jin over which line to get in.

"They take a person from *each* line," he insists. "So we have to split if we want to get on together." Once he sees me, he gives me the barest wink.

"Why would they do that?" Lena retorts in a high pitch.

"He's right, Lena," I say, leaving Cale's handhold. "We should get in each line so we don't get staggered."

It's not technically lying. It's opportunity-manufacturing. Cale should be the one to ride with her. We're leaving it to chance once we queue up. Jin stands in front of me in one line, Lena in front of Cale in the other. The four of us are next to each other.

Now I just pray they call on my line before Lena's.

By some heavenly divination, Jin and I end up ahead in line. One person stands in front of Lena when they summon Jin up to a car.

Right according to plan.

"Oh." He makes a show of false concern. I'm so glad I recruited him. "Sorry, Lena! Guess I was wrong."

All I manage is a shrug and a silent beg to God that she considers it an honest mistake.

"Joy!" Her shrill reprimand urges me to avoid looking back at all costs.

The metal safety bar falls on our laps and Jin leans over, waving and mouthing "sorry" at Lena before facing the tangerine sunset.

Cale and Lena are practically on the opposite side of the wheel when they board. It's like the fair gods were smiling on our sneakiness. If we're lucky, Cale will admit his feelings for her as they gaze on the gradient orange, rose and periwinkle sky.

I know it's a long shot, but I'm in a hopeful mood.

Breezes like this breathe peace onto me, coupling with the dull sounds of riders on coasters and plinking games in the fading day.

"Thanks for assisting me today," I say to my ride partner.

"I think it merits a high five," Jin says. My sunburned cheeks sting when I smirk. I give the man the high five he's owed. Then I return to soaking in the lavender and tangerine sky. There's no better vehicle for this meditation than a rickety seat on a Ferris wheel.

"So, tell me about yourself, Joy," Jin says. The sparkle in his eyes hasn't faded all day.

"College?" he asks.

"FredU. Finance major."

His eyebrows go up. "Exciting."

I laugh.

"So finance is your dream?" he asks more genuinely.

I fiddle with my ride belt. "No. But it's practical. I figure I'll have money if I work with money. Bakers aren't the first ones to go hungry. My mom always says that."

He nods in acknowledgment. "Okay, so, let's say you go impractical. What would you do?"

The wheel stops and we're suspended above people, under the orange sky.

"A singer. But that's not really--"

"That's not any more impractical than a baseball player."

My eyes widen. "How did you... did you know my brother plays?"

A sly smile appears. "Lena mentioned it."

"Well..." I start, gearing up for an argument. But, I don't exactly have one. "I guess you have a point. What about you?"

"Business Law, but I actually like it. I think I want to help small businesses. There's a lot of opportunity for translators, so I'm focusing on super boring law language in Korean and English. I have an internship opportunity in Seoul, actually. It would jumpstart my career, but I still haven't decided if I want to go yet."

"Wow." Actually, impressive. "Cale was right. You are a one-upper."

He laughs at my snarky observation.

A thought occurs to me. "Does Lena know? About the internship, I mean."

"No. I wasn't going to tell anyone until I made up my mind. So, I guess we're in each others' confidences now."

I smile and probably blush. "Guess so."

Wind combs the escaped strands of my dark blonde hair and the sky is slowly saturated with a blue hue. The ride lights cast a more striking glow. I didn't realize until now, but this feeling is what I'm chasing this summer. A collection of breezy, sunburned twilights.

"Thanks for all this, Joy," Jin says. His palms hold up his face as he admires the picturesque sunset. "Today was pretty perfect."

I can't keep from smiling. Today was more than perfect.

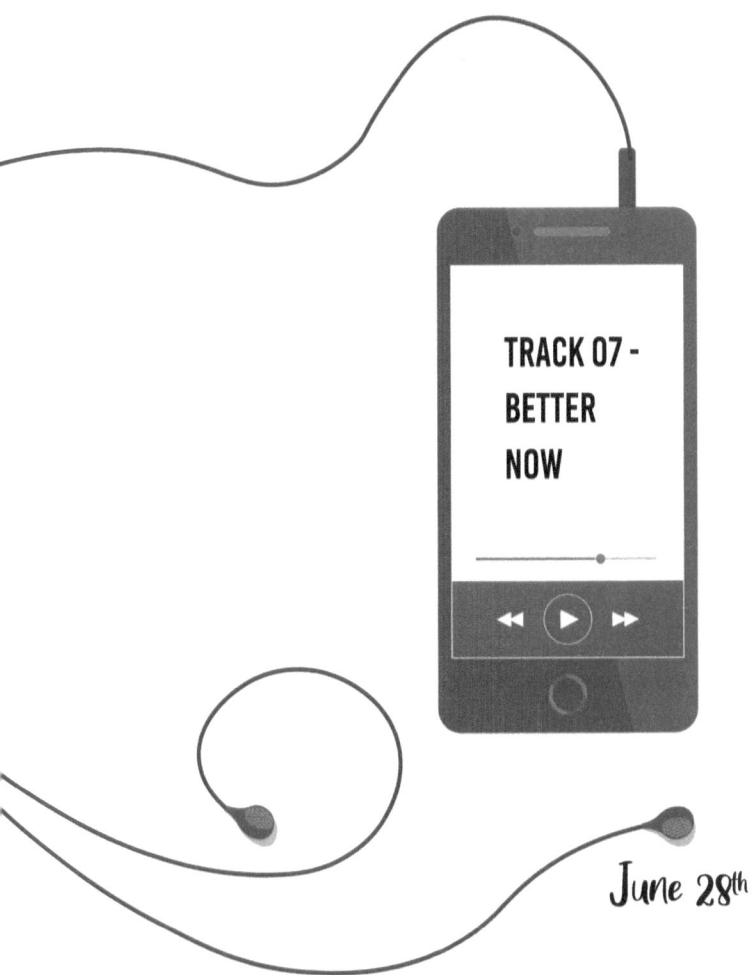

TRACK 07 –
BETTER
NOW

June 28th

Ok but what happened on the Ferris Wheel?

THIS IS HOW I START MY TEXT CHAIN WITH CALE right when I wake up. I would have asked him right after I got home last night, but I experienced a hard post-fair crash. I haven't escaped the layers of my bed yet.

I *did* manage to talk to Lena before she got into her VW yesterday, though. When I apologized for the mixup, she smirked and said, "Well... Cale's Jim Halpert impression is impeccable." She kept giggling, even after she shut the door and waved goodbye to me before taking off.

So yeah, once I was conscious enough to text Cale, I did.

Thankfully he doesn't make me wait very long.

Cale: Who wakes up before 7 in the summer SHEESH

Joy: DETAILS MR. THOMAS

Cale: Okay okay

In the minutes that follow, my eager heart pounds watching his ellipses flash on and off. Did my effort amount to anything? I guess it was kinda mine and Jin's effort. I'm glad he agreed to help.

Even if Jin is still probably the one who will end up with Lena.

Buzz.

Cale: SO, we got on the ride and Lena was kinda pissed cuz I think she was jelly that you were riding with Jin. I figured I had two choices: 1) get my empathy card out and be a shoulder to cry on or 2) pull out the Caletastic charms. I went with 2, obviously. COMEDY is my specialty bb
Cale: Anyway, I asked her what was wrong because PLOT TWIST I was gonna try 1
Cale: She ignored me, but then there was a bee
Cale: And I kinda freaked out and flailed around and rocked the gondola thing
Cale: Then Lena flicked it away like it was NOTHING
Cale: She also LAUGHED AT ME. THE NERVE.

I laugh at him too, right now. The texts come in one after the other. He must be fast at typing, but the progression cracks me up. I can totally picture it.

Cale: We talked about fair food and The Office after that but... yeah
Cale: I think Imma play the long game. Callin it a win :D

So, not as successful as I'd hoped. But it's not nothing. Like Cale said, probably a win.

Joy: I'll keep thinking up schemes

Cale: Your services are appreciated
Cale: Thnx for inviting me

As if Cale has to thank me for that. I thank him for bringing himself. He's a force of hilarious nature. Even if I'm exhausted from all the walking and sun and human interaction, the aching is practically a trophy knowing he had a good time and inched a little closer to Lena.

I whip my white comforter off and relish the coolness of conditioned house air on my legs.

Today, I have zero plans. Carson's off at physical therapy and then odd jobs at Victoria Lake Resort. Willow Haven's claim to fame is "the town you pass through to get to Victoria Lake." We're not that big. But at least I feel like I'm included in "we" now.

I get to eat sugary cereal while browsing Hulu by my lonesome. It's amazing.

This is another feeling I'm chasing, I think. Lazy meals, binging shows I never got to watch during the school year, and soaking up the slightly wider edges of my solitude.

I break up my Nothing Day with more AirBnB browsing, paying particular attention to the long Independence Day weekend. One has a hot tub *with* an ocean view and a hipster cafe walking distance. Just have to make sure the beater can make it.

My phone buzzes.

Lena: So how far have you and Cale gone?

Joy: Omg Lena

I shouldn't be surprised, but I'm still beet red. I envision her sitting out by her glittering pool, wearing the pink bikini, or maybe the teal one-piece, having a second to herself before suddenly thinking, "I need to ask Joy about her sex life."

Lena: What? You guys were good friends before it's not like you can't go a little faster

Joy: I haven't even kissed him yet

So far I'm glad the topic hasn't come up between me and Cale. The hand-holding mishap was essentially the height of my mutual romantic affection experience. Actually, I hate to call it a mishap when it wasn't all that bad. It just wasn't *real*.

And I'm unsure how to address the rules of this game.

I wonder how many girls Cale has been with. He had a girlfriend at the beginning of the school year, but they broke it off early. He sang a few ballads at the time, but otherwise kept his usual class-clown composure. Apparently she thought they'd be better as friends, which isn't really surprising. Cale has a thousand friends.

And that's exactly why I shouldn't be wondering if he's going to try to kiss me during this deal. He's a great friend. He'll understand if I'm too nervous to hand over my first kiss for a fake relationship.

I just have to actually talk to him about it.

Lena: OMG YOU CANT BE SERIOUS
Lena: I thought I taught you better than that

Joy: I like taking it slow
Joy: Not everyone is like you
Joy: Lol

I add the last text so she doesn't think I'm being judgy. What's wrong with taking things slow? It's not like I'm dysfunctional. I'm not even really dating him!

Lena: Oh hey, you want another double dog-sitting job?

Joy: YES!! Do you even have to ask??

Lena: Awesome! The fams are taking an impromptu trip to Cabo :D
Lena: You doing anything for the Fourth?

The Fourth? Meaning, the only week this amazing AirBnB is available? I flip over to my booking app to double-check. It's completely booked except a few days around the Fourth.

I was so close.

But I basically already accepted the dog-sitting job. I groan because I'd rather have money.

Joy: Just eating hot dogs and reading magazines in bed like every year

Lena: Mom said they'll pay you extra since its last minute, and the dogs might get freaked out. But I told her you could handle that :D

Oh yeah. I've neglected to mention Cale's whole part in the dog care last time. It seemed better unsaid after he'd seen her bedroom and noticed her collection of raunchy teen vampire novels (no, I'm not joking).

Lena: And this time, IT IS ON
Lena: I'm determined to get Jin to myself

Joy: Good luck <3

It feels odd to wish her luck with Jin and then actively plot for her to be with Cale. Like he's psychic, I get a message from him.

Cale: Sooooo, you got plans for the Fourth of July?

Joy: Actually, I just took another dog-sitting job

Cale: OOH! I am SO THERE

Ellipses pulse. Did he just invite himself over to Lena's house? He knows she won't be there, right?

Cale: We def gotta hit up Americanafest!

I recall seeing the poster for that around town. Red, White, and Blues, it said. *Very original.* It looks promising enough. Lots of bands playing and food carts serving.

And Cale has a way of upping the ante in the fun department.

Joy: Sounds great!
Joy: But I feel like I should clarify that Lena will be out of town, so...

Ellipses.

Cale: Girl like I don't love spending time with my FGF!
Cale: We'll make her WISH she was in town
Cale: I'm the party selfie MASTER, Becker

FGF = fake girlfriend. I laugh just reading his personality. I feel a little better about losing my beach house prospects.

Now back to more urgent business: America's Next Top Model, Season 8 Finale.

Okay, so my Nothing Day is not turning out as fun as I'd hoped. ANTM got repetitive, I snacked myself into a stomach ache, and a shower sounds like the worst way to distract myself on a hot day like this. Maybe the intense boredom is the reason I decided to text Carson.

Carson: It's been hot out. No AC. Good though, shoulder's healing
Carson: Lots of sexy girls to distract me

Joy: Ew! Don't tell me that!

Carson: Ur the one who asked

Joy: I meant, like, how are you feeling? Is it fun? Does your name have the most gold stars yet?

Carson: LOL u know it
Carson: But I still miss you

Yeah right. Carson's not fooling me. He only misses me when I'm not serving his athlete's image. He's probably confusing me with pitching. Since I'm at all his games, he thinks my absence is the reason he feels off.

He's probably lonely. Probably because he drops people like bats and dashes for someone new.

Ugh. I'm too dried out and salty. Like a hot potato chip.

If I don't text back, he'll just get mad.

Joy: Miss you too

Carson: Once ur at FredU we'll see each other all the time, don't worry

Perfect. Once I'm in the vicinity you can make demands of me and my schedule face-to-face instead of by rare text. I can even hand you your finished homework if you like! So much easier!

Gosh, I really am a salty potato chip.

But part of me knows he still needs me. That's really why I texted him.

I can't forget that I needed him once. Even though he caused a hell of a lot of problems for our family, he protected me. And things are better now.

Out of nowhere, Lena calls me, which is highly suspect.

"Hello?"

"Oh my god, Joy! It's horrible!" Okay, she's panicking.

"What? Are you okay?" It's the dogs. No, the flights. I don't know. It's hard to tell on her tone alone.

"I'm fine, but..." She whimpers. It doesn't sound serious. Or, at least, not to anyone else but her.

"Jin broke his wrist! He said he's not coming to Cabo!" I hear a frustrated sigh.

"Oh," I manage to respond. So I was right. It's not actually an emergency.

"I can't convince my parents to let me stay behind," she tells me. "They don't want to waste the ticket. And they want to *bond*. That the whole point of this trip was to spend time *bonding*. Ugh!"

Poor Lena. Being forced to spend the holiday weekend in Cabo. I stifle a laugh.

"Sorry." Single-word answers are all I have at the moment.

I let her vent about the not-really-a-crisis until she's ready to hang up.

Once she's gone, it suddenly occurs to me that Jin will be home alone this weekend.

And, in the next house over, so will I.

TRACK 08 -
JUST A
FRIEND TO
YOU

July 1st

Oh gosh, the backroads to Lena's house make me so queasy. Why do I take them so fast?

The beater sputters into the curving shared driveway of the wealthiest families I know. Jin Park's petite mom, Jan-di, stands near the fountain in her cream blouse and bright fuchsia capris. She waves her hand wildly at me. There's an envelope in it.

Wow, she has a lot of energy for such a small person.

The hum of my car's engine turns off, leaving me in that calming split-second of quiet. Immediately, Jan-di is shouting my name.

"Joie!" My name almost sounds like "Joey" when she says it. It's kind of adorable. I step out of my car and slam my door. The air isn't cool this morning. Not hot, either. It's the perfect in-between, where you can't feel it at all.

Jan-di's straight, white teeth shine at me, so I smile back. She smells like orchids and orange peels.

"Thank you so much for help, Joie!" she says. Her accent is thick with mixed up consonants and improper emphasis. Jin has no accent. Or, I guess, he has a perfect American accent. Jan-di's voice is high, soft, and smothered in Korean-influenced intonation.

I can't see her eyes through her sunglasses, but I know they are just like Jin's. Winged, flat, and colored like melted chocolate. I saw them in one of Lena's pictures. Kid's got good genes.

She hands me the envelope, but I push it away. "Oh, um, I thought since Jin was home, you wouldn't need my help."

She purses her lips and shakes her head tightly.

"No, no, no. Jin cannot take care Zany," she tells me. "His arm so bad. He can no walk her." The way she says his name is like a shiny metal sound. *Cheen!* It suits him.

Jan-di shoves the envelope at me again. I grab it to keep it from falling on the ground, but that apparently secures my acceptance.

"Thank you, Joey!"

I nod. "No problem."

"And make sure he eat! He forget so much!" Her dry, raven hair swirls in a short breeze. She looks too young and tiny to have sourced such a tall, 20-year-old son.

Said 20-year-old man steps out of the Park house, down the paved stone path. His cast is a blinding neon green and glows on his white t-shirt. Honestly, he could only own one shirt and I wouldn't know it.

I cast a shadow over my eyes with my hand and call out. "Hey there!"

"Hey, Joy. Do you need help with your stuff?" he asks. I'm certain it's a habit. I point to his cast as if he's unaware that his wrist is broken.

"I've got one good arm!" He waves the good one around a little.

"He's so good boy," says his mother. She pats his shoulder on the uninjured side, then skitters back down the path to her house. It's peculiar that she insisted Jin's arm was too broken for walking the dog but not for helping me with my stuff.

He walks up to my car as I rifle through my things. I feel like I should hand him the pillow and blanket since they're not heavy, but I'm still mortified that I own them. But, I guess he has seen them before. Damage is already done.

"Here." I push them toward him. His long, pale arm wraps around them, and I try not to notice that he examines them for a second. Lisa Frank and Barbie, like before.

I dive back into my car to hide my blushing.

"Apparently you're so crippled, you still need me to take care of the dog," I say as I pull my bags out of the beater.

He scoffs. "I don't know why. My legs work perfectly fine, and I can scoop with one hand."

"Oh no, please! I could use the money," I admit, hoping I don't sound nearly as desperate as I am.

"Oh, really? What for?"

I emerge, close my car door, and head to the Garcias' front door. "Well, I need *some* savings for stuff my scholarship doesn't cover. But, if you must know, I'm planning to buy myself a weekend alone."

"You like being alone?"

I feel my heart rate speed up. "No! ...I mean, yes. But not all the time. It's just..."

It's hard to explain. I have an itch, sort of, but it's in that spot on my back that I can't reach. And a couple of days at a beach house is the backscratcher I need.

"Just... what?" he solicits. We stand on the Garcia porch, pausing in front of the double doors.

"It sounds refreshing. That's all."

Jin lifts his broken arm up, his exposed fingers rubbing his chin. I see one of his brows lift.

"Are you making fun of me?" I ask him. He immediately shakes his head.

"No! I just think you're interesting. You just got paid to spend a week alone at two huge houses, and yet your dream is to... pay for that very same thing."

"Ok, when you put it that way... I mean I wasn't *really* alone."

Shoot! It slipped out. I open the front door and hope the transition is enough distraction that he won't ask. Please don't ask.

"You mean the dogs, or... someone else?"

He asked.

I lower my voice. "Cale came by. Zany was freaked out. Cale's a dog person, so he helped with her. Plus, he'd never seen Harry Potter, so yeah. We spent some time together. Nothing crazy. Except for the two seconds he forgot to take his shoes off in your house."

Jin gives me an exaggerated expression of shock. "Betrayal!"

I laugh with him. He hands me my possessions and I hug them like a teddy bear. He still seems unfazed by the fact that I sleep on rainbow leopards.

"I should give you my number," he says, in a way that would inspire soft-focus and sparkles.

I gape at him. "What?"

"Um, just in case you need something," he amends, and scratches his head.

"Oh. Sure." I fumble for my phone and we exchange numbers.

"Guess I'll see ya 'round." Jin's voice is smooth. I catch myself biting my lip as I watch him leave.

I smell heaven on a cookie sheet and glance to the kitchen. Seeing Fernando in his frilly apron is like rewatching a favorite comedy. And this time I'm not splayed out on the floor, so it's even better.

Well, not for Lena. Nobody should be so upset to go on a vacation to Cabo.

She says nothing when she sees me. Unless you count a pitiful sigh as a greeting.

Fernando and her mom, Angela, assure me Diamond has never had issues with the Fourth of July fireworks. They head out to the limo that just arrived and Lena hangs back for a second.

She hesitates. "Jin's really friendly. Just... don't take advantage of that."

I blink, a bit shocked. "I won't."

Her shoulders relax and she smiles on one side. "Okay."

"Hey!" I gently push her shoulder. "Have fun, will ya?"

She rolls her eyes and fights a smile. "*Fine!*"

Then she slogs to the limo. Does she really think that something could happen between me and Jin? If she does, she's crazy. But, it could just be that I'm getting what she wanted, and I can't fix it. It's not as simple as taking braids out of my hair.

Lena will perk up when she hits the blue ocean under the Mexican sun. If not then, the tan, muscular beach men won't hurt.

I shut the door, enclosing myself in an echo chamber of silence. Apart from the soft scuttling of Diamond, who pants at my side.

I head straight for the kitchen.

The cookies are still warm and melty. Diamond follows and begs for a cookie with that goofy puppy smile.

If I could give him chocolate, I'd cave in negative two seconds.

"Hey pupperz," I say with a mouthful of cookie.

Eventually, the corgi and I snuggle up in the den. This Korean romance drama cheeses hard, but I can't stop watching. It has nothing to do with the fact that the lead love interest looks like the guy one house over.

Nope.

My go-to excuse is that reading subtitles forces me to pay attention to the screen instead of trying to multitask.

I'm a little stiff after a few hours of that. It's a good time to make myself dinner. When I peel the throw blanket off and rise from the supple couch, Diamond wakes into immediate jitters. He races to the stairs, probably heading for the kitchen. Fast for a corgi.

My bare feet touch the cold tile of the foyer.

Knock knock.

I see his distorted figure and neon green cast through the floral glass pattern on the door.

Should I open it?

What am I thinking? I can't leave him out there.

I open the door and perfectly warm air flows in with the evening sun.

"Hey, Jin."

He greets me with a warm smile. How can he just hand those out like they're nothing?

"Hey, um, I ordered too much Chinese food. Thought you might want some. Besides, you technically still have to feed Zany." His blush-color lips twitch in a smile for a second.

"Right! I should."

Oh my God. I just agreed to have dinner with him.

Diamond brushes against my leg. I look down at him and hope he's the only one who can see my nerves.

In an only-for-dogs voice, Jin says, "Come on boy!" Diamond happily waltzes out.

Ginger and red pepper in thick sauces send an aroma hovering in the air when we walk into his foyer. I still feel like we are way too casually dressed to be walking around in his museum of a house. Nevermind the goofy-looking corgi and hyper black lab.

"Do you like tea?" Jin asks me when we get to the kitchen. With one hand, he pulls out plates from the mahogany cupboards and then reaches back for a yellow box. He sets it down. It reads "Jasmine" in gold letters.

"Sure!" Wow, yeah. That enthusiastic attempt at lowering my awkwardness had the opposite effect.

The tea kettle hisses. I don't think I've ever had jasmine tea.

Jin attempts to shovel chow mein onto the plates. "Attempts" is a generous word, actually. I giggle cruelly, if that's possible.

"You can pour the tea, how about that?" I say, reaching for the white takeout boxes. I brush his arm. My senses are super haywire because I'm not sure if I should be here. Is this what Lena meant by taking advantage of his friendliness?

I choose to act like it didn't happen. Because, like, what the heck is the big deal about brushing arms, right? It doesn't mean I *like* him.

The hot water is done and Jin pours it into the mugs. I'm struck by the aroma of jasmine. Peppery, floral, and slightly citrus.

"Where have I smelled this?" I say as I pull the cup close to my nose. The steam hits my face.

I'm taken back to the fair. When Jin leaned in to tell me something. He totally smelled like jasmine.

"What is it? You remember?" he asks me. He sips from the edge of his cup, slurping to cool the tea.

Do I tell him? I mean, I *can*. This isn't a *thing*.

"It was you. At the fair." I desperately seek a segue. "Do you drink it a lot?"

He nods, and slurps his next sip. "I'm a tea nerd."

"Really?"

"My family in Korea sends me tea for my birthday. It's way better over there."

Jin opens a cupboard full of teas. He owns that fact about himself, along with many others, proving he's a good conversationalist. His wrist break story is a dull one, he tells me. He tripped on a porch step and landed wrong. I can relate. The cast should come off in less than two weeks, but he didn't "feel like" going to Cabo with it on. I mentally roll my eyes at the idea of a rich person not "feeling" like an exotic getaway.

Jin rubs his mug and sips. The halt in conversation is palpable.

"Was it really your wrist that made you not feel up to going?" I don't know why I ask, but it feels like there's more here.

"Ah, yeah. You got me," he says. "I've been worried about taking the Korea internship. I kinda wanted the headspace. But now that I have it, I just want… distraction."

I lean in. "What's bothering you about it?"

"It's a really great opportunity. I can do in a year what I'd get done here in two years. And I'd make connections with people over there, so jobs would be easier to find."

"But..." I prompt.

"I don't want to go. Or I guess, I don't want to leave. It doesn't feel right, I don't know."

"Can you put it off?"

"See, that's the thing. I can't, really. They want me to come in August. And it's an honor to get selected. They only pick five people in the whole country."

I get the sense that the pressure saddens him for some reason. I take a second to think about what I would do, but it's obvious to me.

"I mean, I would go," I say, but I kind of hate it when I try to be a fixer. "You should do what you think is best, but I wouldn't want to miss the chance, I guess."

He sighs. "Yeah. You're probably right."

We leave it there, and our conversation flows again, like we worked out a kink.

Jin gets out of me that I was vice president of the glee club at Willow Haven. I always think it's strange when people are impressed by what is essentially a compulsion. But I like that he thinks I'm cool.

And then he brings up Cale.

"So, it's definitely fake? Because I saw you two holding hands."

"All for show. I wasn't even expecting that." I have a bite of the spicy, tangy General Tso's chicken and keep talking with my mouth somewhat full. "I was relieved to tell someone, actually. Thanks for being my accomplice."

"Anytime." He smiles at me. Again.

"So, do you have plans for the Fourth?" I sip some tea. It's just barely not too hot to drink, and the flavor is delicious. Not near as soapy as I'd expected.

"Well, not anymore," he says.

"Clearly! Cale invited me to Americanafest, so I'm gonna go to that."

"Even though you're not dating?" There's a sly smile before he slurps more tea.

I automatically roll my eyes. "Friends can't hang out?"

"Of course they can. Just like this. We're friends, right?"

I nod. "Yeah, I could use another friend. You wanna come with on the Fourth?"

He pretends to give it some thought. "Yeah. Sounds fun!"

I sip my tea, hoping that Lena won't be too upset that I get to spend time with Jin. We just established *friendship*. Not taking advantage of friendliness, just reciprocating it.

I speed up our farewell by feeding Zany and washing dishes, which was basically just the two plates and two mugs we used for tea.

Diamond follows me back to Lena's. I wish I could stop thinking about Jin. My mind forces me to replay the various smiles he offered me this evening. My heart is a schoolgirl, and it just met a member of our favorite K-Pop idol group.

I need to calm down. He said it. We are just, *barely*, friends.

TRACK 09 –
WOKE
UP LATE

July 2nd

*I*WAKE UP BLISSFULLY ALONE with the heavenly glow of morning to greet me. The tangible silence tells me I'm not at home. No road noise. No dad in the kitchen, whistling and crackling bacon in a pan. No Carson and whatever growl-inducing frustration hits him first in the day.

Lena's clock reads 9:09 AM in glowing teal block numbers. I yawn and stretch, relishing the puffiness of her blankets on my rested body. What should I do today? I check my phone, kinda wondering if Cale has texted me, but I didn't actually tell him I started dog-sitting yesterday. Hanging with him might be fun.

He didn't text me. But at 8:59, Jin did.

Jin: Do you like french toast?

I think it's because I'm still half asleep. That must be why I text him back without reading his question as an invitation.

Joy: Definitely

Jin: Oh good! I need help cracking the eggs. I already made a mess of it so I gave up haha

Jan-di *did* say I should make sure he eats. Who am I to defy a strict Asian mother?

Joy: Lol be right there

I pride myself on being ready in five minutes. I don't need much. My hair is post-sleep messy so I put it in a loose bun. I check myself in the mirror and brush my teeth. Put on a bra, some deodorant, a hoodie and yoga pants that have never once been used for yoga. Then I'm out into the blinding yet cool morning.

Jin answers the door with a lick of hair still sticking up. Did he look in a mirror after he got out of bed? Not that it matters with him.

In the kitchen, I witness the mess of egg guts and white shells in, and around, a metal mixing bowl. After examining the carnage, I make judgy eyes at the culprit. He scratches the back of his head with his good hand.

"My mom usually does the cooking," he says.

"You're hopeless." I waste no time making this mess right. First clean up, then ingredient prep. It's a good thing I make French toast for myself often. I whisk the eggs, milk, vanilla, nutmeg, and cinnamon with a fork.

"What are your big plans today?" Jin asks.

"Um, not much really. You?"

"Fighting boredom. I could use a break from Rocky movies."

I glance at him briefly before placing the soaked bread in the pan. It sizzles and my mouth is already watering. The mixed scent of vanilla and butter rises from the pan.

"Well, my plan is to binge the first season of The Walking Dead," I watch the edges of the toast for browning.

"Can I be honest?" he says. His tone is serious, like he's stepping away from our light conversation.

Our eyes meet. Why is my heart pounding? "Sure."

"I've never seen that show." He winces. "Is that bad?"

A stupid amount of relief washes over me. I laugh. "Oh my gosh! I thought something was wrong."

I hastily flip the bread over with a spatula. I didn't miss the perfect timing, thank goodness.

He apologizes for freaking me out. I get another piece of bread soaking in the egg mixture.

"I haven't seen it either. Figured I should start," I admit.

"So we have something in common! I was beginning to think you were more experienced than me." It's so casual and easy coming from him.

"Well, unless we watch it together, I will be," I say, and I feel my pulse in my face because that totally sounded like an invitation.

"Then I guess we're in it together," he says. I flip the French toast onto a plate. Then he smirks, and it's really cute, but I'm freaking out. I push the plate to him. He covers his toast in syrup and eats it, and compliments my French toast making skills and I AM STILL FREAKING OUT.

I feel sort of like I betrayed Lena, but it was just a comment. I didn't *mean* to invite him.

But I also don't stop him when he follows me back to Lena's house after breakfast.

Zombies eating people is the most unromantic thing we could be watching together. Despite the brief hot and heavy scenes in the first episode--which are weird to watch with *anyone*, I remind myself--the show is nothing but gore and suspense. Harry Potter with Cale was more romantic, by a long shot.

Comfortably seated on the sectional, but keeping *friendly* distance, we watch three episodes without much interruption. Halfway through the first (oddly short) season, I pause it for a break.

"What? We have to watch the next one!" Jin says as if it's obvious.

"This is why I usually stop watching in the middle of an episode. You're not that invested in the middle."

Jin gives me a look of horror. "How can you do that?"

"I don't like the suspense of not knowing what's going to happen!"

"Really? I love that part." The way he says it makes me want to love that part, too.

Diamond waddles into the den. On that note...

"I should walk the dogs."

"Right. Forgot you were working."

We leave the den, and just when I'm convinced that Jin has had enough of me, he asks if he can join the walk. For fresh air. So I have him bring Zany over.

After securing the dogs on leashes, we take our walk. The sun's at a pleasant intensity, not too harsh but still causing a sheen of sweat. It's actually a bit too nice of a day for watching TV.

But somehow, I don't care.

Zany yanks hard on the leash, so I let Jin have Diamond. Jin jokes about Walkers racing out from the dense trees on the side of the road. I do kind of wonder what it would be like if zombie moaning interrupted the sweet bird songs.

We agree I'd probably kill more zombies. At least while he's still injured.

I really wanted to be alone for this long weekend. *Wanted.*

Now all I want is to finish the first season of The Walking Dead.

But when we get back to the house, I'm famished. I make him some boxed mac and cheese, despite that it's truly the one thing he could make with a broken wrist. I share my secret ingredient: salsa.

Yes, I'm serious. Jin's not buying it until I start eating from my own bowl. He wiggles his fingers for me to pass the salsa. Right when I do, my phone buzzes. His too, a second later.

It's a picture from Lena. Tan sand, harsh sun, teal waters in the background. Her black, sparkling bikini top holds her well. She gives the camera a rose-pink smile, with peace sign fingers. I don't know how many tries it took to get this picture just right, but she nailed it.

Guilt sinks in my abdomen. "It's Lena." I try to sound... happy?

Jin peeks at his phone screen.

"I bet you're wishing you were there right now," I say, with a pinch of regret. "Looks like she's having fun."

Jin pours a bit of salsa in his bowl of mac and cheese. "I'm having fun, too."

"It's not *Cabo*."

"Eh. The Walking Dead is preferable in my state."

He makes eye contact for a second. Jin's eyes are so dark, they always have a twinkle in them.

I think I'm starting to enjoy his company too much.

"This is weirdly good," Jin says, chuckling with a mouth half-full of my odd food combo.

I stare at Lena's flawless picture. She's off in Mexico, trusting me with her dog and this guy that she's in love with. I might've already crossed over into "taking advantage" territory.

"I should probably shower after this. What time is it?"

He checks his phone. "Whoa! It's almost 4!"

I stuff my mouth with the salty, rehydrated cheese noodles, relishing the vinegar tomato flavor that mingles with it. I don't know what else I should say. I may be okay at banter, but I've always been terrible at being blunt.

I don't want vagueness to get me in trouble again.

"We'll finish the season together, right?" Jin asks me.

"Yes! I'm not a Netflix cheater," I say, kind of surprised by how easily it comes out.

"Good to know, Joy. I'll remember that for later."

▶

Lena's shower is heaven. The water falls with just enough pressure, not the needle spray I get at home. Her iridescent tile makes me feel like I'm some kind of mermaid princess. When I'm good and done, I dry off with a fluffy, luxurious towel.

I used Lena's bluetooth speaker to listen to music and heard the text chime a couple times. I'm hoping it's Cale with details for the Fourth. I wonder if I should invite him to watch The Walking Dead with us (since I'm absolutely positive it also wasn't approved by his mom), but I hesitate before checking my phone.

I kind of like that I have a thing with Jin. And I kind of like that I have a thing with Cale, too.

I check my phone... it was Jin.

Jin: It really has been fun not being in Cabo :)
Jin: When should I come back over to finish TWD?

I didn't expect it would be him. Or that his words to send my mind spiraling into repeated visions of his perfect smile. A Jin Park tornado of happiness.

I shake my damp head. What's a good hour for a perfectly friendly friend to come over after I wake up? I'm almost settled on 11 when he messages me again.

Jin: How about a late dinner? Like 8?

Wait, *tonight*? I bite the edge of my lip, kind of shocked at how badly I want to say "yes."

I was looking forward to spending my weekend with my waking hours heavy in the "alone" category, but I'm not peopled out. Or... not with Jin.

There's a sheer veil of worry on me about how Lena would take it if she knew that I spent more than half a day with Jin. But it's not like it's that different than Cale. Purely platonic.

I squeeze my eyes shut and press send.

Joy: Sounds good :)

One episode in and I'm invested hard. Wrappers from the pitas that Jin drove out to get are crumpled on the coffee table. We're both cozied up under *very separate* throw blankets on the couch. The huge TV screen fills the dark room with shifting light. OLED really does look better.

Sweating heavily, the zombie-fighters on the screen argue against the background of singing cicadas. It feels like a Southern summer came in through the TV. My eyes start to betray me near the end of episode five. But I can't stop! Jin was right; the suspense is the best part!

In the final seconds of the episode, a door dramatically opens for the dirt-covered characters. I jolt awake at the floodlight on the screen. Jin is glued to the screen.

I check my phone and it's not even ten PM yet. I should not be tired, and I'm definitely not stopping. The next one is the finale. We agree we have to watch it, so I let it play.

The AC blows in super lightly on my face, how I imagine floating on a cloud would feel. The blanket is silky soft...

I'm so warm... relaxed... the voices from the show are dull chants...

Shoot, I closed my eyes again. I try to refocus my attention on the show.

But the TV's off.

I wake all at once, barely registering the den in low light. As usual, watching TV is best done with eyes *open*.

There's a crick in my neck from the position I slept in on this couch. In the middle of my yawn, I look beside me. There's a tousled head of black hair lying still. *Jin.*

I bolt up! Where's my phone? *Gah!* Here, 6:03 AM. Oh my god.

Jin and I slept on the couch. Together. All night.

Shoot!

How the heck can he just *breathe* so *peacefully!?*

Okay, okay. I press the heel of my hand on my forehead. I have to figure out a way to keep Jin from telling Lena about this *without* revealing that she has feelings for him. She'll definitely be hurt if she finds out I let this happen.

I can't tell if I'm anxious or hungry or both, so I sneak out of the den and leave Jin to sleep. Once I have some cereal in my stomach, maybe I can handle this. When I get to the doorway, though, I look over at him. Sleeping Jin is so...

Nope. No way. I'm booking it to the kitchen.

Diamond is waiting for me, whimpering by the sliding door into the backyard, so I let him out. Zany's probably wondering what the heck happened to Jin.

Ugh, I'm a sore disappointment even to the dogs.

The stupid cereal box even feels heavy, which I know is literally impossible. I'm all nerves. I slam it down on the counter. *Nothing happened.*

Carson would freak if he found out. But he won't. There's no reason that would happen. God, I wish my brain didn't always try to process things through the Carson filter. I think it's my way of trying to control things ever since *that night*. But this is nothing like that.

It's over. Breathe.

It wasn't your fault. Everyone walked away.

Suddenly I'm sinking. Immersed in the icy pool of *that night*. The house party. Colored string lights, drinks I refused, the heavy beat of an unrecognizable song, and disorienting currents of wasted teenagers. *Breathe.* The dim hallway. That song shook the walls and I'm pinned to them. The beat pounds in sync with my heart.

Stop. Stop. Stop.

Tyler forces his drunk lips on my neck. I feel sick all over again.

The cereal bowl scrapes against the granite counter as I push it away. I'm not hungry anymore.

Diamond paws the door and I go let him back in, having barely resurfaced from drowning in my memory.

"Um... good morning." I swivel on my heels. Jin. Gorgeously disheveled and totally unaware that I was just underwater. *Breathe.*

Oh, God, but now I'm breathing like a fool!

"M-morning! Jin!" I stammer.

Diamond's in the house and I shut the door and HOLY CRAP what am I supposed to say?! Is he just gonna play it cool? Should I do that? No, I *hate* that! I'm so not cool right now! But I don't know how to play it down.

"I'm really sorry," Jin says. "For sleeping here. I should've gone home when I got tired. That's on me."

Wait. *He's taking the blame?*

"No, it's fine," I say. Diffusing is automatic. I don't control it. "I should've told you I was tired. I just wanted to finish the episode."

"No way. I was in the same boat and I should've gone home. Staying the night was not cool."

Wow, I'm really not used to a guy insisting it's his fault. I'm at a loss for words.

He stiffens, gathering courage. "Well, I mean! I don't mean it's 'not cool' like it was *horrible*. It wasn't!" He rubs his face and groans. "I'm sorry. I personally think it's a big deal to stay overnight with... a girl. So, you know..." He clears his throat. "I don't take it lightly."

Is he flustered? What is happening?

Am I just staring at him? Nod! Do *something*! Say something!

"It's okay. I don't blame you for conking out." *Conking out?* Oh my God, am I my dad?

Jin sighs in relief. "Are we okay, then?" he asks. And then he gives me a calm, friendly, hopeful smile that obviously I am no match for. Let's be real.

"Of course," I say, and I try to smile, but it hits me that I am already out of social energy. Finally met my quota. "But you should probably check on Zany."

"Right!" He nods once. Twice.

"Right," I echo and watch as he... doesn't leave.

Is he waiting for... "Oh! I'll text you the details for Americanafest tomorrow."

"Great," he says. That gets him moving and smiling that stupidly handsome smile again. "See you later, Joy."

"Bye..."

Apparently I was holding my breath because I heave a sigh when I hear the front door close.

I'm relieved to be alone, but I also feel guilty for it. He was so cute, waking up like that. Trying not to offend me by insisting he was wrong to stay over. *Insisting.* Carson would never insist he was wrong.

I feel this slight dethroning of turmoil in my heart. *It's over now.* The words are a fraction more tangible. He insisted it wasn't my fault, and suddenly the grip my past has on me is weaker. Can it be that simple? Are my demons just knots that can be tugged and loosened like thread?

Upstairs, I retrieve my phone. Cale's been texting me a bunch.

Cale: There's a SINGING COMPETITION JOYYYYY

Cale: At Americanafest, forgot to mention that part

Cale: ...and I already signed you up. :D :D

Before I read his next message, dim anxiety rushes me. But it's the good kind. The kind that I ride like a wave right onto a stage before a performance.

Cale: Think you can beat me???

Shoot him the gif of Ice Cube saying "It's on" very intense-like. My pre-performance panic is always diminished when music gets involved. Or maybe when Cale gets involved.

I don't care if it's tomorrow and I haven't practiced anything. I'm already sounding off scales and imagining the bliss of belting out a ballad.

I will definitely beat Cale!

July 4th

HOPEFULLY I'M NOT FAILING AT CHANNELING LENA'S MAKE-UP SENSE. Effort is important on this day, the anniversary of our nation's founding. Good Lord. Is there a foundation that covers inherent dorkiness?

I weave my hair into a braid crown. The sunshine has given me lighter gold streaks, so the crossing of my strands is cooler than I'd expected. My patriotic foresight was actually in check this year because I actually have an outfit. A striped cherry red-and-white off-shoulder top, kind of a vintage 50s feel, with navy high-waisted (not-too-short) shorts with stars in place of polka dots.

When I check my made-over look in Lena's massive mirror, I like it. My freckles pop, and the green in my hazel eyes, too. Blood rushes to my already blush cheeks. I'm knocking on *his* door today. I wonder if he already texted me.

I pick up my phone, realizing it's on vibrate and there's half a dozen messages and a missed call from Cale.

Cale: Hey, what time should we meet?
Cale: The contest starts at 12. Check-in at 11.
Cale: Should we drive together? I can pick you up from Lena's
Cale: Actually, I don't trust that beater. I'll come get you
Cale: ??? What time? Hello?
Cale: Nvm, I'll be there at 10

It's 10:02 already!! I race down to the front door, and sure enough, he's on time. Or two minutes late, which feels like 20 minutes early as I mentally list my morning failures. One, I didn't prepare for Cale being this early. Two, I still haven't fed the dog. Three, I never ate breakfast.

And four, I haven't yet gotten to knock on Jin's door.

Chill! It's going to be a great day. The weather is perfection, I have two really awesome friends to hang with, and I'm going to a festival where there's a singing contest. All my nerves are like bubbles!

I wave to Cale once I notice he's spotted me, then check my phone again.

Apparently I missed Jin's texts too.

Jin: Should we ride to the festival together? What time are you thinking you'll go?
Jin: I'm an early riser so I'll be ready whenever ;)

My heart leaps a little at the winking face. It's just an emoji, *sheesh!*

I should go tell Cale I'm running behind schedule. I exit the house and walk up as his driver's side window slides down.

"Ooh, automatic windows are so nice," he says with feeling.

I laugh. "Wow, rub it in."

He slaps the outside of his car door. "So hey, since you weren't answering, I did the manly thing and decided for you."

"Sorry. My phone was on silent."

He tuts and rolls his eyes, but it's exaggerated enough I know he's kidding. "Well, you ready?"

"Um, almost. I still have to feed the dogs. And ask if Jin wants a ride or if he's driving himself."

Confusion registers on his face. "You mean Lena's Jin?"

Yeah. You know. Your romantic competition. I guess I forgot to mention that I invited him.

"Uh, yeah. Is it cool if I offer him a ride with us?"

Cale's playfulness dissipates as he considers it, which I wasn't expecting.

"I guess so." His tone sounds the tiniest bit offended, but maybe I'm reading him wrong.

I decide to ask Jin to drive himself. I don't want Cale to feel like he's playing chauffeur to the guy who could upend his chances with Lena. Cale agrees to wait and I head over to Jin's house.

I lift my knuckles to knock on his door, but he opens it before I make contact.

"Morning!" he says, extra cheery. I process him in pieces. Voice, then smile, then sunglasses, then cherry red tank. It reads "AMER" and then "ICAN" but in alternating blue and white, to emphasize "I CAN." I smile back at him.

"Morning..." I say, amused.

"Did you get my text?"

"Yeah, um, is it okay if you drive on the way there? We could ride back together and save Cale the trip."

He beams in the bright morning sun. "Sure! Guess I'll meet you there."

"Okay." I turn to leave.

"Joy?" he says, so I look back. "You look great, by the way." His grin lingers.

My feet and well, honestly, my entire body stay stuck for a second.

Everything except my heart, which is freaking out. Can't this sunshine melt my frozen self a little faster?

"Thanks," I finally say. *Loosen up!* "You, too."

When regaining my agency, I resist the urge to run as I head to Lena's house.

I don't really catch my breath from his perfectly innocent compliment until after I get food into Diamond's bowl.

He said I looked great. Ugh. It's stupid to keep replaying it in my head. But I do.

I pile myself into Cale's car. There's a rising desire in my chest to share what just happened. But it was probably nothing. I'm sure he says that to Lena all the time.

Stay cool, Joy.

"Doesn't need a ride after all?" Cale's cheerfulness has mostly returned. I'm back to reality.

"Nope. He'll probably drive me back, though, if that's cool."

Cale nods. "That's cool, that's cool."

He'll probably drive me back. Just me and him.

It wasn't just me who put some thought into patriotic dress. Even though that sounds obvious, I'm not just talking about other people. I'm talking about this whole "old town" part of town. Red, white, and blue striped Americana banners decorate the antique lamp posts. Main Street is closed for pedestrians and the shops have their doors wide open. Booths litter the sidewalks, covered in shiny patriotic balloons. The hum of the crowd and distant live jazz music fill the air.

We walk through the sea of people wearing America's colors. Occasionally, there's a rebel color like cotton candy pink or canary yellow. Jin's neon green cast sticks out that way.

Nothing is better than food carts. The smoke and salty, spicy aromas waft around us and my mouth waters. Since I was breakfastless, my nose is on high alert for something hot and probably meaty.

Part of me is sad to miss out on my family's baked beans and Dad's barbecue chicken, but I already told myself I'd settle for leftovers. It's the first Independence Day in which I'm claiming my own independence.

However, my stomach seriously expects some food right now. Hamburgers and hot dogs in red plaid cartons walk by me, in the hands of less worthy eaters. There's shaved ice and fritters and curly fries the perfect color of crispy, dark orange. I ache for them. Like almost literally.

"We gotta go check in!" Cale says, nudging me away from the blissful morsels of fried sustenance. Jin and I keep up with Cale's energetic pace.

"Did you eat yet, Joy?" Jin asks. I shake my head.

We head straight to the table labeled CHECK IN. The guy at the table is wearing a shirt far too small, and seems very uninterested in fun. He hands us a clipboard with a list of names and songs for us to choose from.

Cale writes his name with flare. He winks at me when he hands me the clipboard. I glance at it.

CALE THOMAS - TAKE ON ME

He literally couldn't have picked a better song for himself.

I write my name in my bubbly penmanship.

JOY BECKER -

I scan the setlist. It's all 80s karaoke. I want a song with power in it. Not just upbeat or punchy. Something to showcase my range. And wipe that smug look off of Cale's face.

Found it.

"You're goin down, Thomas!" I say as I pencil in my song choice.

I hand the clipboard back to the guy at the table. Completely monotone he says, "You must be present to accept the title after the competition. Results at 3pm." And then he sighs.

All I can say is *my* mood is the opposite of this guy's.

My stomach gurgles at me. I get that odd sucking feeling, like my stomach is trying to escape my body and get food on its own. I scan for nearby carts, but I notice Jin's missing.

"Where's Jin?" I ask Cale. He shrugs.

I turn around and search the crowd, trying to spot a lime green arm somewhere.

"Joy!" I hear on the side I haven't checked. Jin weaves through people. With a pulled pork sandwich on a flimsy paper plate that might as well be fine china.

"I got you some food," he says.

Who is this angel sent from Heaven? I close my gaping mouth, fearing drool might escape.

"Thanks." And I snag the food because I can't *not*.

"What about me?" Cale says, making a wide gesture at himself.

"I only got one hand, man."

I laugh because that's actually a good excuse.

The smoked meat is sweet with barbecue sauce, coupled with cold, dripping coleslaw in a pillow-soft bun. My mouth tingles. There's a bite of spice and a tomato-y tang. My stomach thanks me even though the food hasn't gotten there yet.

I could kiss him. At the moment, though, that would be a gross gesture.

The festival has filled out a lot for lunch. I'm loving the sun rays and soft breeze and this *perfect* sandwich. So far, the best Fourth ever!

Cale secures himself a couple of fish tacos, while Jin insists he's not hungry. As we chat and eat and laugh, I'm shocked that I'm here with two really awesome guys. *Me!* But Lena Garcia has a romantic monopoly on both. And she's not even in the United States of America right now.

I'm okay with it. I want all of these people to be happy, no matter how they arrange themselves. I just have to stay out of it, have fun, root for my friends, and head to college with an awesome summer in the books.

In a way, I feel more freedom without the pressure to impress either of the guys.

Bluegrass floats in the air as we walk around. There's a sign for upcoming shows and I'm locked onto it when I see the name of one of the bands.

The Crux Constellation. They're here? Despite the heavy rotation they have in my playlist, I've never seen them play because they hail from Seattle.

"Hey, you like them, right?" Cale says looking over my shoulder.

"Yeah, but... it says it's their farewell tour," I say. Wow, that puts a damper on things. But getting the chance to see them today is pretty cool.

"Guess we're sticking around!" Cale says. I'm so happy that he gets it.

"Guys, it's noon already," Jin interjects. I'm flooded with jitters. The competition!

We shuffle over to the tent, and free folding chairs near the stage. The MC, a tiny woman in her forties with excess perkiness, battles miserable feedback and gets the show up and running. It's not Broadway, but it's something.

Cale and I are a few down in the set, so we sit with the audience and watch. It's like bad karaoke. We politely cheer with the sparse spectators, but then there's this dangerously good twelve year old girl. How can someone that young handle ABBA like a pro? She calls herself Little Dragon.

"Because she breathes fire!" Cale says into my ear when she hits a particularly difficult note.

We join the applause for her as she bows and grins big with gleaming braces.

"Wow! What a fabulous performance! To follow *that* act, we have Cale Thomas!" the MC says.

His arms fly up and he moves for the stage. "Here we go!"

"Break a leg!" I call after him.

Once on stage, Cale yanks the microphone from the stand. Fake drums sound. Cheesy synth rolls in and his back faces the crowd. His only dance move is the snap of his finger to the drum.

Snap. Snap.

The song builds with a guitar strum and I giggle because I know what's coming.

Cale was *made* for "Take On Me."

The melody synth hits. He moves his hips, wide and flouncy. He swerves around, continuing his ridiculous but entirely appropriate dance.

He's definitely a Will Smith.

And his voice hits the speakers with the lyrics and cheers erupt for Cale. They didn't know what I knew. Cale owns his crystal clear voice like a pro. From the way he handles vibrato, you would not think he's breaking a sweat with that wiggly dance.

He's infected everyone in the crowd with his insanely entertaining energy.

Jin leans over. "He's good!"

I eye him. "I know!"

Cale delivers the smooth, long words of the chorus, and it leads up perfectly to the final word. That crisp high note garners intense cheers. He has them eating out of his absurd jazzy hand. There is no Left Shark in this kid.

I sing the echo in the second chorus. I catch Jin grinning at me.

When the karaoke-quality guitar solo hits, Cale starts half-break dancing.

We. Eat It. Up. His model poses, his perfectly timed robot, his *sprinkler*! Little Dragon has some serious competition.

The song slows for the third verse. He falls to his knees and I can hear in his voice that he overdid it. But he reaches his hand out to me and sings the words.

To me.

I pull my fists to my face and blush. He winks at me.

Cale Thomas. No wonder everyone in this crowd is into you!

He gets up and dances again for the upbeat ending. After he hits that brilliant, high note a few more times, it's over. He bows and the enthusiastic cheers prove his worth.

I'm beginning to doubt my ability to one-up him.

Once he's off stage, my pulse quickens. I'm next. Performing always gives me nervous energy, but I embrace it. That way it pulls my introverted self into scary places. I also have a jolt of Cale-induced energy to work with, like I was plugged into his electricity.

The little MC clears her throat. "Up next, Joy Becker!"

Before I know it, I'm on the stage. I take a measured breath.

The karaoke piano plays the lead up. I adjust the mic.

Sharp inhale.

"Don't Stop Believin'" leaps from my throat. Journey's greatest hit. It was my life when I moved to this town a year ago. My one daily comfort. This song is muscle memory for me, so I play with vocalizations as I fall into the song. It's like home.

Armed with the surge I got from Cale, I claim the stage. I lean into the mic, not dancing with abandon, but tensing and pulling and pushing myself as I move through the emotion of it. It's not just the melody or the cheap synth of the karaoke version. The words, the way I command them, are my existence right now.

I love the way my heart bursts when I build up to the high note. That sweet echo of *my* voice reverberating in the speakers sends chills through my body.

I'm brimming with a songful of emotion and soul and vision, in sync with the power of music. It's like I have those wings on the cover of Journey's *Greatest Hits* album. For me, this is total freedom.

The guitar solo resounds and I have a few seconds to share it with the audience. My face hurts from smiling, Cale whoops, some even look starstruck... like Jin.

Holy... focus. I'm not done yet.

I hold the emotion until the last note. The outro ends and it's over. I fan myself while the people go nuts. I put myself out there, everything I had, and they loved it!

I descend from the stage, dripping with sweat, but I don't care. I run over to Cale and Jin. Cale wraps his arms around me and spins in a half circle.

"Girl, that was amazing!" he says as he releases me.

I'm out of breath, longing to be back in the middle of that song. I love and hate when it's over. I'm so harmonized with being alive when I sing.

In the corner of my eye, neon green. I look up and there's Jin, with a lingering look of awe. Brand new flutters wash over me.

"That was awesome," Jin says like he's catching his breath.

"Thanks!" I bite my lip and fan myself again. This heat, I swear.

My phone buzzes rhythmically in my shorts pocket, so I grab it to see who's calling.

MOM

There's a sudden drip of cold dread on my hot excitement. Buried deep is the part of me that knows she wouldn't call me like this without a motive. I brace myself when I answer.

"Hey, mom," I answer, scouting out a quieter space.

"Joy! Where are you?" she says, sharply.

I knew it.

I give the truth a shot. "I'm with my friends."

"You're supposed to be with your family! Or did you forget about us?"

Just like that, all the happiness I was feeling seconds ago escapes through the hole she just punctured in my ego.

"I didn't forget, I just…" I can't think of how to word it, but she jumps on me before I can.

"You *just* acted selfishly."

How dare I, *a grown adult*, make my own plans?

"Mom, I'm sorry. I didn't think it would make a difference if I was home or not."

The silence between our passes is super short when Mom is angry like this.

"You didn't *think* at all, Joy Diane!"

Psh. Middle name usage. It's pointless now.

She carries on. "Did you know your brother came home? When was the last time you called him?"

"Carson's home? Why is he home?" That doesn't sound good.

"Is everything okay?" Jin asks me. I turn and avoid him. My burning eyes land on a brown patch of grass.

"He lost his job! I can't believe you wouldn't even check on him!"

Yeah, right. Like the phone only works one way.

"What do you want me to do, Mom?" It always ends up with me asking this question, and obeying whatever she says. I hate it, but that's how it is.

"Just come home. I know you have to get back to the dogs, but at least spend a couple hours with your family. Your brother is really down."

I *really* wanted to stay here, but now I can't. I have no idea why Carson lost his job, but I know my brother. His feelings are as real, and definitely a lot more intense, than mine. There's no doubt he needs me. I have to go.

"Okay, Mom. I'll be there soon." I hang up and enter back into the world of Americanafest.

"Wait, what?" Cale starts, having heard my conversation. "You can't *leave*! You gotta stay to claim the prize."

But I can't win anything when my brother's involved.

"Are you really okay?" Jin asks again.

"Yeah," I sigh. "My brother just lost his job and my family wants me to spend the day with them. Can you drive me there?"

Jin nods, his brow still tense with concern.

"It can't wait?" says Cale, annoyed. "What about the prize? And that band you wanted to see?"

I shake my head. "You should stay, Cale. You beat me anyway, Mr. Glee Club President." I smile to lighten the mood. It doesn't really work. Cale lost some Joy.

"Hey, come here." Cale reaches his long arm around me and pulls out his phone with his other arm.

"Say 'singing champion!'" I see his big grin on the screen. I smile for the camera as best I can. It was fun while it lasted.

Cale kisses the top of my head and snaps the picture.

My stomach does a mini-flip. He just kissed me. Once he has the selfie, I stare up at him.

"What?" he says with an oblivious smile.

I guess it's fine. Why not kiss your girlfriend on the head, right? It's more *keeping up the image*. Even though it caught me off guard, I feel better.

He quickly sends me the selfie.

"Selfie King's gotta selfie," he says with a grin.

I really don't want to abandon my friend with all this positive energy for the soul-sucking aura that Carson is no doubt emanating.

"Sorry, Cale. I really wish I could stay."

He makes eye contact. "Me, too."

The deepness of his voice makes me think he means it. Like he doesn't regret that I'm not Lena. Coupled with the disappointed look on his face, you'd think I was his real girlfriend. He even slaps Jin on the back and tells him to take care of me.

Am I letting these lines get too blurry?

I wave goodbye and walk to the car with Jin.

It's a shame I spend the car ride to my neighborhood doing mental circles around my frustration. Jin is polite in silence the whole way.

Carson always wins. I shouldn't have forgotten.

TRACK 11 -
CATCHING
FEELINGS

Still July 4th

MY DEAD END STREET IS PACKED WITH LAWN CHAIRS and charred remnants of used fireworks. Five minutes after Jin drops me off, Mom gives me a tight squeeze, then shoves barbecue chicken in my hand.

Food usually makes me very forgiving and she knows it.

In a way, I wish she would keep seething. That way I'd have a reason to ignore her. But she always forgives and forgets. Rinse and repeat.

"Hey, sis!" Carson says, opening his tanned, muscly arms wide for a brother bear hug. The curls of his head tickle my face. He doesn't seem depressed to me!

Carson didn't actually *lose* his job, I find out. He got caught making out with one of the girls staying at the resort. Her parents made some threats, but she was twenty (older than *him*), so they slapped him on the wrist for misconduct or something. He's on unpaid leave until that family leaves the resort.

Mom was embellishing. Shocker.

I'd wallow in anger, but there's no point. Actually, part of me feels guilty for assuming my family wouldn't want to see me today because I was "working."

Alas, I was wrong. Happens a lot these days.

As long as Dad keeps pumping out bratwurst and chicken, I'll try to be happy. Sparklers make me kinda happy, so I grab one.

My phone buzzes.

Cale: GIRL YOU WON
Cale: OBVIOUSLY
Cale: They gave the title to the 12yo kid with the INSANE pipes
Cale: And yours truly got 2nd place!!

My sparkler flickers and hisses. It's a bittersweet victory. Three dots appear.

Cale: You were beautiful and amazing today

I stare at his words. It sounds weird, but for Cale, that text is understated. I'm used to his loud, elaborate compliments. Snarky gif wars. Exaggerated hand gestures emphasizing his enthusiasm. But somehow the simplicity feels... bigger.

I can't leave him on *read!* I should reply.

What does he even mean by that? I don't know what to say!

Joy: Thanks :) so were you :D

Oh God, kill me now. Instantly I want to take it back. "So were you??" I squeeze my eyes shut and hope it's dorky enough that he'll take it as a joke.

Cale: Hahaha, you know it!

I breathe. Was I holding my breath? Cale's into Lena. We're friends. I stare into my sparkler and remind myself of this plain fact.

"That's not from your boyfriend, is it?" Carson asks me. He's looking over my shoulder, waving his own sparkler close to me like it's a housefly.

"So what if it is?" I swat at his fizzing sparkler. "It's not like I'm sneaking around."

He scoffs. "Sexting counts, little sister."

"It's not! Here, see for yourself." I hand him my phone.

He examines the last few messages. He sees the picture, peers at me, and then hands my phone back.

"Um yeah, that was sexting if I've ever seen it."

"Are you crazy? How on earth was that 'sexting?'"

"I know what a guy is thinking when he calls a girl 'beautiful.' It's sexting." There's a smug look on his freckled face.

I roll my eyes. Carson thinks he knows everything about relationships and guys' intentions and how to woo girls, yet he's still single.

It's not near dark yet, but fireworks start going off. They ring in my ear, and I suddenly think about one, pudgy, slobbery face. Diamond. I hope he's not scared.

I say goodbye to my family. The fact that a paying job is on the line is enough to convince Dad to give me a ride all the way up to the boonies. I'm grateful it's him. Now I don't have to have any more anxiety-inducing conversations about boys with my brother. Or my mom.

In fact, the whole ride is completely silent and I'm 100% for it.

It's been an intense day. Up close explosives are not a necessity.

The house is still and quiet, like it's been abandoned for years. Just the creak of the door gives it life. The leftover smoke and sun linger on my skin. I could fall asleep right here on the foyer floor. I'd probably summon Jin again if I did that, though.

Diamond is totally asleep. Guess I worried for nothing. I take a picture for my story with the caption "the chillest" and post it. The silence is barely broken by distant popping and shimmering. I bet I can see some sky flowers from up here.

My phone vibrates. It's Jin.

Jin: You back?

Jin: Yeah. Diamond is sleeping. How's Zany doing?

Ellipses.

Jin: For how high-strung she usually is, fireworks don't seem to bother her.

More ellipses.

Jin: There's a great view from my balcony.

Yes. That's the first thing that comes to mind. Even though I could just curl up under Lena's fluffy blankets and pass out, all I want to do is go to him. Can I do that?

I don't know where keeping it friendly ends and "taking advantage" begins. Actually, I doubt this twinge of guilt has anything to do with Jin's company.

I don't want to disappoint Lena. Which reminds me that I still have to make sure Jin doesn't let the couch sleeping incident slip.

Buzz buzz.

Jin: It would be a shame if it were wasted on just me.

Jin: But it's okay if you're not up to it.

He doesn't make it easy to say "no," does he?

Joy: Be right over :)

I'm hopeless. I like him. The evidence is right here on my screen. And blundering in my heartbeat.

God, I like him.

But I'll be careful. It'll be nothing more than watching explosions in a dark sky and agreeing that Lena doesn't find out about him accidentally staying over. That's all.

So... I'm walking over to his house now.

When he opens his front door, he greets me with a smile and I remove my flip-flops. Jin guides me up the stairs into a low-lit, pristine bedroom I haven't seen yet. His parents', probably. There's a balcony through French doors that are draped with sheer curtains. I see the first firework sprinkling over the horizon before I step outside.

Pop!

The loud booms and soft shimmers are muffled by distance. Jin leans on the edge of the iron rail. He looks peaceful in the dim flashes of color. That warm, summer night wind finds me, my heart rate lowers.

It really is a good view. Of course, the sky is only part of it. I have to pull myself together. GOODNESS.

"I wanted to clear something up, Jin," I start, all peace fleeing. "About yesterday."

"Sure," he says.

"If my brother found out you'd slept on the couch with me, he'd probably flip." It's easy to use Carson as an excuse. Easier than revealing Lena's feelings, anyway.

"I won't say anything," he says, while looking at the view. "Don't worry."

"Like, not even to Lena," I add, for posterity.

He smirks. "You don't have to say that again."

Okay. Good. He gets it. We're cleared up.

Pop! Fireworks are like champagne, spritzing the stars. Happy Birthday, America.

I glance at Jin's cast. "It's too bad you missed out on Americanafest *and* Cabo." I keep my eyes on the glittering sky. It's too pretty to look away.

"I'd rather be here," Jin says. I peek at his lit-up face, not expecting at all that he'd be looking at me.

But he is.

Oh man, I'm glad it's dark and he can't see me blush so hard. I land my eyes back on the sky, but I'm not really watching. I can't look at Jin.

Bang! Pop!

But I do say, "Me too."

TRACK 12 -
SPACE AGE
LOVE SONG

July 13th

S O FAR, MY TACTICS FOR AVOIDING JIN HAVE MOSTLY SUCCEEDED. I pretend that the call feature doesn't work on my phone with Jin's contact. I have no reason to call him. Except that I want to.

When food or music aren't enough to distract me, I look at the listing for the beach house I booked for this weekend. Sometimes that helps. Mostly not.

The night of the Fourth, I acknowledged that I'm catching feelings for him. Which means I also have to avoid him. I've spent this week with the bulk of my focus on scheming again, even though I'm sure it'll fail. Given my own feelings about Cale's competition and all.

Jin has texted me a few times. More than a few.

But that's beside the point. The *point* is that I had to try really hard to accomplish three things:

1. Find some event that worked with both Lena and Cale's schedules,

2. Try to get them to cozy up at said event, and

3. Keep Jin away.

I expected the third would involve making him sit apart from Lena. I was wrong.

The first was simple. There's an 80s double feature night at the old Main Street Theater tonight, and they both are free. And so is my mopey brother. I invited him because he loves *Ferris Bueller's Day Off*. Also, he whined about being bored and wanting to hang out with me all day.

Dressing up for 80s night is encouraged, so I went with a simple Jennifer Grey *Dirty Dancing* look. High-waisted jean shorts and a white crop top. Lena showed up with a flamingo pink off-shoulder sweater, leggings, and a side ponytail. Even that doesn't look dumb on her.

The second task remains to be seen since we haven't seated ourselves yet. I just have to get them seated next to each other. I'm currently scanning the wine-colored velvet seats and formulating possible seating arrangements.

The third task turned out to be easy because even though I fully expected Lena to invite Jin, she didn't. I don't know why. It's taken a lot of mental energy for me not to ask where he is tonight. I might've been looking forward to having an accomplice, even if he's counterproductive to Cale's relationship goals.

I've limited texting with Jin. He told me more than once how impressed he was with my singing. Even though a lot of people tell me that, my heart still flutters with him. I've been really careful to keep responses to a single word or emoji. But not the winky emoji. Never the winky emoji.

Oh, I have an idea for how to arrange the seats!

Lena, Cale, and Carson are beside me in the aisle, the lines of each of their faces lit by the track lighting by our feet.

"Hey, I'm gonna use the bathroom real quick," I tell the others. "Squeeze in, I'll take the edge."

"I'm coming with you," Lena says without skipping a beat.

I deflate, hopefully not visibly. But my mission hasn't failed yet. I just hope that my bladder is full enough to keep up my deception.

We walk into the green tiled room with fluorescent lighting, but before the door fully shuts Lena says, "What's going on, Joy?"

I whip around. "What do you mean?"

"I *mean*, are you happy in your relationship?"

I frown. "Yeah, why?"

"Because... I don't know. I'm starting to wonder about you two."

Oh no oh no oh no.

"We're fine," I try to assure her.

"Was Cale really fine with inviting Jin to Americanafest?" She folds her arms. "I saw his neon green cast in your picture."

I freeze, looping between guilt and irritation. "Was there something wrong with that?"

"You told me nothing happened!"

Guilt is winning at the moment. "He had no plans, so I invited him. Cale didn't have a problem with it."

Her jaw tightens. "How did you *know* he had no plans?"

Irritation is winning now. "He told me. Was I not allowed to talk to him?"

She doesn't answer for a second. Her brow turns up and she releases tension. "You're right. I shouldn't have thought you wouldn't even talk. It's just..." She looks at herself in the mirror. Even under fluorescent lights, she's stunning. But past all that, where people don't often see, she's conflicted.

"I asked him to come. I didn't say it was a group thing, but he wasn't interested." She sighs. "Things aren't really happening between me and Jin. And I can't decide if I'm, like, scared it'll never happen, or if I'm fine with it because romance could wreck what we have." Lena looks at me, and then groans into the universe. "Ugh! But I want to kiss him so bad."

For once, I understand the feeling. I watch her eyes shift on her own reflection. I don't want to hope that she won't be with him. She's moving up to Seattle for him. I doubt he's told her about Korea, though. For once, I kind of pity Lena.

"By the way," she segues, "you and Cale have gone further, right?"

I look away, flush with nerves. "You have photo evidence of how far we've gone."

She puts up a judgmental finger. "Wait, that forehead kiss is how far you've gone? How can you hold back like that?" She grips her glittery phone and pulls up the picture. "Cale's so awesome. And he has *such* nice kissing lips."

I raise an eyebrow at her and turn to lean my hip against the garish bathroom counter. "Are you jealous of my boyfriend's nice kissing lips?"

To my surprise, Lena's eyes go wide. She blinks rapidly but says nothing.

My heart leaps for a second. *What if she actually is?*

"I'm not jealous," she finally says, "I just don't get how you can be so slow. It's torture!"

"Well maybe I'll invite him to my beach house this weekend," I say. Entirely joking. The mocking inflection and goofy expression convey it. There's no way I'd invite a boy to stay over with me.

I only do that by accident. Guilt wins again.

"You can't do that!" Lena says with an odd urgency.

It startles me. "Obviously I was joking."

"No! I mean, we have our lake trip this weekend."

I frown. "What lake trip?"

"Carson didn't tell you?"

"Carson? You made plans with Carson?"

"He texted me out of the blue and said we should book my cabin when he goes back to working at Victoria Lake. Our moms worked it out. They never told you?"

All at once, I'm fuming. It's suddenly very clear what happened. I storm out of the bathroom and head across the geometric carpet to Theater 1.

Carson whined about being bored all day. Carson texted Lena. Carson saw my beach house booking. Carson planned a family trip behind my back.

Carson definitely jacked my phone.

In the low, shifting light of the trailers, I find his spirally hair and bolt to him. He's shoveling popcorn in his mouth completely unaware of my fury. I reach the row.

"We need to talk," I say, not bothering to keep my voice or anger toned down.

He furls his eyebrows at me like there's no way I should be as mad as I am. Prick.

I yank him by his buttery hand out of the theater and into the hall, passing Lena as she sits next to Cale.

"So what's this I hear about a lake trip?" I accuse.

There's zero amusement in me, but he chuckles anyway.

"Damn. Lena ruined the surprise."

I roll my eyes. "You did it on purpose!"

He scoffs. "How could I do that when you never talk to me anymore?"

"I *know* you searched my phone. Find anything interesting?"

His brow goes up like he's the one who caught me in a lie. "Yeah, actually."

My stomach sinks. "What?"

He narrows his amber eyes at me. "Who's Jin?" He pronounces his name like *gin* instead of *gene*, which makes it more irritating. "You seem pretty cozy with him, for a girl with a boyfriend."

I can't tell if he's figured out that Cale and I aren't really dating or if he thinks I'm cheating.

Carson rubs the back of his neck, looking smug like he has me pegged. "Then you plan some secret trip to the beach. I *know* you didn't tell Mom about it."

I go slack-jawed. So he thinks I'm cheating. "Are you seriously trying—"

"Guys!" I hear, in a partial whisper coming from the entrance to the theater. It's Cale. My throat constricts. "You're missing the movie!"

Carson turns around, positioning himself directly in front of me. "We're fine, Cale. Be back in a minute." Carson doesn't exactly *sound* intimidating, but he is. It's all under his breath and in his stance. Cale definitely catches on.

"Okay, see you in there!" Cale flees, and I don't really blame him.

Deep breath. Carson turns back around.

"You had no right to go through my phone," I say. I keep almost all of my rage controlled, but there's still a tremor in my mouth and a worm in my chest.

He sighs, as if he's the one being reasonable. "Joy, when you don't tell me what's up, what choice do I have?"

He's infuriating! "You didn't even call me when you lost your freaking job, Carson!" I'm so exhausted trying to keep his feelings in check while weighing the risk of having my choices used against me. "You could have just asked me! I didn't think I had to tell you that I wanted a weekend to myself! You didn't have to sabotage it."

A tear rolls down my heated face. Normally I wouldn't unleash like this, but I'm so done with his games.

He throws up his hands as if he's tired of this. As if *he's* the victim. "I'm going back to the movie. We can do this later," he says.

As he swaggers back into the theater, it hits me. I'm not afraid he'll have an outburst. He already did all the damage he wanted to do.

No. I'm not staying in proximity to that jerk for the next four hours. Cale's romantic exploits be damned. I'm leaving.

I pass the muffled sounds of screeching brakes and explosions in some other movie. My stomach turns at the saturated smell of popcorn.

I don't look back even for a second when I walk into the parking lot. I slide into my car and drop my forehead onto my steering wheel. For once, I thought my brother and I might actually have a nice time. How idiotic of me.

I don't even know all of what Carson found out from stealing my phone, but I know I have to change my passcode. And worry a little bit about him texting Lena, now that he has her number. I seriously doubt she'll fall for his games (since she plays with the best of them), but I am worried he might make her think that I have a crush on Jin. Which is true, but I don't want her to *know*.

Honestly, I wonder if that would even matter anymore. In the short seconds between her doubting her own feelings and asking me about Cale, I was almost... happy.

You know, right up until I found out my brother purposely stole my phone and sabotaged my beach plans.

I sigh as I insert my keys into the ignition, but I pause before turning the beater on. The old-school theater lights flash into my car. It's not that I don't want to go to the Garcias' cabin at Victoria Lake, but I wanted some event to call my own. To think. I'm facing the drastic life change of starting college, with Carson around all the time.

The truth is, I'm likely to give in and go to Victoria Lake. Not to appease Carson, though. I'm *really* struggling to care about him right now. More because I want Lena and my mom to be happy. Canceling my solo trip isn't that hard. It's the kind of painful that's intense for a second, like ripping off a bandaid.

I try to start my car, but it just shudders.

My phone buzzes.

Carson: You better come back soon

Jerk. I don't text him back. Instead I slam my phone on my passenger seat and groan in frustration. If I have to deal with him for at least the next week and half, I'm seizing this night for myself.

I try my engine again, but it just sputters and never lights.

I stare at the FredU phone case that sits in a flashing stream of yellow light.

I know I shouldn't call him. I was doing so great with all the avoiding. Screw it. I call Jin.

The phone rings. He picks up right away.

"Hey, Joy," he answers, his voice as pleasant as ever.

I stifle the edge left in my voice. "Hey! Um, you aren't by chance up for giving me a ride, are you?"

It's quiet for a long second, but it might just be that my heart is pounding extra fast.

"Sure! Where are you?"

Wait, really? "Uh, at the movie theater. The one on Main Street."

I sniffle. He heard it. *Great.*

"Are you okay? Is something wrong?" I look out my windshield at the flashing bulbs of the vintage movie sign. 80S NIGHT DOUBLE FEATURE.

"Yeah, I'm fine. My dumb car just won't start."

"Oh, bummer. Well, I'm already downtown so I'll just be a few minutes."

"Oh. You are?"

"Yeah. I had a late dinner with my parents. See you soon, Joy."

"Bye." I hang up. Stare at my phone. Did that just happen?

I put my phone in Do Not Disturb. I don't really feel like dodging notifications tonight.

I get out and slam my door with residual anger. Then I see a glimmer in the driver's seat.

My keys. I locked them inside. Well, at least I'll have an excuse for why I left it here overnight.

Ugh. This is so me. I lean against the car and kick her with my heel.

A loud engine rumbles nearby. The kind that you know can't be an economical car.

Or a car at all.

I catch sight of the Harley that rolls into the parking lot, ridden by some guy covered in black leather and blue jeans, like James Dean. It's not until the motorcycle stops right in front of my car that I realize it's a Korean James Dean. Of course it is.

He cuts the engine and takes off his helmet. That does it. Jin's the sexiest guy I've seen in my life, no holds barred.

"Hi," I say, still dazed. "You didn't mention you'd be on a bike."

"It was the first day I could take it out after my cast came off. Oh, crap! Are you afraid of motorcycles?"

I shake my head, despite the fear that clearly grips me.

But that's not any worse than the dread that punches my gut when I see Carson jogging my way.

"Hold on," I say to Jin.

I meet my brother halfway. Oh, how I loathe his stern look of disdain. "What's this?" he accuses.

Any other day, I swear I would keep the peace. Not today. Not after what he did.

"Jin's taking me home," I tell him. I'm high-key frustrated. "I locked my keys in my car. And believe it or not, I don't *want* to go home with you right now. So let it go, okay? Go and enjoy the movie you were dying to see all day!"

"Hey!" He's offended. "I wanted to spend time with you! I should be the one to take you home!"

"Carson! Will you listen?! I don't want to go home with you!"

"What's the matter?" Jin says. He's off his bike. I've never seen him look this serious.

"He's my brother." It's not an answer to his question, but it also is.

"Is this that Gin guy?" Carson almost seems amused.

"Oh my god! It's *Jin*! He's my friend." This is so juvenile.

"No, no. I wanna meet the guy who begged my sister to come watch fireworks, even though she has a boyfriend." Carson steps forward. What an ass.

Jin doesn't shrivel backward like Cale did earlier.

I put my hand against Carson's chest. "Be cool! He's just my friend, okay?"

Carson looks down at me. "I can't let you go with him." He looks up at Jin. "Sorry."

"Shouldn't she decide that?" Jin asks, a small flame in his words.

"She's my *sister*," Carson fires back.

"Yeah, not your dog. You don't own her." Jin shakes his head like he shouldn't have to make that argument.

Carson presses his chest against my hand. I panic. "Carson. Carson! Please, don't."

He looks back at me, seeming at a loss for what to say. He's not angry with me. "You're not going, right?"

It's like he thinks we share one brain. One heart. But we don't.

I glance at Jin, then back at my brother. I can't believe I'm doing this. Because it's guaranteed to blow up in my face later.

"Yeah, I am," I say. And then I back away.

Carson stares at me, hurt that I didn't choose him. Eventually, he accepts it bitterly. "Okay, yeah. But you just tell *him*—" he points at Jin— "that he can look up my name if he wants to know what I do to guys who mess with my sister."

I look at Jin to gauge his reaction. His brow is up, like he wants to know if Carson is done yet.

"See you at home," Carson tells me, the words steeped in bitterness. And then he walks back to the theater, whipping the door open with all his force before he disappears.

I don't know what he'll do now. Probably dismantle everything.

Jin holds his helmet out for me. "Come on, I wanna take you somewhere."

TRACK 13 -
STYLE

Still July 13th

I'M NOT SURE IF I'M READY FOR THE TERRIFYING THRILL of riding on the back of a motorcycle. I hold Jin's helmet in both hands and chew my lip at his proposition.

"If you're up for it," he adds.

I so am. It's at least a thousand times the thing I would rather do than go back inside the movie theater.

"Where would we go?" I ask.

"There's this place across the river that makes donuts fresh at night. I hung around after dinner so I could get some."

Late night donuts?

"It's my treat," he adds, with one of those irresistible smiles.

I nod. I motion to lift the heavy helmet on my head, but I pause. "Wait. Don't you need a helmet, too?"

Jin leans over the satchel attached to his bike and pulls out a smaller helmet. "That one's better protection. You should take it. Oh! And this, too."

He shakes off his jacket and gives it to me. Obviously he's wearing a white t-shirt. I put the jacket and helmet on, feeling about fifty pounds heavier. The helmet flattens my hair and muffles my hearing, but it's worth it when Jin gets close with that jasmine scent of his and secures it for me.

And it's even more worth it when I slide behind him on his Harley and wrap my arms around his waist before we lurch out onto the road.

Immediately I sense danger. It feels ridiculously insecure. Like, I feel more secure on a kitchen chair, and believe me, I fall off of those easy enough!

The violent wind races past, with the streetlights and cars that seem so much bigger from on top of a motorcycle. I cling to Jin for dear life every time we are near a semi-truck.

When I catch my breath, I think about how Jin feels under my arms. He's skinny. I can feel his ribs and flat stomach. I love how his fluttering t-shirt tickles my fingers.

My stomach flips when another semi-truck passes us. I squeeze Jin and feel him laughing.

I've taken this route a dozen times, but not like this. Once I'm past the fear, there's a thrill that I've never experienced. We're suspended between life and death, tightly bound together by my flimsy muscles.

It's the closest to an adrenaline junkie I've ever been.

Once we exit the freeway, he finds a spot to park and the slow down feels like we're treading mud compared to the freeway. I'm desperate to take this helmet off and hear properly again.

But now that my physical body is safe, all I can think about is if Jin's going to ask me what Carson meant.

He can look up my name if he wants to know what I do to guys who mess with my sister.

My head feels light as a balloon once it's free of the helmet. Static and all. Jin carries it for me and gestures to the street block lit by yellow and pink neon signs. Our path to this niche donut shop.

Jin walks beside me, looking like a pillar of classic style. I look like I was swallowed by black cow hide and then electrocuted, most likely.

I'm just *waiting* for him to ask at this point. I'll be in a torturous mental loop until he does.

"You're not gonna ask?" I start.

"About what?" Obviously he wasn't obsessing over it like I was.

"About my brother. He only threatened you so you'd bring it up."

"Maybe that's why I'm not asking."

Hmm. That's nice. Someone who refuses to play Carson's game.

I examine the black sky. It's hard to see stars in the city's light pollution. As we walk, I wonder if I should just tell Jin what happened.

I see one tiny, flickering star. There are some that shine through all the fake light, I guess.

"Promise me you won't actually Google my brother's name."

Jin nods reassuringly. "I promise."

So far, he's been good on his promises. I should leave it there.

I see people lined up before I see the shop. This hole-in-the-wall place must be amazing. But the draw could be the novelty of donuts at night. Or both. This part of town looks too sketchy for this many people to crowd for mediocre donuts. Sure enough, I read the neon sign, in bubblegum pink: FRESH DONUTS NOW.

Once we're near the window, I catch a glimpse of the rotating display hosting tons of odd-looking donuts. Cereal, crushed oreos, pink, orange, purple. Some look normal and delicious. One of them has bacon on it.

It smells divine, like icing and grease with sugar dust in the air.

Most of the donut names on the chalkboard menu are innuendo or straight up profanity, yet people order like it's nothing. I go for the chocolate one with Cocoa Puffs on it. Jin grabs the Oreo one with peanut butter drizzle. Of course, the clerk with electric blue hair is pierced and tatted because it would be offensive if she weren't. She takes Jin's cash and barely even hands us our donuts before she shouts, "NEXT!"

We walk out and now I get the appeal. It looks delicious, but mostly it's weird. An escape from the mundane.

"So you were going to brave this by yourself?" I say to Jin.

"Yeah, but I'm glad I didn't have to."

We take the emptier blocks back to his Harley. I bite into my triple chocolate cake donut. It's soft and even warm, the cake gives to my teeth. I don't think two whole minutes go by before mine is gone.

I clear my throat and peek at Jin, halfway through his donut. To be fair, his donut was larger.

He's really not going to ask. Not even in the silence.

Here goes nothing.

"My brother beat up a guy that was forcing himself on me," I blurt.

Jin chokes on his donut.

"Oh my god!" I put my hands to my mouth. "Sorry! Sorry."

He puts his hand up. "It's okay! Don't be sorry. I just wasn't expecting you to say that."

"After what my brother said, I felt like I owed you some kind of explanation."

He clears his throat. "Joy, you don't owe me anything. I don't care what your brother said." I appreciate the sympathy in his eyes. "But I'm sorry for what happened to you."

I shrug. "It's over now. But it was a big deal at the time. The guy Carson beat up went into a coma for like a full day. Plus, he was the mayor's kid. The only reason Carson didn't go to jail was because our families reached an agreement. We'd all stay away from the media and none of us would press charges. It saved their reputation, I guess. Political people are obsessed with image, you know?"

He nods. "That was last year?"

"Yeah. In Salem."

His face is tense. He says "hmm" in acknowledgement but his mouth

JOY'S SUMMER LOVE PLAYLIST

is shut tight.

"Anyway," I go on. "My mom worked for the mayor, so she left her job. And Carson lost his scholarship to OSU because even though we couldn't talk to the news, local media published stuff about him anyway. Which is totally bogus because they made him out to be some monster who unleashed his wrath on an innocent politician's kid. He's overprotective, but he's not a monster." I sigh. "That's why we moved up to Willow Haven last year."

It's easier than I thought, retelling my past to Jin. I can tell he's at a loss for words, so I point to his donut.

"You gonna finish that?"

"I'm really sorry, Joy."

"It's fine. It's your donut."

He shakes his head, catching up to my humor. "No, I mean... you know what I mean."

Even though I was kidding, he still offers me his donut. I refuse, but remain impressed with him. Continuously. The pink and yellow neon hues bounce off the perfect lines of his slightly sad face.

I'm happy for his concern, but sometimes it sucks to hear that people are sorry for something they have zero control over. They wish it never happened, I get it. But that's the burden of sharing. When someone believes you, you hurt them.

So, even though I was the victim, my autopilot reassures everyone who's sorry.

"I'm okay now. I mean, it still comes back. And I still feel guilty because I just watched, frozen, while my brother smashed a kid's head in at a party."

This part. This is the part that hurts the worst. No matter how many times my therapist told me to remember *it wasn't my fault*, I carry it that way.

"I always felt like I should have tried to stop him," I say, my voice a pitiful wisp. The echoes of therapy play in my head. *His mind was gone, his body was on a mission. You could not have stopped him.*

Always followed by a flicker of the shameful thought: I didn't *want* to stop him.

"He could've stopped himself," Jin says.

My heart stops for one beat. Somehow him saying it makes it feel true. Words coming from a guy who actually exhibits self-control, and remorse, and doesn't let himself get manipulated.

Jin Park is the opposite of me and my brother. I'm sure Carson will hate him for it.

But I love him for it.

I swallow. "I'm sorry my brother was such a jerk to you earlier."

Jin shakes his head with a mouthful of donut, like I shouldn't be apologizing for him. We arrive at his bike and he leans on it.

I continue trying to make up for Carson's failings. "He's protective, clearly. But I was really upset because I found out he was planning this lake trip with Lena next week--totally behind my back--and now I have to cancel the beach trip I just booked."

"Why do you have to cancel?"

Because I don't want to upset my brother. Because he'll tell Lena whatever he thinks he knows about me and Jin if I don't appease him, if he hasn't already.

But I can't exactly tell Jin that.

I cock my head. "It's not like I don't want to go, it was just a sucky thing for him to do. Carson's just... afraid of losing me, I guess."

It's really weird when the truth that's been under the surface just flows right from your own mouth and you weren't expecting it. But that's it. Carson doesn't want me to leave him.

Jin finishes his last bite of donut. "What if I said that my mom and I got invited to the cabin next week and I could, maybe, go too?"

My eyes go wide, feeling like my body is champagne bubbles. "Like, for real?" I sound the tiniest bit too eager, but if Jin's coming to the lake then I'll happily cancel my plans.

"Would you like that?" His question is adorably wary.

I can't say this out loud, but *hell yes, please stay in a cabin with me!*

"Yeah. I'd like that." I don't try to hide my smile.

TRACK 14 -
BAD LIAR

July 17th

I'M BEGINNING TO THINK LENA WAS ON TO SOMETHING with that whole "you can't pack for vacation in a couple hours" thing. It makes a big difference when you're *trying* to look cute. Mom and I are supposed to leave in an hour, but I'm skeptical of my ability to decide by then.

I'm about to give up on that and just pack all of Carson's hand-me-downs, since my vintage stuff is really not conducive to camping activities.

I don't think Carson said anything to Lena. She's been strangely silent on the subject of Jin, so I really don't know. But sitting with my traitorous romantic thoughts made me realize that I should try not to be so excited. Jin is still off-limits and Lena is worth my loyalty.

I've had friends betray me before. I won't be one of them.

Oh, I give up. I stuff old sweatshirts and gym shorts into my suitcase. I should probably just admit the truth to Lena. At least about Jin.

Maybe Cale, too. I don't know. I don't want to foil Cale's plans, either.

Ugh! What do I do?

Like a silent movie on repeat in my brain, I see Jin's smile in the glow of neon signs. The flickering light of fireworks. The different times he opened his front door. I imagine what he looks like by the light of a bonfire.

Buzz buzz. It's Cale.

Cale: I've got a surprise for you, Becker!

Ooh! I'm intrigued. I wonder what it could be.

Cale: I've been keeping it a secret for a while

Joy: Well? What is it?

Another car? One that doesn't need new spark plugs or a timing belt? Maybe one that doesn't need an oil change every three months just to run?

Cale: You will be graced with my presence
Cale: AT VICTORIA LAKE
Cale: BOOM

He sends me a gif of a mic drop.

Joy: You're coming??? What?! How did I not know this?

Cale: Me and Garcia have been keeping it quiet
Cale: Imma cannonball that lake SO HARD

My shoulders loosen when I laugh. That dork.

Wait. He schemed with Lena??

Joy: I can't believe you connived with Lena!

Joy: Does she know it's all a ploy to get her to like you?

Joy: How's that going, btw?

Ellipses. Ellipses.

Cale: It's hard to get the girl you like to notice you

He sends me a gif of Jim Carrey, arms outstretched, saying "LOVE ME" which is definitely something I could imagine Cale doing in real life.

Joy: Lol good thing you'll have lots of time with her at the lake

Cale: good thing indeed :D

Maybe he'll pull it off. Getting himself inserted into our multi-family vacation is a genius move.

"You're not packed? What, you don't want to go?" Carson says, leaning in my doorway. His tone is like I'm twelve years younger and not twelve months.

"No, I do. Just..." I turn away from scattered clothes to face him. "Did you say anything to Lena on eighties night?"

He drops the arm that was propped up. "I didn't tell her anything. I just said you started to feel sick so I was taking you home. Then I left."

He *covered* for me? "Why?"

"Why do you care what I said to Lena? What if I said something to your boyfriend?"

"Because... Cale won't misunderstand. But Lena will."

"Why? 'Cause she likes that guy... Jin whatever?"

"God, Carson! I'm not going to explain it. You're the worst person to tell secrets to."

"She does, right?" he solicits, but I ignore him.

I stand up and gesture to the door. "Just get out. Please."

He suddenly registers my words. "What do you mean I'm the 'worst' person to tell secrets to?"

I glare at him. "Seriously? You constantly hold stuff over me! I can't tell you anything without you bringing it up as some sort of collateral."

He doesn't leave. "What are you keeping from me now?"

I'm so exhausted with him. "Get out!"

He doesn't. He bolts into my room and grabs the suitcase so freaking fast.

Slam! Oh my God! He threw it against the wall.

When did my hands cover my face? I don't remember doing that. I'm tense all over. My clothes have littered my room.

"Dammit, Joy! What are you keeping from me, huh?" His voice booms, but it also rings with fear. I bring myself to look at him.

It's not anger on his face. It *is* fear.

"Carson..." I mutter.

He folds, crouching to the floor. "I'm sorry."

My pulse calms down. What does he think I'm keeping from him?

Mom crashes into the room, her mouth and eyes round. "What happened?" she says repeatedly, placing her hands on Carson's shoulders.

"It's nothing. I'm okay. I'm fine."

I'm confused. Those words are coming from his mouth, not mine.

What's with him? First he *doesn't* tell Lena or Cale about Jin picking me up and actually covers for me. Then he flips out when he thinks I'm hiding something from him. And then he... calms himself?

This isn't my brother.

Sitting shotgun next to my mom reminds me of the time the whole family visited Victoria Lake when I was little. But this time, my ears have grown AirPods and we don't play the alphabet game the whole way.

The trees pass by to my summer playlist, keeping me company for the hour drive. Then we arrive.

Victoria Lake.

Vintage-style signs direct our car to the lodge, swim park, and lakefront. Mom follows the arrows for Cabins 91-130.

The further we are from the resort entrance, the more nature takes over. The cedars tower high and the roads are less manicured. I see some gravel roads leading to the cabins. I had no clue the Garcias would settle for an unpaved driveway.

Familiar cars are parked by the cabin. Lena's mom's Land Rover. Jin's Mazda. Cale's Hyundai. Now my mom's car is parked among them.

When I get out, it sounds like the moms are competing to see who can greet with the highest pitch voice. Normally I'd eavesdrop like a proper introvert, but this cabin...

I mean, it's not a cabin. It's a mini cedar mansion. Lena's family must like double story windows, because the angular panes reach into the sky. So big, you can see right through the house to the backyard.

I grab my things from the car. Angela, Lena's mom, directs everyone. She has a handle on life that I can't comprehend. I don't know how we're made of the same chemicals. And there's a reason Lena is gorgeous: because her mom is. Angela is the Greek side, with black hair in shiny, loose curls and the same bright green eyes as her daughter.

Lena bounds down from the front deck to greet me, her hair swinging behind her like *Baywatch*. "The boys are getting my room since it has two twin beds. The moms have the other two guest rooms, so you and I get to share the pullout in the basement. Promise it's not drab *at all*."

I laugh because I love it when Lena pretends to care about things like whether or not I care about a basement being drab. "Great," I say. "Where's..."

I hope I don't seem eager as I look for him.

"Cale?" she finishes. I nod. *Sure. I meant to say Cale.*

JOY'S SUMMER LOVE PLAYLIST

Angela overhears and says, "Oh, he's in the kitchen with Jin. Cutting watermelon, if you're hungry."

"I am so hungry, it's not even funny," I say to Angela, and she scrunches her nose at me in acknowledgement. Her attention goes right back to my mom's probably invasive questions.

"Go ahead and find the boys. I gotta talk to my mom," Lena says.

The boys. Of course she lumps all of the male species into one term.

I run inside because I really want to see... the fruit. Just the fruit.

The place is gorgeous. I feel like I'm constantly entering beautiful homes with arms full of my unworthy belongings. Yes, I did bring my trademark pillow and blanket.

This cabin is huge and airy, with exposed beams in the super high walls. That pleasant brown-red of cedar colors the inside, until the white and black fur floor coverings break the scene. The grey boulders of the fireplace climb one side of the living room.

"There she is!" Cale's voice bounces against the walls and I look over to see his two lanky arms open in reception. One of his hands holds a watermelon triangle. I drop my stuff on the espresso leather couch. The contrast of it is ridiculous. Fashion Barbie, enjoying a luxurious leather couch. I mean, she's a billionaire, so why not?

I smile at Cale but... I'm distracted by Jin putting force into the chef's knife as he cuts the watermelon. I approach the kitchen island and he has the nerve to smile at me.

I pluck a triangle for myself and take a bite. It's so perfectly sweet, firm, and overly juicy. At least food is also distracting.

Jin's eyes flit up at me for a second. He makes another cut, smirking. "I see you brought your usual things."

"Of course!" I say with a mouthful of watermelon. It's already dripping down my fingers.

Cale snags a new piece. "Clearly, she's not a shy one," he says to Jin.

Jin laughs. "No. I knew that already."

Oh, goodness. It seems I have a reputation among *the boys.*

The front door shuts and Lena walks in. She beckons me to leave my snack and check out the basement, so I grab my things and follow.

Down here is certainly darker, but the track lighting gives it a movie lounge vibe. There's a huge black leather sectional that should really be two couches. Lena's already pulled out the bed. The beams make it seem like the walls are higher than they are.

"Movie nights are so fun here!" says Lena. "Perfect for *cuddling*."

"If it comes to cuddling," I say. "I'm glacial, remember?"

"I wasn't talking about you," she says with a laugh. "But jeez, get a move on. You can't even cuddle?"

"I can't even flirt yet. I don't know how I ended up in a relationship."

Yikes. Lying still stings. I kind of don't want to do it anymore.

"Lena, can we talk?" She gives me her attention. And I freak out internally. I can't do it yet.

"It wasn't too awkward when I left you at the movies with Cale, was it?" I say.

"No! We're buddy-buddy now," she smiles. "Actually, that's how I set up your surprise."

Yes. The surprise.

"Oh, really? Thank you! It's a good surprise." I hope I'm selling the *I'm happy my boyfriend is here* thing. I mean, I am happy to have Cale around, but Jin was the bigger prize.

Ugh, I wish I didn't feel so guilty right now.

She flashes a smile. "I'm also super glad Jan-di convinced Jin to come. At first he said he didn't want to ruin a girl's trip, you know, when it was just you and me and all the moms. Guess he changed his mind."

He did? Holy crap, *he did?!* Was that for me?

The hopeful part of me wants to think so. Because if he even has a sliver of the same feelings as me, I'd be over the moon. And really conflicted. Now I'm not sure which feeling is right.

But the fearful part—the greater part—watches Lena tap the spines DVD cases on the shelf. She's in love with him. She picked her college so she could be near him. Even if Cale did get her to notice him, he'll be at FredU with me. Honestly, we'd probably all be better off if Jin and Lena end up together. Cale would survive the rejection and so will I.

But that hopeful part of me is a lot bigger than it was yesterday.

We spent the day swimming at the lake, and I can't wait to spend long hours doing that all over again. I had a pineapple snow cone hand delivered to me by my brother. For a while, Lena and I just tanned and watched Jin and Cale race across the strip of sand, crash into the lake, swim to the buoys and back. I had my bets on Jin, but Lena bet on Cale and she was right. Jin lagged a tiny bit behind. It was wildly amusing. Among other things.

One perfect lake day down, four to go. I'm actually glad I cancelled my plans.

Lena walks up fresh from her shower, interrupting my reading. I'm not really paying attention to the magazine, though because I keep thinking about college. I don't know why I'm starting to question my choices now. In my head, my major was always finance because it made good sense. But now I'm wondering if I should've explored other schools. I bring it up to Lena.

"God! We have at least a year before we have to figure out that crap, Joy."

Lena stands over the bed, fluffing the down blankets and smoothing them so we can get to sleep. The basement carries more of Fernando's taste than Angela's. I think this is the only place he's allowed to display Dallas Cowboys paraphernalia. I get up and drape the Cowboys throw over my arm, dark blue with a silver star. I wait for Lena to tidy our bed.

"And that plan is approved by your mom?" I ask.

She grabs the blanket from me. "I tell her Portuguese. But when she really interrogates me, I stick with political science."

"Political science?"

"I mean, I'll take a class to see if I like it. When Mr. Allen did Puerto Rican week in Lit, I started to really wonder about the politics of my heritage. So *yeah*, I'll double major in poli-sci and dance." Her laugh is like caramel, sweet and smooth and a little sultry. "You still majoring in *finance*?" she asks, using some awful form of a British accent conveying mockery and fanciness.

I throw a pillow at her. "At least I never argue with my mom about it."

Lena finishes making the bed, then turns and drops backward onto it. "I wish I had your mom."

My right brow goes up. "No. You really don't. I wish I had *your* mom."

"Oh my god, Joy. You have no idea how wrong you are. My mom has a deep, deep dark side."

Lena always talks about it, but I sure haven't seen the "dark side" of Angela Garcia. She's treated me wonderfully. She's a pillar of success in the community with her commercial real estate business. She even told me that I'm her favorite of Lena's friends.

And seriously, as if Fernando Garcia, keeper of the world's best chocolate chip cookies, would stay married to someone with a "deep, deep dark side."

I plop next to Lena on the just-made bed. "Can I ask you something?"

"Mmhmm." I can tell she's sleepy.

"When did you know you'd fallen for Jin?"

I feel kind of bad for gauging my own feelings against hers, but that's why I'm asking.

Lena bolts up to sitting. "Don't be so loud! Oh my God!" She rakes her hair with her fingers, laughing at the nerves.

And then she tells me the story.

It started with her getting her braces off in middle school. She was a kid when she got them on and a woman when they came off. The sudden sex appeal was brutal on her self-esteem, which surprises me. She got a lot of attention, good and bad.

"All fake," she says. "I got asked out every day. It was like a game to them. No matter what I did, I lost."

Oof. I've never related more to her.

Going into the summer before high school, Jin's family decided to take Lena with them to Korea. Lena lights up when she talks about it. I can picture the scenes as she describes them: the top-notch, steaming Korean food, being bombarded by different customs, learning ritual phrases and making them laugh when she mispronounced things. I'm not jealous that she's well-traveled, but going abroad with people who take care of you like family makes me wish I were her.

Her brightness fades. "Then came the first day of high school. It was a freaking horror show."

She takes a deep breath, like I do when I'm steadying myself.

"What made it so bad?" I ask.

"I'm not stupid, you know?" She's not really asking me. "I know what I look like. But the first day of classes, word spread that there was a *new hot chick* in school. People flooded the halls during first period just so they could get a look at me through that stupid slitty window in the door, like goddamn paparazzi. I thought it was gonna be eighth grade all over again. But, then I found Jin at lunch and sat with his friends to eat. He knew what was up, so he just told people to back off and they did because they respected him." I don't usually hear Lena's voice so low or genuine like this. "There's no other guy out there I respect as much as Jin. I don't really know when it happened, but... I realized that I can't lose him."

Wow, that makes me feel selfish. Here I am with a schoolgirl crush like all those other girls Lena mentioned and here she is way beyond just *loving* Jin Park. He changed the whole game for her.

I fixate on one corner in the ceiling, where the crown moulding doesn't quite meet. Is Jin worried what Lena will think of his opportunity in Korea?

I wonder if she's the reason he's struggling to decide.

"Anyway," she says, yawning. "I'm wiped out."

"Me too," I say, though it's not really true. But it doesn't matter what I say. The dark lashes of her eyes are already closed even though the lights are still on.

It doesn't matter if I'm a bad liar or a good one. I doubt I'll ever have a chance with Jin.

TRACK 15 - FOREVER YOUNG

July 18th

THERE'S SOMETHING SO WONDERFUL about the way summer leaves a layer of different things on your skin. Smoke from a bonfire, sweat and tan from direct sun, the musty smell of lake water in your hair. And if we're talking about me, the dried watermelon juice on my arms.

For hours, Cale and I have been swimming in the lake like we're a pair of preteens. With adult-sized cannonballs. I beat him breath-holding, he's clearly a faster swimmer, I'm better at Marco Polo, and we're about matched in splash wars.

He's definitely got me beat in the bright smile department, though.

I'm not sure if you can call the sand patch a beach, but it's packed with swimmers and tanners. The docks, too. I'm out by the boundary of buoys around the swimming area. I can see out into the grander portion of Victoria Lake, where people fish and zip around on jet skis or sit in swan-shaped pedal boats. I definitely want to learn to water ski someday.

Bobbing in the cool lakewater, I glance over to land and witness squealing little kids in adorable baby rashguards, ketchup-covered hot dogs in their pudgy hands. Lunch sounds like a good idea.

Especially once I spot my brother walking to the snow cone stand to start his shift.

"I'm heading landward," I tell Cale, and paddle myself in that direction.

"Understood, Almond Joy! I'm gonna float on for a bit." Sure enough, he splays himself out and relaxes on the water surface.

I make eye contact with my brother and he smiles at me from beyond the dude so clearly flirting with him. Even if he was a jerk for upending my plans, I can't stay mad at him. I still see the kid who grew up with me. The one who smashed ice cream in my face as often as he willingly shared a single cone. He adjusts his hat and does "the nod."

It's our thing. At baseball games, he finds me and nods from the pitcher's mound.

I nod back. I always will.

Water from the swim drips down the length of my body, tickling my legs. I slick back my dirty blond hair and run toward our group's spot. The sand sticks to my feet, then the hot concrete path pricks them, and then my soles are caressed by supple green grass. I don't blame the moms for not swimming among overeager kids.

Jin claims he forgot his bathing suit, but I overheard Jan-di say she wanted to spend time with him because she "never see him when he at school." It seems like he's engaging the moms pretty well.

Lena clearly prefers sunbathing to swimming. Might more accurately be called "summertime man-catching." But, even with her bright pink bikini that hugs her youthful Latina curves, she straight up ignores how "nice" the men are toward her today. The guy she fell for is probably the least superficial guy in her life, maybe apart from Cale.

But even he makes elaborate plans to get her attention, I guess.

I yank the blue striped towel from the ground and use it to dry my face and scrunch excess water out of my hair.

A toddler in a forest green swim diaper waddles up and touches my leg. He has adorable round eyes with impossibly long eyelashes, big rosy cheeks, and brown curly hair that reminds me of Carson.

"Hawoh!" he says, looking up at me with a toothy smile. What did I do to deserve such a cute smile? Seriously, I've been getting way more than my fair share lately.

Jin kneels down to him and holds up his hand for a high-five. "Hey, little guy," he says, and the boy slaps his hand.

Awwwww! I feel like Kristen Bell seeing a cuddly little sloth.

"Oh my gosh! I'm so sorry!" says the mom. She's a petite woman with long wavy hair, who snatches the boy up with a confident grasp that only moms seem to have.

"It's okay!" I tell her. I kind of love when kids break social boundaries like that.

Jin stands up and says with utmost charm, "I hope my future kids are as cute as yours."

"Ha, thank you," she says graciously, and I know she blushes because, like, *how could you not?!* I'm blushing behind my towel and it's not even my kid!

So Jin Park wants kids someday. Noted. Man, I didn't think that sort of thing got to me.

"Your boyfriend is really nice, Joy," says Angela, and I revert back to reality. She's stretched out in a lounge chair with her wide-brim hat, flipping through a home decor magazine.

"Where did you meet him?" she asks.

"Glee club," I answer. Jin takes a breath to say something, but Angela commands the verbal baton.

"Your bathing suit is so cute," she says, like my answer didn't even register.

"Really? Thanks." Her comment surprises me. It's just a plain and modest navy one-piece with a sweetheart neckline. I mean, it's fine. Lena's is way more glamorous.

"You should dress more like her, Lena," says Angela, not skipping a beat.

"Mom!" Lena says, like a bite. She turns her head the other way, having none of it.

"You dress too sexy. Guys minds go crazy--"

"Mom!"

Angela doesn't stop for even half a second. "Jin knows! Tell her."

My mouth drops open, but I close it right back up. Jin cocks his head and I notice he's stopped breathing. He lets out air with a small laugh.

He doesn't dare remain unresponsive. "I don't think it should matter what girls wear. Guys will always think things." Safe answer. I'd verbally agree with him if it wouldn't offend the Garcia matriarch.

"What do you *prefer*, though?" she asks him, pulling her sunglasses down to peek at his face.

His brow lifts. "I don't think--"

"Oh come on, Jin. You're like my own kid. Like a brother to Lena. Your opinion matters to us. Come on."

There's the dark side.

Lena is stoic, with arms folded and glare in the opposite direction. No matter what he says, Jin is doomed at this point, I think.

"I prefer a girl who's confident, no matter what she wears," he answers.

This guy. Pulling a rescue move on a collision course. I hinder a smile and wipe my neck of the sweat beads I earned during this conversation.

Angela pulls her sunglasses back into place. "Well, I don't know who raised you, but she did a pretty good job."

Lena uncrosses her arms mouths "thank you" to Jin.

So maybe it wasn't "deep, deep dark" like Lena had described, but I see now why Angela Garcia is not to be messed with. Unless, of course, you're the irresistibly benevolent Jin Park.

I slam cards on the glass coffee table. "Told you not to mess with me, Thomas!"

"Again!?" Cale groans.

"Tired of being slaughtered at this game?" I taunt.

Jin laughs, still shuffling the cards in his hand as if I didn't just beat him, too. Three times in a row.

Our second lake day was a success. Once we finished hamburger dinner at the cabin, the moms cleaned up and called it a night, presumably to read similar romance novels. Lena went for her nightly shower, so I got left with *the boys*. I did what all teenage girls would do and hustled them into a game I'm good at.

The smell of fresh shampoo hits me and I notice Lena's walked up. She shakes her damp hair, dressed in a cute fluffy cardigan and leggings. It's the opposite of me with my post-swim blonde mess and hand-me-down hoodie and gym shorts.

"We're doing s'mores, right?" she asks.

"Did you say *s'mores*?" Cale asks in monotone. He smacks the table, startling the cards right out of my hands, and darts to the kitchen.

"Guess that's a 'yes'?" Jin says with a grin and I just laugh. He helps me pick up the scattered cards.

And our hands touch. I feel electricity. That's the only word I have to describe it. I'm staring at the table and Jin's hand takes a second too long touching mine, or is that me?

I retreat.

"Sorry," we say in unison.

"I got this," he offers. I nod. I'll let him take clean up. Yep. I'm gonna go outside and shake this tingling feeling off my hand.

Before I reach the sliding door to the backyard, though, I pass by the mudroom. Out of the corner of my eye, I see Lena reaching for something in a cupboard.

Cale is with her. I seriously doubt s'mores ingredients are in the mudroom, but right away I sense that they're having a private conversation. I won't eavesdrop, but...

Sometimes I overhear.

"You know you've got game, Cale. There's no need to hold back."

What?! I fumble opening the sliding door. Is she... is this actually working? I dash outside and try to forget about what I just heard but also I'm obsessing over it.

In the twilight, I start the fire with some old newspaper and a lighter. I always hold my breath in the moment before a small fire grows into a blaze. I wait for it to catch.

Cale and Lena were just *whispering* in private. Maybe I've been too pessimistic and Lena's hesitation is because of Cale.

I sink into a fabric lawn chair coated with pollen and dirt. The bonfire glow flickers and I'm the sole admirer for a minute. Closing my eyes, I breathe in the faint smoke in the air. The image in my mind is Cale hand-in-hand with Lena.

"Hey," I hear. It's Cale. "I got something I wanna tell you."

"Yeah?" I say. *That the girl of your dreams finally noticed you??*

His mouth twitches to and from a smile before he pulls his hand out of his pocket and holds a small paper out to me.

I take it. "A business card?"

???

"Yeah. Read the name."

The Crux Constellation. Robbie Gonzalez, Manager.

"What's this for?" I turn it in my hand. It has their constellation logo.

Cale takes a seat next to me. "They saw us at the festival. Well, and they saw you sing. They said you should call them." He smiles with his pearly white teeth, then bites his plump bottom lip.

They want *me* to call them?

"Weren't they doing a farewell show?" I ask.

Cale shrugs. "You know, kid, I don't know everything! But I think they liked what they saw." He looks into his lap and says reservedly, "What's not to like?"

I catch his dark eyes. He looks away.

"Well, anyway..." he says, scratching his head.

"She's not out here, you know. You don't have to pretend to like me."

"I don't pretend to like you, Joy." The fire pops.

Was that a confession or... just him saying he likes me in general? I can't tell.

I open my mouth to say something, even though I'm not sure what, but the cabin door slides open. Jin and Lena walk into the backyard, and she shakes the ingredients to show us that they have all been acquired.

Food. Distraction. Thank God!

I grab a poker and secure a marshmallow on it. I try my best to attain perfection. Tan all the way around. Cale is the burn and bubble type.

I'm still so confused by his mood. By what Lena whispered to him. Was she flirting? It sounded like flirting. But what the heck did he mean by "I don't pretend to like you?"

Did his feelings change? This whole time, this has been about him and her. Not me. That "surprise" was nothing more than him doing legwork on his own plan. He came here for Lena.

Even though he's been spending all of his time with me. Sitting next to *me*. Waggling his eyebrows at *me* as he eats his chocolate-and-graham-cracker sandwich. He's goofy and fun and adorable...

My marshmallow catches.

"Shoot!" I blow it out. Though a tiny bit charred, it's still perfect. I put my s'more together, and then glance across the fire at Lena and Jin. They talk in some attractive, orange-glow conversation that I can't hear. It's unreal the way her hair falls on her shoulder, dark and long and just messy enough. She's way beyond "league." The amber flickers of light caress her cheekbones and soft lips. I'm just the girl who's thumb fiddles with a new hole in the sleeve of her brother's rejected sweater.

Jin laughs generously at something she says out of the side of her mouth. It's probably one of the hundreds of inside jokes they have. They're primed for each other.

God, I have no chance. He's just a fantasy and I've already hurt Lena by letting my feelings get to this point.

Cale grabs my s'more hand, breaking me out of the trance I was in. He's leading it. *My* dessert. To *his* mouth.

I resist. "Hey! You have your own!"

He smiles with a full mouth, a small piece of melted marshmallow on his face. "Mine's not sweet enough!"

In what universe is it possible for a s'more to not be sweet enough?

Suddenly he pulls my arm hard and with the momentum, lands a kiss on my cheek. My heart feels like a book getting all its pages flipped at once.

I don't pretend to like you, Joy.

Lena noticed and she grins, eyes sparkling with satisfaction. There's no way she's jealous.

I yank my arm back, but remember to turn on the courtesy. Nervous laugh. Force a smile.

"You really shouldn't mess with a girl's s'mores," I tell him.

"But they're *my* girl's s'mores." His dark eyes glimmer with a smile.

That was real. Wasn't it? Is he playing still or was that real?

Nervous laugh. Force a smile.

I stick another marshmallow on a stick and start roasting again. Pretending I'm not freaking out is the best course of action. This could still be an act, so... yeah. Play it cool.

Cale's lips move in a circle while he chews. He grins at me, having won my first s'more.

Crap! This one's set ablaze too. I continue making another sandwich with it anyway. Please distract me, little dessert!

I peek over at Cale and he's giving me his best impression of a sad puppy.

"Make. Your. Own," I say as I lift my s'more to *my own* mouth.

He snatches my wrist and I instantly resist. "Cale!"

I pull away and start giggling, mostly because his wide open mouth is goofy enough for me to know he's being playful. Back and forth, I give it all my effort and then...

My s'more flies out of my hand.

It smacks Cale square on his cheek on the way down. He tries to catch it with his big, pink tongue, but misses. It plops sadly on the ground.

Cale whimpers, positively dejected.

The image of his tongue contorting to catch the food replays in my head and I cannot stop laughing! I snort, which makes me crack up even more! *Wheeze!*

"I'm glad to know my massive fail was so amusing," Cale says sarcastically.

My stomach hurts! There was no chance for that poor tongue! I snort again.

"Okay, okay! I'll make one for *you* now!" Cale says. I nod, fighting residual laughs.

I'm glad *something* calmed my nerves. I look over at Jin and they come back.

He was watching me, if that grin means anything. Lena garners his attention back to her.

One thing is really unclear to me right now: Cale's actual feelings.

But two things are very clear. One, that I've definitely fallen for Jin.

And two, I can't have him.

If Cale has somehow shifted focus onto me, that might change things. I mean, Jin will be gone no matter what. Cale's around. Maybe it makes more sense to choose him.

I just never thought there might be a choice.

"There we have it," Cale announces. I lean out of my lawn chair to grab it, but he holds it out of reach.

"Mmm, I think I need payment."

I stand up. "Um, no! You owe me that sugar sandwich."

His finger points into the air. "But this one was made with love. It can only be bought with a kiss." He taps his cheek.

I shake my head and giggle. "No!"

"Fine," he says, and holds it out to me. But once I reach for it, he pulls it away again.

And then his free arm is wrapped around my back, pulling me up close to his body. My heart flutters and I look up at him in surprise.

And then he kisses me. And not just a peck on the cheek. His mouth is warm on mine, lingering, sending sparks through me like the embers of the fire pit.

A *real* kiss. My first real kiss.

My eyes blink rapidly as my brain catches up. I feel his exhale on my cheek as his hand presses my back, bringing me closer to him.

My heart is leaping and in shock, all at once.

"She said NO!" Jin's commanding voice cuts through the crackling fire.

Cale suddenly releases me and I stumble back. Smoke and crickets color the tension.

Jin's standing up, glaring at Cale, who's frozen in Jin's smoldering anger.

"Jin! Jeez," Lena says, rising from her chair and pulling her cardigan more closed.

Cale looks between me and Jin, a little panicked and unsure. Jin's stern look is harsh by the firelight.

"It's okay," I assure Jin. Keep the peace.

Don't let him get out of control.

My old turmoil swirls up from my stomach like vomit. Jin's not Carson. Cale's not Tyler.

It's not going to happen again.

"S-sorry... Joy," Cale says. The s'more cracked in his hand a little, but he holds it out to me as a peace offering.

I take it and thank him. Eat it. Nothing happened. *We're all walking away.*

Jin quickly simmers down from battle-ready to annoyed, which is relieving. When he turns to me, his eyes ask if I'm really okay. I nod. I am okay.

But my heart feels like it just got tilled.

I don't think I have room for Cale. Real or fake. I want Jin so much. It's clearer than ever.

But I know I can't have him. So I have to get over him somehow.

July 19th

*I*T WOULD BE AN UNDERSTATEMENT TO SAY THAT I DIDN'T SLEEP WELL, because my dramatic, thumping heart didn't really let me sleep at all. What a *pain!*

It would be an understatement, then, to say I "woke up" early. Or is that an overstatement? Really, I got out of my borrowed pullout bed around 5:50 AM, praying that no one else would get up at such a crazy hour and I could finally be alone. I cannot sort through my feelings and socialize at the same time. Apparently.

When I was a kid, my family came to Victoria Lake for almost 3 weeks. For an eleven year old from the most boring part of Oregon (other than Boring, OR), the mid-summer break from life at a lake resort might as well have been years in a magical hidden kingdom. We memorized every trail, counted a hundred ant hills, learned how silly we could make campfire stories if there was enough Pepsi to keep us awake.

One thing I remember vividly is the Secret Pond. It might more accurately be a secluded pond with a waterfall, since I doubt the only people who discovered it were a couple of kids. But it's off the beaten path, enough that I doubt anyone will be there this early. So, now's as good a time as any to find it.

After putting my bathing suit on under gym shorts and a baseball tee, I pack my mustard yellow Fjallraven backpack with a towel and a water bottle. I'm planning to bring some snacks, and then I'm gone for a couple of hours.

Alone. The only way to sort my heart out.

I head upstairs into the fresh dawn coming in through the massive windows.

The fridge door closes and my heart throbs. *Now* I remember that there's one other person who gets up this early.

Jin.

He stares at me, holding an orange juice carton and glass. "Good morning," he says, looking like a deer in the headlights.

"Morning." I try not to make conversation as I head to the sink to fill up my water bottle. The granola bars are on the counter behind him and so I'm, um, not gonna pack those.

"Going somewhere?" he asks.

"Yeah. Going on a hike. Be back before breakfast, probably." I purposely use as few words as possible. I've already spent way too much time with Jin on my mind. Like, his face, or the way his voice sounded, or his stance when Cale kissed me.

He downs a glass of orange juice faster than my water bottle gets filled.

Get out before he says something!

"Bye!" I say. I walk fast, trying not to seem like I'm escaping. Probably failing at that. Oh, well.

I hit the pavement and try to find peace in the quiet drum of my sneakers. What brings it is the birdsong and sun rays that warm up the leftover coolness of night.

There's the sign. CAPER TRAIL. Carson once said it was named after an unsolved mystery involving stolen jewelry they found buried here. He also said the jewelry belonged to Queen Victoria and that's why they named the resort after her. My kid-brain marveled at his twelve extra months of wisdom. Even though that was bogus.

Something about this place brings out a lot of memories of Carson. The good ones first, when we were best friends. The sour ones where he suddenly became obsessed with his image. The bad ones, then the really bad ones. *Breathe.*

It strikes me as odd that, right after he slammed my suitcase against the wall before coming here, he didn't storm off or scream profanities.

I'm okay. I'm fine.

Rubbing his eyes with the heels of his hands. The anger actually leaving. Something was different.

My shoes crunch on the gravel and I trace the edge of the path with my eyes, searching for the split boulder. That's my marker. My legs are already warm from trekking up the hill. I can already tell from the bright sun rays that it's going to be hot. I doubt it's even 7 AM yet.

The split rock emerges into view. I remember Carson jumped up and perched like a grasshopper. Then he leaped off and clung to the side of the hill. It's maybe a 70-degree angle, covered in ferns and trees and some weed-like plants.

I bet I can beat you to the top, that boy told me.

Bet not! I was always up for a challenge. Carson launched up the side, gaining traction with his grip strength and determination. I don't call him "Racecar" for nothing.

My feet stop right in front of it. Maybe this hill can help me feel better like it did back then.

I didn't come here to think about my big brother, yet I can't stop. Maybe this is what I've been putting off. At the end of summer it'll be me and him again. College classes, baseball, vague commitments to associations and an excess amount of Northwest coffee. It feels like a lot. These feelings I have... they've been a welcome distraction.

I've been staring at this hillside for a little too long. I'm still gathering the courage to climb it. Even though little Carson is long gone and he won't be reaching his hand down to help me up, this hill reminded me how much I love him. And maybe, I can still love him even if I don't want--

"Joy?"

I jerk my head to the left. It's Jin, in his AMER-I-CAN tank that flaunts his shoulders at me. What is he doing here?

And why did it have to be him?

He jogs closer.

"Why are you staring at this..." He can't think of a word to describe what I'm looking at. Probably because I'm not staring at anything in particular. I'm just gaping at a wall of plant matter covered in dew.

"Lost in thought, I guess. Why are you here?"

He scratches the back of his neck. "I, um... I don't really have a good reason." There's blush around his shy smile.

Maybe it's selfish, but I laugh. He's nervous. Questions flutter around me like butterflies. Should he really be here? Should I really want him to be? Does he like me the same way I like him?

Am I really going to ignore Lena's feelings and let this go on?

Though it should all be answered with "no," my soul is yearning for "yes."

Burning for *yes*. So maybe I am the burning type.

I point to the part where the hill curves to a stop. "There's a pond up there. I don't know how else to get there except climb up from this rock."

"How do you know?" His curiosity is achingly endearing.

I grip the straps of my backpack. "I stayed here one summer when I was a kid."

He nods and examines the same hillside. "Then let's go find it," he says and he doesn't wait for me. I follow him like the fool I am.

Jin scales it like it's nothing. I'm not nearly as nimble or long-limbed. And believe it or not, vines and ferns are not great for climbing. They tend to break under the weight of any-size human. Jin clears the top while I continue to struggle. I'll fall if I'm not careful.

If only tumbling down the hill were the only danger.

"Here." His hand descends to me. It's just within reach.

A flood of those feelings race back to me. When I was a kid, I couldn't imagine anyone better to lift me up. It's no different right now.

Jin Park is the person I lend my weight to, guiding me to the point of no return.

Who am I kidding? That point was long ago.

Coated in dirt and sweat, I pull myself over the edge, into another world that is seldom broached. There's no path, no disturbance. Just the singing birds and sunbeams, the smell of earth and drying dew, and the flush of excitement.

"I hear it," Jin says, smiling on one side. The faint rushing of a waterfall. I look around. Nature rarely lends to familiarity, but this feels the same as it did years ago. We tread through the brush toward the sound and I spot the rocky clearing.

I race there like I'm eleven again, snagging Jin's hand on the way. I didn't think about it.

I've had butterflies with Jin for a while, but I don't remember when I crashed so hard in love. It could have been when he reached for my hand a second ago. It could have been when he stood up for me last night. It could have been when he showed up on his motorcycle or when he invited me to watch fireworks. It could have been when he grabbed my hand and helped me up from the tile foyer floor. It doesn't seem to matter now. I'm already done for.

I drop his hand.

"Sorry," I say, assuring him with a small smile. "I got carried away."

He shakes his head, then beams at me. "It's fine."

Then, the sight captures him. I'm taken with his impressed expression.

It's almost as enrapturing as this place is.

There's the small waterfall, the fence of trees, the rocky shore, and the glittering pond reflecting a pale blue sky. Jin walks to the water and the reflecting sunlight gleams onto him like he's some kind of angel.

My backpack crashes to the pebble-covered ground. I lift my baseball tee off and bend down to unlace my shoes. Jin's steps are wobbly on the rocks as he walks toward me. He pulls his shirt off in one swift motion.

"You're not dressed to swim," I say. That was his excuse for not swimming last time.

"I don't care about that." He grins and uses his toes to remove each of his shoes. Then he dashes to the water and crashes into it without a care.

It looked like an ocean when I was a kid, but now... it only feels that way.

Smooth, water-worn rocks massage my feet as I walk to the pond. Jin lays facing the sky, floating atop the settling ripples.

I shuffle into the cool water, my steps wavering on the rocky ground. Soon I let the coldness envelope me and go under. Water falls away from my face when I surface and a shiver travels through my entire being. I position myself to float on my back like Jin, allowing my legs to float up. A breeze blankets me as I stare into the clear morning sky.

I'd stay here forever if I could.

The water beneath me shifts. It feels like a giant fish and freaks me out! I squeal and fold, instinct kicking in. I try to escape before using reason.

Jin breaks the surface looking as smug as I've ever seen him. His black hair lays flat and shiny, his cheeks round in laughter.

"You scared me!" I splash a wave at him. He pushes a bigger wave back at me and it hits my face, pulling my hair in a wet sheet over my face.

I laugh at myself. At this crazy circumstance. This beautiful morning, where Jin Park followed me to a secret paradise and smiled when I grabbed his hand. Where he made fun of me and now looks at me as if I'm the best part of all of it.

Without a doubt, I share that look.

He bites his wet lip. My heart races even more than it did when I was on the back of his motorcycle. Like we're suspended in danger all over again.

Am I really doing this?

Yes.

This is all I want. Maybe I never wanted to be alone. Maybe I always wanted him to show up, unexpectedly, and fill my days with this.

But... *Lena.* I know why she's head over heels with him now. Everything about him is inviting, not just his perfect, genuine smile or his warm laugh. It's the way he approaches you with respect and obvious desire for connection. His infectious happiness. His refusal to shy away from conflict and confidence that shows up even when he doesn't know what to do.

I wish I could be like him. But I'm not. I can't escape the image of deep hurt I might see on Lena's face if she knew everything. I'm not ready to disappoint her.

Diving under, I drown my thoughts in white noise. *Get out. It's not too late yet.*

With droplets racing down my limbs, I brave the stones, which are gaining heat in the aging day. Upon reaching my backpack, I open it and pull out the towel and dry off.

Why haven't I stopped this already? I've already betrayed Lena's trust far beyond the boundary of forgiveness.

I look over my shoulder and Jin's following me out, slicking back his hair. Smiling.

Maybe... I'm starting not to care what Lena thinks.

I shake the towel open and lay it over the pebbles. It's rock hard and lumpy, but it'll do. I sit, placing my abdomen against my thighs, laying the side of my face on my knees, letting the hot sun wick away the pond-water from my body.

Jin walks over to me.

"You didn't have to get out just because I did," I say. He takes a seat next to me.

"I wanted to." His words are so simple, yet for me, they're loaded.

His arms are wrapped loosely around his knees and he looks distantly at the waterfall.

"I really want to hear you sing again," he says like it's a thought escaping.

I turn my face into my knees, blocking the sun, hiding my blush. "Really?" My voice is muffled by my legs.

"Well, yeah. You're amazing."

I turn my face again and meet his eyes.

I give him a courtesy smile. I'm lost for any other type of reaction that might be appropriate because my heart is losing it's cool, *for real.*

"Please?"

I lift my head. "What, like now?"

"Are you doing anything else?" There's a hint of wariness in his request and it's adorable.

I push my legs out in front of me and lean back on my hands. A flood of joy washes over me. "I guess not."

But his anticipatory stare chickens me out.

"You can't look at me like that!" I protest.

"Okay, fine!" Jin shuts his eyes, the anticipation still ever-present.

What should I sing to him? It sounds childish, but there's one song that feels perfect. *Rainbow Connection.* It's Kermit the Frog, yes, but he's existential and magical. He tugged on my spirit when I was a kid. I could sing it then, and just as passionately now.

Slow, soothing. In my head, guitar strums and violin sings, but just my voice pours out...

Rainbows. Shining, full-spectrum, their essence visible to everyone. It's a song about how people desire deep beauty and meaning, yet it's still elusive.

No wonder this song is on my heart.

At some point in the verse, I close my eyes, too. A vision of a glittering rainbow tickles my mind.

I give in to the song like it's just me. Singing to the earth, the moss, the water, the trees. Giving them life with the vibrations of my voice.

This feeling is probably magic...

The last word spreads out, growing, pulling my soul open. Then the sun is eclipsed by something. I open my eyes. Jin is close, staring. Longing.

"Can I kiss you?" he asks desperately.

Time stops. I nod. "Yes," I hear myself say, matching his desperation.

This distance, it's gloriously gone. He's kissing me, softly at first, palming my face and pulling me closer.

The music goes on in my head, the orchestra, the voice someone else's, serenading this moment. I'm floating, flying, kissing *him.*

His lips are the sparks of fireworks, the smoldering of a bonfire, the sweet taste of summer fruit. He's kissing *me!* I graze his shoulder with my fingertips.

Jin sends chills of wonder throughout me. Each move he makes, I'm further lost in a wilderness of magic. This is what my first kiss should have been. What every first kiss should be. The long-awaited relief of yearning I've been feeling for I don't know how long.

He pulls away and I witness him anew. This is the Jin Park I don't have to question anymore. I have my answer.

But I also have a brand new problem. My bliss wavers. I can't.

Jin leans to kiss me again, but I push my hand on his chest. He doesn't hesitate to respond.

"What's wrong?" Now his bliss wavers too.

I can't do this to Lena. I told myself I would never be a traitor like my old friends were. If she loves Jin at all like I do... I can't keep doing this.

Regret burrows in, a little at first, then a tidal wave.

"I'm sorry," I whisper.

"Why?"

My heart shatters. I shake my head. I should have stopped this a long time ago. Maybe she'll forgive me if she gets him.

I get up and distance myself. Jin stands up with me, confused. "Joy, what's wrong?"

I haphazardly stuff my shirt and damp towel in my backpack while searching for the point of exit.

Why does this have to hurt so much? It was so perfect.

These sharp rocks prevent me from running. I slip my sneakers on without lacing them. They hang loosely on my hasty feet.

"Where are you going?"

"I can't do this," I tell him without stopping.

"Why not?" I hear his slight exasperation. Bless him for being angry. Even that is perfect.

Don't look back.

It's time to tell Lena the truth. I should not have been so selfish. Ever. Couldn't I have just told him "no"? Why did I have to let everything be "yes" today?

I try to keep steady. I'm almost to the brush. Almost to the hill's edge.

Jin's hand lands on my shoulder and I whip around. He breathes heavy with a stern expression... no, that's hurt. His dark eyes secure mine.

"Don't run," he tells me. "Please, stay with me."

"I'm sorry." I break into a run toward the edge. I almost reach it, but I pause. *Don't run.* I don't want to. What am I supposed to do?

I turn and see him standing there, shirt in hand, his chest still glistening. He takes one step, so I do, too. Backward.

Not my first mistake of the day.

TRACK 17 -
I'M DOWN

Still July 19th

WHEN MY BODY FIGURES OUT THAT I NEED AIR TO SURVIVE, I suck in a breath. My ankle screams in pain so bad that my other muscles are tense. I tumbled down the hillside and landed my ankle on the split boulder at a weird angle. I'm also covered in scrapes from all the sticks and brush that I rolled down on.

I guess that's just the Joy Becker way. Give something your best shot, wind up injuring yourself. Trademarked.

My ankle throbs as I try breathing evenly. Jin slides down the hillside on his feet, as a stable person does. It looks like he grabbed the shoes that flew off my feet when I lost balance and rolled down here.

Of course he offers to carry me. It's like poetic justice. I try to avoid his affection, only to be unable to refuse being held by him immediately thereafter.

Jin helps me up on my good leg and I put my backpack on, tears streaming down my face. Then I pull myself onto his back, gripping his shoulders and collarbone as he wraps his arms around my legs. It feels like our hearts are too close and tangled.

The persistent pain in my ankle isn't as difficult to handle as the fact that I like being close to him. The bliss of being held hurts because I know it's fleeting.

He carries me silently down the path. The scent of dirt and pond water is on his skin, like fresh rain. I lay my head on his shoulder and try not to think at all. Not about how he holds me. Not about how hurt Lena will be. Not about how complicated Cale makes this, or Carson, or the fact that once summer is over, none of it will matter anyway.

"Did you follow me?" I ask him, my tone muted.

He sighs. "Yes."

There's an extra vibrant tick of my heart. "Why?"

"Because I wanted to. I wanted to be alone with you, and I didn't realize it until I was already on the path."

I don't respond, because that's exactly what I thought. What I hoped.

The sun is intense now.

"I'm sorry. That sounds creepy," he admits.

"No, it's okay. We've been alone a lot already. It's not like I don't trust you." I feel his tense shoulders relax.

Twittering birds and Jin's shuffling feet are all I hear for a minute. My lips tingle, replaying the kiss. It still feels unreal. It's also another thing I have to tell Lena.

There's a bench a little ways off, under some tree shade. Jin asks, "Is it okay if we stop?"

"Mmhmm," I say.

Though Jin is careful about setting me down, hitting the bench makes the pain shoot up my leg. I wonder what I did to it. I've never broken anything before. The radiating pain is unrelenting.

"Do you have any ice?" Jin asks me, grabbing my backpack. I don't.

When he finds my water bottle, he kneels to the ground and holds it to my ankle.

"Why'd you run?" His question punches me in the abdomen.

I can't tell him about Lena. And anything else just doesn't seem like enough of a reason.

"I don't have a simple answer, I guess."

He makes eye contact. "Are you trying to protect Lena's feelings?"

I hesitate, but it's pointless. "You know about that?"

"She's not subtle."

I let out a knowing laugh.

"But I don't feel that way about her." I can tell it's hard for him, but also definitive. "She's like my sister."

"Right. A supermodel sister who isn't in any way blood related to you." My word, was that a twinge of jealousy in my voice?

Jin doesn't skip a beat. "It's not just that. I appreciate her and everything she's done for me. But, even if we had no history, she's not my type."

I don't mean to say it out loud, but I say, "And I am?"

"Is that so hard to believe?" And then he checks me out. Not subtly.

Goodness.

I laugh off my nervousness. He's been so chivalrous this *whole* time! Have I been too dense to see that he's attracted to me?

"What is it about me, then?" I ask. I don't know why Lena isn't better. She's been beside him forever. She's packing up and moving near him. She's ready, willing, gorgeous, fun, strong.

"Your confidence. Definitely." Wow, that took zero time for him to think about.

"What confidence?"

He looks up at me with a furrowed brow and adorably conflicted smile. "How do you not see it, Joy? You laugh openly, you sing freely. And share yourself with everyone. You wear what you want, eat what you want, and you fully enjoy things that Lena wouldn't bother with because it's too basic or some dumb reason."

"Did you just call me *basic*, Jin?" I ask, amused.

He laughs, then sets the water bottle down. He sits on the bench, really close to me. Touching. Making eye contact.

"Joy, you're adorable." His look is most definitely *adoring*.

A breeze brushes by us. I'm still a bit in awe of all this.

But then he switches gear. "What I can't figure out is how you keep sacrificing so much for everyone else. Even your running away was for Lena's sake, right? Unless... you don't *want* to be with me."

"Are you crazy? Of course I do!" And I mean it. So much. "And it's not just because you're amazingly handsome. You... Jin, you are a rare kind of wonderful."

He seems kind of stunned as if my words are particularly meaningful. "Wow. That makes me happy."

I'm lost in the look of his flushed cheeks and perfect lips and exquisitely messy, damp hair. His hand brushes my cheek and he draws closer.

Jin smirks. "Because I've been holding back."

My eyes flutter wide. I almost don't register what he's said before he kisses me again, deeper and more commanding. Like there was a longing he held back before. All the blood leaves the sharp pain in my ankle and rushes to where his hands are. The back of my neck tangled in my hair and firm on my hip, keeping me from floating away.

Jin pulls away, but it's like there's an invisible rope tying us together. And the best part of it all is how he looks at me. Like, how is this happening?

How did I get to this incredible moment of time? With *him*?!

I don't care if I'm injured. I could be suspended here forever, pain and all.

Like a slamming door, our moment stops. His mood shifts and he scoots away.

"What is it?" I ask.

"I'm still holding back," he says, frustrated.

"*That* was holding back?"

"No! I mean, there's still that whole deal with you and..."

"Cale," I finish. "Right."

Jin rubs his temple. "I've been so upset over it. And until now, I just felt like I didn't deserve to be. We met, like, a month ago."

Wait, *for real?* It's hard to believe.

Those dark brown eyes latch onto mine. "I know I'll intervene if he touches you. I can't play along, Joy."

I grasp his arm. "I get it. I don't want you to. Just, give me time to talk to him."

Worry burrows into me, though. I lace my fingers together. "I don't know if it's all fake to him anymore, though."

"That's more reason to end it." His words are confident and definitely at least a little jealous.

I wonder if I couldn't bring myself to talk boundaries with Cale because I didn't want to let him down. Maybe I sensed that things were different. He'll forgive me, but that's not all there is to it.

"It's not just Cale, though..."

Jin squares himself to me. "Lena is going to get hurt either way. Let me worry about her."

"You weren't the one who betrayed her trust. I was. I have to talk to her."

Jin grabs my hand. "Let's do it together, then. You don't have to do everything yourself."

We make eye contact. These peaks and valleys of emotion, like the terrain we're on, torture me and heal me. I want him so much, but traversing this won't be easy.

"You're a rare kind of wonderful, too, Joy. I don't mind fighting for that." Though he doesn't smile, I sense his happiness. It's the same as mine, hidden in some secluded, vibrant place. Like the pond where we finally kissed.

"How's your ankle?" he asks.

"Throbbing." I sigh. "Just like my heart, Jin Park."

He laughs and looks off. "I love that you say things like that."

Huh. He actually likes my dorky commentary. I take an eyeful of him. "I can't believe you exist."

He turns to me, drawing close as he says, "Do you need further proof?"

I smile in the moment between him leaning in and his lips pressing on mine again. Okay, I believe it. He's real.

It stops too soon. How does anyone ever let go?

Jin thumbs my cheek. "I'm saving the next one for when there's nothing in the way."

I'm spinning, but I somehow still have a quip. "That's a shame."

"Good motivation, though," he replies. I nod.

One really good thing about being clumsy: when you fall, you fall hard.

TRACK 18 -
SUCKER

Still July 19th

THE OFFICIAL DIAGNOSIS IS THAT NOTHING IS BROKEN, but it still feels like everything's on fire. My ankle. My sunburned shoulders. My fear of telling Lena. My heart when I see Jin. My lungs when I think about breathing a word of this to Cale.

At least the ankle will heal.

When Jin and I came back from the First Aid Center, explaining what happened was... a balancing act of truth. We said we went on a hike together.

Not untrue. Not really enough to calm the radiating heat of Lena's anger at seeing us return to the cabin together. At least Cale was eager to believe it and move on to being my dedicated helper, ice packs at the ready.

Since I'm really good at ruining things today, I break it to Carson that roller skating is not on my agenda. He's working at the skate rental desk today after seeing the resort's physical therapist. His response was "that sucks," so it could've been worse.

So I am doing my part insisting everyone else still go while I watch. Frankly, I don't feel the need to prove just how ungraceful I am. Point's been made.

The moms, who have become the Sisterhood of the Trading Romance Novels, tell us to go on our own. I'm starting to think I should bring Angela and Jan-di to distract Mom on all family vacations.

All over the resort are staff clad in dark green t-shirts driving golf carts to get people around. We snag a ride, which isn't the easiest on my ankle, but it's less torturous than walking.

Carson is waiting at the rink, leaning against the rail that goes around the outside. It's an open air rink, covered by a gazebo. Brown pillars hold up the roof. You can feel the wind, smell the evergreens, and even inhale the dust from the gravel parking lot while you skate.

I hobble over to Carson on my recently procured crutches. He scrolls on his phone, then looks up. I messaged him about my ankle so he wouldn't be surprised, but something feels off about his expression. Like he wants to frown, but he's trying not to.

He even smiles at me. But his eyebrow twitches when he sees Jin.

My internal danger meter goes off. I forgot they met once before.

I'm pleading with God to keep this light and airy.

"Glad you still came," Carson finally says to me. Not cheerful, but not about to burst.

"I'd hate to ruin everyone else's day. I don't mind the sidelines."

Carson breathes a bitter laugh, but I don't know why. I'm always on the sidelines for him.

"Well, I'm going to leave you all in the dust," Lena announces as she passes by us. She heads to the skate rental counter, Jin following.

My heart rate bounces rapidly, but I resist the urge to look at him.

Cale's hand falls on my shoulder. "Can I get you a concession, Almond

Joy?"

Oof. His light touch cuts deep today. "Just a soda," I say with a smile. He obliges my request.

"Hey!" Carson grabs Cale's attention. "I'll take first shift with her. I'm not on duty for another 30 minutes. You go get some skates."

Cale's eyes bounce to me, but he nods. I'm pretty sure Carson scares him.

"You don't have to babysit me," I tell my brother.

"I wanna talk." But it doesn't sound like he wants a friendly chat. It's a command.

I don't resist, but maybe I should. What's up with him? Maybe it's selfish, but I don't want this day to be soured by my brother.

We grab a table right next to the rink, where there's a half-wall separating tables and the skaters. There's a beat from the mid-grade speakers. The Jonas Brothers' "Sucker," but some kind of remix with more synths and bass. I'm alone for a second while Carson grabs my soda from Cale. Lena hits the vinyl floor like some kind of pro. Her hair whips behind her as she floats along with the grace of an Olympic ice skater.

She wasn't joking.

Jin looks like a toddler learning to walk, but with lanky limbs. I chuckle. He doesn't look at me though, because all of his concentration is taken up by trying not to fall.

Cale is somewhere in between them. Not miserable like Jin, but not the smooth glider that Lena is either.

The paper soda cup slams on the table. Beyond the blue PEPSI label, all of Carson's facial muscles are tense just short of revealing a specific emotion.

I grab the soda slowly. "Thanks."

"So, how are things with your boyfriend?" he pries.

"Fine." I want to keep this as minimal as possible.

But part of me knows it's not going to be a small conversation.

He squints at me. "Are you cheating on him with that Asian guy?"

I choke on my soda and start coughing. Once I catch my breath, I say, "N-no."

It's technically true. I'm not cheating. I'm just not actually dating the guy he thinks I'm dating.

Carson grits his teeth.

No. *No no no.*

"Why are you lying to me, Joy?" His mouth is a tense, straight line.

"What makes you think I'm lying?"

He knows. I'm petrified watching him pull out his phone, thumb through something with purpose. He flips the screen over to me.

A picture of me and Jin, kissing on the bench. From this morning.

I'm too stunned for words. How could he have gotten this?

"There's a PDA channel on our work Discord. I was checkin' the channels and woke right up when I saw this, y'know?"

"Carson, please let me explain this."

"Sure. Tell me why you've been lying about that guy?"

I glance out, certain there's worry all over my face. They're rounding the rink, close to passing me and my brother by.

Fake a smile. *Fakeasmile!*

Lena whips past us and smiles back, enjoying herself too much to pick up on the ominous air. Cale keeps a hefty amount of distance, which basically proves to me that he's afraid of Carson.

Jin catches on. I'm sure he does. His eyes are tuned into mine for the second that he passes us by.

Carson's eyes burn into me. "Now they're gone, Joy. Talk."

My voice is hushed. "Cale and I are faking it. He said he liked Lena and wanted to spend summer with her, so I went along with it. That's all, I sw--"

Slam! Carson's hands hit the table and my soda falls over, spilling everywhere. I jolt all over. My heart is pounding in my head.

"I'm not an idiot!" he yells.

I hold my breath and shake my head. I know he's not an idiot. If this were flipped, I would think he was lying, too.

Carson lifts his hands off the table and reveals his freshly cracked phone screen, the image of me and Jin still displayed.

Jin's body slams against the barrier. "Everything okay?"

Carson's jaw juts out in anger. But he sighs deep and meets Jin's solid gaze.

"Carson," I beg. *God, don't throw a punch.* I look at Jin. "It's okay, you can go."

"Yeah, we're fine," Carson says. Even though I fully expected him to fight, he doesn't. He just walks away, leaving the rink for the parking lot, not even turning over a chair as he goes.

Carson has been suspicious for a while. *What are you keeping from me, huh?* He thought I was cheating on Cale. And now, he thinks he's got proof.

"You sure you're okay?" Jin asks me. Soon, Cale and Lena crowd around him.

"What's with him?" Lena asks, judgment thick in her voice.

My hands cover my face.

It echoes in my head, over and over again.

Carson always, always, always wins.

But this time, when he could've bested me, he walked away.

TRACK 19 -
REWRITE
THE STARS

Still July 19th

WHILE I'M STUCK FIGURING WHAT THE HECK I SHOULD DO about my brother, Jin cleans up the spilled soda. He kneels on the ground, dabbing it with a wad of paper towels.

"Seriously, what the heck? He invited us here," Lena says, still standing in the rink with her arms folded.

"I'm gonna rest at home, I think." It's the first thing I've said since Carson left.

Jin looks up at me. "Should I come with you?"

"Jin! Come on," Lena says, "It's not like she needs a babysitter."

"You can stay if you want, Lena," Jin argues. "I'm trying to be nice."

Cale walks up to the table, skates in hand. "You're a real MVP, Jin, but I think I should escort the lady. It's kind of my duty."

Lena scoffs. "Gosh, now you're all ready to leave because Carson had a hissy fit. Guys, he's a jerk. We shouldn't let him ruin our day."

"You're right, Lena," I say, "But I kinda want to be alone. You guys should stay. Have a good time."

I'm wobbly getting up, mostly because this chair is so unstable. *Everything's* unstable.

They let me go, and I'm grateful for the lack of resistance. I don't think it's been even an hour since I left the cabin, but it feels like I lived through two weeks of turmoil and bliss today. I take a bitterly quiet golf cart ride back. It's not even one o'clock when I walk into the empty cabin.

I flop myself onto the living room couch, right in the direct afternoon sun that shines through the giant window.

Carson could wreck a lot of hearts with that picture. I finally let myself cry about it.

At least now I'm actually alone.

I wake up. My tears left a dried trail to my ears. For a second, I'm not sure where I am. Every crevice of the ceiling and piece of furniture or decor is mysterious. I've never known this leather couch I woke up on.

As soon as I realize where I am, I also realize none of today was a dream.

Even though seeing Jin makes me feel like it must be.

"Hey, you're up," he says.

I unstick myself from the couch and clear my throat. Jin's in the armchair next to me with a gentle smile and every wonderful emotion hits me like that waterfall.

A muffled laugh sounds and I notice that everyone else is eating outside. Cale is doing some silly dance with his hands, which seems like something he'd do when surrounded by women.

"What time is it?" I ask with a yawn.

"Past six. How are you feeling?"

I heave a sigh. "That's complicated."

Lena waltzes into the cabin. "Oh hey, you're awake! Guess what we're gonna watch for movie night? It's one you've been begging me to watch."

Cale follows after, grinning. "The *best* movie of the decade!"

"We'll see about that," Lena bites back.

I furrow my brow, wondering what movie...

I hazard a guess. "*Greatest Showman*?"

Cale claps his hands and points to me. "Yes! Thank you! Can you believe Lena's so uncultured?"

Lena scoffs. "I'm gonna go make sure we have it." She crosses through the living room and heads downstairs.

I swing my injured leg off the couch and wince. Still tender. "I could use some help."

Jin grabs my arm and drags it around his neck. His fingers are warm on my hand and his neck muscles make my arm tingle. He slides his other arm around my waist sending sparks along the path.

"No problem, Joy."

His voice is so cool, my heart flutters.

"Thanks," I half-exhale.

It isn't until Cale is at my side that I remember he was literally right behind us.

"I got your right, Almond Joy!" His hold is sloppier and he pinches my side trying to maneuver around Jin's arm. When I'm secured, I glance at Cale, whose close-mouthed smile and wandering eyes make my stomach do flips. He's too eager to mistake the gesture as just friendly.

How did I end up like this? Between two guys who both seem like they *want* to hold me?

"I'll start the popcorn!" Lena calls as she bounces up the stairs. She pauses when she sees us.

I give her a crooked smile.

Why do I feel about as unlucky as I am lucky?

The popcorn wafts with a strong buttery aroma and my mouth waters. I should want more sustenance than just this over-salted movie snack, but I reach into Cale's bowl and grab another fistful.

The orientation of the young adults on this sectional is as follows: Lena on the right end of the couch, leaning against the armrest with her legs folded neatly under her. She intermittently scolds Cale for humming along. Jin sits next to her, quiet and still (other than blinking). I can't tell if he's paying attention to the movie or desperately trying to not look at me the same way I'm (failing at) trying to not look at him. He's only about an inch away from my injured, outstretched leg, meaning my petite self is taking up most of the couch. Cale is on my left, confined to the corner, hogging both the bowl of popcorn and the Cowboys throw blanket.

"You don't have to be such a blanket hog," I chide as I pluck more popcorn from the bowl.

He raises his eyebrows far too high. "Oh, really? We're goin' there?"

I giggle and stuff my face with popcorn. Plead the fifth.

He sets the popcorn on the coffee table and opens the corner of the blanket. "Well, then, snuggle on up, Becker. Or are you all talk?"

I hold my breath. I can't *snuggle*! But we're still technically faking and Lena is eyeing me.

But... Jin. We both brushed it off when Cale grabbed my other side and helped me down the stairs. Jin didn't seem jealous, but he also told me in no uncertain terms that he couldn't stand by and watch our little charade go on.

"Oh God, Joy! We don't care!" Lena assures me.

But I care! And I avoid looking at Jin because I *know* he does.

Cale flashes a goofy grin at me. "Come on! We can be cuddle buddies."

And the waggling his eyebrows makes me question if this young man has ever been serious a day in his life. My laugh relieves some of the tension, but I still feel wrong obliging.

And I still don't want to disappoint him.

We're at the part of the movie where Hugh Jackman holds out his hand to Zac Efron in an attempt to strike a deal.

Jin finally looks at me and raises his brow, expectant of my choice. Unlike Zac Efron's character, I'm not going to compromise.

It's clear who I'd rather not disappoint.

"Actually, I kinda have to use the bathroom," I say. "Could you give me a hand, Lena?"

"Oh, sure." Lena doesn't bother to pause the movie as she gets up to help me. I leave my crutches and hop into the hall, keeping steady with a grip on her shoulder. The bathroom is at the end of the hall, the movie noises becoming faint whines.

I'm glad to be out of sight of the boys. One makes my heart flip because I'm still buzzing with thrill at our shared feelings, while the other makes my heart flop because he's my friend and I don't know how to make him happy.

Distance is good right now.

I let go of Lena's shoulder. "Thanks."

"You're having second thoughts, aren't you?" she asks.

The urge to release it all rises up in me. Second thoughts? I never had first thoughts. But I'd far prefer having this conversation with Cale first.

"Yeah, maybe," I say. It's only a slight bluff. Not a full-blown lie.

"Why?" She sounds annoyed.

"Because I am. I like Cale a lot but... I don't know if our thing is working." Not a lie.

"Oh my God, Joy. Is *that* why you were with Jin this morning?"

I'm stiff. And kinda peeved she's acting all superior. "No!"

She folds her arms. "Do you like him? Just tell me."

Lena has always intimidated me, even when we shared chocolate chip cookies or cracked up at some dumb meme or studied together in a subject that I know better. She's used to getting what she wants. Now I see she can also be very patient to that end.

She's waited years for Jin. I've tried over and over not to take her jealousy personally.

But I didn't have to wait years for him. We fell together like a chord falls out of a guitar when the fingers press the right strings.

Lena's going to get hurt either way.

"Maybe I do like him," I say.

She throws her arms down and uses a hushed voice. "What? Joy!"

Then she rubs her forehead and sighs like she's handling a disobedient child. "You know he's just nice, right? Like he helps people because he cares about everyone?"

I blink at her with my mouth ajar. She thinks I'm Jin's *charity case?!* It takes everything in me not to shove it in her face that Jin came onto *me*.

But then she dabs her eyes, careful to preserve her mascara. I soften. I've never actually seen her cry before.

"Lena," I say as tenderly as I can. "I *tried* not to."

She wipes another tear away and launches into rambling. "When he went to Willow Haven and I was, like, a sophomore, girls were *all* over him, okay? Jin totally just doesn't realize that being so nice comes off as, like, flirting. You know?"

"I know. I get that." *Shut up.*

She sniffles. "The point is that he turned them all down. He's not a player. So, like, I just don't want you to get hurt because, you know, he's sweet and everything. If Jin *actually* likes someone..."

The next words out of her mouth are basically slow-motion. Here's a bona fide expert on Jin Park, about to tell me what he's made of. If he *actually* likes me.

"...he's obvious. And by then he's serious." She takes a deep breath and wipes her cheek again. "Being friendly is, like, his default."

He's obvious. And by then he's serious.

I fake a knowing nod. I have to pretend like her words didn't just send my heart beating into a frenzy.

Jin was certainly obvious. Kissing-me-three-times obvious.

Miraculously, I speak monotone. "Okay, well. Thanks for the info. Still gotta pee."

"Oh God, sorry!" she says, and she turns around to walk back to the movie, but she stops. "Hey, Joy?"

I crack the door open and turn to her. "Yeah?"

"I just... I care about you. Other than him, you're my only real friend."

I feel like I'm punched in the gut. Lena's only real friends are conspiring to break her heart.

Locked in the bathroom, I pull out my phone. There's at least one variable I can try to control.

Joy: Let's talk tomorrow, I'll tell you everything

Joy: I just don't want the pic to hurt my only friends

...

Carson: K, I'll listen

TRACK 20 -
FEEL IT
TWICE

Still July 19th

WELL, THIS IS AN UNEXPECTED TURN OF EVENTS. Cale's leaving. Tomorrow.

Cale stuffs his backpack full of crumpled t-shirts and attempts to zip it up, without success. I lean against the doorway to his and Jin's shared room, trying to decide if I should make the effort to break off our deal or wait until I see him again.

After the movie, I came upstairs to eat some leftover tacos (you know, *proper* food) and asked Cale if we could talk. He told me he still had to pack and the whole intended conversation got derailed.

"Why are you leaving tomorrow?" I ask him as I watch him fumble with his belongings. Jin's bed is the neat one, looking as if he never slept in it. Cale's looks like a failed omelet flip.

He pauses packing. "My mom only let me come because it's halfway to my sister's wedding. Can't believe she's gettin' hitched tomorrow." He wipes a false tear. "They grow up so fast!"

"Isn't she older than you?"

"Not the point!" He points at me for a second. Then goes back to frantic stuff-gathering. "I'm sorry I didn't say anything. I would have taken you as a plus one but Dee's keepin' it small."

Now it's like he's not even trying to cover up that it's me. I'm worried that breaking things off could sour his sister's wedding. My hesitation, with the butterflies fluttering in my still empty stomach, make me wonder if *my* feelings are also more than just fake.

I'm so confused. But I came here for a reason.

"So what did you wanna talk about?" he asks.

I open my mouth but can't speak. I want Cale to be happy so much it hurts. I'd give up the car, if it would keep that silly demeanor chugging on. I guess he must want me to be happy too, since he actually did give me his car.

"Oh, nothing serious. Just wondering if you were going on the jet skis tomorrow, but..."

I sigh. Lying doesn't ease the butterflies at all.

"If I wasn't heading off very first thing, I'd sip iced tea and watch Jin and Lena wipe out all day long with you, Almond Joy."

Cale snaps his fingers when something else occurs to him. "Hey, but we got Carson's practice game next week, right? Your mom said I should go with you."

I stiffen. "Wait up, *my* mom told you about Carson's game? She didn't even tell me."

"Oh, really?" Cale looks worried, but a sly smile curls on his lips. "Am I becoming a favorite?"

"Trust me, Carson has a monopoly on 'favorite.'" I should try not to sound so bitter in front of Cale, but being polite seems like an excessive burden. Carson literally threw my suitcase at a wall and broke his phone because I was "keeping something" from him, but he can't tell me that he's playing again? And Mom assumes I'm able and willing to go?

Cale furrows his brow in my direction. "Hey, you okay?"

I meet his round, gentle eyes. He can tell that I'm not.

"We don't have to go, Joy. I know things get tense with your brother."

I sigh. "No, I'll go. I don't really have a choice."

"Of course you have a choice," he argues, like it's simple and there's nothing more to it.

Cale doesn't get it. I know I have a choice, but the worse choice is *not* going. That choice would mean Carson would get God-knows-how angry. Since Mom babies him and Dad ignores him like he does everything else, I would have zero support in that decision. Except maybe from Cale, but he's got a wimpy track record with my brother. Not to mention that I'm the sister. Siblings are the only people who can really get it when life hands you a bad card.

I have to choose going.

I clear my throat. "No. I want to support Carson, I'm just annoyed I found out secondhand. That's all."

Cale's busy hands give up on his overstuffed backpack. He walks over to me carrying the scent of his laundry detergent. My eyes strain looking up at him, he's so much taller than me.

And then he puts his finger on my chin.

"Look up, Joy," he says. And he's smiling, like he's taking the gentle approach to cheer me up for a change.

Don't do this, Cale. Don't kiss me.

Along the soft edges of his features, his skin glows and I wonder if I should've been honest. Almost every second of the day, Cale is kind and thoughtful and hilarious. He's so good.

Why can't I tell him about Jin? Even now I'm wondering what Jin is doing, what he's thinking. I don't want him to catch sight of me and Cale.

I pull my chin from his finger, which lingers in the air like a tree branch that's lost a blossom.

"You don't have to worry about me, Cale Salad," I tell him, grabbing the crutches that lean against the wall. I hobble off, still pondering these butterflies. They're there, but they dwindle.

I don't think I'm sparing Cale because I'm falling for him. I think it's because I'm loyal to him. Maybe a romantic spark could've started with that before Jin.

But I'm not before Jin anymore.

When I enter the living room, I find Jin sitting on the couch next to Lena. He looks up with hidden hopefulness. Before I can give him a sorrowful, bare shake of my head, Lena looks up from her magazine. "Everything cool?" she asks.

I try to sound happy, but not too happy so Jin doesn't think we're in the clear. Because we are not. "Yeah, but I'm gonna go to bed. I'm pretty wiped."

Jin gets off the couch. "Let me help you."

"I got her, Jin!" Lena says, quite literally shoving him down into the leather. "God, do you always have to be so chivalrous?" Her tone is like a grapefruit: kinda sweet, kinda bitter.

Neither of us resist her. Maybe Jin feels the same way about telling Lena as I do about Cale. It's so hard to ignore that I'm crazy about him.

I doubt I'll be able to sleep much.

July 20th

I did sleep. Minimally. By the time I check my phone and see that it's just past five in the morning, I can't get back to sleep.

Jin texted me last night.

Jin: So, you talked to Cale... How'd that go?

My fingers wake up before my brain does.

Joy: We talked about my brother. And no other subject, unfortunately.

I know he's not going to read it yet, but I owed him that much.

Lena is still snoring like a dainty pug. It's as good a time as any to get out of bed and test my ankle.

Better. Still aching like someone took a nail file to the muscle, but better.

I'm parched. Orange juice is calling my name. I discover I can hop up the stairs one-legged. The living room is dressed in a nice shade of robin's egg blue, light enough to see everything.

I bounce over to the armchair and rest my overworked healthy leg. Is it too early for Jin to be up?

As soon as I hear faint footsteps, I have my answer. Seeing him sets my heart smoldering like a campfire. His mussed hair, foggy eyes, wearing that same plain t-shirt crumpled a bit from sleep. I want to kiss him again. And run my fingers along the nape of his neck. And sing to him under the sky and watch the sunset on a Ferris wheel and listen to him talk about his childhood.

I'm bombarded by these desires crashing together like bursts of fireworks. I love it.

"Morning, Joy." He grins and his eyes tell me he feels it, too.

I respond with a similar grin. "Morning, Jin."

As he walks past me, he catches a bit of my hair and lets it slide through his fingers in the sexiest way possible. His eyes linger on mine, even though he walks farther away.

It almost aches to watch him pour juice from a carafe into a glass.

"You hungry?" he says.

"Oh, always."

My answer makes him laugh a little. He pours a second glass and puts the juice back, then brings it over to me.

"For your effort," he says. There's a sad smile.

I don't take the glass. "I'm sorry."

"It's okay." He stretches his juice offering out more and I take it. "I know it's not easy to break news."

Jin averts his eyes. He must be struggling with letting Lena know. How can I blame him?

"Eggs?" he asks, heading back to the kitchen.

I sip my juice and give it a thought. "French toast?"

"Whoa, that's a bit romantic. What will our moms think?" He smirks and I laugh thinking of when I took over making French toast for him.

We have inside jokes. Me and Jin. I could get used to that.

"What's romantic?" Angela emerges from the hall. She pulls her black curls into a ponytail as she walks toward the kitchen.

My laugh halts. "Nothing," I answer, trying to sound light.

"It's a joke," Jin says, sounding far lighter than I did.

"Because it's French?" she asks, then reaches into the fridge to get the eggs.

Sheesh. She was totally eavesdropping.

"Yeah," Jin says. Maybe it's because I know him a little better now, but there's a hint of reservation in his answer. He totally suspects that she was listening, too.

I'm actually happy when my mom's clueless energy enters the open space and offers to whip up German style crepes instead of French toast. It's weird that she's up so early, but I'm not asking questions. Conflict-avoidance is my specialty these days.

We all end up at the dining table while my mom does her 1-2-3 crepe recipe: one cup of flour, two cups of milk, three eggs.

The others are a bit slower to rise. Jan-di is the first after about an hour, Lena about a half-hour after that. She doesn't speak a word to me. Or to anyone else. She grunts for a mug of coffee as her first conversation of the day in exactly the same way her dad does.

As soon as she has her *second* cup, we'll have the Lena we all know and love. Too bad she drinks it like a caffeine-addicted sloth. At least the conversation, or rather debate, the moms are having about the staying power of *shiplap* is riveting entertainment.

Finally, an hour later, Cale gets up. He practically darts into the living room like he's hopped up on six shots of espresso.

"ImlateImlateImlate!!" He plucks a rolled up jelly crepe and it dangles out of his mouth while his backpack swings around on one shoulder. He slides his feet into his sneakers and takes the floppy crepe out of his mouth.

"I'd give a speech about how grateful I am for all this, but I've already wasted too much time explaining why I'm *not* giving a speech, so THANK YOU and GOOD DAY!"

This kid really needs to learn how to utilize the alarm feature on his phone.

Cale stuffs the crepe back in his mouth, cheeks full like a chipmunk's.

We ring in a chorus of polite goodbyes. The door slams and leaves us in an awkward quiet.

Now that he's gone, I regret putting off the conversation. Sometimes you don't know if you made the right choice until there isn't a choice anymore.

"Cale really is something, Joy," my mom says with admiration. She glances at Jin's empty coffee mug and offers to pour him more. With his mug in one hand and the coffee in the other, she says, "How do you like it?"

"Oh, I'll take it how you like it, Mrs. Becker," he says with an insane amount of charm.

Angela slices a bite of her crepe and lifts the fork just in front of her mouth. "Isn't he just a dream, Karen?" She eyes him and bites. "I wonder why you're still single."

"Give break to my boy, Angela!" Jan-di says with her own mouthful of crepe.

"So, Joy, think you and Cale are gonna last?" Lena blurts out before blowing the steam off her coffee.

We all kind of stare in shock at her.

"I'm not sure where my daughter left her tact," Angela says, "but I'm sure she just means to ask how things are going with you two."

Sure. That's why her comment was juxtaposed with the topic of Jin's relationship status.

"Things are fine," I answer safely. "We get along really well."

"You must be kinda sad he's gone now," Lena says.

If only she knew why.

I stab my eggy pancake with my fork. "I don't think I'm more upset than his mom would be if he missed his sister's wedding, so I'm okay."

"Oh," she says, finally straightening her back from the gollum hunch she had over her coffee. "Well, I'm sad you'll be missing out on the jet skis today."

I sigh. Today is jet ski day.

Yay.

Lena's less snooty when we get to the rental shack. It's probably because she gets to ride a jet ski with her arms around Jin.

Now I *really* regret running from him.

The moms decide they'll take turns keeping me company (which is wildly unnecessary, but there is no talking these women down). The off-duty moms, starting with Jan-di and my mom, ride a tandem paddle boat.

This clear, 85-degree Saturday afternoon was apparently very tempting to the local population, because all of them are at this lake spot. Lots of little kids run around and squeal and cry. There's an ice cream puddle on the pavement and hardly any sand peeking out from under all the laid out towels on the manufactured beach. I'm lounging in a fabric folding chair on the grassy section, failing to get lost in my book.

I can't keep my eyes from wandering over to Jin in his navy swim trunks and bright orange life vest. His slight slouch is more obvious from this distance.

Maybe it's just me, but that K-Pop idol of mine sure glitters in the sunshine.

Lena rides up on a sunflower yellow jet ski, wearing an apple red life vest. Her glistening skin reminds me of the shining coats of mustangs in classic paintings, especially with her high ponytail whipping behind her like a majestic tail.

Angela sits next to me, sipping an iced coffee through an emerald green straw and flipping through a magazine in the shade.

"The Parks are leaving early tomorrow. Yuno's back from his business trip already," Angela says, without even looking up, though it's hard to tell what her eyes are doing under the wide sunglasses that cover half her face.

Yuno. Jin's dad, the lawyer, and the reason he's studying law. That sensation of recognition hits me again.

My eyes fall on the bright blue paddle boat in the distant part of the lake. Mom's laughing while Jan-di's arms flail about.

"They seem like they get along well," I say without much thought.

"Hmm?" Angela says. My gaze is on my mom and Jan-di, but somehow she traces it to Jin and Lena. He's helping Lena off the yellow jet ski onto the dock.

"Oh yes. They always have. Jin and Lena," says Angela.

I look at her. She takes another sip and smiles. "They'll be good together."

What now?

I stiffen. "What do you mean?"

She clears her throat and puts her drink in the grass. "They're suited to each other. Life's gotten in the way, but it's just a matter of time. Lena's never stuck to any other guy before. It's always been Jin."

I square my shoulders to her, eyeing her with subtle frustration.

"What if they don't want to be together?"

She takes her sunglasses off and pierces me with her bright green eyes.

"Why do you care, Joy Becker?" She says my name like I'm a lowly peasant and Jin and Lena are royalty.

Lena was totally right. Her mom is a piece of work.

It's odd to be stuck in a public place, where your world stops, but the rest of the world still goes on around you. Kids lick melty ice cream, teenagers laugh in fits, someone lathers sunscreen on someone else. And here I am, an inch from unraveling.

I want my seams to give and throw every contradictory punch I have at her. *Actually, Jin chose me and has never looked at your daughter that way, so THERE!*

Jin's voice echoes in my head, though. *It's not easy to break news.* I owe it to him, even to Lena, to let Angela have her assumptions and play her games. I won't bite.

I want to run, but that's literally impossible at the moment, so I lie.

"I *don't* care."

Angela folds up her magazine and places it beside her. "Joy, you may think that us moms don't pay much attention to what goes on with you guys. But we do. We have to." She folds her sunglasses, knowing she has my attention. "We have to protect our kids. Our homes. You didn't think I would let some random friend of Lena's have total control of my house without some checking, did you?"

A sharp breath escapes me. Tears manifest and I dread whatever hangs on Mrs. Garcia's lips.

It had to happen. Sooner or later.

But why the hell now?

"I am well aware of your family's past, Joy. And it didn't bother me. You are not your brother and you've been a good friend to Lena. And I spoke with your mom about it. She told me everything."

I can't stop the trembling in my lips, or the tears that trail down and sting my sunburned cheeks. I feel like a wrecking ball collided with my chest, hearing that my mom shared my past. I know it affected all of us but... it *happened* to me.

"Don't worry, I never said anything to Lena. But, there's something else you should know."

No venom is on my teeth, but I wish it were, because I'm buzzing with hatred.

I was *trying* to make things right. Trying to work past the scar tissue and be happy without tearing anyone down because I've been down enough for a lifetime. Now I feel it twice. Inadequate. Hateful. Worthless.

My burning, wet eyes glare at her, waiting for her to finish. "What?" My voice is coated in anger and hurt.

She sighs, her shoulders relax, and she looks at me with pity.

"Jin's dad is one of the Mayor's lawyers. *Tyler Fuller's* lawyer."

Unsteady air escapes me. I cover my face. *No.* Jin was new. The one who pulled me out of that pit.

How is it possible that his dad protected the monster that derailed my life?

That's why I couldn't shake his name or his face. *Yuno Park.* I only saw him one time, at the end of the hospital hall, in a crisp black suit. Standing next to Mayor Fuller and his wife, while their unconscious son was wheeled into the hospital room.

It's like a puzzle piece of my memory fills in the picture where his face wasn't clear. It was him.

God, this whole time my past was chasing me.

I can't stay here. My shaky arms lift me off the lounge chair and I grab my crutches.

"Where are you going, honey?" she says, not bothering to move a muscle.

What a calculating opportunist Angela is. She definitely had suspicions about Jin and I, and she saved this game piece.

Well, I guess she wins.

Maybe it's not that Carson always wins. Maybe I just always lose.

I honestly don't even care that she dug around my past and got my mom to reveal personal details of the night I was violated. It stings, but that pain is so trivial now.

Before I get far, I search for him standing on the dock. He gleams.

I trusted him.

Jin waves at me and my world falls apart like someone's deforesting the evergreen woods in the background. His hand drops. He knows something's wrong.

And it really is. Because the last person I thought would lie to me was Jin Park.

That was last year?

There was no reason for him to know the timing. He suspected. He knew.

And he never said anything.

TRACK 21 -
SOMEBODY
I USED
TO KNOW

May 3ʳᵈ, last year

"I'M ONLY GOING SO I CAN KEEP YOU FROM DOING SOMETHING STUPID."

I grinned at him, my cheeks dusted with glitter, a lace choker around my neck to go with my black sequin dress that wasn't too short, or so I thought. It was the pride of my closet before that night.

"You know I never make a fool of myself, Joy Bear," Carson said to me. He wore a sly grin and an ocean blue tank that he knew garnered female attention.

His shirt would be covered in blood before midnight.

The memory is almost like a ghost's whisper. "No d r i n k i n g ..."

Tyler Fuller was the golden boy of the whole town. I'd known him since I was a kid because my mom had worked for the Mayor for a really long time. We had roots in that godforsaken place. Tyler had asked me to be his girlfriend more times than I could count. I always rejected him, but

I tried to be friendly for my mom's sake.

I wasn't expecting him to be at Molly Hannigan's house party. He said he'd never get caught dead partying.

God, the irony. It's the kind that stabs and hurts and isn't funny at all.

The beat was far too heavy to know what song was actually playing. I found the punch bowl, which reeked of whiskey, I think. I didn't bother to taste it. Molly made the rounds like an overly chipper *maitre'd* dressed in a yellow knit crop top and tight burgundy leather skirt. Way more revealing than me. Her matte lipstick smile greeted me and my brother, before she insisted she had to go to another part of her massive, unsupervised house.

That was the last moment I considered her a friend.

Carson made it to the string-lighted backyard before I had two seconds to get my bearings. Parties were not my thing, but Carson was finishing his senior year and wanted to go. I didn't know anyone there except him and Molly.

And Tyler.

He came up behind me smelling like booze and inappropriate thoughts.

"Joy, didn't think you'd come!" I remember his curly smile as clear as a bell.

I may have politely smiled back, but inside I was in shock. "Hey, Tyler."

"You look really good tonight." I watched his eyes cover me and immediately made plans to burn my outfit later.

"Thanks."

Thanks. Ugh. I wish I never said that.

I don't know what else we said. The next few minutes felt like hours as far as memory serves. I was on edge, I know that. I refused drink offers. And he drew in closer. And closer.

His arm was around my shoulders and his breath was hot in my ear. "Hey, let me show you something."

"I don't know, Tyler." My shoulders felt like they were up to my ears.

"Come on!"

"...okay."

I didn't stop him. I followed because I wanted to be nice. I didn't think it would end the way it did.

I realized later that Tyler didn't know Carson was at the party. They hated each other and everyone knew it. I had always tried to play peacemaker, which gave Tyler the wrong idea. Despite the post-trauma counseling I got in the plea deal, it's hard to feel like it wasn't my fault.

Even though I rejected him so many times before. Even though I resisted when he pushed his body against mine in the dark. Even though Molly walked by, saw my look of desperation, and continued to the bathroom.

Everyone else would figure Carson snapped because he was drunk.

He wasn't drunk, but I guess he did snap.

Tyler had me pinned against a wall in a dark hallway, and during that time Carson was looking for me. He was already angry about something. But then, he caught my voice. Whimpering, stuffing my crying down, trying not to move as Tyler pressed his unwanted lips on my neck.

His hands wandered too far. Criminally far.

Carson ripped him away from me by the collar of his polo. I was stuck in an elongated moment. I watched Tyler slam to the ground. I saw the terror on his face before Carson's first punch landed.

And I was so... relieved. For a very short fraction of a second, I was relieved it was over.

But it had really just begun.

My brother brutally beat him, landing blows with all the accuracy and muscle he'd earned pitching baseballs. The bones of Tyler's face cracked under Carson's knuckles. Tyler managed to stand up in an attempt to flee. His face filled with fear as blood and saliva fell from his mouth like thick red threads. Carson yanked on Tyler's shirt and shoved him down again, eyes wilder than I'd ever seen.

Carson didn't let up even after Tyler went unconscious. I watched and listened as people struggled to decide who to side with: the golden child of the mayor or the promising baseball star. They chose the one who wasn't conscious.

Some of the brawnier partiers finally lifted my brother off and held him down until police came. Tyler's face was bloodied and swollen and, most of all, unmoving. A few people swore he was dead.

The next twenty-four hours were the most grueling of my life. My brother was in police custody. I wasn't sure if Tyler was going to live or die. I held a deep pain that I wasn't sure I could ever talk about. My mouth was shut tight every moment I wasn't forced to speak.

Then I started to pray that Tyler would live because his death would've made it all worse.

I talked to police officers and lawyers. I felt like I wasn't really the one talking, though. I observed myself recounting what happened. They found witnesses, though I'm not sure who they all were. I was both glad they corroborated my story and furious they did nothing to stop it. It was and still is conflicting.

But most confusing was how desperate I was for none of it to balance out. I didn't want justice for my brother, or justice for Tyler, or justice for myself. I wanted us all to walk away. That's it.

In the end, it was actually Tyler's mom who convinced me to press charges. She knew what her son had done. I've thought about what her reasons were for encouraging me to do it. Maybe she was ashamed. Or maybe it was because, even though he hurt me, I still valued his life. I've wondered if she might've known what I was feeling. Maybe she went through it herself before.

"You have power here, Joy. You should use it. If you don't, they will learn nothing," she told me.

I knew she was right, but I told myself it wasn't enough. These men didn't deserve to learn from this! They didn't deserve to become better people at my expense, to be saved from the consequences of nearly killing someone or to be spared a reputation with a plea bargain. For it to work,

I'd have to be willing to share my side in court, if Tyler was stubborn enough to fight it. And I was convinced that he was.

But then I realized that Mrs. Fuller wasn't just talking about Tyler and Carson. She was talking about *every* onlooker. The Mayor, the rest of my family, other women who were in positions like me, my friends, maybe even my future children.

I willed myself to stop thinking about it and just do it.

I told the Fullers that I would press charges against Tyler if they pressed charges against Carson. I was 100% ready to face court. But, in the end, they settled.

We all walked away. Even Tyler.

The media doesn't like settlements wrapped in shiny red bows, though. They like to rip things apart so public scrutiny runs free like blood from a prey. It was illegal for them to report anything about my part, since I was a minor, so Carson got the brunt of it. Lost his baseball scholarship to OSU. Forced us to move from Oregon to southwest Washington. Never quite healed from it all.

At least Tyler lived. When he woke up, my relief was mostly for his mom. I don't wish him dead, but I hope I never see him again.

It was one of those events that you find yourself measuring everything else against. What's really so bad when your brother almost killed someone and it was your fault?

But, I know it wasn't my fault. *He could've stopped himself.*

Now, I'm sitting outside the locker rooms at Victoria Lake, reliving it. But it's different this time. Like I'm more sober.

When Jin told me *they* could've stopped, it changed me. But in the end, he still lied by omission. There's no possible way he didn't make the connection. How many mayor's kids get beat into a coma?

I run my fingers through my sweat-damp hair and suddenly understand why people pull it out when they're frustrated.

I'm so tired of feeling elated just to get stuck in a self-destructive loop, debating whether or not I'm worth such amazing feelings. I'm so tired of crying over it. I just want to be done already!

Maybe I'm allowed to just sit in my twisted up feelings while I process the crazy curveball that got thrown at me. Maybe I finally *know* I wasn't the one to blame.

Maybe, even though my heart is broken, I'm still resilient.

"Joy?" Carson says as he exits the locker room. "You finally talking to me?"

TRACK 22 -
SAY
SOMETHING

July 20th, this year

S OMETIMES I HATE THAT I'M SO CLOSE TO CARSON. It's hard not to be attached when you have no memory of a world without someone. We share brokenness because we're a pair. The Becker kids. Even if I heal, there's always an ache in my soul over him.

"There's something you deserve to know," I say. Carson takes a seat on the metal bench just outside the locker rooms. His curls are dark and damp from his post-shift shower. The shade is still so hot, it's like I'm watching him dry.

"About time," he says. I involuntarily roll my eyes.

"I don't care if you don't believe me. I never cheated."

"Bull—"

"Shut up! Can you listen for once?"

His brow turns annoyed but I'm sure my expression reflects it back.

He folds his arms over his chest and slumps back.

Deep breath. "I was telling you the truth. I made a deal with Cale, that we'd fake a relationship because he's got a crush on Lena. That's why he gave me his car."

"You really think he gave you his car because he has 'fake' feelings for you?" He uses air quotes around "fake" because, well, he has a point.

"I'm not sure anymore."

He studies my face. "You were really faking it?"

"Yeah. But I care a lot more that you believe I wasn't cheating."

Carson sighs and sits up to put his elbows on his knees like the athlete he is. "It's not that I don't believe you. It just sounds so... stupid."

He's not wrong. But him saying that is a healthy portion of relief for me.

"I still don't like that other guy," he says.

I smirk. "Only because he stood up to you."

"No, it's because he freakin' seduced you when you had a boyfriend! Fake or not!"

"Carson, obviously I told him!"

"Pfft! And he believed you?" Carson grins as if he's just witnessed something supremely idiotic. His scoffing makes me realize how easily Jin accepted my word. We didn't even know each other that well.

Is that a good trait or a bad one?

The warm breeze brushes against us. The woods that surround the employee locker rooms are a mix of quiet stillness and bustling nature. On any other day, I'd drink up the summer heat and fresh air, paying no mind to the impressions this metal bench is leaving on my bare legs.

Today, though, the forest's serenity offers no escape from reality.

"I didn't actually come here to defend myself, Carson."

"What else is there?" he asks with the vague annoyance that's a staple of his utterances.

I tell him about Jin's dad. As I do, every hint of his usual smugness fades and his amber eyes go distant into the trees. He didn't expect this to catch up to us again, either.

"Guess it's not gonna work out after all, huh?" he finally says.

I fight tears hard and say, "Guess not."

But I wasn't ready to say that. I wasn't ready to call it because I never gave Jin the chance to explain. Carson and I are so interconnected that he spoke for both of us. I can't dangle his livelihood over spikes just because Jin's smile won't leave my mind.

"You really like him, don't you?" I'm surprised he's watching me. He hardly ever leaves his own head.

I sniffle. "More than I thought I would. A lot more."

"Well then, screw it!"

My head whips to face him. "What?"

"Figure it out! You don't always have to spare me. I can take one for the team sometimes."

I gape at Carson, in a spiral of emotions that's going both up and down at the same time.

"He lied to me, Carson! He knew about our past and said nothing. I don't blame him for who his dad is but... he should've told me."

"Oh." Now he gets it. "That sucks."

I pat my face dry with my wrist. "It's not like it stops there. Lena's been in love with him forever, so it's just way too complicated."

He looks a bit skeptical. "I thought she went through flings like crazy."

"Yeah. Jin's the reason for that."

"Huh." He sits in this place of wondering about everything. The level of emotional investment he's putting into it surprises me.

Then I have to rewind. "Were you really about to let me date a guy that you hated? Like what have you done with my actual brother?"

Carson chuckles. "My old techniques weren't working so I'm flexing new ones."

I furrow my brow. "Techniques for what?"

"Protecting you."

That's the first grain of sweetness I've gotten on a long, bitter train of conversations with Carson. I smile.

He's finally learning. Took his sweet time, but Carson is getting there.

"When were you gonna tell me about your *game* next week, huh?" I punch his firm upper arm and he laughs.

At least one thing in my life doesn't have to be beyond repair.

The hot wind from the golf cart ride heals my swollen face, like it's taming the flames of my uncertain heart. Carson drops me off at the cabin so I don't have to hobble all the way back from the locker rooms by the lake. My armpits are so sore from the crutches. Profuse sweating is zero help when attempting to balance on metal sticks.

Carson helps me into the air conditioned cabin, but he has to go to physical therapy again. So, once again, I'm alone. With my thoughts. I take my usual spot on the leather couch. It's been imprinted with my body and turmoil. I'm a lot antsier than usual, though, so I get up and hop to the kitchen for ice water. It's all I can stomach with these balled up nerves.

The cold water traveling down my throat reminds me of being enveloped in the pond. Alone with Jin. I'd stopped fighting for long enough to fall. The bliss was explosive, but ignorant.

Maybe he wanted to tell me, but couldn't. Like how I was with Cale.

I know it's hard to break news.

Was he talking about this? Even if he was, does that change anything? He still kept it from me. He still kissed me. He knew who I was and he let me fall. But maybe I shouldn't blame him.

No. I *know* the right thing was to say something.

I stare at the vaulted ceiling. My breath feels shallow, not just because I'm lying down again. I have to talk to him. But how?

My mom's voice enters the cabin before she does. Heat radiates inside the cabin when she opens the door. Jan-di gives me a sun-kissed smile and waves at me as if she's not only fifteen feet away.

And they don't ask me why I came back early.

Angela walks in after them, her towel and hat under one arm and clear vinyl tote back dangling from the other. She says "hello" but clearly she's keeping our last conversation under wraps. Judging by how everyone else acts when they see me, I'm sure she covered up what actually happened.

What an ugly woman.

Lena follows after her, thumbing her phone. "Oh hey, Joy! Get too much sun?"

I nod, but her eyes are already back on her screen.

And then Jin walks in. Whatever lingering smile was on his face fades entirely when we make eye contact.

I can't keep it. I look away immediately.

Don't cry.

His hand falls onto the couch back.

"Hey," he says in a low voice. "You okay?"

DO NOT CRY.

I don't look at him. "Fine."

He lingers on my monotone answer.

Everyone else goes on about the fabulous weather, the amazing nature, some guy with a weird tan line. They loved every minute of today.

Feels like I'm on another planet.

"You wanna help me start a fire?" Jin asks in almost a whisper.

I finally meet his eyes and I don't know how to feel. I caught insane feelings for him. I still dream of our next kiss. I'm still twisted up with hurt. I can't answer him.

He shakes off my silence, but I can't decide if he knows. He goes into the backyard and starts fiddling with the fire pit. The other women have barely stopped talking. Not really surprising that none of them perceive my actual state of being.

Jan-di leans on the back of the couch, the edge of her bob tickling her jawline.

"Joey, you should go to talk with Jin," she says, with a small, courteous smile.

Or is it something other than courtesy? Maybe Jin actually talks to his mom.

She holds her hand out. "Come up." I take her hand and strain to get off the couch. She carries my crutches as I limp to the door.

The sun casts a harsh glow on everything. Jan-di shuts the door behind me. Jin lifts his head. He's tense, so he knows *something*. I take a seat and my crutches crash to the ground.

Jin pulls newspaper out of the cardboard box labeled "BONFIRE" and crumples it into balls. I hate that I'm watching him. How can he be so beautiful as ink spreads onto his fingers?

"When were you gonna tell me about your dad?" I ask.

Eye contact. Yep. He knew. He squeezes his eyes shut and his shoulders fall forward.

"I'm so sorry." He's quieter than the rustling of newspaper in his hands.

"It had to come from *Angela*, right after she goes off about how you and Lena are meant to be together." My lip trembles. There's a wavering anger in me that I never expected would be directed at Jin.

I don't want to scold him. "How long did you know, Jin?"

"When you told me last week. Donuts. First time I made the connection." He drops what he's doing and kneels down in front of me with urgency. "I swear I was gonna tell you. That's why I followed you yesterday."

I can't tell if it hurts or not, knowing it wasn't just blind affection that drove him to come after me. "So why didn't you?"

He opens his mouth to talk but nothing comes out for a second. "How was I supposed to tell the girl I like that my dad almost ruined her life?"

My stomach flips. He'd been trying to figure it out because he liked me. His remorse softens me. I'm weak for his weakness.

He keeps talking. "Everything was too perfect, Joy. And then you ran and I just... I didn't want to give you another reason."

I shudder, but it's because it makes sense. I doubted him and I shouldn't have. *Deep breath.* "It's okay. I get it. I don't blame you."

Is it that easy to forgive him? I want it to be. But there's still worry in his brow when he bites his lip. He stands up and gets back to his forgotten task of lighting the fire, fiddling with the lighter.

"What is it, Jin?"

He throws the lighter in the unlit pit. "I'm stuck on you, Joy. I meant it when I said I would fight for this. If you want me to."

There's something foreboding in the way he says it. Like I still don't know everything we're fighting against.

I frown. "Jin..."

"There's something else I have to tell you," he says, avoiding eye contact. My heart is in my throat. I'm caught in that suspense and I hate it. I've always hated it. How can someone love this part?

It pains him to get it out. "I accepted the internship." Now he looks at me. "I fly out in two weeks."

My eyes fall closed, my face gets hot. I'm awash with unforeseen despair.

He's leaving.

Jin draws near again, and I sink further into the chair. The daylight has faded and everything is turning blue. He grabs my hand. "I want you, Joy. More than I expected."

Tears stream on my cheeks and I'm so shaky. I told him he should go. *Why did I tell him to go?*

I pull away from him. "This is too much."

I get up. He doesn't stop me, though I can tell he's holding back again. I grab my crutches and turn away. It's too hard to watch him.

"Joy, please," he begs, his voice wobbling. "I want this to work. So much."

I whip around before I've taken a step. "But you're *leaving*, Jin!"

My voice catches. It doesn't matter how strong I thought I was or how desperate I am for him.

He stares at me, lost for what to say.

"And you should go," I say. "But you should know that you're the brightest spot I've ever had in my life." Another fresh tear rolls to my chin.

I leave the rest unsaid. There are too many conditions to follow "but" and too many ways to say "goodbye" and too many well wishes I don't really want to give.

I turn my back to him.

"So are you, Joy."

I shiver as I press the heel of my hand to my eyes. I can't respond. So I focus on getting back inside the cabin. I shut the sliding door, sealing him off from me.

Precariously balanced on my crutches, I heave a sigh.

"What was that about?" Lena's sitting in the armchair, facing away. She looks over her shoulder.

I reveal my sore eyes to her and she gets stiff.

"Are you crying?" She rises and gets a closer look.

"I don't want to talk to you, Lena." My voice is low and cruel and I don't care how it makes her feel. It couldn't possibly be worse than me.

Her eyes grow wide. "What did I do?"

"Nothing. It's not even about you." I hobble past her. "Believe it or not."

I don't get far when she says, "I warned you, didn't I?"

I pause, gripping the handles of my crutches with white knuckles. Moments like these give me sympathy for Carson's outbursts. Hurling objects at walls, shoving things off of tables, screaming everything that I know would hurt her.

But I'm not Carson, and honestly, she's right.

She warned me that I'd get hurt. And I did.

TRACK 23 -
GRIP

July 25th

*D*AMN. I COULDN'T GET THE DIRT STAIN OUT AFTER ALL. It's just a pale grey splotch, judging me for bringing it along to the secret pond and dropping it carelessly on the dirty rocks.

The sun is some kind of uncomfortable devil today. It glares at us in a makes-you-wish-you-lived-in-the-Alaskan-tundra type of way. Thank goodness I brought my Mariners cap because I could see nothing without it blocking the bright beams. It's Carson's first day back on the field. This stain is foreboding, though.

I didn't think I was superstitious, but my fortune hasn't been great lately.

After Jin and I had our... I don't know what to call it. After that, my mom found me crying into the Cowboys blanket, alone in the basement. She asked what was wrong. I didn't know what to tell her, honestly. I said the "fight" was with Lena (because it kind of was). She asked if it was about Jin, and so I said, "Sort of." Then she actually switched likable-mom mode on and asked if I wanted to go home.

So that night, we left. And for the whole car ride, she didn't press it. She asked if I wanted to talk a couple times, but I just redirected the conversation to Carson. He healed up nicely, thanks to the specialized doctors at the resort rehab center. Apparently Victoria Lake is known for its muscular rehab program. Good news for Carson.

Anyway, Mom was apologetic for failing to mention the practice game. And forgetting to mention that I was the only family member who'd be able to make it.

Now I'm here. I have three unread texts from Jin burning a hole in my shorts pocket. But it's so hot out, I wouldn't notice anything burning a hole in anything.

"They actually sell Cracker Jacks! Like you got no idea how excited I am that they're a real thing!" Cale scoots past the other onlookers on his way back to our blistering plastic seats.

God, I'm glad he's here with me today.

"Why wouldn't they be real?" I laugh. Then I gasp. "Is that a slushie?!"

Cale hands it to me, candy red and glorious. "Figured you could find a use for it," he says.

"Today I could pour it in my shirt."

Cale laughs, but it drowns in the crowd's cheering when the ballgame song hits the speakers. I stand straight up and join the choir. My ankle isn't even sore today. The doctor yesterday said I can use it if I'm comfortable, finally. A week of crutches is long enough.

Cale screams the part about Cracker Jacks, wildly waving his box in the air.

"Play ball!" everyone shouts in unison.

I suck down the slushie and it cools my insides. I'm glad I didn't actually pour it down my shirt.

I really needed a day where not thinking about Jin was actually filled with something fun. Where I don't see his face whenever I blink or stare off.

I mean, I guess it's not really that day yet. I can't stop thinking about the first text he sent to me. I did read that one.

I still mean it.

Four loaded words.

I started a thousand messages, but never sent anything back. After that, he sent the same four words, once a day.

I still mean it.

Even though I read it in the notification, I let the number in the red circle grow. He hasn't sent one today. I'm kind of scared he won't.

The truth is, giving myself over to Jin means a ton of bitter confrontations and one really painful goodbye. I dread standing on the other side of airport security and watching him leave. And then the flood of all the smiles and touches and the things he said in his smooth voice just overwhelms me with desire. Straight desire. I want him.

Jin pegged me pretty well, too. If it had been flipped, I probably would have approached with equal caution. I would have done anything to make him feel safe before dragging us through the mud. But I darted for the exit anyway. He still pursued me. And not in a way that was disrespectful or selfish.

It takes a lot of energy to not grab my phone. My fingers itch. I've been doing a terrible job trying to get over him.

CARSON BECKER flashes on the screen with my brother's baseball portrait. It's time for the Gophers to take the field. The crowd goes crazy because his followers finally feel heard. This is their comeback as much as his, even if it is just a practice game.

"Woo!" Cale hollers, up on his feet and pumping his fist. "BECKER! BECKER! BECKER!"

I yank his arm. "Cale! Would you calm down?"

He plants himself hard in the chair. "When has asking me to calm down EVER worked?"

"Never," I admit. "But he's not a pro, so cool it!"

He snatches my slushie. "Yeah yeah, whatever you say." He slurps while eyeing me, and I ignore him by watching my brother step on the mound.

Carson spots me. He nods once from the down there. I nod once from the bleachers. And I grin. It's the first time in a while that "the nod" made me feel special.

I can practically see his muscles flex as he grips the ball. He eyes the umpire, winds up and hurls the ball. *Strike!*

That's my brother.

"That's her brother! WOOOO!" Cale wails, and I have to shush him again. He's twelve times louder than anyone else.

While sweat drips down my back, Carson gets the first two batters out. This next one is a strike away. They haven't gotten any runs yet. They're about to go to the second inning in under 10 minutes, which I rarely see.

"He's on fire!!" Cale says. He pops a Cracker Jack in his mouth. "You think he'll make it big?"

"I think he could. I'm biased, though."

"Speaking of big breaks, you ever email that guy? The band manager?" Cale asks me, his eyes on the game.

Crack! It's a hit. The opposing player jogs to first base. So much for a no-hitter comeback.

I turn my attention to Cale's question. "Nah. I'm too nervous to find out what they want."

He nudges me. "You gotta shoot your shot, Becker!" He's smiling big, but then he turns his head and bites his lower lip.

He turns back to me. "There's something I gotta tell you, actually."

Shoot your shot. My pulse races. I'm almost certain I know what he'll say.

For a split second, he looks down. Smiles. Flips his brown eyes up again.

"My feelings aren't fake," he says. "I really like you. Like for real."

He blows air out of round lips, like he just released a weight. Then he smiles with uncertainty.

We're doing this now. "I guess I kinda figured that out," I say, wagering a little smile. But that weight has been transferred over to me. It feels like I'm balancing Cale's heart on my head, but I'm the same old, clumsy Joy.

I don't know what to say.

Cale squeezes his eyes shut and, like it's all one word, says, "Actually, I kinda liked you this whole time. I was never into Lena."

My brow tenses. "Wait... the *whole* time?"

I stare off at nothing in particular. The whole time?!

His knee bobs up and down. "Yep. That crazy ploy was actually meant for you."

How did I miss it?

Thinking back, it's obvious. Always covered by a joke or song and dance routine. A diverted text chain. Nervous fake-fake affection.

Girl like I don't love spending time with my FGF!

You were beautiful and amazing today.

It's hard to get the girl you like to notice you.

The opposing team scores a run and a small section of onlookers cheer, while jeers moan everywhere else. Point for the away team. Meanwhile, I'm running backwards to process the fact that Cale has had real feelings for me for months.

Not like a week and a half. *Months.*

I punch his arm. "Why didn't you ask me straight, *Thomas*?"

"Ouch!" He rubs his arm, then meets my semi-annoyed gaze. "Would that have worked? Better than a convoluted master plan to convince you secretly?"

"Yes, you doofus!" Until I say it, I didn't know it was true. The scary part about jumping in is not knowing if the other person will go with you, but I think offering your hand is sometimes enough. Just knowing he felt that way might have made my feelings bloom.

"So you're saying I could've tried the traditional route?" he says.

I throw my hands up. "You mean the *normal* route!"

He folds his arms to mock me. "Well, I guess that depends on how you feel, Almond Joy!" He unfolds his arms. "Sorry. I'm really bad at 'serious.'"

"I know." My eyes fall on Carson, focused on his pitch. Before he throws the ball, there's suspension. People are antsy to know the outcome, even though it's a couple seconds away.

Just like Cale is, waiting for me.

"I know I've been kind of a wimp around him," he says, and I find him looking at Carson too.

I shake my head. "That's not the problem."

Serious doesn't seem to be an issue for Cale right now. "So it's me, then?"

"It's Jin."

His brow twitches in confusion. "Oh." It takes a second to settle, but it does. "Of course it's Jin."

I sigh. "But that doesn't even matter because he's going to Korea next week, so."

The heat bears into my flesh. I feel sour like forgotten fruit.

But Cale... laughs. Like, a lot. He slaps his thigh.

"Why are you laughing?" I ask him.

He nods once. "Wow, my plan backfired big time." He gives a post-laugh sigh. "I knew I shoulda been jealous of that guy! Man."

"He should be jealous of you, too!" I glance at him. "It's not like I felt nothing."

Cale looks at me, his eyebrows up. "Really?"

My heart thumps. He's hopeful.

In a split second, I imagine what it would be like with Cale. Easy. Fun. Lots of sing-offs and stolen bites of food. Everything I love about being friends would still be great as a couple. And I could kiss him.

But I'd rather kiss Jin. I don't know if I'll always feel that way, but right now, I do.

Cale scratches his head. The game's been at a bit of a standstill with foul balls. It's hard to pay attention.

Cale leans over toward me and his forehead almost bumps against the bill of my cap. His shoulder touches mine.

"Joy, I'll stick around for you. As a friend or... as whatever you want."

Cale doesn't give himself enough credit. He is really, really good at serious.

His hand reaches up to my hat, lifting it off my head so there's only humid air between us.

"All *I* want," he says, "is a shot." He looks at my lips.

I can't decide which side of this war should win. Jin, who'll be gone. Or Cale, who's staying here. Both of them lied. Both of them had good intentions.

Right now, I can figure out which one holds up.

I give Cale the shot. I kiss him, lingering on his full, salty lips. He's a good kisser. Soft and considerate.

I want to want it. But it's not enough. I never thought of Cale when I was with Jin. And now... I can't escape Jin. This feels wrong.

My chest twists and I break it. I take a deep breath in. Why did I do that?

My phone buzzes. I yank it out of my shorts.

Jin: I still mean it.

Me too.

"I'm sorry, Cale." I look up at him, but his eyes are on my phone.

"It wasn't one-sided, was it?" he asks. I give him a bare shake of my head.

The crowd bursts into cheers. Carson struck the hitter out, just before another run. My eyes land on the mound. On Carson. He's looking right at me.

A gripping glare.

Oh God. He saw me kiss Cale.

And now he thinks I lied.

TRACK 24 -
HEARTLESS

Still July 25th

THE STRINGS OF OUR FRIENDSHIP ARE FRAYED. Not broken, but weaker. Our "deal" wasn't exactly broken; it was never really a "deal" to start with. But there was still the matter of the car.

Cale and I didn't talk much the next eight innings. The Gophers won, in no small part due to Carson's rage, which was obvious to me. One game, it gives them a ten run lead. Another he injures his shoulder. Unpredictable.

People shuffle out of their seats, most of them pleased with Carson's comeback win. I grab Cale's sweaty forearm and pull him aside, into the shade.

"I'll pay you for the car."

"Don't! Don't do that," Cale says, physically waving the notion away. "The Beater is yours, no strings."

I shake my head. "I'd feel better if I paid you, though."

"And I'd feel *worse* if you did." He rubs the back of his long neck. "I'd kinda like to not feel any worse."

I'm so sorry. I want to say it, but I just nod.

Cale stretches his arms, I imagine more to cut the awkwardness than because he's sore. "Okay, well, I'm gonna go back to my car and blast that AC."

"See you soon?" There's a lilt of hope in my voice.

He wants to smile but he winces. "Maybe... later."

The distance in his words hurts, but I can't blame him.

"Okay," I say. Then I watch as he escapes through the gates to the grassy parking area.

I want to cry. But I'm also somewhat relieved. But it also sucks to be relieved when you know you just crushed your friend's heart.

I *thought* I was helping him out, even though I wasn't thrilled about fake dating. Now, I'm not sure. If I'd just told him I didn't want to do it, maybe things would've been better. Maybe I should just stop being so compliant.

I'm not eager to go to my car. The AC is still out. Shade is better than a mobile sauna. I wish Mom and Dad had taken the day off work and driven me in one of their present-century vehicles, but they never do that for practice games.

I lean against the hot brick wall. I'm not sure what I should do right now. Usually I wait for Carson to get out of the lockers post-game, but I don't want to stick around today. Nothing good could come from it.

"Hey, are you Joy?" It's a blonde member of the Gophers team, can't remember his name. He doesn't wait for my response before he says, "Your brother's looking for you."

"Of course he is," I mumble. I peel myself from the wall. "Thanks. Tell him I'm coming."

So much for avoiding him.

The guy started jogging back before I finished thanking him. I take a slower pace to the lockers.

Here's to untangling whatever Carson has in his head.

I only wait outside the locker room exit for like thirty seconds before he comes out, freshly showered and changed. I can smell the musty sweat coming off his duffle bag but I ignore it.

"Come with me. I got a surprise," he says walking past me. No greeting. No amusement.

No anger, which is honestly the most terrifying part.

I follow him toward the parking lot. "What do you mean you have a 'surprise'?"

"I just got a surprise." This serious tone forms a pit in my stomach.

"Can I just explain what happened?" I start, though I immediately regret it.

He spins around. "Explain what? Why you were kissing your *boyfriend?*" His flash of anger dissipates and he starts walking again. "You don't have to explain, Joy. I don't give a shit."

My heart stops. It's obvious that he means the opposite of what he said.

I grab Carson's arm. "What's going on with you?"

He yanks his arm away and keeps walking. We reach his truck and he opens the passenger door, tossing his duffle bag in.

"Carson!" Why is he ignoring me?

The door slams.

"I said I got a surprise for you! Just hold your goddamn horses, Joy!"

I meet his angry eyes and recognize this state. There's no talking to him now. If I try, he'll fly off the handle. I don't want to give in, and I definitely don't want to know what his "surprise" is, but I'm certain it'll be worse if I argue.

"Now," he says, rounding the front of his truck, "You gotta just sit in here for a minute. I'm gonna be over there." He points to the chain link fence twenty feet away. "You'll know it when you see it, little sister."

"Why can't you just talk to me like a normal person?"

"I didn't get this far by being normal."

You'd have gotten farther if you could reign it in sometimes. I keep the thought to myself. It's not worth it.

I do what he asks and sit in the driver's seat with the window down. At least this side of the lot is shaded by the stadium. Carson leans against the fence, checking his phone. I put my elbow on the open window and rest my head on my hand. This is so dumb.

Over the next few minutes, more people leave the stadium grounds. There's hardly any stragglers. This side of the lot must be where the teams park because there are still cars but hardly anyone is out here.

What is he trying to show me? That he can manipulate me into sitting in a hot car for no reason?

"It would have been less weird if you just invited me to watch you play."

Dread fills me. I know that voice.

Anyone but her.

"I thought you hated sports," Carson says, as she walks right in front of his truck, with her silky hair over a flowery crop top and distressed shorts.

Lena.

"Are you kidding? I don't hate watching sexy guys throw a ball around!" she argues, and then she throws her arms around his neck. He grins at her.

And they kiss. Lena's making out with my brother.

WHAT?!

I slam the door. I don't even remember getting out of the car. I barely register my ankle soreness as I pound my feet toward them.

"WHAT THE HELL!" I hear myself say. Lena whips around with eyes wide as baseballs.

"Shit!" she says involuntarily. "Joy! Oh my God!"

Carson's angry eyes meet mine. What nerve he has to be smug right now.

Lena's head bobs between us like a ping pong ball.

"Really? *Her?*" I say to him. I'm furious with her, too, but Carson is the one I truly don't understand. He's my *brother*.

"Joy, please don't freak out!" Lena says with her hands up.

I glare at her. "Freak out? Why the hell should I freak out when my brother is making out with my best friend *behind my back*?"

"Please listen! This is nothing. It's a fling!" she stammers. "It's nothing."

"It's not nothing!" I scream, sounding more shrill than I'd hoped.

She folds her hands and pleads. "Please don't say anything to Jin. Please, Joy."

Ugh. I want to vomit, I'm so disgusted with her.

Carson laughs. "Wow, girls are scary. Always lying to each other."

Lena shoots a glare at him. "You're an asshole, Carson!"

She thinks he's talking about her, but his eyes are locked on me.

"Me? You sure about that, Lena?" says Carson, not looking away.

Tears well up in my eyes. Inevitably, he would do this. I knew it would happen.

"I'm *not* lying, Carson."

"So you told her, then?"

My lips tremble, shut tight. He nods, knowing the answer.

"What the actual hell is going on here?" Lena says, catching on.

His eyes flick to her and he reaches into his back pocket. "You shouldn't be so worried about Jin, Lena. He knows what he wants."

I'm frozen in this god-awful heat. I can only watch him deliver more hurt.

He hands his cracked phone to her.

Damn it.

"What is this?" she says so muted that I'm not sure it's her voice. "You *kissed* him?"

I frown at her. "Are you serious, Lena?"

She rubs her temples, like she has a right to be frustrated with me. "I was extremely freaking clear, Joy."

"Who were you kissing just now? A ghost?"

She points at me, her brow tense. "You *never* said your brother was off-limits!"

"Did you say Jin was?" I square my jaw. "You didn't think you had to, right?"

She scoffs. "Well, why the hell would he go for you when you have a boyfriend, huh?"

"Cale was *never* my boyfriend! None of it was even real!"

Lena folds her arms. "Is that what you told Jin? Please tell me he bought it."

The humid air piles onto me as I try to figure out what's behind Lena's annoyed tone. "Did you know?"

"How can you keep this up, Joy?" Carson says. "You were making out with Cale like three hours ago."

"Wow, really?" Lena says, shocked and nearly amused. "So Jin was just a fling to you?"

"No! That's... ugh!" Are they both insane?

Lena rolls her eyes. "You know what? I'm over *both* of you."

"Fine with me," Carson says, not even looking up from his phone.

Lena takes off the direction she came. I chase after her.

"Carson doesn't know what he--"

She turns on a dime, every muscle committed to the action.

"Are you really stringing Jin *and* Cale along? *And* lying to me about it?"

"So you did know," I gather. "About the deal."

"Yeah," she says and off-sets her jaw. "The *deal* was my idea. Didn't expect you to go behind my back."

We're in a draw of betrayal. She knows she's a hypocrite. I know I'm a hypocrite. I could explain my side, and she could still come back with her side. Nothing will get solved.

But I've got enough fire left for one last round.

"You *forced* me to lie to you, but I told Jin the truth. Is it really surprising he picked me?"

Lena's face is tense with hurt and restrained anger. She tuts. "So then why kiss Cale?"

I sigh. "Because I was trying to give up on Jin."

Her jaw drops just enough that I know she wasn't expecting me to say that.

A pair of truth-wrought tears fall along my cheeks. I walk away.

And then I run to my car because I can run now.

I reach my blistering hot metal beast. My chest heaves. How did I not know they were meeting up? How dense am I?

My key makes it into the door, but I leave it there and drop to the grass.

I was trying to let Jin Park go.

But I can't. *I still mean it.*

Still July 25th

WHEN WE WERE KIDS, Carson used to cheat at hide-and-seek. He used to pretend he wasn't there when I found him. Most kids would grab the hider and shake them or something but we had a bogus rule that I always followed. Our rule was that the seeker would lose if they touched the hider at all. I tried everything to get him to acknowledge, but no matter what I did, it would result in me losing to him. I tried using the same tactic on him, but he'd pretend he'd gotten bored of looking for me and leave me in my hiding spot for however long I'd stay there.

The thrill of playing with my big brother strung me along for a while, but I gave up eventually. Then I refused to play it with other kids. Better to be out of the game than to lose when cheating is so easy.

I really didn't think that a brother could cheat on you, but that's what it felt like to see him kissing Lena. I was just starting to trust him. When he said I should try to make things work with Jin, I wonder if he was just interested in Lena. If it was really all about him, like it always is.

He cheats to win. With me, anyway.

It's a broiler inside my car. I slam my fists on the steering wheel, practically burning the skin on my hands.

"Please! Please," I cry, tears nearly dry from overflowing for so long. I take off my hat and violently toss it into the passenger seat.

I turn the key again and it sputters, but nothing happens. Then I hand roll the window up, ready to abandon the damn thing in the parking lot.

It's poetic justice. I broke Cale's heart, and his car is loyally screwing me over.

Just call him. You know you want to.

I click the lock down and slam the door. I slide my phone out of my back pocket. To hell with it.

I call Jin.

Ring. Ring.

He's not gonna answer. That would be so appropriate right now. I'd walk home before asking Carson or Lena for a damn ride.

"Joy?"

My throat catches. "Hey."

"Hey." I can hear a smile in his voice.

I swallow. "I still mean it, too."

"I hoped so," he says. I smile. He's perfect.

"Are you busy?" I ask.

"Not anymore." So perfect.

"Good because my car won't start."

"Where are you?"

"It's too hot for a bike."

He laughs. I missed his laugh. "Car it is."

I spot a mirrored '50s diner across the street, like a beacon. "Meet me at Glen's Diner. It's off of Highway 90."

"Glen's Diner, I know that place. I can be there in twenty minutes."

"Twenty minutes," I echo, no doubt in my mind that it's as fast as he can get here.

"Cool," he says. I can hear jingling keys like distant twinkling stars, growing my hope. "See you soon."

"See you soon, Jin."

"Hey, Joy..."

The streaks of tears tighten my skin as they dry on my face. "Yeah?"

"It's really good to hear your voice again."

I grin. I can't help it. "Yours, too."

"Bye." *Beep.*

I look at my phone in a daze. I fell hard. I'm almost glad my car is a beat up hunk of useless metal.

Within exactly eighteen minutes, I jay-walked across the street, used the bathroom, praised God that I found a five dollar bill in my pocket so I could buy something, slid into a sparkly teal vinyl booth and ordered a strawberry milkshake. The sugar doesn't really help the nerves, but it cools me off.

Nineteen minutes. My milkshake is halfway gone as I avoid staring out the window.

The old-school bell twinkles when Jin opens the door to the empty diner. There is no better situation to describe "a sight for sore eyes." None.

His hopeful, relieved smile. That same white t-shirt on his skinny shoulders and blue jeans a tiny bit too loose. I'm glad I abandoned my hat in my car, because I would hate for anything to obstruct this view.

"Sorry about your car," he says first thing. The waitress brings him a laminated menu and walks away without so much as a "hello." It seems rude, but it occurs to me that she might've ignored him because he won't take his eyes off me.

"It's okay. I'm used to it."

"Need me to take you somewhere?" His genuine concern melts me. That he offered to play chauffeur so easily makes me smile.

"No," I tell him, still soaking him in.

"Do you *want* me to?"

The mysterious depth under his words squeeze my heart.

"Yes." It's instinctual. He starts to get up and hesitation floods in. "But can we talk first?"

He sits back down. "Of course. Anything you want."

His attention is latched onto me, which pulls me deeper into my affection for him. If this time apart has done anything good, it's strengthened my feelings.

"I broke off the deal with Cale today." Jin nods and I continue. "Apparently it was never fake for him, so..."

"I'm not really surprised. How'd that go?"

"He took it well. For getting his heart broken."

He leaves the talking space for me to fill, yet he's not forcing my hand. I can tell him anything. Everything. But I'm afraid to admit that I was trying to let him go.

Looking at him, though... my fear seems so unfounded.

"I'm sorry. I thought I was over you but..."

"I couldn't stop thinking about you either, Joy." A grin flickers on his gorgeous lips.

I play with the straw in my milkshake. Jin is so easy to adore. "I'm sorry I didn't text you back." The regret hurts. I was fooling myself by trying to stay away.

He grabs my hand. "No, no, no. I messed up. I should have told you about my dad when I figured it out."

"But you were right." I squeeze his hand. "I would've gotten scared."

"You still didn't deserve to hear it from Angela Garcia of all people."

I love him.

Jin leans over on the table and lowers his voice. "So, no pressure, but... can we get out of here now?"

I smile and nod. I'm out of the booth before he says another word, abandoning my shake even though it's half full and strawberry's my favorite.

I push the door open, breaking into the heat to the sound of a tinkerbell. I feel Jin's hand on my shoulder and I turn around.

I'm swung into his embrace in a moment. He kisses me.

Jin wraps his strong arms around the nape of my neck and small of my back. Surprise and bliss cascade down my body like honey. There is nothing else but me and him.

Goodness, Jin Park. If everything had to fall apart, I'm glad it was for you.

I don't know why I thought I could convince myself to let him go. I'm elated, pulling away from this kiss, looking into his glimmering eyes again.

Funny how quickly happiness can fly away.

"Joy! What the hell are you doing?"

Carson.

He found me. It takes everything in me not to pretend I'm invisible.

Jin runs his hand down my arm and squeezes my hand. He's in this fight with me.

"Why can't you leave me alone?" I say, trying not to raise my voice.

He rushes us, no care for making a scene out in public. "You still need to explain what the hell that was about."

The light beaming off the mirrored diner feels more intense than the sun itself.

I wipe sweat off my forehead. "Why don't you just ask Lena? Apparently you two are very intimate."

Jin's arm straightens and he shoots me a brief look of confusion.

Carson waves that off. "Bullshit, that was just kissing."

"Oh, so it's fine when you do it behind my back, but not when I do?"

"I'm not the one who's cheating!" His eyes flit over to Jin, making sure he heard. The cars driving by sound like slow bullets. I look up at Jin, stoic in the face of my erratic brother. I can't tell if he's disregarding everything Carson says... or if he's wondering if he's right.

"Is it really worth it, Joy?" Carson gets up close to Jin, looking him in the eye, but keeps his words and venomous tone for me. "Mom told me your little boy toy here is going to Korea next week. Apparently his mom is super proud. So what's the point in cheating with him?"

Jin cracks. "She's not cheating."

Carson laughs like it's a bad joke. Every nerve I have is anticipating more, but Carson doesn't tense up like he's ready to throw a punch.

He takes a step closer.

I pull my hand out from Jin's and point at my brother. "You're just scared because his dad is Tyler's lawyer, and you think all that stuff is gonna come back to us. It won't. It's over."

He looks at me, verging on hurt. "Really? You think it can be over after I lost everything?"

I stiffen. It's almost hard to breathe when it's this hot. These late July days are never usually this brutal.

I've been filled with so much regret ever since OSU called the meeting and pulled Carson's scholarship. I always felt like it was my fault. Repeated to myself that it wasn't. That it was over.

But it was never really over for him.

"I'll be happy when he's on the other side of the world," Carson says.

Jin rests his hand on my shoulder. "I'm not going anywhere."

I whip around. "What? But your internsh—"

"I'm gonna drop it." His eyes go soft on mine. "I told you I would fight for this. And I still mean it. If that means staying here, so be it."

I study his resolve. I know he means it, and I want him to. But the regret over Carson's lost future still yanks on my gut. In my mind, Jin staying was never an option. The Korea internship was his future, because it's what's best for him.

"You can't do that, Jin," I say. I've already ruined too many futures.

Carson scoffs. "You'd really give up your fancy internship for a girl who cheats?"

I look over my shoulder. "I told you, Cale was never my boyfriend."

Carson tugs on his shirt to air it out. "Yeah yeah, keep it up." He looks at Jin. There are flares in each of their eyes. "You believed that shit? Even though she kissed him today?"

My gut sinks like it's full of lead. Jin cracks a little more, a line in between his eyebrows forming. He brushed Carson off before, but now he's not sure what to make of it. He's looking at me with uncertainty.

"Did you?" he asks.

I raise my hands defensively. "Let me explain that."

His eyes widen. "You did?"

"Jin, it's not like that," I say, but this is like that scene in every movie where someone gets caught in their deception. And it does quick work of making things worse.

The subtle expression of hurt on his brow, the slow shaking of his head. He's wondering about it all. Rifling through every memory for some inconsistency to the theory that I lied about my relationship with Cale.

"You kissed him, and then you called me?"

I try to regroup. "Okay. I thought it would make me stop thinking about you." *Damn it!* I sound even worse. Textbook example of being caught in a lie.

He steps back. "You wanted to stop thinking about me? Why? Did you feel guilty?"

No no no no! Why can't I say anything right?

"Finally, he figures it out," Carson chides.

Jin's dark eyes linger on me, searching for a way to reconcile this chasm my brother ripped open so carelessly. "I believed you," he says to me, like he's upset with himself. "Maybe I shouldn't have."

I shudder. I can't watch this. I cover my face, blocking out the sun, Jin's hurt, my brother's smugness. I cry into my already damp palms.

I don't know how to fix this. I really don't.

I look at him, the rims of my eyes certainly red. "I'm so sorry, Jin."

He frowns, hearing my apology as confirmation. He breathes out like he's in physical pain. "Me too."

My breath hitches as he walks away. I can't bring myself to stop him. This was inevitable, wasn't it? All the reasons we couldn't work fill in the widening space between us.

An ignorant couple opens the door, the bell ringing amidst the carnage of this fallout. Jin gets into his car and I cast my gaze to the gray sidewalk under my feet. His car starts up.

And then he drives away.

I lift my head, hoping that Carson isn't still populated in front of me. But he is.

"Are you happy now?" I ask, muted and angry.

His beastly shoulders stiffen as his fuzzy hair dances in the hot, shifty air. "You shouldn't have lied."

"I never did, Carson. You're just so used to doing it yourself all the time, you can't believe that I might've had an honest reason for all of this."

He crosses his muscly arms. "What the hell would that be?"

I step closer to him, biding my angry hurt so I can speak clearly. "That even though I fell in love with him, I was already trying to let go. For you. For Lena. For Cale. Even for him." I don't know if Carson gets it, but I don't care. "So there you go, Racecar. It's just you and me again. You win."

"Joy, I wasn't trying to beat you or something," he says, with an oddly calm inflection. "You're just not who you were."

I shake my head, tapping into anger. "Did it ever occur to you that being this way is suffocating?"

The answer is all over his silent, slack-jawed face. It never did.

**TRACK 26 -
THIS IS
ON YOU**

July 29th

... auditioning as our lead vocalist... it's your call... crossing our fingers...

I'VE REREAD THE EMAIL PROBABLY TWENTY TIMES. I look at the date again.

August 2nd, 4 pm. Yep, that's troubling.

Choppy warm air from a dusty fan travels over my heat-lazed body. The three o'clock sun hits my bedroom window with ferocity. Apparently it's a heatwave this week.

It must be to melt my icy heart.

Might be working. It's kinda racing when I read the email again.

It's from Robbie Gonzalez, The Crux Constellation's band manager. Turns out he decided to stop waiting for me to reach out and grabbed my email from an unused Facebook profile. Apparently, they don't want to disband just because January, their lead singer, is headed off to London for grad school. I haven't responded because... well, I'm too much of a mess to write an email.

They want me to audition during a surprise pop-up concert, but there are two problems: the location and the date. The concert's in Seattle, which is a four-hour drive. And that's the day of FredU's final mandatory orientation. The one I have to show up to if I want to attend classes.

It's also the same day Jin flies out from Seattle.

So obviously I'm desperately avoiding that geographic location during that specific span of time. It would hurt too much to be that close to him as he flies off into a better life without me.

Good thing I have the solid excuse of college dreams. If only they felt like *my* dreams.

I press my phone to my chest. I should just write the email.

There's a knock at my door.

"Joy Bear?" Carson says through the seam. I say nothing. I just stare at the nick in my door, willing him to go away.

"I want to make it up to you. Please come out." His voice is small, and it's not just because it's muffled by the door.

He's never said the words "I want to make it up to you."

"Why?" I say. The door cracks but not enough for me to see him.

"Lena's ghosting me, so I messaged Cale. He said you never lied about anything."

I throw my phone onto my down blanket.

The air shifts when I yank open my door. "Oh, so you believe me now?"

He jolts, like he's a little kid afraid of a disciplinary smack. "Will you come to the backyard?"

I stare up at him.

"Please?"

I follow him down the hall. I've been forced to pass that wall of pictures these past few days and my stomach lurches every time. Those happy kids feel so far away and fake, it hurts. I've mentally practiced a thousand conversations with my brother, but none of them went well.

Carson always wins. Even in my dumb mind.

He stops us in the kitchen. "I bought like four watermelons. Picked the best looking ones and knocked on them and everything. And I got you an iced coffee." He holds out a sweating plastic cup. It's black coffee.

At least he remembered that I liked watermelons.

"I always get a headache if I skip coffee," he says, daring a smile.

He's right that I've got a massive headache. "Well, I can't sleep if I drink caffeine after three PM," I say, "And I never drink it black."

His smile falls and he puts it back on the counter. "Oh." I feel bad for a split second. Then I remember what he did and I have no sympathy anymore.

"Well, I cut some watermelon up. It's in the backyard." He tries to sound light, but it fails.

I go with him through the back door anyway.

It's fatally hot out again, like the sun decided it likes physically assaulting the skin. I thought the AC inside was broken, but I was wrong. Dad must've just turned temp up to give the poor unit a break from working so hard.

Mom's frosted glass tray sits on the patio table, under the umbrella's shade. It's filled with watermelon triangles. There are three other whole watermelons on the table too, like Carson said.

Carson squares himself to me, making direct eye contact. "I'm sorry I didn't believe you."

I snag a triangle and bite the sharp tip. The flesh is already warmer than it should be, but it's sweet and juicy. I squint at my brother. Should I even consider forgiving him? Since he hasn't apologized about shacking up with Lena, I'm undecided.

"That's it?" I finally say because my patience is hanging on a frayed thread.

He swallows. "Uh, no."

I won't lie, his struggle is gratifying. He's so full of himself all the time that genuine apologies are like speaking a foreign language.

I take another bite and raise my brows at him.

"I'm sorry for yelling at, um, Jin. And making out with Lena." He sounds like he's admitting he stole a cookie.

I'm chewing watermelon in my mouth when I add, "Behind my back."

"Yeah," he says, dejected. "That. I'm sorry, Joy. Um... can you forgive me?"

Now that he's done it, I've decided. I savor this watermelon a bit before answering.

Yum. "No."

"Okay..." Definitely not what he was expecting.

I scrape my bottom teeth against the pink part that's left, sucking on the juices. And maybe I'm a terrible person, but I enjoy watching him finally lose at something.

"What else should I do?" he asks. At least it's a genuine question.

I flick the rind onto the deck. "Nothing," I say, and I pluck another watermelon slice off the tray. I expect him to get mad. To flip the table or tell me that I'm a bitch or smash a window. And I promise myself I won't react. I won't give in this time.

But Carson doesn't get angry. He takes a sizable breath, and definitely concentrates on something inside his head for a minute.

I keep eating. It really is a good watermelon.

"Why?" he finally asks. "Why can't I make it better?"

"Good question," I say, and I have this little idea. "Let me show you."

I take the biggest watermelon in both hands and carry it over to the grass, setting it on the ground. Then I turn around and walk back to the deck, while Carson watches me utterly confused.

I snatch the baseball bat that's leaning against the house next to the door. Maybe he'll get it if he sees it in a familiar context.

So I stand over the watermelon and point at it with the bat. "This represents my heart, okay? Here's what happened when you showed me your little *surprise*."

I swing the bat down onto the watermelon with all my strength. The thunk leaves a sizable crack, most of the inner flesh visible, but it's still held together. I look at Carson's upturned brow. Good. At least some regret shows through.

But there's more.

"And here's how I feel now that I have no remaining friends, mostly because of *you*." I throw another swing onto it, which splits it in two mangled chunks.

Juice drips down the wooden bat. I sigh from the effort.

"But you didn't stop there, did you? You *could have* stopped, but you never do."

Carson's mouth tenses downward.

I smash the watermelon remains again. And again.

"I've only ever fallen for *one* guy, Carson! But you showed up and told him I lied when I *didn't!*" I slug the poor fruit one last time, but I'm shaky and out of breath. I stare down at the pile of pink pulp and green shards.

My voice lowers. "And I let it happen. Because Jin deserves better than what you made me." I toss the bat into the grass. "So what do you think? Do I have the heart to forgive you?"

Carson's eyes travel the span of our backyard where I murdered the watermelon. And there's a glimmer of regret on the rim of his eye. I've seen him cry before, even as a grown man. He's not void of emotion. The world has been cruel to him before.

But this is different. He looks at me and breaks. *For* me. He hurts *with* me right now. And he can clearly see that the cruelty was his.

He falls to his knees, witnessing the carnage. "I am so sorry."

Even though it's the most genuine sentence I think he's ever said, I'm not giving another inch. Not today. "I know you are."

I walk past him to go inside.

"Joy, please," he begs.

I pretend I haven't heard him and walk through the door. He deserves to face this alone.

When I'm inside, I find Dad in the kitchen, still dressed in his navy work suit. I pull the door a little too hard when I close it. Between the sharp sound of it shutting and Carson crumpled to his knees on the other side of the glass panes, Dad knows something's up.

He grabs an apple and takes a bite. "Your brother okay?" he asks. Fewest words possible, as usual.

I adopt his method. "No."

He stops chewing, uncertain how to proceed. "What happened?"

"Today, he didn't win." I weave past him and head for my room.

But Dad speaks again, "Was there a game?"

I halt. He's already talking more than I expected him to.

"Not anymore," I say.

"Joy." I meet my Dad's eyes through his coke bottle glasses. "What happened?"

"He always just has to win, you know?" I say, my throat catching. I clear it.

My dad blinks. "That's not true."

I slam my hand on the counter. "It is! He's a bad sport."

"Not true, Joy."

"Don't defend him! You're the one who's supposed to take my side."

"I don't pick sides."

We stare each other down. He's met his daily conversation quota, so I'm hoping he already exhausted himself and stops expecting me to elaborate.

He doesn't. Carson doesn't get his stubbornness from Mom.

"Carson loses to himself all the time," he says. "Most of the time, *you* pick up the pieces."

"What if I don't want to do that anymore? Why can't he handle life without me?"

"He's trying." Dad's so sure of it, I know there's something in what's unsaid.

"Really? How?"

"Therapy. Last couple months."

I'm a bit in shock. "No one told me that."

"Carson didn't want us to."

I can gather what's unsaid now. Carson wants me to be proud of him. Needing therapy bruised his ego. And he's enough of an idiot to think I'd consider him weak for going.

Was that what that was? Him *trying*?

Even though he sucks for hooking up with Lena, and he sucks for charging at me and Jin the way did, and he really sucks for thinking it could all be forgiven with some cut up fruit...

I don't hate him as much as I did a second ago.

TRACK 27 -
MAKE IT
WITHOUT
YOU

August 2nd

I STARE AT MY OUTFIT IN THE MIRROR as if I'm waiting for some revelation of what's missing. I can't put my finger on what's wrong. This cream Peter Pan collar top with the pearl detail is nice. The pleated A-line skirt is a flattering coral color. I even pulled a braid strand back, so I'd feel more... me, I guess.

I fight the urge to text Lena a picture and ask her advice.

Even if we'd forgive each other this second, the reunion would be a small reward in a pit of grief. Jin's leaving today, and neither of us get to have him. It's kinda funny. Lena and I would probably bond over the shared trauma if it wasn't the very thing that tore our friendship to pieces.

Good riddance, cruel summer of minor injuries. At least you were stupidly short.

I still have a couple weeks before classes begin, but attending

Orientation today feels like it's the death of the summer in between high school me and college me. That's kind of why I picked the last possible slot to attend.

"You can do this," I whisper. I'm not entirely sure why I need to hear it. This is exactly the plan I started with. I took a detour but I'm still taking the original path I had planned.

I pick up my phone on instinct. There are three contacts my thumb avoids like they're upturned thumbtacks.

Cale. Because I broke his heart.

Lena. Because she broke mine and I broke hers, too.

And Jin. Do I even need to say it?

But my thumb kinda wants to be pricked for Jin. To set things straight. To tell him I still mean it, even though I disengaged completely. But there's a reason I haven't.

I want him to be free.

Knock knock. It's Mom's knuckle.

"Come in," I say, smoothing my skirt.

She presses the door open with more caution than necessary. "Hey, sweetie." There's a pity smile on her face. "I talked to Jan-di. I'm sorry, honey. I wish I'd known--"

"It's okay. I'll be fine." Even if I'm still sucking up something whenever he's tangentially mentioned.

"Your brother is very remorseful."

"Okay, Mom."

Her lips twitch, as if she's not sure about what to say. Or she doesn't know if she should say it. The crows feet around her eyes reveal the latter.

"If you hadn't been so secretive--"

"Okay! I get it." My heart twists.

"Joy, I don't mean to blame you."

I nod. "Okay." That word makes up half my verbal utterances lately.

She mercifully decides not to say more and puts her hands on my shoulders. Her eyes meet mine. And then she pulls me into her arms.

I don't want to at first, but I bury my face into her shoulder. She squeezes tighter.

"Are you really okay?" she asks.

My eyes tingle. "I will be."

"Joy," she says, pulling away to face me. "I always say Carson and you are my pride and my joy, but..." She brushes my cheek with her thumb. "I am so proud of you. No matter what you do, I'm proud to have you as my daughter."

I've never actually heard her say it so clearly. I mean, I guess she didn't have to. I feel now that it was always true, but hearing it gives my heart a glimmer of happiness.

"Hey."

Mom and I look back at my door. It's Carson. He slaps my door frame. "I'll be in the truck." Then he's off.

Mom rubs both my arms at once and sighs. "Time for you to live your own life."

I stare at her for a second. It feels weird to hear her say that, too. "Okay," I say, but... I might mean it.

She smiles at me as I move past her to leave, but I turn around.

"Mom?" I say. She waits for me to say more. "Um... it wasn't Carson who destroyed the watermelon the other day. It was me."

Her eyebrows go up.

"I just... I didn't want you to think he snapped or something. Actually, I think the therapy's working."

Mom nods, and I can see she's fighting tears. "Okay, sweetie. Now go. It's mandatory." Her smile has gained a few wrinkles since I started high school, but it's the same one she had before I went off to my previous freshman year.

I head out of the house and land in Carson's truck. I agreed to ride with him because I know he's trying. Once Dad told me about the therapy, I softened up.

I will always love him. Not because I owe it to him, or because he needs me to, but because I need to love him. And from now on, I'm doing it my way.

Today, that means letting him drive me to orientation. We get on the road, less than twenty minutes until I officially declare an end to my summer.

"So, I had this thing planned," Carson says. He doesn't take his eyes off the road. "I don't want to call it a 'surprise.'" He laughs like there's a bad aftertaste with the word.

"Probably better not to," I say.

"I'm, uh, supposed to give a speech at your orientation. They picked a couple student representatives or whatever, and I chose your orientation day. So, I'm gonna go up on stage."

"Oh." My eyes trail away from his cautious smile. I almost feel bad for having such a flat reaction. I pick at the peeling pleather on the car's bench seat.

"I just wanted to be there for you, too," he says. His curls droop around a semi-sad expression. There's something different about him. Like he's practiced calming himself for long enough that he doesn't have to try so hard anymore.

"I'm looking forward to it, Racecar." I hazard a small smile. He joins me.

When we get to the overfull parking lot, I survey my surroundings. Campus is... fine. Landscaped with a few flowering bushes, trimmed grass on small hills, and mature trees to shade the concrete walkways. There's a large angular fountain in the middle of the rows of buildings, mismatched by the decades they were built in. Some little kids play in it, waddling and squealing as the fountain shoots sparkling streams into the air, soaking up their last bits of summer.

The time when the toddler walked up to me at Victoria Lake tickles my memory. I'm kind of jealous of those carefree kids.

The Student Union building is utilitarian in essence, working overtime to represent literally every side of identity with multicolored flyers in the windows. Carson and I split before I head into the ballroom and find the alphabetical line A-J.

For a brief second, I remember Mr. Allen Jr. and his sarcastic passes with Cale during glee practice.

I miss Cale.

I figured the best course of action was to let him have space until he made the first contact. It's been brutal going to bed at night knowing it's still not "later" enough. I know I'll see him once classes start. We're in the same FreshQ, which is the nauseating term for the "freshman qualifying course" that all students must endure. Cale will make it bearable. If he'll talk to me.

My arms are overflowing with school merch that I know I'll never use. I pass by the booths. Study Abroad. School of Business. Beekeeping Club. Dentistry.

Right. Because free toothbrushes will sell me on a lifetime of dentistry.

"WILL NEW STUDENTS PLEASE TAKE THEIR SEATS!" blares through the speakers a little too loudly, in some man's monotone voice.

I plant myself in a cushioned chair, facing the stage draped with lackluster navy curtains. The man speaking into the mic has the energy of a bored cat. He introduces a video: *The History of Frederick University*. I zone out halfway through the title. Spoiler: it's remarkably boring.

"Wasn't that soooo great?" says a chipper blonde woman into the mic once the video's over. It's like FredU can't decide the energy they're going for here. Reminiscent of the singing contest at Americanafest.

"Up next, our resident *baseball* star, Carson Becker!" she says, and my heart skips. I don't know why I'm nervous for him. Entering the stage wearing a baseball cap, he salutes charmingly and wins hearts in three seconds flat. When he hits center stage, mic taps echo from the tip of his finger.

"Hey everyone! F-U!" he chants, and there are laughs, a cheer or two and a whole lot of eye-rolls. I'm in the eye-roll camp.

"I'm a pitcher for the Gophers," he says, his dimples are visible even from way in the back. "I really found my center in baseball. As a kid, I liked trying to see how far I could hit or how fast I could pitch. But I learned something real fast. No matter what your gameplan is and no matter how hard you train, there's nothing like the pressure of the game. I also learned that I'm not a great hitter. I strike out a lot."

Carson pauses. His eyes flutter to the ground and he measures a breath. The audience grows silent.

"But I keep playing. In baseball, striking out is basically inevitable. You have to deal with it. Now, here's something that I did not learn so fast. In life, the same thing is true. You're gonna strike out. Even if you trained hard, or planned it all to a T, or you're left counting on your lucky charm." His eyes pick me out of the crowd. "You'll fail your team."

My pulse latches onto his words. He goes on, "In my life, I kept trying to force wins where I should've accepted defeat. It doesn't matter if you win or lose. There's always another game coming. Another ball hurtling toward you. What matters is that you play."

Everyone else may think this speech was meant for them, but I see it in his eyes.

It's for me. Just me.

Suddenly, everything else fades away, we're standing on the field.

"Even if it means you lose, show up and play your game." His voice is like an echo.

I'm holding my breath like I'm on home plate and he's on the mound readying a pitch.

"If you don't play, you don't win."

It hits me. Carson doesn't always win... *I never play.*

I'm still in the bleachers of my own life.

Carson must've thanked the audience, because everyone applauds.

I can't be here. This isn't my game.

I stand up. Sporadically the crowd joins me. And amid the cheers, I leave the ballroom because Frederick University is Carson's game, not mine. It's time for me to leave his field and go figure out where mine is.

Because like Carson said, I'll never win if I don't play.

When I'm in the hall, the crowd's cheers fizzle out and someone mumbles into the mic what's next in the mandatory orientation session. It no longer applies to me.

My heart races. I see his contact, push my finger on his number. Hard.

TRACK 28 -
CLEARLY

Still August 2nd

H E DIDN'T PICK UP. IT KIND OF FEELS LIKE KARMA.

"Joy, wait up!" Carson jogs down the maroon carpet toward me. When he gets close, I realize he's farther from me than he's ever been. My big brother doesn't need me to hold him together anymore.

"I have to go," I tell him.

He reaches deep into his jeans pocket and keys jingle when he lifts them out.

Then he gives them to me.

"I know, Joy Bear." And there's a Carson smile that's meant just for me. Adoring, protective, and now, crooked and bittersweet.

My fingers wrap around the truck keys. "Thanks, Racecar."

We both jump into an embrace without warning, like we read the other's minds. His tight bear hug squeezes the air out of me, but I wheeze it out willingly.

Then I ask, "Wait, what about you? How will you get home?"

He grins. "I'll find my own way."

I'm finally in the driver's seat of Carson's truck. It's awkward and roomy. I dreamed of driving his truck, but I never expected him to hand me the keys. He dangled them above my head often enough. I don't hate the memories now, though.

My ringtone sounds. *He called back.*

"Cale!" I answer, nearly squealing.

"Hey, Almond Joy! What's up? How you been?" He sounds like his normal self, which is a relief.

"I'm okay," I say. And I'm not lying. I lay my forehead on the steering wheel. "I wanted to apologize."

"But you already did, and you didn't even need to. I shoulda... I don't know. I should have done this whole thing different." His laugh is light, but nervous.

I chew on my lip. "There's stuff you should know, Cale. I mean, I don't know what you figured out, but you should know the truth."

There's a beat of silence. But then he sighs. "You don't gotta do that. But I'll listen."

Before I manage to start off on my speech, I pause. It feels wrong to tell him like this. I look down at the keys in my hand.

Cale breaks the silence. "Wait, aren't you supposed to be at orientation right now?"

"Yeah. But I'm, um..." Where was I going, anyway? Where's *my* game?

"Hey," I say with new inflection, "Are you up for a day trip? Because there's somewhere I really want to be and I could use the moral support."

"You know, Almond Joy," he says, his voice low enough to fill me with anticipation, "I can make that happen."

"What, the beater wasn't up to the escapade?" Cale asks as he plops into the passenger side of Carson's truck.

My heart's a rush just seeing him. I don't address his question.

"It's good to see you, Cale."

His face softens and he smiles on one side. "You, too." He slaps the dash. "So! Where we headed?"

I twist my grip on the steering wheel. "Don't worry too much about the destination, Cale Salad. The journey might be all you can handle."

"Whoa." He puts his hand on his chest like an offended old lady. "Was that vaguely threatening or is it just me?"

I laugh and pull out of the parking lot of Cale's apartment complex. "I don't think it was a threat."

"You don't *think* it was?" He flashes me an expression of increased worry.

I missed having him around.

GPS is unnecessary for now. I just have to head north for a few hours. I'm guessing there will be signs to warn me when I get close. But as I enter the freeway, my main concern is clearing the air with Cale.

I'm still struggling with how to start the whole story.

"So... you gonna explain what happened with orientation today?" he asks before we've even gone a mile from his house.

"Yeah. But it's a long story so sit tight."

"I ain't perfected my duck and roll out the car move yet. You're good."

"Everything has to do with the reason we left Salem more than a year ago." And from there, I tell him about it. About Tyler Fuller and the police and Carson. He gets real quiet and I leave the cab empty of noise for a little while. He stares out the window as we leave town, but it doesn't seem like he's struggling with what to say. I think he's just sitting with it.

It's not uncomfortable, being silent with him. I'm not sure how long we're there. Sitting in a length of utter quiet without any awkwardness is a good marker of friendship. We let each other think our own thoughts.

"That never shoulda happened," he finally says, his voice muted and contemplative.

"If it never happened, I wouldn't be here with you. I'd be living a fake life, still trying to please everyone but myself. Honestly, I think that's what I was doing until I left FredU today."

I explain how things changed after graduation. How I developed feelings for Jin, despite trying not to. Then I'm regaling what really happened when I twisted my ankle, or rather right *before* I twisted my ankle.

"So you literally fell for him?" Cale says. I'm glad his humor has remained intact.

"More like I crashed and burned for him. Against my own will. But... even though we both wanted it, it's impossible."

And I explain why. Jin's dad. My loyalty to Lena. Him moving to Korea. And the whole blow-up after Carson's return game.

It's the first time I verbalize the truth even to myself. I let Jin believe that the fake dating thing was a lie because I didn't want him to give up his internship for me.

I believed you... Jin's regret stung. Like he was shocked at himself for being so reckless.

By the time I've finished the entire story, my throat is dry from talking so much. We're nearly to Seattle.

Actually, it wasn't the whole story. I guess there's time to address the part I left out.

"About the game... or, the part where we kissed," I start, pursing my lips with hesitation. "It wasn't out of pity. I do like you, Cale."

"Wait, really?" His surprise is evident in the high pitch of his voice.

"Yeah," I sigh. "You're the obvious choice. I'm happy whenever you're around. You bring light everywhere you go, and more importantly, you're here." I glance at him. I want to want Cale. I want water games and clever puns and interlaced, two-toned fingers. I really like being with him.

But... I *love* Jin. And I won't run from that.

The exit for the SeaTac airport warns us a quarter mile ahead.

"Girl, you're gonna miss the airport exit if you don't get over."

I refuse to move.

"You think I didn't figure it out? Jin's leaving today. We're heading to Seattle. Simple math."

I shake my head. "But I can't make it right anymore."

"Like hell, Becker! I see it all over your cute little face, you are still hung up on that Korean Prince Charming. Get your BUTT into that lane!"

I hold my breath. We pass the SeaTac exit.

"You missed it!" he shrieks.

"Jin's plane left this morning," I say with a large portion of sour regret. "My mom talked to Jan-di right after. He's already gone."

I linger on Cale's shock for a second longer than I should, then look back on the grey stretch of freeway.

"Do me a favor, Cale Salad?"

His mouth hangs open before he answers. "Are you serious? I thought we were gonna dash through TSA in a grand romantic gesture this whole damn time! You swindled me! I want drama, Joy!"

I hand him my phone. "You'll get drama. Route me to Alki Beach."

"Fine," he says with mostly false resistance as he plucks my phone from my hand.

The road noise and artificial clacking of my phone's keyboard are all I hear for a minute. Google's pleasant female voice starts us off.

"I hope this mystery trip makes it up to me," Cale says, settling my phone into the mount.

My lungs fill with nervous air. "Forgive me?" I keep my eyes on the sun-baked road. "For still choosing him, even though he's gone."

"Kid, there's nothing to forgive."

I didn't expect my summer beach trip would involve Cale, my brother's truck, or a beach so small it should really be called a "sliver of sand." But here we are.

Cale snagged the pin of the exact location from Robbie's email. He also confirmed from various social media platforms that The Crux Constellation is indeed setting up a surprise concert and fans are freaking out.

"What song are you gonna sing?" Cale pesters.

I bite my lip. "I didn't exactly pick one."

"Well, they know you're coming, right?"

I avoid eye contact.

"GIRL."

"I'm taking a chance here, Cale. If it's meant to be, then it'll work out. Right?"

"You really got no plan?" His high voice judges me.

The exit becomes visible. HARBOR AVE SW.

"My *plan* was to call you. And somehow I convinced you to jump into the car and we ended up at the top of the state. I achieved my goal. We're good again, that's all I wanted."

"Hey, my grand master plan to win your heart may have backfired, but we were always good, Joy." His seriousness on the latter part cuts straight to my soul. I take in how he looks, as Cale as ever, but I find something deeper now.

"I don't deserve you."

"No one does, Almond Joy." He folds his hands behind his head. "I am a generous gift."

I laugh. "I'm glad you recognize it."

The sun beats in through the gradient tint on the windshield as we spend the next few minutes slowing down on the residential streets.

Modern beach houses and aged brick apartment complexes confuse the horizon before the water comes into view against coin-colored sand. My heart rate picks up the closer we get to the plaza.

I once told my primary school friends I'd seen the Statue of Liberty because I'd witnessed the miniature version of her at Alki Beach. Calling this place "the beach" feels as lackluster as calling that tiny hunk of bronze "the Statue of Liberty." I'd envisioned lying back on the massive, breezy oceanside of the Oregon Coast. But here, the wind comes off the water and people walk around in shorts and sunglasses, so it does the trick.

I parallel park next to a seafood restaurant that advertises too many types of cuisines. When I cut the engine, it's real. A few blocks up, I see bulky guys carrying speakers to the makeshift platform at the plaza.

"You ready?" Cale asks. I don't move, so he elbows me. "You ready? YOU READYYY?"

I giggle, but I'm still terrified. "I don't know," I sigh.

"Hey," he says, "There's not really such a thing as 'ready.'"

I meet the gleam in his brown eyes. It isn't until this moment that I realize how bad it hurt not to have him around. I'd been uncertain of our friendship, but he never was. There may not be such a thing as "ready," but there is definitely comfort in being supported.

Cale pumps his fist. "Let's do this, Becker!"

A gust of violent wind whips my hair across my face when I get out of the car. I don't know how I'm gonna keep it cool when I get on stage.

If I get on stage. I have no idea how forgiving "Robbie Gonzalez the band manager" is.

The Statue of Liberty Plaza is paved with rectangular stone and people are already seated on the grass and benches, even the stairs. The statue obstructs where people will crowd, but their fan base is loyal enough not to care.

Cale flashes his white teeth at me as we walk. My gut does flips the closer we get. I recognize the band and their respectively distinct hairstyles. Fiona with the magenta bob, Krista with the emerald side-buzz, Geo with stick-straight blonde hair down to his hips, January with the bleached pixie cut, and Javed with absolutely normal, shaggy black hair.

Even if I didn't plan to come, I did my research.

Robbie Gonzalez is the one guy I have not seen a picture of, but there's a stocky man covered in tattoos who looks like the name might belong to him. The sides of his head are shaved with a dark plume of gel-covered hair on the top. Also a full beard. The hair might mean he belongs with the band. My hasty plan is to ask him if he knows who Robbie is, but he spots me and his eyes light up.

"Joy Becker?" he almost yells.

I step closer and raise my hand sheepishly. "That's me. Sorry I never emailed back."

"And you brought your partner in crime, I see!" Robbie slaps Cale on the back and they both laugh, but Cale rolls his shoulder when Robbie isn't looking.

"I'm stoked you're here! I just wish we'd set up for you. It's been crazy all around today." He has a genuine, friendly laugh that puts me at ease. "What do you say if we have to take 'Back To You' after our first fiver?"

"Fiver?" I wish I knew the lingo and didn't sound like a little kid.

"Oh, yeah, it's a five-minute break. Like forty-five minutes into the show the band will cool off."

Back To You. I know it. I've played it five hundred times.

And specifically avoided it for the last week.

"I can't," I say.

Robbie's positive energy dissipates. "Oh. Wow. I'm sorry, I thought you came because you were still interested. I should've asked." He rubs the back of his neck. "I can hardly think straight today!"

"No, I want to sing! I just... I don't know if I can do that song. It's too..."

Robbie's brow goes up waiting for me to finish. But it's hard to say it.

"Raw," Cale finishes. He points to me and frowns. "Lost love. Too raw."

At least Cale's bluntness has benefits.

Robbie perks up the way someone does when they're excited, but also feel they shouldn't be. "Well, what song do you want to do? I can tell you if it's in our set and send you on up. Just gotta warn the band."

"How about *Cosmos*?" I say. One of my favorites. Upbeat and well-practiced in the shower.

"Yeah yeah yeah! I'll let January know you're taking that one over." Robbie grins and shakes his head in disbelief. "This is gonna be good."

I hope he's right.

"He's right," Cale says like he's reading my mind. "You're gonna kill it!" He whips out his phone and taps the back of it. "And I'm gonna document."

"Okay, so I just have to enjoy the music and keep my nerves from causing me to implode."

Cale lands his wide palm on my shoulder and squeezes. "You got this!"

Despite his encouragement, performance anxiety scratches at the edges of my soul and begs me to run.

But I'm not a runner. Not anymore. I found the game I'm meant to play. If only I'd realized it sooner.

An airplane cuts the sky overhead, a whooshing noise trailing behind it.

Jin's voice echoes in my mind. *I really want to hear you sing again.*

As thrilled as I am to be on the ground, right where I am, I kinda wish I was singing up in the sky, somewhere over the Pacific Ocean. I wish I was with him.

But I'm not.

The true farewell show of The Crux Constellation is void of dancing lights or quality speakers. It's no more than a fiery set of humans who meld with the energy inside each of their songs. January exudes sex appeal I'll never match. She's way more rough-edged than I am, too. But I'm not deaf; I know our voices are crazy close. Raspy in all the ways that count, powerhouse on cue, feminine and light when it works.

I don't know what Robbie sees in me. I'm nothing like their current frontwoman, but maybe that's the point. My voice does justice to the songs and I'm still me. The girl at Americanafest wasn't trying to be January Evans.

Their heavy drums and stretched-out synths carry listeners to worlds where robots fall in love and waves crash against bleeding hearts. The drummer can also play the fiddle and the basswoman gets lost in her chords like she's unafraid of drowning in the song.

The people around me eat it all up. Cale has become a total fangirl, "woos" and all.

Meanwhile my stomach turns into foam each time they end a song. The buzz of anticipation is like a drug that heals you and makes you sick. My limbs feel like they've fallen asleep.

I sober up when Robbie shoves me toward the stage and says, "Okay, kid! Your time to shine!"

My heels skid on the paved plaza ground. *Deep breath. You can do this. You'll never be ready.*

Like singing for Jin. I look at the water, imagining the sparkling waterfall. Remembering how the water reflected sunlight against his face.

I slam my foot onto the platform and force myself up there.

January talks into the mic, "Hey, we got a friend here today to sing for you CruxConvicts! She's little, but she's got one hell of a voice on her! Give it up for Joy!"

Everyone cheers louder than they should for me. She pulls the mic from the stand and hands it over, mouthing "good luck."

I grab it, feeling like I'm suddenly drunk on something strong. The crowd's bigger than I expected. Or the nerves are, I can't tell.

Cale lifts his phone up, undoubtedly recording.

I lift the mic up, ready to say whatever I planned about the song *Cosmos* and what it means to me and that I sang it into a hairbrush like a proper dork.

But I freeze. It's not right.

The last time I sang, Jin kissed me. I haven't piped out a single note since then.

I blink like mad, willing long-built tears to stay back.

"Um," I say into the mic, my breath reverberating in the speakers. "I can't sing the song I came up here to sing. I'm kinda stuck on something else."

People grow quiet and I feel my honest self reaching through the cracks of what's broken in me. I don't care if it's awkward. It's real.

I'm stuck on you, Joy.

I meet eyes with January, and some of the people in the crowd. There's a lot of raw expectation, but some of them have honest, supportive expressions. They don't even know me.

Well, one of them does. I'm glad he's here.

I step to the precise center of the platform. "I'm gonna sing a song you might know. Maybe it means something to you like it does to me. But it's the only thing on my heart right now, so it's all I have to give."

In my mind, instruments swell, but everyone else is baited on the silence before my voice flows into the mic. I close my eyes.

And sing *Rainbow Connection*.

I pay no mind to how I sound or how people react. I'm sitting on the rocky floor next to a pond, the hum of my voice floating into the sky with ethereal song. The lyrics mean something different now. They don't tell of an unattainable dream swirling out of reach like a balloon.

The Rainbow Connection is our journey to seeing true beauty. Or, that's what it means to me.

By the second verse, the pianist lifts notes into the song, the guitar strums beachy chords and the bassist carries depth under it. The song takes on new life and the crowd travels to another plane of appreciation. Songs are that way. Like a vehicle for your soul, taking you off the grid of reality for however long they last.

I sing the bridge, reaching the moment where Jin stopped me. I let the word carry out too long, and the silence after, too. With my eyes closed, I can see his face like a vivid picture. The moment replays in my head.

How did I get so entwined with Jin so quickly? How can my heart be threaded to him, stretched out over time and space and this moment of a song?

I sing the words of the next verse, like I'm gently plucking flowers from the ground for a bouquet. And this is far more beautiful than the last time I sang it.

Before, I couldn't finish. I wasn't finished. Jin interrupted my life and brought a halt to my heartache, like the apex of a hill, before rolling quickly down and crashing at the bottom. But I've completed the journey now. I climbed the mountain, and now I live at the end of the rainbow.

I finish the song, with some Kermit fans who happened to join me, and something clicks.

I am my fairytale dreams, my tumultuous past, and my uncertain future. My essence is a spectrum. Both real and ethereal, like a song can be.

I'm beaming when I notice the cheers. But even bigger than that is my own sense of wholeness. The crazy part of finally feeling whole is that you don't feel unbroken. You're different, a new thing altogether. Changing back isn't the right path to normal. It's not even an option. Accepting is.

I have no idea if I belong on this stage, but I know I belong somewhere. And I don't have to try fitting into someone else's life. I will find my game and I'll play hard when I do.

Cale whoops in decibels high above the rest of the crowd, bringing me somewhat to reality.

Oh, God. I just threw professional musicians off their own concert to sing a kids song about rainbows.

I shove the microphone back into January's hand, garnering feedback on the speakers. At least she's smiling at me right before she takes over again.

Cale's right at my side to help me off stage. "Joy Becker, you tantalizing muppet-lover!"

I laugh at him but something catches my eye. Someone standing on the sand, not far off, staring me down.

I meet a set of familiar, pear-colored eyes.

Lena.

TRACK 29 -
HOMECOMING
QUEEN

Still August 2nd

HAT'S LENA.

When she won the title of Homecoming Queen, Cale told me all about the girl with the shiny hair and big reputation. She was so glamorous and sparkly, I thought I could never make friends with a girl like that. Not again.

Molly Hannigan was Junior Homecoming Queen at West Salem High. A partier, charismatic debate team president, the girl with a boyfriend in college, one of my friends. I figured Lena wouldn't be any different. In some ways, I was right. They both did a pretty good job betraying my trust.

But Molly never came back.

"That's Lena," I say, staring at the girl on the beach. Strands of her silky black hair dance across her face and collar bone. "What's she doing here?" My question comes out like a breath.

"Okay, so, don't freak out but I texted her," Cale says, stringing the words together rapidly. "She came up today for U-Dub orientation. She... feels bad about everything. That's what she told me, anyway."

She watches me, fiddling with her sweater, gazing off into the water for a few seconds before landing her eyes back on me.

When I left Salem, I had no one. Every person I counted on turned out to be a fairweather friend. They chose Tyler's side, believed lies about my family, ignored me crying in the bathroom stalls. I felt like I was floating above myself, forced to watch a tragic film that never relented. Molly, Amber, Gavin, Thea. Names I used to say daily. Faces that greeted me warmly in the morning. They became sideways glances and whispering heads.

All I wanted was for one of them to talk to me. I thought at least Molly would.

I learned a long time ago that loneliness isn't worth protecting. Carson did that, with rage-covered shame. I resolved never to be the kind of person who made reconciliation impossible.

None of my friends ever tried.

Not until right now.

"Joy? Are you mad?" Cale asks.

I look up at him and shake my head. "No, I'm not mad at all."

And then I run to her.

It takes me five seconds and I hear her start an apology, "I'm sorry about me and Car—"

I crash into her and wrap my arms around her waist before she can finish.

A second later, she hugs me back, laying her head on the top of mine.

"I really suck," she says. I distance myself and notice she's crying.

"No, you don't suck. You did a sucky thing, but you don't suck, Lena."

"God, Joy, do you have to be such a mom?" She taps the edge of her eye with her fingertip.

Cale walks up to us and points at Lena. "Stop! Just stop! I'm a sympathetic crier!" I can't tell if his throaty voice is real or genuine, but it's welcome regardless.

I turn back to Lena and she heaves a sigh. "I am sorry, Joy. I got jealous and tried to strangle control out of something I had no control over. Like my mom. Shit." I note a few freckles on Lena's glistening cheekbones. "I should've never met up with your brother. Or tried to keep Jin to myself. I knew he liked you and I just..." She sniffles.

"You knew?"

She nods hard. "Oh yeah. He had the hots for you, like, the first day you met."

I blush, recalling the on-the-floor moment we first saw each other. "Really? How do you know?"

"He *told* me!" She laughs with a twinge of bitterness. "Jin's basically halfway between a friend and a brother. He's not shy with me."

"But you're still in love with him."

"Yeah, well..." Lena looks off, her vision landing on the hazy blue hills in the distance. "I don't know if those were *my* feelings or my mom's visions of a perfect future projected onto me. She was the one always telling me my boyfriends were wrong for me, no matter what. She was right sometimes, but not always."

The air is fresh but heavy with humidity. The crowd cheers behind us, but it's out of place with Lena's turmoil. She's felt a lot more loss than I ever realized.

"The point is," she says, "Regardless of how I feel, I know he's *not* in love with me. He didn't even tell me he was leaving until yesterday." Her lip trembles.

"I'm so sorry, Lena," I whisper. I don't know what else I should say.

The wind picks up and she tightens her cardigan around her shoulders. "I was at the airport this morning before he left and I told him the truth. He deserved to hear it."

"What did he say?" I ask. What I really want to know is what he did, but I'm afraid to ask that.

"He thought about it for a sec. Then he said, 'If she wanted to clear it up, she would have.' And then he hugged his mom and left."

I feel a shudder in my heart.

Lena's judgemental tone kicks in. "Why didn't you set things straight, Joy?"

I stare at her, my brow knit together as I try to form an answer.

She folds her arms. "He would've heard you out! He *wanted* to hear you out."

I still can't answer. I avert my eyes to the nearby fish and chips place, the bike going by, the driftwood lying on the sand.

"Why'd you let him go?" She's near yelling.

I pinch my mouth closed, fighting tears. Why is it so hard to say?

"Isn't it obvious, Lena?" Cale says, breaking his uncommon silence with uncommon gravity. "She'd rather suffer than ask Jin to jeopardize his future. That's who she is."

My wide eyes meet his. Since I told him my past, he sees the patterns of my choices. If it saves someone, I pour myself out. Even when I shouldn't.

"What if Jin *wanted* his future to be here?" Lena bites back, even though this fight isn't with Cale. She shakes her head and lands her pretty eyes on me. "Maybe we should just let these stupid boys make their own choices."

Her eyes flit to Cale when she says "stupid boys" and, to my surprise, he nods in agreement.

I look up at the clear, blue sky. "He already did."

"Guess so," Lena sighs.

Cale clutches me and Lena each on the shoulder, giving us each a start. "Are you both legit crazy right now?" We gape at him, since he's clearly the crazy one.

He continues, "Just cuz he's flying over the ocean don't mean it's over! Take it from a dude: he wants c-lar-i-ty." Cale enunciates each syllable on "clarity."

"What am I supposed to do now?" I ask Cale, as if he's the keeper of such knowledge.

"Call him. Leave a message." He drops his hand and gestures a check mark in the air. "Simple!"

My lungs fill with uneasy breath. It's almost too simple. *Call him.*

I can do that.

I yank my phone from my skirt pocket and find his contact. His silly winking face is his contact picture. My heart pounds as my finger hovers over the number.

Tap.

Straight to voicemail, as expected. *You've reached Jin Park, leave a message and I'll call you back when I can.*

I hope that's true. Wow, I desperately hope it's true.

Beep.

"Hey. It's Joy. Um..." *Deep breath, Joy.* Each word comes out separated from the others. "I just wanted to say that, um—" I swallow. I know this isn't right. "I hope you'll be happy in Korea. And I'll miss you."

I hang up in a rush.

"Joy! What the hell was that?" Lena shrieks.

Air shudders out from my lungs as I look between her and Cale, both surprised.

"You don't get it!" I say, the entrails of desperation escaping into my voice. Halfway through the voicemail, it hit me. "I can't make it harder for him. I don't want him to regret leaving."

They're both frowning at me, trying to make sense of my tangle of emotions. If I can't, I doubt they will.

"I don't want him to regret anything," I say. It's not really to Lena or Cale, though. I know I have to make a plan and reconcile, like my old friends never did.

I stand up taller. "I'll make it right. Later, I promise."

"You better," Lena says, but the snare in her words is a farce. She cares about me.

"I will personally hack your phone to keep you honest, Becker."

My eyes rim with tears as I look at them both. "I don't deserve to have you as friends."

"Oh, come on," Cale says, throwing his head back dramatically, snapping it back to me. "We all know who the real MVP of our friendship is, Joy."

Lena nods. Both of their eyes are on me.

I gape at them. Words don't exist, just disbelief. And honor.

There's a tap on my shoulder and I whip around. It's Robbie the band manager.

"Hey!" he says with a beaming smile, "Thanks for coming out. They're about to wrap up. You should stay and hang out."

I suck in a breath and try to level my emotion, with minimal success. "Sure! Yeah," I say. He's about to leave but I catch his attention. "Hey! I'm sorry for changing things up. Something came over me, I guess."

He shakes his head. "It's cool! I don't speak for everyone, but I like a little unpredictability in a show." He winks and laughs, simultaneously young and grown-up. Then he points his thumb back to the stage where January screams into the mic. "See you over there!"

Robbie walks off, weaving into the crowd and patting shoulders like he knows everyone.

"He's cute," Lena says, her chin slightly up as she checks him out.

That's Lena.

And I, for one, am glad she came back.

TRACK 30 -
HANDMADE
HEAVEN

August 3rd

THE MEMORIES OF THIS SUMMER flip through my mind like fanning the pages of a book. The challenges, the rewards, the strikeouts. My future is uncertain now, but I also kind of needed that. It's bitter and sour like a grapefruit, but refreshing like watermelon. Now that I think about it, the memories themselves are like that, too.

I don't regret that it all happened, because in the end, I stepped up to the plate and swung. It sucks that I missed. But I don't regret playing.

My headphones are crackling a little, which means I've loved them well. A dreamy summer song helps me relish a stillness so rare in my life so far. The song is interrupted by the chime of my text tone.

Lena: Meet me at the fallen tree in 30 minutes
Lena: Don't be late

Wow, two seconds into making up and Lena's returned to her old, demanding ways.

I missed her.

I finish out my heavy rotation and head for the front door. It's finally not oven-weather today, but I can't walk the field in sandals, so I opt for Converse. I tuck my newly acquired Crux Constellation t-shirt into my acid-wash jean shorts and pull my hair half-up into a bun. Then I stare at my reflection in the entry hall mirror, freckled and sun kissed. This girl looks different than the one who's faced this mirror time and again. I'm not the pushover, can't-miss-a-game-or-get-a-B kid anymore.

I'm the college-dropout who never went to college. The singer who flubbed the biggest opportunity of her life. The magnet for minor injuries and Korean lawyers.

The girl who somehow charmed Jin Park into falling for her, then convinced him to fly to the other side of the world.

I wonder if he checked his messages. He never called back. It's 6 AM there. Not that it matters with jet lag.

Am I giving up again? I don't know. If I could, I'd get on a plane and find him, just to tell him face to face. But I didn't make *that* much money this summer. Maybe I'll ask Lena what she thinks I should do.

Still staring at my own gold-flecked hazel eyes, I remember how it felt to kiss him. It's like it ended two seconds ago. Potent memories always sting, because if they're bad, they still hurt. And if they're good, they're already gone.

"Where you headed?" Carson asks, shoveling midday cereal into his mouth.

I'm out of my trance. "Meeting Lena."

He blushes. "Oh. Hey, can you, um…"

I adjust my bun, my eyebrows lifted at him.

"Can you tell her I'm sorry for being an asshole?" he says.

I smirk. "Sure thing, bro."

"Joy. I know Mom was kinda annoyed about what you did yesterday, but you're gonna do great, no matter what you do." His dimple appears beside a really great brother smile. He'll be cheering me on from bleachers this time.

I smile back. "Thanks, Racecar. Go put on a shirt."

I walk out into the bright, breezy summer day, stuffing my phone into my back pocket.

"Joey!"

Immediately to my left Jan-di Park is leaning against her slick white Mercedes parked by the sidewalk. It looks like she was talking to my mom.

I can't help but smile seeing her. "Jan-di! How are you?"

She grins, her eyes creasing. "I'm doing so good."

"You going somewhere, sweetheart?" Mom asks me in that light tone of voice she uses when she's talking to me in front of another adult.

"Yeah, meeting Lena." I look back at Jan-di. "How's Jin doing? I bet you miss him."

Her smile doesn't fade, but her eyebrows go up. "Oh, yes! Every mom miss baby, Joey. But he so good."

Jan-di sure is good at keeping a smile on. Then again, I guess I am, too.

"Tell Lena I said 'hello,'" Mom says, in that gentle way of urging a child away from the adult conversation.

"I will. Bye, Jan-di." I wave goodbye to the pair of oddly pleasant moms. Moms are so good at keeping a cool head around each other, especially when their children make drastic life decisions they don't approve of.

I'm not sure how Jan-di felt about Jin's decision, but I know Mom wasn't too happy with mine. I'm not going back to Frederick University. The fallout wasn't as awful as I expected, though. Less a shrill "the world is ending" and more a reluctant "back to the drawing board."

Walking along the sidewalk, I note the hum of a lawnmower and smell some faint smoke from a barbecue. It's a remarkable summer day. I wonder if the secluded fallen tree will feel like it did before. Chatting

Lena up about future plans and Puerto Rican culture, promising to bake cookies next time I go to her house. I guess I don't have to convince her to watch *Greatest Showman* anymore. And she doesn't have to ask if I'm eyeing anyone.

Before I leave my neighborhood, I stare out at the field on the other side of the street. The golden swath of grass, lined by rows of tall trees that sway and rustle. I can't see the fallen tree from here, but I know right where it is. Into the middle of the woods, just beyond the line.

That dead, scraggly log has the tendency to inject life and brightness into my friendship with Lena. We crafted an emotional oasis out of nothing but air, tree bark, and solitude.

I cross the street and jog into the field. The dry grass tickles my legs all the way up. I brush my hands across the tops of the tan strands. After traversing the uncut field, I pass under the sporadic shade of the trees, birds singing in pure confidence. The rustling leaves hush every other sound. It's been a while since I soaked up an atmosphere like this.

The trees peter out and I walk into the hidden clearing. My eyes fall on the centerpiece: the fallen tree. In a stream of amber sunlight, perched on top of it... isn't Lena.

It's Jin. Looking up into the sky like a contemplative work of art.

Am I dreaming?

He turns his head, slowly. A current of wind strikes us both.

I study him. His neutral expression, the lines of his bony shoulders, that same white t-shirt. The sun rays cast him in harsh yet angelic light.

I slowly walk toward him. I'm not sure if the ground will give way. He leaps from the felled tree. When his feet hit the ground, my heart pounds and I stop. He really is here.

"I thought you were in Korea," I say.

He takes a second to answer. "I'm not."

"Clearly." I sound annoyed even though I'm not. I adore the way shadows hug his cheeks and lips and long neck. I can't believe I'm looking at him.

I don't know why it's taken me until this moment to realize that Lena's text and Jan-di's diversion were a set up. They both knew I'd meet Jin here.

Confusion and happiness swirl together in my heart. I'm happy he's here, but I can't read him. I don't want to screw up again.

Deep breath.

"Do you not want me here?" he asks.

His question surprises me. "I just thought you were gone, that's all."

"That's not why I'm asking, Joy." There's heaviness in his serious eyes.

The bewildered part of me grows. What does he mean then?

I scan the parched ground to keep composure, but I can't keep myself from catching the way he's cloaked in the glow of the afternoon. I feel like I'm not ready for this. *There's not really such a thing as "ready."*

"I'm really sorry for everything, Jin. I am."

His brows pinch together, like he's pained. "Everything?"

"Yes! I hate that I hurt you. I didn't mean to. I just... I thought if you were unattached, it would be easier for you to go."

"You thought breaking my heart would make it easier?" There's a thread of irritation in his expression. He angles away from me, and he's right to.

My jaw trembles. I was so stupid to think it was better that way, but I was convinced.

"I couldn't let you give up your future for me." My eyes sting with tears and my voice fills with emotion. "I didn't want that to happen again."

I bury my face in my hands, sobbing into the darkness of my palms. Carson lost everything because of me. Jin was about to do the same thing. I didn't want to hurt him, but I couldn't let him do that for me.

But... Jin's the one who showed me that I can't bear the responsibility of other people's choices.

Jin clears his throat. I lift my wet face out of my hands and my nose tingles. I'm sure it's red. I'm a splotchy mess and he's painted porcelain.

"I'm not your brother," Jin says. "I wasn't giving up anything I didn't already want to give up."

I narrow my eyes. "But you went to the airport. Lena said you went through security."

Jin nods. "Yeah. I got on the plane. Because I was hurt. It's not like you just ended it, Joy. You let me think every amazing thing we had was..." He holds his breath before blurting, "Fake. Like you were never all in."

His hurt flickers when he sets his jaw and fear constricts me. It's like a neon "Open" sign has shut off and I missed my chance to walk in. He won't look at me.

He walks toward the tree, facing away. He hunches over with his palm on the bark.

"Nothing was fake, Jin," I insist.

He glances over his shoulder. "That's what Lena said."

Jin suddenly walks up to me. "I have to tell you something, Joy."

My stomach flips. I nod, bracing for whatever it is.

What is it?

His dark brown eyes study my face, like he's not sure how to say it.

"When I sat down on the plane, I couldn't fasten the seatbelt. I didn't know why. But I couldn't stop thinking about you. Wondering why you'd let me think you lied." He steps closer and my heart races. "Then I thought about who you are. How you've given up so much just to benefit other people. The deal with Cale. Running off to spare Lena's feelings. What you did for your brother. You always sacrifice your own feelings for other people. That's why you let me go. It was for me."

His voice is so dreamlike. *Am I dreaming?*

Jin reaches out to brush a golden string of hair behind my ear and his finger brushes my cheek and, boy, I am definitely not dreaming.

"Jin—"

"I'm not done," he says like a command. "Tyler Fuller wasn't worth your mercy, Joy. Maybe your brother was. Knowing what Tyler did, I definitely understand Carson better. That made me realize I'm not meant for translating business law. Not when people like you are standing up without someone behind them. Protecting those people... *that's* what I want to do. *That* is a rare kind of wonderful." He looks down, almost embarrassed. "I want to be worthy of that."

"You are, Jin." I'm flush and so, so certain. "You are."

I can't describe the light that turns on in him. It's not just an "Open" sign. It's like an entire skyscraper lights up.

"I don't deserve that," he says. "Not from you. You're far more wonderful than I am."

His sudden, unrestrained adoration pummels me.

Jin draws closer. The scent of jasmine dances with the breeze that whispers into the inch of space between us.

I'm breathless. No one has looked at me this way. Even my parents were always bent on shielding me. They didn't look at me like this. With...

Admiration.

I can't move. This moment is so big. I can already hear the swell of an invisible orchestra, building to what he's raring to say next.

In sunbeams, Jin's eyes gleam. His breath goes shaky.

"I'm all the way in love with you."

Just like that, I am fearlessly deeper in love with Jin Park.

"Me too," I whisper, just before impulse takes over. I reach up and grasp the back of his neck, standing on my tiptoes, catching his brief look of surprise before I pull him into a kiss. His arms find me, tighten around me and lift me off the ground until I'm above him.

This love doesn't feel like falling. It feels like flying.

Jin was hidden in my life long ago, tucked away in the background when I thought I would never see light again. But here, I'm bathing in light, inside and out.

All we have is a melody of birds, the beat of rustling leaves, and each other. It's the sweetest song I've ever heard.

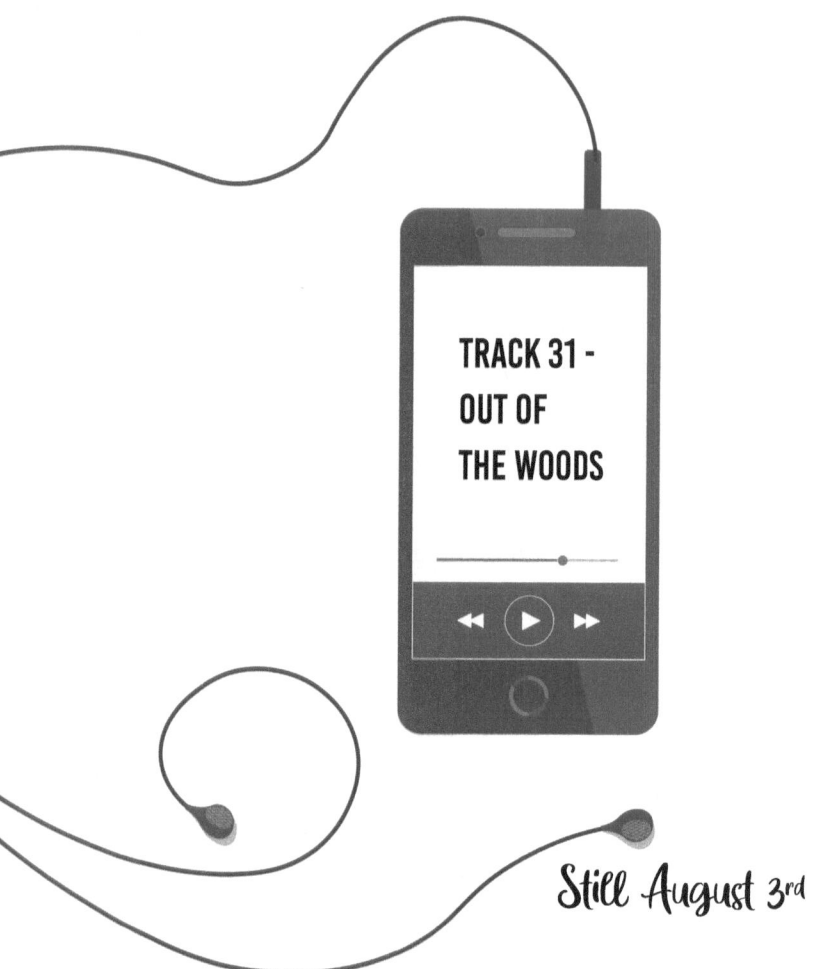

TRACK 31 –
OUT OF
THE WOODS

Still August 3rd

COLOR ME SURPRISED. This is not how I thought this day would go.

Jin and I are stealing time at the fallen tree, talking between dreamy make-out sessions that leave me giggling every time. I don't know how I moved into this sheer bliss, but with the falling sun and cooling air, it gets easier to want Jin's arms around me. It's like a drug, the coupling of our lips touching and my heart bursting. Every part where he touches me, my hands, my back, my hips, my jawline... it tingles.

The sun has turned into a rainbow and lights up everything like neon. The colors of my life.

We sit on top of the log facing each other. Jin confirms what Lena told me. He was into me from the first moment we met.

"That was the most embarrassing introduction I've ever had," I laugh.

"It didn't seem like it. You brushed it off. And you were super cute, too, so I took notice."

I avert my eyes, blushing. "Yeah, I took notice, too."

I take an eyeful of him, his one leg dangling off the side of the tree. I press both my hands on the scratchy bark, leaning into them so I can get closer.

He meets me in the middle, with exactly the kiss I wanted. One we each take a full breath through.

"So what did you think when you thought I was taken?" I ask when we've parted.

"That I had to back off."

"Of course you did." I should've known. "You're an actual gentleman."

"Yeah, well, I'm also naïve. My mom told me not to believe you, but I did because I wanted to. I'm too honest. Might make me a terrible lawyer."

I palm his cheek. "Or one of the best."

He smirks. "You don't have to say that just because you're my girlfriend."

Girlfriend? I gape at him, pulling my hand back because I'm caught off-guard.

"Oh." He reacts to my abrupt shift at his word choice. "I never asked, did I? I—will—"

"Yes!" I say, unable to contain my smile. "Absolutely yes."

I don't know why the thought of Jin being my honest-to-goodness boyfriend gives me a fresh wave of butterflies, but it does.

His fingers graze mine one by one. "So why *did* you kiss Cale that day?"

There's a flicker of insecurity in him. He looks down and continues tracing my fingers.

"Cale said he wanted to shoot his shot, so I let him," I say, my tone somewhat somber. "But it was all wrong. You texted me right then and... I knew it was you."

We make eye contact and my heart's ticking resounds deep in my chest. The corner of his mouth curls up.

"But Carson saw it," I add, hating to ruin that smile. I explain what happened from that side. Carson didn't believe me, then he did, then he didn't again. Now that I know Carson has been talking to a therapist, it makes sense to think he just struck out that day. But the fact that he can pull himself back together now makes a huge difference.

"So how will your brother react to me being your boyfriend?" Jin asks, just a little smug.

"He'll survive," I jest. The truth is, Carson might feel mixed up, but it won't matter. I'll fight for what I have with Jin. I hope I don't have to, but I will.

"One last question," he says, scooting toward me. "Why were you in Seattle yesterday?"

"Lena didn't tell you?" I'm kind of surprised.

"Nope. She just said you drove all the way up there for me. But, the timing was off, so I'm missing something."

"I didn't actually go up there for you. I knew you were gone. Or, I thought you were."

"So why were you there?"

I put my finger up and reach for my phone with my other hand. When I pull it out, I find Cale's TikTok, where he posted the video of me singing for The Crux Constellation.

Ten thousand views. And counting.

"Oh my god!" I say, laughing in shock. "I'm viral!"

I give my phone to Jin, leaning in close so we can watch it together. The emotion is clear. It's weird to view it from this side. Singing that song was healing and ethereal in the moment. Now I see a girl with a broken heart, letting her voice carry her through something no one else can really see but they can somehow relate to.

"I was supposed to audition for the band, but I couldn't do it. After the show, even though they said I sounded good, they didn't say they'd contact me. I'm pretty sure I missed my chance." I say all this right before the part when I stop singing because Jin had kissed me there before. The video captures my hesitation, but only me and Jin can tell what's there.

"I was thinking about—"

"I know." Jin gently puts his hand behind my head and draws me in.

Here he is again, kissing me, interrupting the song. Is it always going to be like this?

God, I hope so.

August 4th, 2:08am

Jin and his mom stayed for dinner. And after dinner. And then Jin and I took to the den ourselves for an episode of *The Walking Dead*.

We didn't really watch much of it, if I'm honest. Too busy kissing.

I cover my face with my blankets. Am I really blushing alone in my dark bedroom where literally no one will see me? My cheeks are sore from grinning so much. I'd rather smile than sleep anyway.

This yearning aches. Like when we said goodbye. Jin kept his eyes on me as long as possible, before my front door closed. I slid down the door and dropped to the floor. Maybe I was hoping he'd come back if I laid in the entryway.

Separation from him feels so wrong. Like someone so in love shouldn't feel heartbroken, but I do. The reality is a thrill, though. He's mine. I'm his. Bless this summer, injuries and all.

All I can think about is when I'll see him next, which is serious cardio for my brimming heart. It keeps me awake, but my eyes are starting to droop.

Buzz.

My hands are faster on my phone's notifications than they've ever been.

Jin: I'm still thinking about you

I type very, very quickly. My cheeks hurt again.

Joy: Me too
Joy: It's hard to sleep

Jin: Agreed
Jin: I'm kind of in awe that today even happened

Joy: How do you think I feel?? I didn't even plan to see you this year!

Jin: Haha I guess that's true
Jin: I'm sorry I didn't just call you. I wasn't sure you still felt the same.
Jin: Lena only said we needed to talk. And your voicemail was discouraging. I thought you'd moved on already.

I audibly whimper when I read that. It didn't occur to me that keeping my true feelings to myself had hurt him. Not until now.

Jin: I'm really really glad I was wrong :)

I can hear it in my head, the text in his voice. Emphasis on the second "really." An actual smile at the end. I wish he was here, saying it in person.

Joy: I love you so much, Jin. I mean it.

Jin: I still mean it too.
Jin: You should get some sleep.

Joy: I'll call you before you drive back to Seattle

Jin: Can't wait to hear your voice Joy. Goodnight.

Joy: Goodnight <3

Grief is the other emotion keeping me up right now. Jin has to go back up to UW to talk to his academic advisor. Apparently his sudden forfeit of the Seoul internship involves signing some paperwork, plus meeting professors to get in classes he needs. He'll be there for a few days with Jan-di, and it is definitely going to kill me. I'm grateful we live in a time where cell phones exist, but they're not much when the real thing is so, so good.

I'm not excited about potentially having a longish-distance relationship. It's not South Korea, but it's a long drive my car won't survive after a few round trips. And it's not like I can just move there. I might have rich friends, but even if they offered to help me get there, I couldn't take it.

I'm playing this game. Me. I'll do this my way.

Since I can't sleep, I think I'll look at Seattle job listings. I reach for my phone and check the time. It's already 2:20 AM. I set it down. I should *try* to sleep.

Buzz.

I snatch it and see it's not Jin. It's an email. I'm about to ignore it, but it's from Robbie Gonzalez. Robbie Gonzalez *the band manager,* Robbie Gonzalez.

"So about that audition..." the email subject line reads.

Holy crap. I fight tremors in my hands and my overworked racing heart to open the email.

I read it.

They want me.

HOLY CRAP. The Crux Constellation wants to give me a shot at being their lead singer!

Nope. Not sleeping. Not even trying.

I waste no time calling Jin. Of course he picks up right away. I don't keep my voice down just because the world is sleeping. I'm squealing. I don't care if Carson brings his fuzzy head here to complain.

Nothing stops me from sharing in this life-altering news with the boy I'm in love with. He couldn't be happier for me.

Or for himself. Since it probably means his girlfriend has to move up to Seattle.

TRACK 32 -
YOUNG AND
IN LOVE

September 7th

"**F**INALLY I CAN MOVE MY WEIGHTS OUT OF THE GARAGE and blare my music." I'm standing in my mostly bare room and Carson's taking up my doorway. It suddenly occurs to me that this frequent sight is one thing I'm leaving behind.

Mom already told him there's no way he's taking over my room. She refuses to do one thing that might deter her baby girl from visiting home, her words. It makes me feel pretty special, actually.

I ignore his comment. "You're gonna come up for some shows, right?"

Carson grins. Then he nods once. And I nod back.

I can hardly wait to see him do it from an audience. I think I get why he wanted me at every game now.

Robbie's email said the band wanted to feel out having me up front, so I drove up that same week and practiced. I also got to see Jin sooner than I expected, which motivated the beater. Dad also fixed her up a bit, thank goodness.

Anyway, they GAVE ME A CONTRACT. After making the drive a few times and practicing more than I thought I could, they wanted me.

I guess going viral has perks. I still have to find a part-time job to make ends meet, but thanks to my Dad's scary good job-searching skills, I've already got a couple interviews lined up. I still have time to apply for part-time school at community college. I'm not mad at that prospect.

"Are you gonna be okay, Joy Bear?" It's hard to ignore that my big brother is actually worried about me.

I walk up to him and rub his face on both sides, making his curls bounce. "Yes, Racecar. I'll be fine."

I wouldn't be so certain, except that Jin will be there. And Lena. Part of it is my faith in them, and part of it is their faith in me. I might be young, and small, but I've tackled bigger arenas than the ones ahead of me.

Knock knock. Lena pokes her head into view.

"Hey, Lena," Carson says. He moves aside for her, a charming cadence covering him instantly. As if I'm not standing right here. "You look nice today."

"Whatever, Carson. You still haven't invited me to a game." His smile falls off his face.

Okay, I still love how she reams him.

"Uh, yeah, well, I thought..." he stammers. "There's one today. If you wanna make it."

Wow. He's trying the coy approach. Haven't seen that one. It's clumsy.

Lena sizes him up. "A solid B for effort. But no. Can I have Joy now?"

"You're just delaying the inevitable, Lena," he says with a sly smile on his face as he walks by her.

"Dream on, Carson," she says, rolling her eyes. Even so, I give her a look that says "is he on to something??"

She frowns like I don't even know who I'm talking to. "Please, that's *way* over," she affirms, running her hand through her long hair. "It's weird that you're moving there before me."

"I know! I'm excited for when you get there, though. My apartment's not far from campus," I say, though I can hardly believe I just said "my apartment."

"Do you have anything else that needs to go?"

I scan my room. "I don't think so."

"Actually, there is one thing. Shouldn't be too hard to move, though." Lena pulls something out of her pocket. It's a silver necklace with a triangle watermelon charm on the end of it. The seeds look like tiny, sparkly black gems.

When I look up, I notice she's wearing an identical one.

"You got this for me?"

"Yeah. After asking around for what you might like. And, well, I hate the ones where, like, you have to put them together to make a whole piece and say something dumb like 'BFFs FOREVER' which is stupidly redundant, so I got matching ones."

I pluck it from her hand and it sways beneath my fingers. "I love it. A lot."

"Good," she says with a huge smile.

I pull my hair to one side so I can clasp it behind my neck. It drops just below the neckline of my pineapple tee, the coral pink popping against the yellow and green like a vibrant fruit salad.

"You ready to go?" Lena asks.

"Yep," I sigh. It's weird, leaving the bedroom that cradled me through the most intense time of my life, but I am ready.

Lena and I walk out to where *the boys* are still loading boxes in my car.

This summer started with a ridiculous deal for this very car. This beat-up, ugly beige, 90s sedan, that practically begged me to call Jin to my rescue on multiple occasions. I couldn't leave her behind.

Cale rubs her roof in nostalgia.

"Be good to her," he says with his eyes closed.

"She's been good to me so far," I assure him.

"I was actually talking to you, Almond Joy. This is my baby."

"It's a big, metal object, Cale," says Lena. "It's so weird when guys talk about cars like they're people."

Cale clings to the side of the car. "Don't listen to her, my precious, beat-up beauty!"

"Thanks for the help, Cale," I say, getting a little choked up. "I'm gonna miss you like crazy."

"No, no, no, no! Stop that! I told you, I'm a sympathetic crier!"

But I don't comply. I snatch Cale into a hug and a tear escapes the corner of my eye. He squeezes me back.

"I'm about to object to the length of that hug," says Jin. The tone of his voice tells me Jin definitely isn't worried about the hug, but Cale's arms fling away from me anyway.

Turns out, Jin makes him nervous. But Jin still makes me nervous, too. In a different, much better way.

I kiss Jin's cheek after he's loaded my last box.

"That everything?" he asks. And honestly, I've already forgotten what he's asking about. I can't believe he's here, about to drive us up to Seattle, to a tiny apartment I'll share with *my* bandmates Krista and Fiona, in close proximity to where Jin will be studying law.

I've been ready for days.

"Just one thing," I say, and I jog back inside my suburban home, straight to my brother's room.

"I'm leaving," I say as I hang on to his door frame.

He bolts off of his bed and envelopes me in a bear hug.

I'm proud of him. So proud. Even though he's sad that I'll be gone, he can fight his own battles. I grip him with all the strength I have in these bony arms.

I feel in his muscles all the sport and rage. He squeezes me until near death, and then he relaxes, letting me linger. This is the last time I'll hold my brother up.

"I love you, Carson," I say into the shirt he's thankfully wearing.

"I love you, too." They say your heart can be on your sleeve, but Carson's is in his voice.

He decides to step outside so he can wave at me as I drive off with Jin. I see Dad is wiping down the beater's windows, doing his best to leave the beast squeaky clean, which is better than "I love you" coming from him. Mom races out of the house with ziplock bags full of snacks for the road. She hands them to Jin and pats him on the arm.

I think she's still a little in awe that I snagged him. In a good way. Like me.

She turns to me, laying claim on the final farewell hug. She kisses my forehead and then stares back at me with the hazel eyes I inherited, stroking my head a few times. Fighting tears.

"I'm so proud of you. I'll see you at your first show," she says tenderly.

"Okay. I love you, Mom. You too, Dad."

"Same," Dad says, and that's more than I expected. It makes me laugh. Or maybe I'm just giddy.

I look up at the clear blue sky, entirely empty of clouds. This is the sky that watched my summer live out, in all it's scandal and glory. I never thought it would end up like this.

Deep breath.

It's a pretty magnificent sky.

Jin takes the driver's seat and I take the passenger seat. Piled in with all my things, including, of course, my wonderful and embarrassing Lisa Frank pillow and Barbie blanket.

"Soooo," Jin says, a mere thirty seconds into our journey, "You said you have some music for the trip."

I plug my phone into the auxiliary port, old school. "It's kinda dumb, actually. I made a summer playlist and added songs as things happened. It's like a record of our summer."

"A musical commemoration of our love story?" he says with a silly grin.

"I know it's like melodramatic middle school vibes," I laugh. "I can pick something else."

"Play it," he insists.

I flip through the list of playlists I've gathered. *Joy's Summer Playlist.* "Are you sure?"

Jin takes his eyes off the road for long enough that I worry his adoration will cause an accident. "Absolutely. Make this summer last as long as possible."

B-Sides

A COMPANION TO JOY'S SUMMER LOVE PLAYLIST

Playlist

TRACK 01 -
REAL
FRIENDS

Lena – June 5th

"**L**ENA!" EMMA BOUNCES OVER TO MY LOCKER. She's decked out in shades of pink and her usual bushy tail demeanor.

She's way too perky for her own good. She actually hops to a stop. "Hey! Cale said he wants to talk to you before you leave school."

I shut my locker door. "Cale Thomas? Did he say why?"

One of her brows goes up toward her huge bow headband. "Why do any guys want to talk to you?"

Gee, thanks for the backhanded compliment, Hello Kitty.

I sigh. Better to just ignore it than deal with it. "Did he say where?"

"Tennis courts. I gotta go. Bye!"

Emma flits off like the condescending fairy she is, glitter and all.

I check my phone. I guess I have time to reject a member of the male species before heading to Joy's house.

Heading out of the main building, I slog to the tennis courts. At least the weather is amazing. I'd spend the rest of the day in my pool if I could.

I shove a piece of gum in my mouth. Easier to dodge unwanted lip-lock situations when I'm smacking my mouth.

Cale's standing by the chain-link fence, fidgeting with his phone, waiting to confess his feelings. He's one of the nice guys, I think. And he's cute, even if he could manage to wear clothes that actually fit. I admit my envy of his Nike collection, though.

I figured Cale Thomas would have made a move on me before now. He's pretty outgoing and he's been single for a while. We've been acquainted in classes here and there for four years, barely striking a conversation beyond "Can I borrow a pencil?" That's how I know he won't be worth it. He doesn't even know me.

He lights up when he sees me, like an eager puppy.

Great.

"Lena Garcia! Thank you for your punctuality," he says.

I sigh and pop a bubble. "Hey, Cale. What do you need?"

Need is a better word than *want*, I've learned. It conveys that I don't care what these guys *want*, and gives me a chance to shut them down if I decide their "needs" are useless to me. The word "want" usually leads them to say "you" and that only worked the first time.

"It's not really a need, I guess. I've grown a *curiosity*."

My brow arches. "A curiosity?" That's new.

"You're good friends with Joy, right?" he asks.

"Yeah." I chew my gum loudly.

"Do you know if... um..." He rubs the back of his neck, eyes wandering off.

"Yeah?"

His voice goes high. "Is she into anyone?"

Oh. So he's not going to ask me out? That's... exciting, actually. I've been trying to get Joy to spill her romantic leanings for months. Ever since we became real friends, I've been way more invested in Joy's happy ending than my own. She's so freaking happy and sweet all the time.

And I know she talks about Cale. A lot.

"Do you like Joy?" I ask, amused.

"You caught me," Cale says with a wince. "I'm nervous because I was trying to get her to come with me to the karaoke thing tonight, but she said she couldn't. Do you know if she's just, like, not interested?" His big brown eyes are hopeful. Cute.

"She can't go because of her brother. She's at all of his baseball games. Which is super dumb. So I wouldn't take it like she isn't interested."

Cale nods. "Okay. That's good to know."

I eye him. "You really like her?"

"I *really* like her."

My smile unveils slowly. This is perfect. It's now my mission to set them up.

I put my hand on his shoulder. "Here's the thing with Joy, okay? She's, like, a people-pleaser. She wants everyone to be happy, but I don't think she really knows what *she* wants. So, even if you ask her out, I'm worried she'll just say 'yes' because she doesn't want to disappoint you."

"Is that a bad thing, ultimately?"

I frown. "Do you want her to like you back or not?"

"Yes. That I do."

"Okay," I say. I start crafting a plan, tapping my chin. "I bet she'd let you be her fake boyfriend."

"But I'd like to be her actual boyfriend, Miss Garcia."

"Just listen. If she thinks you're into *me*, then I'm sure she'll let you pull your moves on her. Then maybe she'll actually start to have real feelings and you can shoot your shot."

He furrows his brow. "And why can't I just ask her out directly?"

"Oh, come on, do you know her? She's going to be stuck at her brother's baseball games all summer. She'll feel super guilty ditching her boyfriend all the time. And she'll feel bad if you tag along with us because she'll think I won't want you there."

Cale lifts a worried brow. "You really think so?"

"Oh yes. It's perfect! Seriously, she won't be so worried if she's doing it for my sake. Tell her... tell her I'll want what she has because I'm jealous of her."

"Are you?"

I gape at him. "Kind of, I guess."

"Wow, the Great and Mighty Lena has a weakness?"

I knew he had nerve. "Shut up."

Cale shakes off my response. "What if she doesn't want to do it?"

"Cale. I know my friend, okay? We've spent every weekend together since our first semester physics project. She loves the idea of me finding a great guy. Plus, I know for a fact that she could use a chauffeur." Cale's not sold on my genius yet. "Look, you asked me if she could be interested. I don't know the answer. But this way, you can put out actual feelers without scaring her off."

He thinks about it for a second. "Okay yeah, that's a good point. And actually, I could give her my beater. I won't need it after graduation."

I clap. "Yes! Even better!" Wow, this feels awesome. Matchmaking for Joy. She deserves a fun boyfriend like Cale Thomas.

"I'll try to get her to come to the glee thing tonight, 'kay?" I say.

"You will?" he squeals and thanks the heavens. He's such a character.

Cale calms, smiling at our devious plan. "You sure you're okay with being the fall guy, Lena? What's in it for you?"

"I just owe her, okay? She's my friend."

I owe her for just being my friend. She's not the type of girl who assumes guys will only talk to me if they have a chance at hooking up.

"Plus, I can handle anything you throw at me," I tell him with a sly smile.

He laughs. "You know, Lena, people don't give you enough credit."

Now I really like this guy for Joy.

**TRACK 02 –
SING IT
WITH ME**

Cale – June 5th

IF I'M OBJECTIVELY HONEST WITH MYSELF, I'm worried I made a mistake giving Garth the venue-picking power for tonight. The dude was all excited and said it was gonna be a big surprise, which is unlike him. I caved. Glee Captain. Made of butter.

Daisy, my trusty Australian shepherd, waddles into my room and looks up at me.

"I'm busy overthinking my faults, Daze," I tell her. She pants at me, all smiley and calm like there's nothing more important in life than her afternoon walk.

I stare her down. "Not yet, girl! Have you no respect for the delicate male ego?"

My bed bounces as I sit. Daisy jumps up and lays next to me while I scour Garth's Instagram for evidence that he hangs out in places that have some amount of swankiness. No luck so far.

Part of me is hoping Joy *doesn't* come so I won't be so nervous about taking her to some country-lovin' dive. Not that I'm against that sort of thing. But tonight's *like* a date.

It's not an actual date, but it's an impression. A shot. If she even comes.

These fish pics are pretty ugly, but Garth sure seems proud of them. Guy's got a shiny smile, like a toothpaste ad, if no one cared about sweaty hat hair.

I flip over to Joy's Instagram account and scroll. Scroll. Scroll...

She's so cute in all those little vintage dresses she shows off by fanning them out. I remember when she walked into glee that first meeting day, so quiet and doe-eyed. I thought I was charitable by taking her under my wing.

What I didn't know was how fun and awesome and selfless she was.

Just thinking about her (and looking at her cute pics), I get all tingly and nervous.

Lena Garcia, DON'T FAIL ME NOW!

I get a text. FROM JOY.

Oh, my heart! Did Lena do it?

Joy: Guess what?? I can make it tonight! Pick me up?

Oh my oh my oh my. I've prepared all year for this moment. I jump off my bed, and Daisy skitters off my bed, abandoning my lovesick ship.

Cale: YASSSSS!!!!! I'm sobbing Becker
Cale: SOBBING
Cale: Gonna be LIT with you there!
Cale: See you at 7 sharp Almond Joy

A development. Hoo boy. All that tripping over myself trying to get

◀◀ 284 ▶▶

Joy to come to karaoke night and I just had to tap into the BFF. Despite the shotty reliability of my vehicle, I'm stoked to pick her up.

I'm not actually sobbing, but, like, my heart is kinda sobbing.

Now onto Phase Two: asking Joy to be my girlfriend. Well, *fake* girlfriend.

TRACK 03 - GIRLS LIKE YOU

Jin – June 16ᵗʰ

"WOOOOO-JEEEEEN!"

I race down the stairs to meet my mom's call, certain she just wants me to load yet another one of her suitcases into the limo. I don't know why she needs so many for one week.

"Umma! What is it?" I say in Korean.

She launches into every thought without a single breath in between. "Why are you so out of breath? Don't you exercise? Here's the envelope. I saw the dog-sitter's car outside. Make sure she gets paid before we leave."

"Okay," I say, panting as I grab the envelope. My mom's observation aside, I do exercise. I *don't* usually run up and down these same stairs fifteen times in one hour bearing the weight of overstuffed luggage.

Jogging across the courtyard over to Lena's is a nice change of pace. The morning is crisp and bright. My favorite part of summer is the breeze that floats across me as I head over.

I slow my pace when I see the door is open, but I'm convinced it's because the Garcias are in and out of their house.

Until I see her.

There's a girl on the floor. She's splayed out like a starfish, random things littered around her. She's just... lying there, all little and serene.

"Um..." I say, unsure of what else I could possibly say at a discovery like this one.

Her eyes peel open, revealing a very pleasant hazel color. She's cute, but she seems more surprised to see me than I am to see her, which is amusing in its own right.

"You okay?" I ask. I grin, offering a helping hand that she accepts.

Once she's up, she says, "I'm fine."

Freckles pepper her nose and her hair falls just below her shoulders, with streaks of gold like she dipped it in sunlight. It dawns on me that this is the dog-sitter. She hasn't let go of my hand, so I guess I'll just introduce myself.

"Jin Park."

She snatches her hand back and laughs. Her eyes are really pretty. "I know," she says.

Oh. She knows who I am.

"I-I mean, I'm Lena's friend. I've heard of you. Joy!" She scrunches her nose like she's embarrassed. "Joy is my *name*. Sorry."

I laugh. I like the pleasant way she corrects herself. It's not insecure, it's ... honest. "Don't be sorry," I tell her. It's something I try to say when girls apologize. "Nice to meet you, Joy."

Despite this odd encounter, Joy seems like a happy person. That, or she's attracted to me. It's kind of unfortunate that I have to consider a dodge strategy, but it happens a lot with Lena's friends.

Just when I expect her to pull some nervous, flirty move, she looks around at the floor where all of her things are scattered and I start picking them up without thinking.

"No! You don't have to do that," Joy says.

I shake my head, unable to leave the mess to her. I'm curious what kind of person sleeps with these brightly-colored items. *Barbie?* Either Joy is immature or she likes what she likes. I'm tempted to think the latter. Partly because I get the impression she's authentic. Like she's the same person with make-up on or off, in sweats or a cocktail dress. Also, I have a hard time believing Lena would want another superficial friend.

"I see you met our dog-sitter!" Fernando says from the kitchen. I look over, but Joy surprises me by stepping in my line of sight.

"Are those for me?" Joy asks with false desperation. I suddenly smell the melty chocolate and butter.

Fernando smirks. "No, they're for TSA!" he teases.

Joy chucks her chapstick at him, which I wasn't expecting at all.

"Resorting to violence, Miss Joy?" he says. They grin together.

Okay, this girl is funny. I think she's been friends with Lena for less than a year, yet she seems perfectly comfortable with Fernando and his dad jokes. That says a lot about her.

"I'll keep your dog alive while you're in Italy!" she partly sings.

This is kind of adorable. I laugh. She looks back at me like she forgot I was standing here.

Maybe she wasn't totally overcome by my looks. Refreshing.

I look to Fernando. "Were we supposed to pay in cookies?"

He doesn't hear me, but Lena's voice comes from above. "Oh, you're here!"

I can't tell if she's talking to me or to Joy, but my guess is Joy. Lena comes down in her travel uniform. Tee, leggings, sunglasses. I've seen it probably a hundred times.

I'm more interested in the girl I found on the floor.

Joy's attention is fixed on Lena in an anticipatory way. Like she's eager to be helpful. Joy's whole look makes me really happy. Lena needed a good friend.

Lena touches my arm, snagging my attention off of Joy. "Can you go up and get my luggage for me? It's a little heavy."

"Sure." Another luggage lugging won't kill me, I guess. "Should I take your stuff upstairs, Joy?"

I can already hear my mom's praises for remembering to take care of the guest.

"Um... okay," she says, and I can't tell if she's blushing or overheated.

When I grab her Justin Bieber bag, leopard pillow, and hot pink Barbie blanket, I wonder why she doesn't seem embarrassed by these things. A point in favor of dancing to her own rhythm, I suppose.

I can't get the image of her on the floor out of my head. With my arms full of her belongings, my interest in Joy is growing, for sure.

I lay her things on Lena's bed. It's funny, these items take me back to pre-teen Lena. All of Lena's present grown-up decor is a reflection of who she's *trying* to be. But I still see her with braces on, stressing out over pimples, getting C's and D's, pretending she doesn't care. She actually managed to pick up her grades this year.

Now that I'm thinking about it, she said it was because of this new girl who was super nice and laughs a lot.

It has to be Joy.

I grab Lena's suitcase and head back downstairs. The scent of cookies hits me hard. I know I'll regret it if I don't ask for one. I leave the suitcase by the door and walk into the kitchen.

"Are those—"

"They're a bribe!" Fernando points his spatula at me and I hang back.

"Oh, that reminds me," I say. The envelope. I yank it out of my pocket, relieved I didn't forget the one reason I came over here. I hold it out to Joy. "This is for watching Zany."

"Zany?" she says, furrowing her brow at the mention of my dog.

"Joy didn't know she was watching two dogs," Lena explains.

"Oh." Well, that's a complication. Our flight leaves in three hours. What do I do about my dog?

"Oh no, no! It's fine!" Joy says right away. And to my surprise, she adds, "You don't have to pay me. The cookie bribe is plenty."

Her cheeks are round and happy. I think she actually means it. But I'm absolutely certain my mom will hold a grudge against me for at least three months if I don't pay this girl.

"No, you've saved us. Zany will be happier at home. And I can't take this back to my mom." I push it forward and whisper, "Take it."

Diamond waddles over and bumps into Joy. She loses balance, catching herself just short of touching me and then plucks the envelope from my hand. "Thanks."

I enjoy her cheerful tone. I'm kind of wishing she hadn't caught herself.

I slide into the limo just ahead of Lena. My mom and Angela launch into a loud conversation about our Italian itinerary while our dads pull out their phones. Normally I'd take the male route and mindlessly scroll Twitter, but I keep thinking about the girl on the foyer floor.

"Why are you grinning?" Lena asks me with a skeptical tone.

"That friend of yours…" She's cute. She's funny. I'm kind of interested.

"Joy?" Lena fills in, her brow raised. "What about her?"

"She was laying flat on the floor when I walked into your house."

Lena snorts. "She was? Oh my god, that is so *her*."

"Really?" I fight the urge to laugh at myself for finding that sort of clumsiness adorable. In my head, I replay how she brushed it off and threw her chapstick at Fernando.

I'll just be blunt. "She's cute. Is she single?"

Lena stares at me for a second before she lets out a single, kind of bitter laugh. "Um, no. She's not."

I scrunch my nose. "Too bad."

Lena smacks my arm. "Hey, that's not true! Her boyfriend is awesome and hilarious. They're great together."

I roll my eyes, but take the point. I'll just have to stop being so interested in this Joy person.

I won't easily forget how we met, though. That's for sure.

TRACK 04 -
ROOTING
FOR YOU

Lena – June 27ᵗʰ

*I*T'S A BLOW TO MY PERFECT, AWESOME, should-have-been-me-and-Jin Ferris Wheel ride when the metal hatch slams closed and I'm sitting next to... Cale.

"Well, she's got tenacity. Gotta give her that," he says to me when the ride attendant walks away.

I tut and roll my eyes. "I blame you for this."

Cale angles his entire front toward me. "Ummmm, what?" He points to himself, his voice high pitch. "How am I responsible for Joy's trickery?"

"You could've put up a fight. She's supposed to be your girlfriend!"

The ride jolts forward and I lean back into the swinging seat. Cale's grip tenses on the edge of the gondola as the fairgoers fall beneath our feet.

"You've got to up your game, Cale," I criticize. "You've been at this for weeks. How much progress have you even made?"

He scoffs. "I'll have you know that I *held her hand* a few minutes ago." He raises an eyebrow as if that's some sort of accomplishment.

Oh, boy. This is going to be a long summer.

I narrow my eyes at him. "Oh, great. At least you've gotten as far as I have with her."

"Hey now, improvement is improvement! I don't want to freak her out, remember?"

I fold my arms. He has a point. I really want Joy and Cale to be happy together, but I grossly underestimated how determined she'd be, shoving Cale on me all day. And what the heck is up with Jin? He's friendly, but he's not a freaking pushover. Why didn't he bother to give Joy the Ferris Wheel ride with her boyfriend?

Their gondola rises at the front of the wheel, while ours falls. I catch sight of Joy nodding. My stomach gets a hollow sensation as we dip closer to the ground.

I don't think Jin *wanted* to ride with me.

But whatever, I'm not going to let that ruin the whole plan.

"Okay, new strategy," I start, but when I look at Cale, his eyes are wide and focused on a spot on the safety bar.

There's a bee.

"What, are you allergic or something?" I ask him.

He tenses and yells, "NO! I JUST DON'T LIKE PAIN!"

"Oh my god." I position my fingers to take care of it, but Cale wails and flails, shaking the gondola. I laugh at his terror before flicking it away. "You're welcome, you big baby."

"FALSE. Only people twelve months old and under can be considered infants."

I burst into laughter, and Cale joins on the tail end. "Was that supposed to be Dwight Schrute?"

"Yes! And I got a lot more where that came from!"

"I'm sure you do," I giggle. My mood's only a fraction lighter than I was. "Cale?"

"Yes?"

"I want you and Joy to work out, but you're gonna have to up your game."

Cale sinks his head and nods. The light in him fades like a dim bulb on a carnival game sign. "I know. I just wanna be careful, you know?"

Jin comes to mind. I sigh. "Yeah, I get it."

I might seem like the fearless one, but right now, I see why Cale is so wimpy with Joy. Because I feel it, too.

TRACK 05 -
BOY WITH
LUV

Jin – June 28ᵗʰ

S HE'S SINGLE. I thought I was unlucky, but I guess I was wrong.

The rice cooker beeps, wisps of steam shooting out of it. My mom makes my favorite, *gyeran-mari*, a Korean omelet with roasted seaweed, carrots, and onions. I like it when she puts chunks of bacon in it, too.

My eight hours of sleep feel more like four. We were outside all day, walking the fairgrounds. I need that rice and *gyeran-mari* to soothe my greasy stomach right now.

"Morning, Woo-Jin," my mom says in Korean.

"Morning, Umma," I say, stretching and yawning.

"You slept in," she observes, floating her eyes up to me for a second, the way she does when she's teasing. "Have fun yesterday?"

I take a seat on the stool by the island. "Yeah."

The thought of Joy's shenanigans makes me smile. And the way she looked when we got on the Ferris Wheel at sunset...

And the fact that she's actually single.

"Looks like it was fun," my mom says. "Anything special about the fair, little boy?"

She calls me "little boy" when she thinks she's caught me. Usually, she has.

"You know that girl? Lena's friend, the dog-sitter."

She nods, whisking the eggs with chopsticks.

I wonder for a second if I should tell my mom. I kind of tell her everything. It's part of our life now. She has to be willing to hear it all, and I have to be willing to say it all. But this is kind of Joy's secret.

Mom sets down the egg bowl with impatience. "Will you speak, child? Why are you making your mother wait?"

"It's just that Joy told me something and... I don't know. It's a secret. But I kind of want to tell you because it changes things for me."

"I can keep a secret, Woo-Jin." My mom loves secrets. She's good at keeping them, too.

"Well, it involves Lena, and since we'll all be in Cabo this weekend, I really don't want it to slip." I'm teasing her at this point. I grin.

She tosses a floaty piece of roasted seaweed at me, but it doesn't come close to crossing the island. I recoil anyway, laughing.

"You must not be hungry!" she says, threatening her very love for me.

"Okay, fine!" I have to tell her. I'm having a hard time dodging thoughts about Joy. If this turns into anything more, I'm gonna have to talk to my mom anyway. "She's not actually dating that guy. Her boyfriend. They're faking their relationship because he's interested in Lena. He wants an excuse to spend time with her."

My mom takes a handful of chopped carrots and tosses it into the egg bowl, keeping her skeptical eyes on mine.

"What?" I ask, defensive.

"You silly boy. Do you really believe that girl? Have you forgotten all the things Lena's friends have said to get your attention? You're too handsome for your own good." She works in the carrots and the onions. Then she shoots me a harrowing look. "You're too trusting. That's gotten you in trouble before, Woo-Jin."

I rest my chin on my propped up hand. "Yeah, I know," I sigh.

The truth is, I *want* to believe Joy. But she also just seems like an honest person. Why else would she have pushed Cale to take Lena to the shooting range thing? And why would he have followed suit? I didn't sense she was doing it to get my attention.

She was trying the whole day to get Cale closer to Lena. But that could be confirmation bias, I guess.

I explain some of these details to my mom.

She pours the eggs into the pan and they sizzle. The scent of fresh carrot and onion fills the air. "Why are you making all these excuses, Woo-Jin?"

I shrug despite knowing full well it's because of my attraction to the girl in question.

"Little boy?" she says, her brow raised. She lays the seaweed layer in the pan. "You know I already know the answer."

I slap the counter. "Fine. I think she's cute," I admit. "But I also think she's honest."

My mom sprinkles bits of bacon into the pan and my mouth waters at the smell of roasted seaweed and butter. She rolls it over and over into a swirl before addressing me.

"I'll let you make up your own mind, Woo-Jin. Just be careful."

"Yes, Umma."

"Good," she says, as satisfied as she can be for not having completely convinced me. She slides the *gyeran-mari* onto a cutting board and slices it. I'm famished.

Then she puts it in a glass container.

"I need you to take this to Angela. She has some Korean clients today and wanted to give them an appropriate snack for their showing."

"What?! I thought that was for me!" My poor, grumbling stomach.

"I'll make you one while you're delivering this one." There's no room for argument in her tone. She holds out the container to me and I take it in one hand.

I head out the front door, offended that I have to give my breakfast to Angela.

When I step off the porch, my foot slips. I try to preserve the container of food, but I overcorrect and fall backward. I brace myself with my hand, but my wrist snaps in the wrong direction when it hits the ground.

Ouch! I'm instantly out of breath. My hand and arm suddenly catch fire.

It feels broken. I lift it up. "Ah!" Definitely broken.

Yeah. This is going to suck when we're in Cabo.

Jin – July 2nd

TAP. TAP. CRACK.

Egg guts and shards of shell slide over my hand. At this rate, I'll have French toast for lunch. I pick shell pieces out with my one good hand, but ultimately give up.

Joy's laugh from last night echoes in my memory. She let me suffer with the takeout boxes just long enough before offering her help.

I'm glad she fell for the "ordered too much Chinese food" thing. It would've been weird if we were alone in two houses next to each other. Instead, we got to really talk. She insisted that Cale's not her real boyfriend and she seemed genuine. I'm glad it's settled.

And she invited me to Americanafest. I grin thinking about it.

My phone clacks with false key sounds as I type out a breakfast invitation to Joy.

Jin: Do you like French toast?

I don't bother to clean as I attempt to freshen up. Brush my teeth. New shirt. I really wish I had more than a thousand white ones. It feels weird to have one look now that I actually want to impress a girl...

Wait. I really do want to impress her, don't I?

She texts back.

Joy: Definitely.

I waste no time writing back.

Jin: Oh good! I need help cracking the eggs. I already made a mess of it so I gave up haha

I watch my screen for her reply.

Joy: Lol be right there

Cool. Yeah. Now I won't have to settle for a bowl of cereal for breakfast. And I get to see Joy again. What does she look like this time of morning?

A few minutes go by and I hear the deep gong of the doorbell. I run my fingers through my hair and open it up. I'm pleased she's in a roomy gray hoodie and yoga pants with her hair pulled back like... like she wasn't trying to impress me.

But she still does. I love a girl who can just show up as just herself. It's confidence. It's... sexy, actually.

Before I realize it, we're in my kitchen and Joy's eyes are narrowed at me.

Right. The egg mess. I now feel like an idiot for leaving it that way.

"My mom usually does the cooking," I say, attempting to lighten my incompetence.

"You're hopeless," Joy says, but her reprimand is a playful jab. Further proven when she cleans up after me like it's nothing. Then she gathers things without missing a beat, except to ask where the spices are.

We haven't said much, but I kind of like just getting to watch her do something remarkably normal like make breakfast.

For me.

My pulse picks up thinking about it like that.

"What are your big plans today?" I ask her.

"Um, not much really. You?"

"Fighting boredom. I could use a break from Rocky movies." It's true. They don't keep my attention like they used to. Probably because I haven't decided if I should go to Seoul. The pressure means nothing keeps my attention for very long.

Well, except Joy. I always seem to forget my anxiety when she's around.

She puts bread on the pan and a buttery vanilla scent wafts toward me as it hisses.

"Well, my plan is to binge the first season of The Walking Dead," she says.

I heard so much about that show in middle school. "Can I be honest?"

Joy's eyes flutter wide. "Sure."

"I've never seen that show. Is that bad?"

Joy bursts out laughing in relief. "Oh my gosh! I thought something was wrong."

I smile on one side. That's cute. "Sorry for freaking you out."

She presses the bread into the pan with the spatula and shakes her head with a sweet smile lingering on her face. "I haven't seen it either. Figured I should start," she tells me.

"So we have something in common! I was beginning to think you were more experienced than me." I'm referring to how pop culture savvy she is. I missed out on all that since I had to learn academic Korean on the weekends. All the free time my friends seemed to have during the teen years eluded me.

"Well, unless we watch it together, I will be," Joy says.

My pulse quickens. Joy just invited me to watch a show with her. That's a level up somehow, right?

Does she like me?

I don't think twice about accepting. "Then I guess we're in it together."

She plops the bread on a plate for me. I'm so excited that I don't think I'd even really taste it if it were bad. The french toast is great though.

And so is the fact that we get to spend the day binge-watching TV together.

TRACK 07 - COOL

Jin – July 4th

O KAY, YES. I'm fully aware that Joy hinted at wanting to be by herself, but I pushed it. And then I fell asleep on the couch with her, and based on her reaction, probably freaked her out.

But I'm *dying* to see her today.

I've been living off of the fact that she invited me to Americanafest and that must mean she wants me there with her.

I'm helpless. I've only known this girl for like two weeks total, but these fresh feelings are intense. I've loved talking to her, discovering what she likes, watching her squeal and hide under the blanket when we watch The Walking Dead.

If I were a more forward person, I would have tried to make a move by now. But I hold back until I can't take it anymore. There has only been one other girl in my life, and that was nothing like this. *That* was heavily influenced by my mom's former obsession with marrying me off to a Korean girl. It kind of started well, but it didn't end well. At all.

This thing with Joy has started off *really* well. If you can call it a *thing*.

I admit it's been really complicated and clumsy, but I've loved every second of it.

It's kind of torture that she hasn't texted me back this morning. I texted hours ago.

Jin: Should we ride to the festival together? What time are you thinking you'll go?

Jin: I'm an early riser so I'll be ready whenever ;)

I am already dressed. It took a whole four seconds.

I need to stay cool. I flip through my Lonely Planet Seoul guide again. If I take the internship, I'll console myself by planning where I'll eat.

Console? What is wrong with me? I need to be more positive like Joy is all the time. She's right that this internship is not an opportunity I should miss. I don't know why I'm concerned. It's only a year.

Car wheels screech outside and I walk to my front window to see who it is. I don't recognize the car, but I'm wondering if it's Cale.

That's odd. She didn't text me to say she was riding with him. Not that she *needed* to, but I did ask for that information.

Cale seems like an upstanding person, but the whole faking thing makes me... I don't know. Envious? He got to hold her hand at the fair. I'm pretty sure he'll put his arm around her or... maybe he'll kiss her or something while they're keeping this thing up in front of Lena.

I blow my stray hair from my eyes. They actually have a *thing*.

Joy walks up to his car and starts talking to him. Little and cute in her patriotic colors.

Okay. I'm walking away. I should resist the urge to watch her. She'll contact me when she's ready. Stop obsessing.

I sit on my stairs by the door and fiddle with my phone. Red, white, and blue colors appear distorted in the glass of the front door.

Before I know it, I whip it open bursting with energy. "Morning!"

Whoa.

Joy's dressed up and made over and freaking gorgeous. Her striped red top reveals her freckled neck and shoulders, fitted to her great curves. And her star-spangled shorts really do it for me. I like that she wears shorts. Because I like her legs. Because I like *her*.

"Morning..." she says and I can tell she's sensed my eagerness. At least she seems amused by it.

"Did you get my text?" I ask.

"Yeah, um, is it okay if you drive on the way there? We could ride back together and save Cale the trip."

Ride back together. I'll take it. "Sure! Guess I'll meet you there."

"Okay," she says and turns to leave.

I have to tell her. I *have* to.

"Joy?" She turns back, so I say it. "You look great, by the way."

She doesn't move for a second except to blink. She gives me a slow smile that warms me like a good, strong drink.

"Thanks," she finally says. "You, too."

Then she leaves, which I admit I enjoy watching. I shut the door.

Then I slog to the couch like I've been struck by lightning and I'm not fully recovered.

I have never seen a girl as cute as her right now. I am overwhelmed.

I flop onto the formal velvet couch in the front room that truly is not meant for flopping. My wrist twinges in pain when I hit the cushions. But I don't care. I'm bursting.

Joy is simultaneously the cutest and sexiest girl alive, no holds barred.

No wonder I was struggling to stay away yesterday.

TRACK 08 -
ICE CREAM

Cale – July 4th, again

S TOP. OVERTHINKING.

Joy's not the kind who plays games. It's one thousand percent more possible that she just forgot to text back about me picking her up. Or her phone is off or something.

Driving up these winding roads is not helping my twisty-turny stomach. I'm excited. I'm nervous. I'm EXCITED. It's just Joy and me.

Maybe things will happen.

You know. Things of a touchy-feely, cutesy G-rated romance nature. If I can man up, I might even make it to the lower PG-13 bracket.

SHOOT! I slam on my brakes. I almost sped right past the gate to Lena's.

I'm only two minutes behind. Still haven't heard the text chime or DM ding or anything from Joy yet.

I drive my barely fancy, new-to-me car down the driveway and swerve around the fountain.

Aaaand there she is. Looking like a *fine* chickadee in that patriotic fit. Oh my LORD.

I stifle a squeal. Joy's as cool as a firecracker ice pop.

She walks up to my car, gleaming in the harsh July sun. My nerves build like I'm hopped up on caffeine, which I am *not* because my Mama says I don't need it. And she's correct.

I roll down my window with wobbly fingers. "Ooh, automatic windows are so nice." I make a show of the luxury with my tone.

Thank the comedy gods, she laughs! "Wow, rub it in."

I'm digging her braid and red lipstick and stars and stripes theme. It's gonna be a good day.

I slap the outside of my car. "So hey, since you weren't answering, I did the manly thing and decided for you." There's a twinge of insecurity in my chest cavity. I'm hoping the playfulness came through and not the creepy false macho-ness.

"Sorry. My phone was on silent," she says. Her eyes turn in the direction of the other house.

I tut and roll my eyes with fake offense. Then I grin, just to be sure she gets the joke. "Well, you ready?"

Please say yes.

Joy twiddles her thumbs. "Um, almost. I still have to feed the dogs. And ask if Jin wants a ride or if he's driving himself."

Uhhh... heart-throbby man candy, Jin Park?!

"You mean Lena's Jin?" I ask. She invited him and didn't tell me?

"Uh, yeah," she sighs. "Is it cool if I offer him a ride with us?"

Okay yeah. This is super not ideal for getting anywhere near PG-13. I got nothing against the kid, but this was supposed to be Almond Joy day, with a side of Cale Salad. I don't even have a proper nickname for this man!

"I guess so," I answer, trying to hide my uneasiness. What am I gonna do, confess right here? I can't just tell her to uninvite him for NO REASON.

How far off the mark am I with Joy?

"Okay, be right back," she says, but her voice is kinda quiet and now I feel bad for making the thing with Jin more *thing-y*.

I suck in a breath and let go of my unrighteous annoyance.

Jin seems like a cool guy. But if he gets up close with Joy, there's a chance he could upend my whole diabolical plot.

Nah. That won't happen. Jin's a flash in the pan. Just a summer dude in the background, heading back to his fancy school come fall. There's no way he'll infiltrate all the history I have with Joy. Plus, as far as he knows, she's taken.

Joy walks back into Lena's house, presumably to feed the dog. I note the way she grins and bites her lip.

Stay cool, man. There's no reason for me to think she's into him. Right?

I close my eyes and repeat my internal mantra: *just be your irresistible self.*

TRACK 09 -
DYNAMITE

Jin – Still July 4ᵗʰ

I WISH THERE WAS MORE I COULD DO. I'm not sure if I'm reading Joy right. And I don't know what I could say to make her feel better. But I really want to.

Until I know her better, I'm helpless.

Am I an idiot for saying nothing when I gave her a ride to her house? I didn't want to come off as distant, but she needed to handle whatever was going on with her family. If she wanted to talk to me, she would have.

Right?

I'm dying for that girl under the sunset at the fair, completely content and happy. The one that was on stage a few hours ago.

Now I'm staring out from my parents' balcony and watching the fireworks flash in the dark sky. As beautiful as they are, I'm still thinking about Joy.

Watching her sing did me in. Better than any concert I've ever been to, but I'm already biased. I'm super interested in her. And her voice is next-level amazing.

She's amazing.

And Cale thinks so too, by the way he beamed at her today. He sang to her when he was on stage. I really hope Lena's into that sort of thing, but part of me knows she isn't. Joy sure was.

Does Cale know that I know about them? It was hard to tell.

I'm never insecure like this. Is this what lovesick feels like? I can't stop thinking about her, the mic in her hand, glowing and amazing. When she hit the long and high notes, I was hooked. No, I was hooked before that. I don't think she knows how awesome she really is, which makes it better.

Good grief, I'm melting.

Is she back yet? I text her.

Jin: You back?

My heart races when she texts back immediately.

Joy: Yeah. Diamond is sleeping. How's Zany doing?

Jin: For how high-strung she usually is, fireworks don't seem to bother her.

My fingers resume typing with their own will. And just like that my subconscious desires are sent.

Jin: There's a great view from my balcony.

Please give me any hint that I'm not totally alone in my feelings. Even though watching fireworks isn't exactly confirmation. I could be a bit more forward, right?

Jin: It would be a shame if it were wasted on just me.

Oh, God! Is that too much pressure? I keep tapping.

Jin: But it's okay if you're not up to it.

I rub my eyes and sigh. Should I at least try not to read into this? I like her. The evidence is right here on my screen. And swirling around in the visions of her that won't leave my mind.

God, I like her.

Buzz.

Joy: Be right over :)

I stop breathing. She said *yes!* I feel starstruck all over again. I have to be cool.

Grinning, I head downstairs. In a couple of minutes, Joy shows up.

"Hey," I say as she walks in.

"Hello again," she says. That is one tired smile.

I can't think of anything else to say, so I gesture upstairs and we head to my mom and dad's room. I lead her to the balcony.

Pop!

The booming fireworks are quieted by distance. They paint the sky with flashing colors that reflect off of us. The breeze pushes her golden hair across her button nose. When the flashes are extra bright, I can make out the freckles on her cheeks.

I have to pull myself together.

"I wanted to clear something up, Jin," she says. "About yesterday."

I sense nervousness and develop some of my own. "Sure."

Her worried hazel eyes sparkle when she glances up at me. "If my brother found out you'd slept on the couch with me, he'd probably flip."

I look off, remembering Lena's brief mention of Joy's overbearing brother. "I won't say anything. Don't worry."

"Like, not even to Lena," Joy adds.

I smirk. *There's no way I'd wake that beast.* "You don't have to say that again."

Pop!

Oh, Lena. I've selfishly forgotten how she complicates things. Her unsubtle affections flow my way like a strong wave and I resist like a dam. And yet, here's Joy, sprinkling magic on me like a firework.

Joy is clearly less reckless than I am. She's protecting Lena. I'm sure she's had enough private conversations to know how Lena feels.

I don't want to back off, but maybe I should.

"It's too bad you missed out on Americanafest *and* Cabo," Joy says. She doesn't look at me, though. Does she think I actually cared about those things?

Because I didn't.

"I'd rather be here," I say with my gaze laid on her. My wrist aches, but right now, I'm just glad it reminds me this is real.

Joy looks at me. Yeah, I'd *really* rather be here.

Averting her eyes in an adorable and wistful way, she says, "Me too."

TRACK 10 – DRIVE

Jin – July 13ᵗʰ

IT FEELS LIKE I'M WAITING FOR A REVELATION.

I met with my parents for a late Hawaiian dinner to talk it over. The internship in Seoul is a great opportunity. An honor, really. I knew I'd have a good chance when I applied.

But I can't remember why I applied. I love my life in Seattle. Coming home for holidays or weekends. Getting both sides of Korean and American life in doses that I manage.

And Sunny isn't in Seattle. I'd be lying if I said I wasn't concerned about running into my ex in Seoul, even though it's a big city.

I hardly ate anything, which I guess is normal for me these days. Unless I'm around Joy.

Even she thinks I should go.

My dad wants me to take it for logistical reasons. I take his advice

I walk with them through the restaurant parking lot to their car. It's getting late, but late dinners are typical with my dad's work schedule.

"You don't need to decide right now," my mom says in Korean.

It's nice to be close to her now. Much less of a handler than she used to be. Like I'm more than just a list of accomplishments.

"Thanks, Umma," I say. They're about to get into their car to head home. It's a relief that she doesn't pressure me to make drastic life choices anymore. I wish it wasn't because she felt super guilty about what happened with Sunny, but it's been good.

My phone buzzes repeatedly. I yank it out of my pocket.

JOY BECKER

I can't stop my reactive grin quick enough. I can't believe she's actually calling me.

"It's that girl, isn't it?" my mom gathers. I nod, looking up from my phone for half a second. She waves her hand at me. "Fine, fine, answer it. See you at home, little boy." She grins at me in a teasing way before closing the car door.

I head to my Harley and answer. "Hey, Joy."

"Hey!" she starts. I love hearing her voice again. "Um, you aren't by chance up for giving me a ride, are you?"

My heart skips a beat. Joy's been coy responding back all week. I thought she wasn't interested... but she wants to see me. Right now.

There's no question that I'm skipping donuts for Joy. I don't care that I waited all day for them. I'd much rather have Joy on my bike with her arms around me.

"Sure! Where are you?" I say.

"Uh, at the movie theater. The one on Main Street."

I happen to be five minutes away from there. The luck lifts my excitement.

She sniffles on the other end of the phone.

A pit forms in my stomach. "Are you okay? Is something wrong?"

I'm tense while waiting for her response. *Please be okay.*

"Yeah, I'm fine. My dumb car just won't start," she finally says.

I exhale in relief. A problem I can actually fix. "Oh, bummer. Well, I'm already downtown so I'll just be a few minutes."

"Oh. You are?" I love that she sounds a tiny bit happy about it. I hope that's what it is, anyway.

"Yeah. I had a late dinner with my parents. See you soon, Joy."

"Bye," she says, and hangs up.

I practically leap onto my bike. Why do I like her so much? I mean, yes, she's pretty and happy, but lots of girls are. I like her freckles and her singing. But, the thing about Joy is… she loves herself.

I crave a girl like that. It's rare. Joy took a whole thirty seconds to prove she was that girl. I'm pretty sure I started crushing on her when she threw her chapstick at Fernando.

My Harley rumbles and my limbs jostle, but it doesn't really feel too different from the thrill I felt before I lit the engine. I wouldn't say it out loud, but I've always kind of wanted to rescue a girl from trouble. A girl I liked.

My mom was right about me being in trouble with this one. But I don't care.

Wind whips into my jacket on the way there and cools me off. I can't wait to see her.

The shifting marquee board lights up the parking lot where Joy's leaning against her car. She's adorably shocked when she sees me, which means the bike has served the unintended but major benefit of making me seem cooler than I actually am.

I cut the engine and remove my helmet, grateful I can catch a better sight of her dropped jaw.

"Hi," Joy says. "You didn't mention you'd be on a bike."

"It was the first day I could take it out after my cast came off," I explain, but now I'm worried her shock wasn't at all about me being cool. "Oh crap! Are you afraid of motorcycles?"

She shakes her head, but she's not terribly convincing. Which is really cute. She's really cute. Her outfit is really cute. I like seeing her legs in those high-waisted shorts.

Then she deflates, her eyes focusing past me.

"Hold on," she says, weaving around my bike. I turn around and notice a built guy with curly brown hair walking toward us. I wonder if this is the baseball player brother I keep hearing about.

He seems pent up in irritation with her, putting me on guard. I might want to come to Joy's rescue, but I also want to respect her. I don't really know why they're fighting but I am pretty sure the resemblance confirms he's her brother.

Joy can handle herself. He sure gives off the "unrighteously angry" vibe if I've ever seen it, though.

My attention piques when Joy tells him I'm taking her home and makes it clear she doesn't want to be around him. I don't know what he did, but I'm happy to let her be the judge of her night. She tells him to go back to the movie, but he protests. Loudly.

I get off my bike.

"Hey!" he yells. "I wanted to spend time with you! I should be the one to take you home!"

She's little, but she puts up a fight. "Will you listen?! I don't want to go home with you!"

She shouldn't have to say it twice.

I step in. "What's the matter?"

Joy looks at me. "He's my brother."

"Is this that Gin guy?" he says, mispronouncing my name the way most people do. I'm usually neutral to it, but the fact that he says it with disdain when he doesn't even know me just adds to my dislike.

"Oh my God!" Joy reacts. "It's *Jin*! He's my friend."

For a second I'm swirling in happiness and disappointment that she called me her friend. Her raging brother gives me no chance to overthink it.

"No, no. I wanna meet the guy who begged my sister to come watch fireworks, even though she has a boyfriend." He steps forward, attempting to intimidate me. That sort of thing always makes me *less* intimidated. I don't blame her for not telling her brother about Cale. Not when this is the kind of person he is.

Joy steps in front of him. She's drenched in worry as she pushes him back. "Be cool! He's just my friend, okay?"

"I can't let you go with him," he says to her, before hitting me with a glare. "Sorry."

Damn, this guy is pissing me off. "Shouldn't she decide that?"

"She's my *sister*."

"Yeah, not your dog. You don't own her." I shake my head. Who the heck tries to control their adult sister? Does he really think that's a valid play?

He puffs out his chest and tightens his fist, like all entitled morons that live in our age bracket.

But Joy panics. "Carson. Carson!" she says. "Please, don't."

Don't what? Joy acts like his threats mean something.

Carson... why does that name sound familiar? Lena must've mentioned him, but his name leaves an odd, sour feeling in my stomach.

Carson looks at Joy like he can't figure her out. His idiotic frustration irks me. "You're not going, right?" he asks her.

She looks at me for a second before telling him, "Yeah, I am."

I like her more and more, and not just because she picked me over him.

But also, *she picked me.* I'm so ready for this idiotic face-off to be over so I can make Joy's night better.

"Okay, yeah," her brother starts with abundant indignance, "But you just tell *him* that he can look up my name if he wants to know what I do to guys who mess with my sister."

It takes everything in me not to roll my eyes. Is he done now?

Carson walks away. Figures. All talk, like most of them.

He rips open the door when he goes back inside the theater.

Joy returns to me, relieved but still shaken up. I hand her my helmet.

I'm not going to waste this night.

"Come on, I wanna take you somewhere," I tell her. "If you're up for it."

As we ride off together, I replay the way she looked at me when she accepted. Man, my fingers were shaky when I secured my helmet on her. I wanted so badly to brush her cheek or graze her arm. Those hazel eyes totally distracted me and it took way too long to secure the helmet. She didn't seem to notice.

I also gave her my leather jacket, totally swallowing her little body and added a hefty bit of thrill to mine. Joy's in my jacket. I selfishly hope it's not the last time.

And I very, very selfishly love the way she squeezes me as we ride my bike. We ride the freeway across the river to the bigger city. I should have considered that factor when agreeing to pick her up. Riding is *supposed* to command 100% of my attention. Tonight... it does not. It's all I can do to keep my thoughts away from the feeling of her amazing figure pressed against me.

When we slow to a stop and park, Joy stumbles off and I already miss the feeling of her arms around me. She seems distracted, but not in the same way as me. I should tune in better.

He's my friend.

That might be all I am to her. She agreed to come with me, but it's not like that's a confession.

Joy takes off the helmet and hands it to me. Her hair has grown a bit fuzzy.

Cute.

It's all cute.

My heart thumps and I want any excuse to touch her. But I can't because she's not giving off the right signals. I switch my focus to the reason we came.

Donuts. Late-night donuts.

We stroll the neon-lit sidewalk. At the very least, it's nice to be here with her. I don't really know how she feels, but...

I want to tell her how I feel tonight.

Maybe once I drop her off at her house. On the other hand, the anticipation might be just the sort of excessive distraction I don't need on my bike. I look down at her pretty, wandering eyes lit up by city lights.

Tonight. When the moment's right. I'll tell her.

"You're not gonna ask?" she says.

My nerves jolt, but it's not like she can read my mind. "About what?"

"About my brother. He only threatened you so you'd bring it up."

That must be what's bugging her. I can ease that worry. "Maybe that's why I'm not asking."

What a piece of work. *Carson.*

Joy angles herself to me. "Promise me you won't actually Google my brother's name."

I nod. "I promise."

What did Lena tell me about him? I only remember that he plays baseball and Joy has to be at all of his games, but he's injured right now. I'm nervous to keep asking Lena about Joy, though. It set her on edge last time.

Guilt tugs me. I've been avoiding Lena. I keep turning down her offers to hang out alone. That's why I'm not going on the lake trip with her and my mom. It sucks because I like spending time with Lena, but she's clearly trying to take a chance with me.

I can't make myself see her that way, even if I wanted to.

Enter the dodge strategy. I've kinda just been waiting for her to grow out of it and find someone else. But now I'm wondering if my hesitation inspired her to come on even stronger.

I don't want to hurt her, but I've caught feelings for her friend. Dodging Lena won't solve anything.

We join the line that snakes around the building leading up to the donut shop. I hope the donuts live up to the hype and Joy remembers this night.

Once we're in the tiny shop, I read the profane donut names and cringe. It might be a hit to my character if she's offended. When I study her, though, she seems enthralled. I love how she stares at the rotating display, her eyes lit up by the bright colors. Her choice is the one with Cocoa Puffs on it. Mine has Oreos and peanut butter.

"So you were going to brave this by yourself?" she asks me as we leave, a cute smirk on her face.

"Yeah, but I'm glad I didn't have to."

Watching Joy scarf down her chocolate donut puts me at ease. She just enjoys food like she never worries about it. I wonder what else makes her this happy.

As we walk and eat, my donut punches me with the sugary sweetness of icing and Oreos. The peanut butter balances it out with a bit of saltiness, thankfully. A few bites in and I'm starting to understand the hype. I'm curious about how Joy's was. What if I asked her for a bite?

Would that be weird? Can we share donuts yet?

I take a contemplative bite of what's left of mine. I might test the waters and offer a bite of—

"My brother beat up a guy that was forcing himself on me."

I choke on my donut. *Holy shit.* Out of nowhere, she... what did she say?

I cough and struggle for air, only for a second. *Some guy forced himself on her?*

"Oh my god! Sorry!" she says, her eyes wide and hands up. "Sorry."

Once I'm breathing normally, my sense of justice rises as I realize what she just told me. It stops once I catch sight of her worry. "It's okay! Don't be sorry. I just wasn't expecting you to say that."

I mentally catch up to what she revealed to me. *Her brother beat up a guy. A guy that forced himself on her.* This sweet, small, happy girl went through *that*?

Damn my thoughts about trying to get close to her. By sharing a donut. God. I couldn't have known what was bothering her, but I still feel selfish.

I stop eating and listen.

Joy sighs. "After what my brother said, I felt like I owed you some kind of explanation."

I clear my throat. "Joy, you don't owe me anything. I don't care what your brother said. But I'm sorry for what happened to you."

How does she deal with that? How does *anyone*? I'm in awe of her. Not only is she trusting me just to be around her, but she actually felt like she owed me an explanation.

She shrugs. It's odd that I wish she wouldn't. "It's over now. But it was a big deal at the time. The guy Carson beat up went into a coma for like a full day."

Carson. Coma. My chest bursts with recognition and dread. *No.*

She keeps talking. "Plus, he was the mayor's kid."

HOLY SHIT. The air is knocked out of me. That's *the* Carson. The guy who got off after almost killing Tyler Fuller. *The mayor's kid.* Carson is the guy—*the pitcher*—my dad should have put in jail. She's...

Joy's *his sister*?!

I'm hyper-focused on every syllable coming out of her mouth.

"The only reason Carson didn't go to jail was because our families reached an agreement. We'd all stay away from the media and none of us would press charges. It saved their reputation, I guess. Political people are obsessed with image, you know?"

I'm gaping at her, but when she makes eye contact, I nod. I'm rethinking everything. "That was last year?" I ask. Maybe part of me is hoping it's a different mayor. A different baseball star. A different girl.

"Yeah. In Salem."

God. It is her. But... I don't recall any mention that she was involved. Suddenly it makes a lot more sense. This adorable, fun-loving, awesome person I've been falling for...

That Fuller kid *touched* her. Bastard.

I'm enraged, but I have to rein it in. My dad's words ring with clarity.

It's more complicated than you imagine, son. No wonder he wasn't torn up about that near-murderer getting a slap on the wrist.

"Anyway," she says, "My mom worked for the mayor, so she left her job. And Carson lost his scholarship to OSU because even though we couldn't talk to the news, local media published stuff about him anyway. Which is totally bogus because they made him out to be some monster who unleashed his wrath on an innocent politician's kid. He's overprotective, but he's not a monster."

I recall that news. I try not to get too involved in my dad's cases, but that one pissed me off. Now I regret my judgment, looking at her. Hearing her pain. Finally noticing the remnants of trauma.

"That's why we moved up to Willow Haven last year," she finishes.

I'm at a loss.

Should I tell Joy about my dad? I feel like I should, but I'm nervous she'll recoil. I like her. I don't want her to worry about my dad's connection to the Fullers.

"You gonna finish that?" she says.

I don't register her words before I say, "I'm really sorry, Joy."

She shrugs. "It's fine. It's your donut."

I look at my donut, confused. Then I realize she's teasing me. "No, I mean... you know what I mean."

And honestly, I'm impressed with Joy. Continuously. For being her honest self even amid sharing a dark corner of her life with me. The fact that she doesn't realize who my dad is makes this *way* more delicate.

I offer my donut because, frankly, she deserves it. And a hell of a lot more.

She doesn't take it, though. She laughs at the misunderstanding and keeps opening up to me, tearing my heart to shreds.

"I'm okay now," she says. "I mean, it still comes back. And I still feel guilty because I just watched, frozen, while my brother smashed a kid's head in at a party."

Regret manifests on her face and she slumps over in my jacket. Damn, she's beautiful in her heartache, hugged by pink and yellow neon light.

I want to fix it, but I'm afraid she won't want me to. Not once she knows.

Her voice is small when she says, "I always felt like I should have tried to stop him."

"He could've stopped himself," I say instantly. I don't care if she disagrees with me. Carson definitely seemed to me like he had full authority over himself. He was even trying to control *her*. There's no way she should feel like she could've stopped him. It's hard to keep myself from trying to free her from that notion.

What an incredible thought. A *freer* Joy.

I wouldn't have thought it possible, but the look she gives me... it's like no one ever told her Carson is his own person. And she needed that.

Did *I* give her that?

"I'm sorry my brother was such a jerk to you earlier," she says, mindlessly running her fingers through her dark blonde hair.

I take another bite of my donut and shake my head. Joy feels responsible for so much more than she should. No matter how many times I tell her not to apologize, she still does.

She's delicate. And this news about her brother twists me up inside. It's like the darkness of the night stung by the glow of neon.

Maybe I'm not the guy she needs.

But I can be, if I approach this right.

"He's protective, clearly," Joy says. "But I was really upset because

I found out he was planning this lake trip with Lena next week—totally behind my back—and now I have to cancel the beach trip I just booked."

Wait. Lena's lake trip? Joy was invited? My mind races wondering if I missed that somehow. But, she just said she made other plans.

"Why do you have to cancel?" I ask.

She cocks her head and I'm super into the way she twirls her hair in her fingers, looking up at the sky and biting her lip. Why do I like the little stuff so much?

"It's not like I don't want to go," she says, "it was just a sucky thing for him to do. Carson's just... afraid of losing me, I guess."

I almost completely miss the part about Carson because Joy just said she might want to go to the lake. And I could be there. At the same house.

I *need* to gauge this.

I stuff my last bite into my mouth and dust icing off my fingers. "What if I said that my mom and I got invited to the cabin next week and I could, maybe, go, too?"

Once I've said it, I'm embarrassed for *assuming* she'd be happier if I were there.

But she lights up. "Like, for real?"

Her reaction makes me buzz with happiness. "Would you like that?"

She smiles big and my word, *yes*, she's happy.

"Yeah. I'd like that," she says.

I'd dance if I were any good at dancing.

The way she looks right now, in her sexy shorts and *my* leather jacket, beaming at me because we'll be at the cabin together... it's an image that'll be burned into my brain forever.

I'll tell her while we're at the cabin. About my dad.

And that I'm crazy about her.

My mom is going to give me hell for changing my mind about that trip, but I don't even care.

TRACK 11 -
WIN YOU
OVER

Cale – July 18th

FIRST, SHE SHOWS UP IN THAT SUPER FINE BATHING SUIT that fits her so well it hardly matters that it's plain and modest. Second, she whips my behind in Marco Polo because I couldn't resist having her arms wrapped around me even if it lasted a few seconds.

"Told you not to mess with me, Thomas!" Joy taunts as she slams the cards on the table.

And now, third, she conquers me and Jin at poker.

"Again?!" I groan.

Three. Times. IN A ROW.

"Tired of being slaughtered at this game?" she says, her freckled nose scrunching up.

No. I'm not tired of any amount of time I get to spend with Almond Joy.

Jin laughs and up comes this *flicker*. A feeling. A dangerous kinda feeling.

Does Jin like her?

If yes... I'm in serious trouble. I've taken things slow with Joy. You know, out of respect. She doesn't seem to mind the little touches here and there. She also doesn't seem up for more. But this guy just *oozes* the vibe of a K-pop idol worthy of millions of fans across the globe.

As I obsess about my lack of charm, Lena somehow enters without my realizing.

I catch the word *s'mores*.

"Did you say *s'mores*?" I ask monotone. I smack the table, announcing my enthusiastic approval of the declared snack. The cards fling from Joy's hands and she laughs.

My mission is clear: KITCHEN. NOW.

The reality is I'm retreating from the vibe of that smooth Korean studmuffin. Just his laugh sends my insecurities buzzing like bees. I recklessly open cupboards, wagering guesses at where s'mores supplies may be hiding.

I know it's cowardly, but I can only process my shortcomings when Joy's not around.

"Psst, Cale!" Lena whispers. I turn to see her gesturing to the mudroom.

Weird. But you know, weird *is* the norm of this summer.

When I enter, Lena's eyes turn in the direction of Joy and Jin for a fraction of a second before she says in a hushed tone, "You gotta make a move on her already!"

I'm hushed, too. "I know! I just don't know how..."

Lena rolls her eyes, then turns to open the cupboard. While she digs around, she makes eye contact with me. "You've barely even touched her this whole time."

I shrug. I know we kinda planned this whole thing at the movie theater like it was gonna be some big shift in my relationship with Joy, but it's just not happening that way. It's easier to just have fun and avoid battling the nerves.

Lena points a long, pokey marshmallow-roasting stick at me. "You know you've got game, Cale. There's no need to hold back."

My gaze falls to my dirty shoes. Joy makes me coy, what can I say?

Lena keeps rooting around the cupboard when she gives up and sighs at me. "Just... give her a peck. On the *mouth* this time. I think she's out there by herself."

My heart pounds when Lena physically turns me around, leading me to the door. She says in a firm whisper, "*Show* her."

Her hand presses hard against my shoulder before she leaves and I... face the door. Take a deep, courage-gathering breath.

And out I go.

Joy's sitting in the smoke.

Smoke follows beauty. My dad always says that. Mostly to stop my sisters from complaining anytime the wind pulls the smoker's plumes toward them. It's missing the meat smell, but the smoke reminds me of Dad's full-day barbecues.

I wish I could talk to him. He's the only man alive who can handle my mom. He'd probably have some good advice if he weren't in the Middle East with no internet connection for a hundred miles.

"Hey..." I say to her, "I got something I wanna tell you.".

OH CRAP, this is it! I'm gonna fess up. Get ready!

"Yeah?" she says in that sweet tone of voice that's like an angel even when it's casual.

Oh man! Am I doing this?!

I fiddle with something in my pocket, buzzing with nerves. What is this thing? A card?

O-M-G it's *the card!* From The Crux Constellation guy. I forgot to give it to her!

I pull it out and hand it to her. I don't say anything which is BASICALLY proof that I'm nervous as heck right now. She grabs it.

"A business card?"

My vocal ability returns. "Yeah. Read the name."

She scans it with her greenish-brown eyes. Smoke really does follow beauty. "What's this for?"

I sit down in the fabric lawn chair beside her, taking a whiff of that campfire smoke. "They saw us at the festival. Well, and they saw you sing. They said you should call them."

And you should, you fantastical crooner! I don't say that, though. I just smile at her.

"Weren't they doing a farewell show?" she asks.

"You know, kid, I don't know everything! But I think they liked what they saw." I look down into my lap. "What's not to like?"

THAT WAS OUT LOUD. How... did she take it? I lift my gaze.

She's doe-eyed, but not like, flattered-doe-eyed. Is that a thing?

"Well, anyway..." I say, my stomach in five bajillion fizzing tangles.

"She's not out here, you know," Joy says. "You don't have to pretend to like me."

"I don't pretend to like you, Joy."

The fire pops.

HOLYYYYYY CRAP. Was that a confession?!

Did I just admit my feelings with ZERO suave?

Joy's reaction isn't flattered-doe-eyed this time either. It's... I mean, if my investigative abilities on people's emotions are not terrible, Joy's definitely shocked at what I just said.

Oh man. OH MAN. What. Is. She. Thinking?!

Jin and Lena interrupt us, thank GOD. I might have legiterally turned into a puddle of embarrassment if they hadn't.

But hey, the night is young. Plenty of time to up my game.

You know you've got game. There's no need to hold back. Show *her.*

Okay, Miss Garcia. You win. I'm giving it my best shot.

So far, I've landed a peck on Joy's cheek. I've secured a s'more from her. And I'm cranking up all the efforts to make her giggle, which seems to be working.

"You really shouldn't mess with a girl's s'mores," Joy tells me with a lingering grin. Her lips are caressed by the glow of the fire. All the smoke should funnel to her because she is gorgeous.

Since Lena's supervising, I gotta strike it bold. "But they're *my* girl's s'mores."

I smile back at Joy. She bursts laughing, and I can't *totally* blame her.

Maybe this is all still a joke to her. But I want her to know how I actually feel. I want to make her heart flutter like she does mine.

As I watch her get another marshmallow over the fire, I harden my resolve. When I get an opening, I'm gonna kiss her. *On the mouth this time.*

Nibbling the s'more, I smile about my sweet victory, but also because I'm jittery over my intentions.

Joy's eyes go wide when her marshmallow catches. She blows it out, her lips in an O-shape. I can't help staring at her.

I want to feel her lips on mine. I'm daydreaming about it. Or twilight-dreaming, as it is.

LORD HELP ME, I *will* kiss Joy by this fire!

I stuff the rest of my s'more in my mouth. I gotta make another play and, apparently, my only material is stealing s'mores from Joy.

Puppy dog eyes, let's go. Joy looks over to me, her s'more in hand.

"Make. Your. Own," she demands. I can hear the joke in her words.

I snag her wrist in my fingers and she makes a show of resisting, but she's still giggling. "Cale!"

I like the back-and-forth we do. The play fighting. Joy's giggling. I keep pulling on her wrist, trying to get a bite of her food so she'll keep laughing. I don't care about the s'more. I want Joy's cute freckled cheeks to be all appley and happy!

I get my wish when the s'more flies out of her hand and hits me in the face. Why I attempt to catch it with my tongue, I do not know. But the whole fling, smack, plop process makes Joy crack up like there's no tomorrow.

She keels over laughing.

SHE EVEN SNORTS. That should not be endearing, but it is!

"I'm glad to know my massive fail was so amusing," I say, monotone. I pretend I'm unaffected by the adorableness occurring in front of me, but all Joy's giggling makes my nerves go haywire.

I want to finally kiss her. *On the mouth this time.*

"Okay, okay! I'll make one for *you* this time," I say, just to give myself something to do. A small measure of time to think. How can I play up that game I supposedly have?

I don't actually come up with a great plan as I assemble the s'more for her. The whole time, I'm imagining what it's like to kiss her. I wanted to use this whole faking thing to get closer, but...

I'm shaking at the thought of pulling a move. I almost crush the graham cracker!

"There we have it," I say, holding up the completed s'more with my plans still incomplete.

She reaches for it, but I pull it back. Idea!

"Mmm, I think I need payment."

Joy stands up and looks offended. "Um, no! You owe me that sugar sandwich."

"But this one was made with love. It can only be bought with a kiss." I gesture to my cheek.

"No!" Joy laughs. Her eyes twinkle in the firelight.

I love that laugh. And I'm kinda crazy about the girl, too. She grins at me, waiting for her rightful dessert.

"Fine," I say, holding the s'more forward. My eyes travel the outline of her sweater, around her waist.

And I'm pushed by Lena's words. *Give her a peck. On the mouth this time.*

Joy steps closer to me and I take the opening, reaching around her waist and pulling her up close and *just do it! Just kiss her!*

So I do. I squeeze her closer to me. And I melt.

Joy's soft lips are sweeter than any chocolate/marshmallow combination anyone could think of. My heart soars and I'm buzzing all over, warmer than the fire next to us.

I'm kissing Joy! I pull her in more. The longer she lets me do this, the more excited I am. The more I'm convinced she might feel—

"She said NO!"

The words come barrelling at me like an angry bull. I break away to dodge the person saying them.

Jin.

The dude is practically on fire, standing there with flickering light on him. Fear encases me.

She said no?

Oh, shit. She *did* say no.

My head is spinning. I thought that was good, but what did I actually do? I look at Joy and she's in shock. No giggly nervousness, no starry eyes. She's worried, her gaze fixed on Jin.

Yep. He's still pissed.

"It's okay," Joy says. But it's only a bandaid.

I'm pretty sure I fumbled this play. HUGE time.

TRACK 12 - SLOW DANCE

Jin – June 18th, again

*I*CAUGHT THAT LOOK. Her grin when that toddler high-fived me. She was hard blushing and I am all for it. The number one thing I want to be in life is a good father, so...

Seeing Joy's pure happiness at that little kid was special. *Really* special.

Too bad Angela ruined it with her particular brand of disruption. At least I'm experienced in handling conversations with her. I felt bad for Lena with the whole bathing suit comments, though. It's tough when your mom is set in her ways.

I've been there. My mom was like that until it broke me. Something about having to pick up the pieces made her chisel at her set-in-stone ways.

I'm at the coffee table, playing poker with Joy and Cale. Joy cocks her head at the cards in her hand. I'm not really playing to win. At least, not at poker.

"Told you not to mess with me, Thomas!" Joy says, slamming her cards on the glass coffee table.

"Again?!" Cale groans.

"Tired of being slaughtered at this game?" Joy taunts.

Her show of confidence makes me laugh. She's playing at intimidation, but she's so freckly and pretty, I can't take her seriously. Even if she tried to be tough, I'd still think she's adorable. It's a disadvantage for her, probably, but she has cute privilege, so maybe it balances out.

"We're doing s'mores, right?" Lena says, walking into our game. Or Joy's victory lap, I should call it. I smell Lena's rose shampoo as she scrunches her wet hair with a towel.

Completely monotone, Cale says, "Did you say *s'mores*?" And then he smacks the table, abruptly standing up and startling Joy into losing the cards in her hand. Joy giggles. That's one thing that makes me nervous. Cale makes her laugh so easily.

"Guess that's a 'yes'?" I say. Lena takes off after Cale, leaving Joy and I to clean up the scattered cards.

Joy's hand bumps mine. She leaves it there. My urge is to brush her fingers, to show her *something* about how I feel, but I resist it. Instead I linger a bit too long.

"Sorry," we say at the same time.

"I got this," I add. She nods and then leaves for the back door.

This feeling is like a slow dance, but my arms are empty.

I forget my task, thinking about her soft skin on my hand. Does she feel the same way? Does she know that I'm here for her?

Cards. Gotta pick up cards.

"*Show* her," I hear Lena whisper from across the room. I look over my shoulder and see the ends of her fingers pressed against Cale's shoulder.

What is that about?

Cale takes a deep breath before heading out to where Joy is.

Show her what?

I'm worried my suspicions are true. That Cale likes *Joy*. I don't know why Lena would know, though.

What if he does? He doesn't seem to be drooling over Lena at all. I pit my eligibility against his in my head. Yes, he's funny, but... I've got the motorcycle thing. Good career prospects. Objectively speaking, I'm good-looking, but that only goes so far with a girl like Joy. I'm not nearly as confident as Cale.

And I'm definitely not as free as Joy. I hold back a lot. But I guess she does, too. She doesn't let everyone know the dark stuff.

That's a point in my favor. She trusts me.

Lena flicks the back of my head.

"Ow!" I rub the spot where heat pricks me.

"Come on, I got the stuff," she says. "Hurry up!"

I follow Lena outside and snag a lawn chair on the other side of the fire from Joy and Cale. Joy leaps into s'more-making, which doesn't surprise me at all. I really want to talk to her, but I'd be stepping on too many toes if I do. So I talk to Lena and she brings up UW.

"I let it slip to my dad that I'm gonna study dance," she tells me. "He's not convinced I'll make the six a.m. class..."

I'm not really listening to her. I'm watching Joy. Her marshmallow catches on fire and she adorably blows it out.

"Jin!" Lena says. I snap back.

"Uh, yeah, your dad is right," I say, hoping it's a convincing response.

Her flat eyes judge me. "So you think I should drink twelve cups of coffee in the morning? Right. Were you even listening?"

"I want a s'more, actually," I say.

She reaches over to the bag of marshmallows and throws it at me. "Then *make* one."

I feel kinda bad for upsetting Lena, but I don't know what she wants from me. "Sorry," I tell her. "He does have a point, though. You're basically half-dead at that hour."

"Not everyone can perk up at the buttcrack of dawn," Lena says out of the side of her mouth.

I laugh at that nostalgic phrase. We once watched this weird Bigfoot movie together, where Justin Long in a mullet said the "buttcrack of dawn" line and Lena couldn't stop laughing. I was twelve, she was ten.

I still see her like that sometimes. A lot of times.

Out of the corner of my eye, Joy's resisting Cale, but smiling. He's making a move for her dessert. Just being funny.

Until he kisses her cheek. Joy's eyes flutter wide. Lena grins.

Yeah. I have a hunch that Lena's not getting jealous like Joy thinks she is.

And I'm on guard, even though I have no right to be. I have no claim on Joy. Plus, we have a pretty big chasm keeping us apart.

My dad.

I can't keep acting like I'm the one she wants. I still haven't told her about my dad's connection to the Fullers. Joy's protected that part of her life even from Lena. Maybe Cale, too.

"Jin! Hello? Your marshmallow is gonna catch fire," Lena tells me.

I pull it from the fire. I don't have to ask for her help getting the other ingredients ready, she just does it. When she smooshes the sandwich together, going on about the different things she's planning to do at UW with me, I note how we just know what the other is going to do. We can tell what the other is thinking. It's seamless.

"Here," she says, holding it to me.

I'm about to take it, but I hear Joy protest. "Cale!"

She resists him again, a little annoyed this time. Cale persists.

The s'more flies out of her hand and lands on Cale's face as he sticks his tongue out to try and catch it, but honestly, there's no chance. It's an epic fail. Joy laughs in fits, and Lena and I join. Cale plays it like he's not pleased with our amusement.

Joy snorts and turns red. It's just so genuine. Vibrant life flows from her.

Cale offers to make a s'more for Joy this time, which is a good move because she's barely keeping it together.

"Jin..." Lena says. I look at her. She gives me a calm smile. "Thanks for coming."

Another guy would feel like the luckiest person sitting next to her this close. Covered in her fuzzy sweater and leggings. Natural and still beautiful by the light of the fire, begging for attention.

"I'm glad I came," I tell her. "It's been really fun." I keep my tone the way it always is with her. Familiar, but distant.

I can tell she knows by the way she sighs, but keeps eye contact.

"Um, no! You owe me that sugar sandwich," Joy says. I don't take my eyes off of Lena, though, because I feel like I'm sort of saying goodbye to her, and I think she can tell.

"But this one was made with love. It can only be bought with a kiss," Cale counters.

If I look at them, Lena will figure it out. She'll know that I'm here for Joy. So cast my eyes down at the s'more in my hand and keep my ears open.

Joy giggles. "No!"

"Fine," he says. I hear a smile in his voice.

I look back up at Lena, who is watching them, and a shocked expression suddenly unfolds.

My head whips in Joy's direction.

Cale's kissing her. Jealousy rips into me.

HOLY SHIT. HE'S KISSING MY...

No. She's not mine. But it's not just jealousy. Joy said 'no' *very clearly.*

Before I realize it I'm standing up, flaming from the inside out. "She said NO!"

My voice booms across the flames. Cale lets go of Joy and gapes at me. I glare at him. I won't mess around.

Joy's had enough shit like that.

"Jin! Jeez," Lena says, standing up. I realize I threw my s'more in her direction without even thinking about it.

I'll never let anyone get away with ignoring her, if I can help it. I hope Joy knows that.

"It's okay," Joy says to me, on the subtle edge of panic. I simmer down. I'm not cool with Cale right now, but I'd rather quell any anticipation of anger. For her sake.

Please trust me, Joy.

"S-sorry... Joy," Cale says, and gives her the s'more. She takes it.

I sit back down, but I make eye contact with Joy to truly gauge what she's feeling. She nods at me. She's okay.

But damn it to hell, Cale stole a kiss from the girl I'm crazy about. Right in front of me.

I don't know how much longer I can hold back.

TRACK 13 -
CAN I
KISS YOU?

Jin – July 19th

*I*WAIT ON THE EDGE FOR HER TO SING, my eyes shut and my body tense until I hear her voice. And when she sings, everything else fades but her. Every sensation of the air on my skin, the heat wicking drops away, the sound of water crashing and wind in the leaves are nothing but a frame for her. She's the picture, the one I came to see.

So I open my eyes, despite my promise to keep them closed.

She carries on, like a dream, like an angel under the morning sun with her eyes closed.

I don't remember when I decided to follow her out here. All I remember is not caring if it was right or wrong. It scares me because I'm usually so in control.

But that's slipping and I know it.

Joy's voice is gorgeous and clear, mixed with this slow song like they belong together.

Belong together. I'm on the edge of that cliff. I want to jump.

Can I kiss her yet?

I close in, casting a shadow over her just as she finishes the highest and most beautiful note.

Joy opens her gorgeous hazel eyes. My heart leaps.

Ask her.

I can't contain my desperation. "Can I kiss you?"

Barely a moment passes. "Yes."

I finally, *finally* kiss the girl I've adored from a distance for much longer than I cared to. That cliff edge is gone. I've fallen off.

I kiss Joy deeply, her lips warm on mine, her skin dewy under my hand. And even now, I question if she really said yes because this is so good. I don't deserve it.

She brushes my collarbone with her fingertips. I pull away and the sight of her is as much a pleasure as touching her. I'm in awe of her, caressed by sun and happiness and shared relief that we dove deep into this together. Breathless, both of us.

I miss her lips already, so I move forward again. But she pushes back.

I respond, trembling on the edge of fear. "What's wrong?"

The happiness is gone. *Come back.*

"I'm sorry," she whispers.

Don't be. I want to say it. I want to, but I can't believe she'd apologize right now.

"Why?" Confusion seeps out in my question. Please, let it be nothing.

Joy gets up, drenched in worry and I'm not on the edge of fear anymore. I'm all the way there.

TRACK 14 -
ALL IN

Jin – July 19ᵗʰ

"**A**RE YOU TRYING TO PROTECT LENA'S FEELINGS?" I ask her, holding the cold bottle to her injured ankle.

Her round eyes tell me everything. "You know about that?"

"She's not subtle."

I've known for years. And it sucks. "But I don't feel that way about her. She's like my sister."

"Right. A supermodel sister who isn't in any way blood-related to you," Joy replies, and I hear the envy in her.

"It's not just that. I appreciate her and everything she's done for me. But, even if we had no history, she's not my type."

Joy's eyes widen a fraction. "And I am?"

I frown. "Is that so hard to believe?"

My eyes travel all the places I've wanted to touch her, so she can see that I mean it. Because I do.

Joy blushes. "What is it about me, then?"

"Your confidence. Definitely."

Her brow shoots up. "What confidence?"

I furrow my brow. She really doesn't know how amazing she is. "How do you not see it, Joy? You laugh openly, you sing freely. And share yourself with everyone. You wear what you want, eat what you want, and you fully enjoy things that Lena wouldn't bother with because it's too basic or some dumb reason."

"Did you just call me *basic*, Jin?" Joy asks with a cute smile.

I laugh. I can't stay down here while she's up on the bench, so I put the water bottle down. It's probably doing nothing for her injury anyway.

I sit next to her and the subtle touching drives me crazy. But I'm still trying to make sense of why she ran. It's definitely not just Lena's feelings.

"Joy, you're adorable," I tell her, my thumb on her freckles. A breeze hits us.

Am I just another guy to her? Worth my looks and nothing else. My insecurities beg me to stay quiet, but Joy's nothing like Sunny. I shouldn't let my past sabotage this.

Just say it.

"What I can't figure out is how you keep sacrificing so much for everyone else. Even your running away was for Lena's sake, right? Unless..." Here comes the insecurity. "You don't *want* to be with me."

"Are you crazy? Of course I do! And it's not just because you're amazingly handsome."

Joy searches her mind for the greater terms. The ones that actually mean something. Then she says, "You... Jin, you are a rare kind of wonderful."

My world bursts with affection. I'm stunned. She thinks I'm *rare*. *Wonderful.*

This... is not just a crush. Joy said the one thing I *needed* to hear.

And I didn't even know it.

I was so destroyed by what Sunny did to me. So destroyed by all the talk of how replaceable I was. How she'd find another guy like me in two seconds. How she'd done just that, even though she was the one who ruined us.

Joy is nothing like my ex.

And I'm afraid I'm already in love.

TRACK 15 -
I DON'T
KNOW WHY

Jin – July 19ᵗʰ

HOW AM I SUPPOSED TO TELL HER NOW? Carson's outburst really affected Joy.

I tried not to overthink it while skating with Lena and Cale. Lena's finally opening up to other people. All of high school, she was hindered by her reputation. Now she's upbeat and happy. Everything seems so delicate right now.

Especially my chances with Joy.

We get back to the cabin and Joy's sleeping peacefully on the couch. The sun touches her skin and I have to keep myself from staring.

Kissing Joy this morning was phenomenal. And Joy singing out into the world, like she was open for me. She let me into a deep recess of herself, where she is truly free and so damn beautiful. I couldn't hold it in anymore.

And she said *yes*. Thank God. Even after she ran, she said I was *a rare kind of wonderful*. It all replays in my head, over and over.

But something went sour when we were at the skating rink. *Carson*. He set me on edge, but I tried to stay away. I failed, ultimately. I couldn't watch Joy take his rage like that.

I don't know what they were arguing about, but it looked bad. I don't get guys like him. What does he gain from intimidating her?

Cale and Lena trail into the cabin after me, separating to shake off the exercise. I grab a drink from the fridge and avoid the beautiful sleeping girl in the sun rays.

The moms walk into the cabin a few minutes later, hopped up on some bubbly conversation. I shush them and point to Joy. My mom excuses herself from Angela and Karen.

She knows something is up.

I walk with her to her guest room. She puts her bag and wide-brim hat on the floral bedspread and glances at me.

"What is it, little boy?" she says in Korean.

How the heck is she so intuitive?

"It's Joy."

"I know it's Joy. What about Joy? Are you ready to tell me why you were really with her this morning?"

"I kissed her," I admit. No point in talking around it.

Mom tuts, her hand on her hip in judgment.

"Umma!" I argue, trying to keep my voice hushed despite no one else in the house possibly understanding us. "I really like her. I've never... I've never felt like this before."

Her eyebrows raise. Reasonably. It's a big statement for me, given my last relationship.

"I mean it," I affirm.

"So you told her about your dad?"

I clench my jaw and sigh. "I don't know how to bring it up, Umma. I'm worried she'll get scared. She gave up everything for her brother. How could I blame her if she chooses his well-being over me?"

My mom softens. "Okay, little boy. I understand. You don't want to lose her." She starts pulling things out of her bag. "But you have to tell her."

"I know."

She points at me. "And Seoul. Tell her that, too."

"I will." I just don't know how.

TRACK 16 –
GETTING
CLOSER

Jin – July 20ᵗʰ

I DON'T KNOW WHAT INTEREST ANGELA HAS in my romantic involvement, but it's obvious she's paying attention. She's probably looking out for Lena, but honestly that makes me a bit worried for both girls. I glance over to Angela and Joy, sitting on chairs in the grass a bit far off.

"Next one you drive, okay?" Lena says as I help her off her yellow jet ski.

Lena is extra cheerful because of the jet skis. It would be fun if I wasn't wishing Joy was out here, too.

"Sure," I tell Lena, but I'm distracted.

I wish Joy would've broken the deal with Cale last night. Is she aching as much as I am for us to be out in the open? It was so hard to sit apart during the movie.

Why did I have to make it contingent on her being done with her fake boyfriend? I guess I assumed she'd do it right away, but maybe she's not as eager as I am. Maybe we're still a little off-center as far as how much we want the other.

Then again, I haven't told her about my dad yet. Or Seoul.

I look over at her again, talking to Angela. I wave.

Something isn't right. Joy looks upset and Angela doesn't move. Joy sees me but doesn't wave back. Instead she gets up to leave.

I book it off the dock and ignore Lena calling my name as I race to where Angela is lounging. She's flipping through some magazine like nothing happened.

"Hey," I say out of breath, bracing myself on my knees. "Where's Joy? Is she okay?"

"She's fine, sweetie," Angela says without looking up. "She said she just got too much sun."

That's definitely a lie.

Angela flips her eyes up to me, peeking above the rim of her sunglasses. "If you ask me, I think she's just upset that her boyfriend isn't here. Joy's too sweet to let anyone feel sad for her, but she told me she misses him."

Ugh. I hate that it sounds like the truth, even though it probably isn't. There's truth in it. Angela is skilled at putting convenient lies under even more convenient realities.

"Maybe I should go make sure she's okay," I think aloud.

"Jin, honey. Why are you concerning yourself with a girl who's taken? Just let her be. There's no reason for you to assume she needs *your* help."

I sigh. If only she knew the truth. I'd tell her, but I've never trusted Angela.

My hunch is she's pushing Lena to me. Felt that the second I left my ex.

Joy's safer if Angela thinks she's winning. Lena too, for that matter.

"I guess you're right," I say. It feels wrong, though. Comforting Joy is supposed to be my role, isn't it?

"Oh gosh, where is my daughter off to now? I should've kept a leash on her," Karen says as she walks up, her voice thick with sarcasm. She pulls her hair into a short ponytail. My mom buzzes with residual fun from their boat ride. They giggle together like they're back in high school.

My mom pinches my exposed arm and I flinch. "Why you leave Lena alone? Go have fun!"

I look back over at Lena sitting on the dock with her feet in the water, taking in the sun with her eyes closed. I don't want to hurt her.

"Joy said she got too much sun," Angela repeats for them.

Karen digs her phone out from her bag that's lying in the grass. "Oh, she just texted me that she's going to talk to Carson. That's good! They need to spend some more time together while we're here."

Carson?

My stomach sinks, and I don't know why.

TRACK 17 -
SAVE US

Lena – July 20ᵗʰ

JET SKIS WOULD'VE BEEN A LOT MORE FUN if Jin hadn't abandoned me, but whatever. Now I'm wishing Cale didn't bail this morning since Joy is crippled and nothing is going right with Jin. Cale would have been a much better jet ski partner. Now that we're actually friends, I kind of miss his craziness.

But mostly I miss my best friend since toddlerhood.

I stare at the back of his head as we ride the golf cart back to the cabin. The moms won't shut up so they're basically a dull whine. Jin's messy black hair shifts in the breeze. Why won't he look at me?

Jin's been distant ever since we left the dock.

No, actually. He's been distant since the day he dumped Sunny.

And Joy freaking *likes* him. Ugh! I made her promise not to fall for him. I guess she didn't actually agree. She just changed her mind about the whole "swearing off boys" thing. My fault, probably.

She just *had* to discover romantic desire with Jin. God, now I'm fighting tears just thinking about it.

Get over it. It's not like anything's going on.

The cart stops in front of the cabin. I pretend I don't care that Jin didn't bother to say a word to me the whole way. I follow the verbally active moms inside, glad at least for the AC.

Joy's already back. She sits on the couch, stretching out her leg. I take out my phone so I can pretend I'm interested in something and not have to talk to her. I'm still ticked she went on a hike with Jin yesterday.

"Oh hey, Joy! Get too much sun?" I don't wait for an answer before I open an app to check whatever notifications. Then I go downstairs to change out of my swimsuit.

Down here, it's dark and quiet except for some soft footsteps above. Am I being too harsh? I invited both of them here. I should at least try to have fun with them. I won't be petty like my mom.

Get over it.

I trek back up the stairs and overhear Karen asking where Joy is, and Jan-di saying she's outside with Jin before carting her off to look at some special brand of lotion or something. My urge is to hang out with Joy and Jin outside, but I also want to ignore them both.

They're your friends. Stop taking everything so personally.

Jin actually came to the cabin, I remind myself. Joy and Cale *kissed.* Traction has been made.

I walk up to the door and right when my hand reaches for the handle, I hear my mom's voice.

"I wouldn't go out there, Lena."

I swivel around and find her in the kitchen. "Why not?"

She pours herself a strong drink. "I'm pretty sure Joy's confessing her little crush on Jin."

My heart thumps and now I'm mad at my mom, too. "How on earth would you know that?"

She lifts the glass to her lips. "I overheard her flirting with him this morning." *Sip*.

My eyes go wide. *What?!* That little...

I glance outside and see clear anguish on Jin's face. I could definitely believe it's because he doesn't want to hurt her feelings.

For once I agree with my mom. I do not want to watch this. So I walk away and slam my butt into the armchair. The leather squeaks under my weight.

I freaking told her! Why didn't she listen?!

Mom's hand lands softly on my upper back. "It's going to be okay, Lena. Jin would never go for a girl like that. With a *boyfriend*." She scoffs and takes another swig of her amber drink. "She should know better. Don't you think?"

If I didn't know that Joy was faking her relationship with Cale, I'd slip right into the same venomous gossip mode my mom's so comfortable with. *What kind of girl does that? Who does she think she is? She knows he's out of her league, right?*

"I feel bad for her," I say to my mom, knowing it'll shut her up.

I put Joy in that little deal. And I might've been a little happy to tell Jin she was taken. I thought she at least wouldn't sabotage my chances with him.

But I also might be responsible for blowing up what we had left.

"I'm gonna go relax for a bit, sweetheart," Mom says and then disappears into the hallway. I knew she'd be merciful if I lied.

As soon as she leaves, I hear Joy walk inside and sigh. "What was that about?" I ask. Then I peek over my shoulder.

She's red, puffy and tear-stained. Her arms are shaky holding onto her crutches.

"Are you crying?" I ask. I guess I didn't expect she'd take it so hard.

"I don't want to talk to you, Lena," she says, her voice bitter, cold.

Um, hold on. Is she seriously blaming me? "What did I do?"

"Nothing. It's not even about you," she says as she shuffles past me.

"Believe it or not."

Wow. Some friend. She goes after the one guy who should've been off-limits and now she thinks *I'm* the selfish one.

"I warned you, didn't I?"

She stops, her back facing me. Her shoulders fall forward before she picks up and hobbles away again.

I don't even feel bad that it hurts her. It's the truth.

I really hoped Joy wasn't fake as hell, but I guess I was wrong.

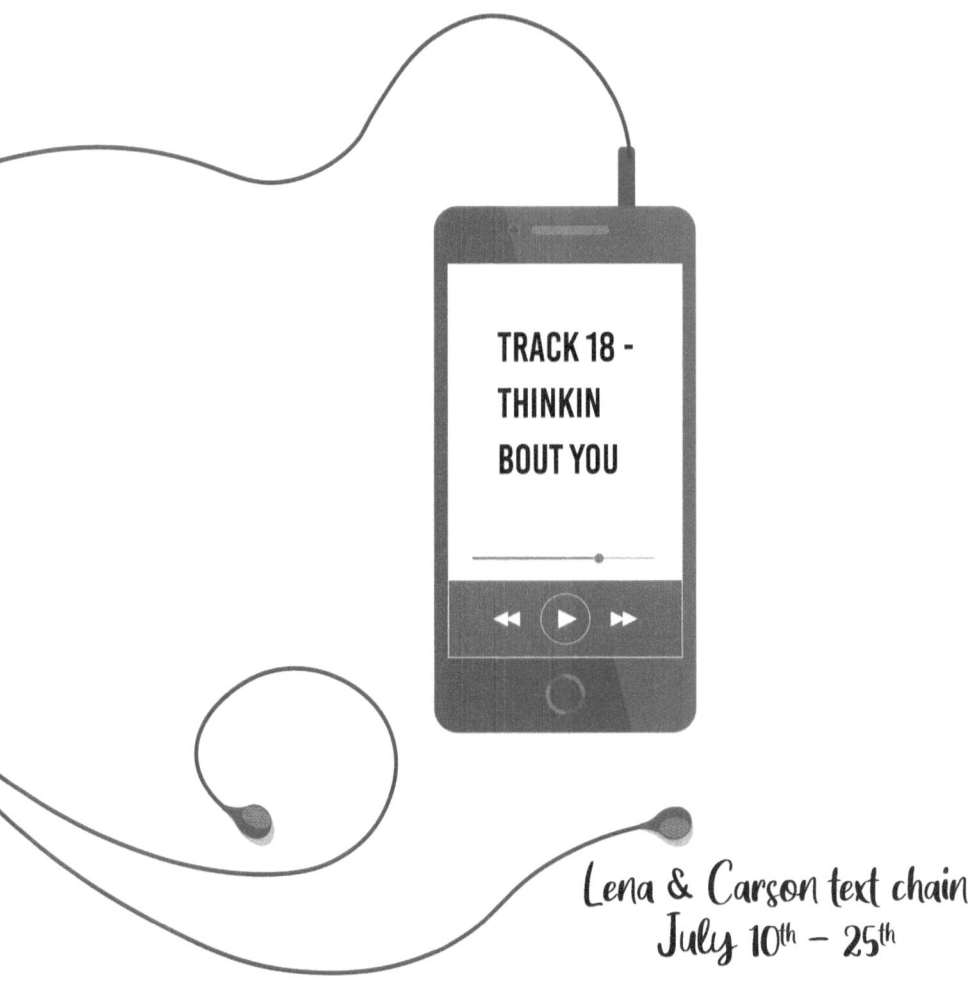

TRACK 18 -
THINKIN
BOUT YOU

*Lena & Carson text chain
July 10th – 25th*

Wed, Jul 10, 5:08 PM

Carson: hey lena, this is Carson

Carson: i wanted to surprise Joy and take her to Victoria Lake when I go back

Carson: she said you guys have a cabin up there

Lena: WTF how'd you get my number? I was pretty proud of how well I've been dodging your creepy ass so far

Carson: Hey whoa im not a creep!!

Carson: ill prove it

Carson: ill be all business

Lena: I'll take that deal
Lena: You want my mom to see when the cabin's open?

Carson: Yeah. im going back on the 17th and i wanna surprise her that day

Lena: We can do the 17th. Next booking is the 22nd so we can stay for a few days.

Carson: Cool!

Lena: K well I'm heading to bed, but my mom wants to know if your mom wants to come. She's going all manic trip planner and inviting everyone and their moms lol

Carson: Yeah i'll tell her
Carson: my mom i mean

Lena: So you *can* be nice

Carson: when i want to be ;)

Sun, Jul 14, 2:44 PM

Lena: I solved the mystery of how you got my number
Lena: You hacked Joy's phone. Nice.
Lena: I knew you were a creep

Carson: In my defense i didnt hack it. She gave me the code a long time ago. And i was trying to surprise her remember?

Lena: You need to stop being so controlling for real
Lena: Did you know she booked that beach house?

Carson: Nope

Lena: I don't believe you

Carson: K yes i did, but i miss my kid sister its not a crime
Carson: And ive been pretty nice to her lately not that u care

Lena: How have you been nice?

Carson: i let her go to that glee thing and i didnt interrogate her new boyfriend even tho i wanted to

Lena: Oh my god, brother of the effing year
Lena: You know you don't LET a grown woman make her own choices, right?

Carson: your right
Carson: i know i suck but im trying
Carson: im doing more than just that but your right, it doesnt really matter wat i try to do
Carson: i have a lot of crap to make up for

Lena: At least you're self-aware
Lena: And learn to use the right "you're" for God's sake

Carson: lol maybe I like it when YOUR mad

Lena: omg I will seriously block you

Thu, Jul 18, 10:20 PM

Carson: i know this was supposed to be all business but you looked super hot today and i'm still thinking about it

Carson: feel free to ignore this, but damn lena

Carson: i don't expect you to look my way, but it's on the table

Lena: ...

Lena: It's on the table?

Carson: definitely

Lena: Okay. Then I guess it's on the table.

Carson: god i hope that means you're interested

Lena: Keep learning proper punctuation and I might be.

Sun, Jul 21, 9:11 AM

Lena: This sucks. Everyone left early. Now I'm stuck here with my mom which is literally the last place I want to be.

Carson: Do you want to hang out?

Carson: My shift doesn't start until 3.

Lena: Maybe

Lena: Okay yes

Carson: Awesome! Can't wait to see you, Lena. :)

Lena: What the hell, is this even Carson?

Lena: Your texts are so unlike you.

Carson: I downloaded a grammar app. Just for you.

Lena: lol

Lena: That's basically the sexiest thing a guy has ever done for me.

Carson: Damn, you're getting my hopes up, Lena
Carson: When can I see you?

Lena: At the lodge in fifteen minutes

Mon, Jul 22, 11:58 PM

Carson: What did I do to deserve you?

Lena: Sweet talk doesn't work on me, FYI

Carson: It's not sweet talk. I'm thinking about you.
Carson: Plus, I'm working tomorrow. It's not like I'm waiting up. I just meant it.
Carson: I don't want you to forget about me.

Lena: Yeah right. Like I could when we went behind Joy's back.

Carson: Can I call you?

Lena: Fine

Wed, Jul 24, 11:51 AM

Lena: When are you back?

Carson: Today. Can I see you?

Lena: Yes. Just lie if anyone asks.

Thu, Jul 25, 4:01 PM

Carson: come to the stadium asap

Lena: What the hell?

Carson: wat? i wanna see you. park in the back lot.

Lena: Why bother with asking?
Lena: Or proper spelling?
Lena: Ugh. See you in 15.

TRACK 19 -
WRONG
DIRECTION

Jin – July 25th

SHE LIED.

I squeeze my steering wheel and stare out at the hills behind my house. I don't even remember the drive here. I can still feel the hot sun glaring off the diner, like I'm not miles away.

I never thought she'd lie. God.

Joy and Cale were... *are* together. She kissed him today. *And me.* It's like a punch to the gut.

Feels like I could vomit. Like Sunny was right.

I'm not enough. Not for a girl like her. I'm not worth honesty. I don't deserve something real. I should've been more serious. More of a man.

Guys like me are cheap and weak.

Like a bad drink.

Sunny still haunts me with the words she spat at me when I cut her out. Joy's nothing like her. Or, I thought she wasn't.

My memory shifts to Joy's hazel eyes meeting mine, the breeze drawing her closer.

You're a rare kind of wonderful.

Did she even mean that?

Tap tap. I jolt. My mom is standing right by my window.

I sigh and get out of my car, braced for the onslaught of Korean reproach.

"Where were you, Woo-Jin? You missed your meeting with the advisor—" I walk away from her without saying anything. Not to be cruel. I just can't.

If I say a word, I'll crumble.

My mom shuffles after me. "Woo-Jin! What's wrong with you?"

I open the door and walk halfway up the stairs.

"Shoes!" she yelps at me.

I look down at my converse, still on my feet. I forgot to take them off.

Mom's tone shifts from irritated to worried. "What happened?"

Looking at her, I fail holding it together. "I'm sorry," I sob. Then I sit on the stairs and bury my face in my hands. "I believed her, Umma."

I feel my mom's hand grip my ankle as she pulls my shoes off, one by one. "You always believe the best of things, Woo-Jin. Much better than believing the worst. It's rare."

I lift my face, the chaos in my heart quieting as my mom pads down the steps and gently places my shoes under the bench.

I never told her what Joy said to me on the bench.

But now, maybe, I can still believe it was true.

TRACK 20 -
DON'T CRY
FOR ME

Cale – July 29ᵗʰ

M Y ALARM BEEP WAKES ME UP. 7:35 a.m. Why the heck do I still have it set this deep into the summer? I don't have band practice on Mondays anymore.

I yank the phone so hard the cord comes out of the wall, then I jab through all the settings until the alarm is done for. Forever. Or, at least until FredU classes start next month.

One of my classes starts at 8:15 a.m. Kill me now.

The lines of morning light stream through my blinds. That dang pit is still there in my stomach. I'm not accustomed to the pang of rejection putting a damper on my fire.

I half groan, half chuckle. It still cracks me up how bad I flopped. If she'd have been my *real* girlfriend, I'd probably still have her.

BEEP! BEEP! BEEP!

I groan again. I forgot about the stupid two-minute follow-up alarm! Each *beep* makes the *pang* hurt worse. Why can I get nothing right in my liiiiiiife?

Joy was the sweetest cupcake I ever met and I let her go. That swoony Asian biker dude snagged her cute little heart. I don't want to be mad, but I'm about to throw this pillow at the lamp or something CRAZY!

Wow. I can't even rage like a normal person. This stupid pang has got me off my game!

Knock knock knock.

I take the pillow I was *going* to throw at my lamp and cover my head with it instead. My voice is muffled and sounds like straight mumbling, but my tone is a recognizable "come in!"

My old janky door squeaks and one of the females in my family walks in.

"Hey baby, you up?" It's Mama.

I take the pillow off my face and look at her. She's got her hair in her brightest headwrap with the orange and blue pattern that matches her silk pants. My mama is the kind of pretty that brightens when she's gentle. It always puts me in a better mood when she calls me *baby*.

Mama sits on my bed and starts rubbing my arm. "What's wrong?"

"I'm so terrible at life and love and I'll never find true happiness so I'm just tryna accept it, okay?!" I sob in a grandiose manner, like it's a joke. But I'm worried it's true.

I pull back my fake pout and bury my face in her shoulder. She smells like her cocoa butter lotion. My false wails shift when the pang seats itself deep in my core.

Am I too much? Like, the kind of *too much* that makes me *not enough*?

Her tender hand strokes the back of my neck, taking me all the way back to toddlerhood. "I got you, baby."

I pull away from her tickling fingernail and look in her eyes. "Mama?"

She palms my cheek. "Yes?"

"Just be real. Am I too much for a girl like Joy? Or... I dunno. Any girl?" My tone is a quiet serious and I wish it wasn't.

She cocks her head and purses her lips. "Baby, you *know* you are."

My back goes straight as a board. "What?! You're not supposed to say that!"

Mama's brows go up like I should know better than to judge her, whilst judging *me*, which of course is her right as the matriarch.

I slump against my wall, my indignance mostly restrained. "How am I supposed to find love then, Mama?"

She folds her hands together. "Yes. You're *extra*. And the one for you will be blessed by all that extra. She'll want it. She'll wonder how she lived without it."

I hang my head. It doesn't really help. "They all seem like they like it until they bounce," I say, my voice reserved and quiet like I'm some other person.

Mama brushes her fingers on my chin and then gets me to look at her. "You know, Dee was the best baby. So easy. She slept all night, she ate whatever I gave her, the only thing she was picky about was what she wore."

"*That* didn't change," I comment. "Also, THANKS, I needed the reminder that Dee was your favorite child."

Mama tuts. "Boy, I do *not* have a favorite child. But I was not prepared for you, that's for damn sure."

I pull my chin back with wide eyes. "Mama!"

"Boy, hush! I can say whatever I want, I'm the mom!" She scowls for a second and I cede defeat. "Anyway, you were a struggle every day. The opposite of Dee. You had all these intense feelings. You were into every drawer and cabinet. I thought I'd never survive you. And one day, I asked God why I got you. I was *done*. But, God said right into my heart, 'I gave you that boy as a blessing. Now act like it.' And I realized that, for all the crazy you brought to this family, you made us happy. We never laughed so much until we had you!" She laughs a little as she says it.

I mean, I knew that. She's said it five thousand times throughout my life.

"What I'm saying, baby," she continues, "is that the right girl will figure out that she can't live without you, just like I did."

Mama's lashes are low, watching me with tender eyes. She always told me I am supposed to be this way.

I *am* extra. And that's the *point!*

I'm so used to being intoxicated by the laughs I get, I didn't know what to do with myself when these pangs in my stomach sobered me up. I miss Joy and I hate the idea of being too much for her.

But I am enough. I know I am.

As Mama says the words, I feel them resonate within me like a harmony. "God has big plans for you, baby."

"Like *The Voice?*" I say with a cheesy grin.

I hear Jayla laugh right outside my door.

"Jayla!" I say, and finally whip the blankets off and get out of bed. Before I exit my room, Jayla pushes my door open, her head all wrapped up with a pink scarf, the same way Mama's is. She's got her hand on her hip, attitude the main component of her beach attire.

"You were eavesdropping!" I accuse, with a point of my finger.

"Was not!" she says and then sticks out her tongue because she's still twelve despite her pretty clothes.

I look over to Mama. "Why are you both up so early? Is it my unlucky day?"

"Wasn't that Friday?" Jayla says, a wicked grin sliding across her face.

I narrow my eyes at her.

"When that girl dumped you?" she finishes.

"I got the drift!"

Mom gets up. "Jayla, leave your big brother alone! He's processing."

"Pfft! Like a computer? Please." She waves her hand and pops her little hip. "What a muggle."

Mom shoots a fiery glare at Jayla. "What did you say?"

And I crack up, because Jayla is the extra in my life. The kind I always needed. And somehow, that gives me a lot of hope for myself.

God has big plans for me. Whether it's romance or not, I got a lot of love already.

TRACK 21 –
FALLING
FOR BOYS

Lena – August 1ˢᵗ

MY BIG, FAT BED IS ZERO HELP. I lie in it—the bed I made—scrolling through my Instagram and trying to feel better about this freak show of a week.

Guys are jerks. That's all there is to it. Every last one of them. Jin. Cale. Carson. This random perv in my DMs. They're all faking random types of affection for me to get something else.

And what really sucks?

Aside from this creep on Instagram, the person they're ALL trying to get to through me is Joy. Every damn guy cares about her way more than they care about me. And like, whatever. It's not like it's her fault. Even if she's not an angel, she didn't ask for any of it.

The biggest jerk in my life, though, is me.

Why the hell did I lead Carson on? Am I really that jealous of her?

I mean, it's not like I was completely lying to Cale when I told him he should tell Joy I was when he brought up the deal. It's always been somewhat true.

But when I figured out that Jin was attracted to her, something cracked. I don't know.

She's cute. Is she single?

Never once has he asked me if one of my friends was single before that. It didn't help that I said she wasn't. That whole "off-limits" crap made it worse!

There's a knock at my door.

"Come in!" I yell, throwing my phone onto my bed. I'll handle the creeps later, I guess.

"Hey, can we talk?"

I turn my head and find Jin. Wasn't expecting it to be him.

"Oh, we can talk now? How gracious of you," I say. He hasn't said anything to me in a week, so I'm bitter like the tea from a cup that was smashed against the wall. So much for taking advantage of our summer together.

"Lena," he sighs, shutting my door behind him. "It's important."

He sits on the edge of my bed.

"What is it?" I ask with little patience.

He frowns at me with his stupid, handsome face. He has the nerve to struggle with what to say, and there's a flicker of the boy he used to be. The Jin who felt helpless when his dad couldn't make it to a piano recital or had to leave his birthday party. Why the heck is he so sad? Did he really like her that much?

I release a sharp breath. "I know about you and Joy, okay? You don't have to pretend nothing happened."

He looks up and chews on his lips, sighing the sigh that means he's frustrated it came to this. "Lena, I wasn't trying to sneak around."

Whatever. Yes he was. JERK.

"I didn't want to do it that way, anyway. It's complicated," he says, fiddling with his thumbs. "But it's over now."

I glare at him, but the intensity is lost in his somber demeanor. He's slumped forward, eyes distant into the ground.

"I *know* you kissed her," I say, just to see what he'll do. Does he care about what that means to me? He looks at me with zero panic. Worried, but not in the way I'm hoping.

It's infuriating!

"Why did it have to be her, huh? She was my friend!"

His brows pinch together. "Was?"

"Yeah, well," I sigh. "I kinda made out with her brother. I don't think she'll talk to me again."

I watch him for any signs of anything. But I don't know what I'm hoping for. If I really want him to be mine, to end up kissing and holding me, would I feel so... hesitant? Do I want him to be jealous, or am I just tired of him being gone?

"I bet she would," he says and it's the last thing I expect him to say. It hits me in the stomach like a brick.

He's right. If I asked Joy for her forgiveness, I bet she would give it.

"Don't worry about me and Joy. It's over. She lied to me. I'm not sure she even felt the same way about me."

I sit up, confused. I knew she lied, but she said she told Jin the *truth*. "What are you talking about?"

Jin hesitates. "It sounds stupid. She told me she and Cale weren't really dating and I believed it. She led me on."

I was trying to give up on Jin.

Oh my god. That petite little idiot. Why the hell is she letting Jin believe this crap? She's not that kind of person at all. Why does that make me so mad?

She likes him.

Clearly, he likes her, too.

She's not heartless! God. I'm the one who's heartless, she's just clumsy.

But if I tell him the truth, I have no doubt my chances with him will return to zero. If they ever even blipped above zero.

Screw it. What kind of friend am I if I don't tell him Joy wasn't actually lying?

"That's not why I came here, though," Jin says before I can say anything. "I'm leaving tomorrow. I decided to take an internship. In Seoul."

HELL. NO. He did not just say that. "What?! You're going to Korea *tomorrow*? And you're telling me now?"

He nods, one side of his mouth pinched in a frown.

My face gets hot with anger, or something like it.

He sighs. "I'm sorry I didn't mention it before. I wasn't sure if I was gonna take it."

"How long have you known?" I'm hurt. My lungs shudder.

"Two weeks," he admits.

"*Two weeks* and you couldn't tell me?" I yell.

"I'm sorry. I didn't want to upset you."

I throw my pillow at him, hard. "Great job, Jin." I'm on the verge of tears, ready to scream. "I thought we were going to be at U-Dub together! You're such a jerk! How could you not tell me?"

He stands up, frustration settling heavy on him. "Well, what the hell should I do now? I love her!" He rubs his eyes and I'm stunned at the depth of his feelings.

He loves her?

"She's the one who told me to go in the first place. Now I just... I guess it sounds like a good idea to leave and focus on something else."

He's barely holding it together when he looks down at me. I'm shocked, but I don't know why. I already knew we were leading nowhere. Why would he stay for me? He never even told me. He told Joy.

What the hell is wrong with her? Why would she break him apart like this?

Jin heads to my door, stalling when his hand hits the door handle.

Damn it to hell. I really screwed up.

"I'm sorry," we say at the same time. I know he's apologizing for leaving me out of his gigantic life decision.

"It's okay," he sighs. "It wasn't your fault, Lena."

But it was. He doesn't know it, but that's why I apologized.

Everything was my fault.

He opens the door but pauses. "If you come up early tomorrow, you can send me off before your orientation. If you want."

With a thousand regrets on my mind, I don't think I could stand one more.

"I will," I say.

TRACK 22 -
SOMEONE
TO YOU

Jin – August 2nd

"I'M THE ONE WHO SET THEM UP... JOY NEVER LIED. I convinced Cale to make a deal with her for the summer."

Her eyes gleaming with tears, Lena confesses. *Joy never lied.* I don't know what to make of it. Warbling voices announce my upcoming flight to Seoul; my inevitable reality echoes in the terminal.

"I just thought you should know," she finishes, and then sniffles.

So, my trust wasn't misplaced. If Joy told the truth, then...why didn't she tell me?

I clear my throat, trying to regain control of my heart. "If she wanted to clear it up, she would have."

I hug my mom, her arms squeezing like she'll forget me if she doesn't grip so tight.

She taps my cheek. "I'll watch your plane from the coffee shop."

"I love you, Umma," I say in English. It feels more natural in English.

"I love you, too," she says back, in her thick accent.

Lena meets my eyes with regret in hers. Her arms are crossed like she's trying not to unravel. I relate.

"Bye, Jin," she says. It sounds more like "I'm sorry."

"Goodbye, Lena."

And then, I head into the ebbing line through security.

Joy left me on the edge for days, leaving my messages unread while I insisted I still meant everything. I wanted to fight for her. For *us*.

Why didn't she call me?

"ID and boarding pass!" the TSA agent yells at me, annoyance in her voice and face. A lady behind me sighs like taking two extra seconds to dig them out of my backpack is going to cause her to miss her flight.

I fish them out, then walk through.

I don't want to cross the multiple barriers to get to the gate. Each one is a more significant step away from home. From summer.

From Joy.

I'm in a haze, shuffling through the towering halls to my gate. It's all straight lines and evenly spaced out signs, seats, gates, charging stations. When I get there, they're already boarding. So I get on. One more barrier.

Before I've really processed it, I'm inside the vessel that will take me to Seoul. There's no going back now. I find my row and secure my carry-on. It's all very ritualistic and familiar. The multi-lingual announcements. The stiff air. The hard, slim seat with a puff pillow and flimsy blanket neatly placed on it.

"Hiiiii!"

The high voice comes from below. A toddler in blonde pigtails grins up at me. "It's a airplan!"

"Rosie!" a woman says in a weak reprimand. Her face bears a similar coloring to the girl.

"I'm sorry," she says to me, then addresses the girl. "Rosie, please say 'excuse me.'"

"No need to be sorry," I say, and then I kneel down and hold up my hand. "You like high-fives?"

Rosie blushes and beams before slapping my hand with all her might.

I smile at her and let them sneak past to their seats.

And then I remember... Joy's face. Last time I did that, she was the one blushing.

That was real.

"You seem good with kids," the woman says to me while getting the toddler settled in her seat.

"I love kids," I say.

The woman rubs noses with Rosie and then says, "They bring a lot of joy into the world, that's for sure."

I'm a bit stunned when she says it. Did I imagine that?

I shake it off and sit so I'm out of the way of the other passengers funneling into the narrow aisles. I stuff my backpack under the seat in front of me and my phone falls out.

I grab it and turn it off. Joy would have called me if she wanted to be with me.

Are you crazy? Of course I do!

Why do I have to hear her voice in my head now? Why do her eyes gleam and her freckles pepper my mind?

Why did she let me believe that she lied?

I put my phone in my pocket and grab the lap belt.

Even your running away was for Lena's sake, right?

I thought I knew her, but I don't. Do I?

I stare at the shiny metal buckle in my hands. I wanted to fight for us. I didn't want to be here. I was ready to stay. To always be there when she needed me.

You can't do that, Jin.

The waves of our connection flood me, crashing together like an erratic storm in my chest.

It's not like I don't trust you.

But you're leaving, *Jin! ...And you should go.*

I thought I was over you but...

...You're the brightest spot I've ever had in my life.

Then Lena's words calm the storm: *Joy never lied.*

It was *all* true. The out-of-sequence memories of Joy paint the clearest picture of her that I've ever seen.

Joy's the girl who would let me walk away. Who would run the other direction if someone would be spared. Who would stand up against her abuser so her brother could be free.

But me... I'm not free. I'm about to be trapped in the sky, heading for a city I don't want to be in.

I drop the buckle.

I can't go to Seoul, and it's not because it's wrong. I *could* love the internship and the work. But I don't care about loving my work. I want to love people. The way Joy does.

I get up, yanking the strap of my carry-on from the overhead bin. I have to give it all my strength. It's practically vacuum sealed.

"Sir! We're about to depart. Do not remove your bag," the flight attendant tells me. Her uniform is pristine and no hair is out of place. Like the internship, she's rigid and proper and imposing.

I have to get back to the girl who isn't. I much prefer her.

"I'm getting off," I tell her, a wide grin plastered on me.

I pull harder, but I'm about to just leave it. I register nothing around me but the moment my suitcase gives. Then I squeeze past people, who struggle to make way. I cross the middle section of seats to make for the exit, brushing legs and probably swiping people with my overstuffed backpack.

I don't care.

Well, I do, but only once I'm off the plane and can no longer apologize.

I'm off. I'm not going.

This was definitely the right choice. I feel lighter, like shackles fell off. As people buzz about in varying directions, suitcase wheels scraping on the speed walkways and shoes clacking on the floor, I chart my way out of here.

Before I know it, I'm out of breath bursting into the coffee shop where my mom said she'd be. I find her staring out the floor-to-ceiling window at a little table.

Her puffy eyes gape when she sees me. "Woo-Jin?"

"I couldn't go," I tell her in Korean. My heart is twisted in happiness and regret. "I didn't want to. I wanted to stay. I can't explain it, Umma. I can't go to Seoul. Not right now."

She stands up and examines me. "I know exactly why you got off that plane, little boy."

I smile on one side. Of course she does.

My mom brushes my shoulder and taps my face. "Your father will be disappointed."

I sigh. That's true.

Then she grins and places her purse on her shoulder. "Just like my parents were when I chose him."

That makes me laugh.

I never thought my mom would understand if I fell in love with a girl who wasn't Korean. I never thought she'd relent on warnings after Sunny almost ripped me apart.

And I never thought she'd call it before I said it out loud.

My choice is mine to make. And I choose Joy.

If she'll take me.

August 3rd

"I'm all the way in love with you."

– JIN, TO JOY

TRACK 23 -
WONDER

Carson – September 7ᵗʰ

L EANING AGAINST THE FRONT DOOR FRAME, I trace Joy's beat-up little car as it disappears from our Willow Haven street.

She'll be okay. She won't need me. She has Jin now and that's... fine.

If he can stand up to me, then she'll be okay. He's a good guy for her.

But her room is gonna be quiet and that makes me sad. I already glanced at her empty doorway from mine. It's weird. The end of the hallway feels like it's under construction. Empty but still off-limits.

I'll be okay. It's probably worse for Mom and Dad. Well, Mom, anyway. She'll be an empty nester when I get set up in my dorm at FredU. Although, I'm considering not rooming in over there. It's not a long drive. I could save the money and my therapist says it would be good for me to have a space away from all the college kids.

She's probably right. And Mom's food is better than the cafeteria. Joy just won't be in her chair anymore.

"You look like you're about to cry, Carson."

I shift. I didn't even realize Lena had walked up to me. I look over at Mom and Dad, still making conversation with Cale. He's good at keeping attention.

It takes me a second to figure out what Lena said.

"Well, I might," I say absentmindedly. I curse in my head for saying that out loud.

Lena raises one eyebrow. "Seriously?"

I take a deep breath and finally look her in the eyes, but I really shouldn't. They're so pretty, I have a hard time remembering what I'm saying.

"Um... do you have a problem with emotional men?" I smirk. That was good.

Lena laughs. "Nope. It just doesn't seem like a very *Carson* emotion."

"It wasn't. But it should be." My eyes sting. I've grown really tired of fighting all the hot tears that scream at me. My instinct says to practice hitting and throwing, but even that isn't always enough. I can't always throw my big emotions at a target on a wall.

I stare off in the direction Joy left.

"I don't want to be embarrassed about what happens inside me anymore," I say, but it was so quiet, I'm not sure I said it aloud.

Until I glance at Lena. She blinks at me, surprised. I think. I have a hard time reading her.

"You shouldn't be," she affirms, before looking away and brushing her silky hair with her fingers.

She angles herself toward me, getting close enough to get my hopes up for more of what we had before. But she hangs back and meets my eyes again. "Um... Carson?"

"Yeah?"

"I'll try to make it to your game tonight." She gives me a pretty smile.

I knew it. I knew it wasn't over.

I grin and Lena rolls her eyes. "Oh my god, never mind!"

"What? What did I do?" Can she read my mind?! What is up?

Lena crosses the lawn, pounding toward her car. I follow.

She spins around and swats me on the arm. "You're so full of yourself!"

"I didn't even say anything!"

"You didn't have to!" But I see a smile flicker on her face. She fishes her keys out of her bag and flips her eyes up to me before opening her car door. "See you tonight."

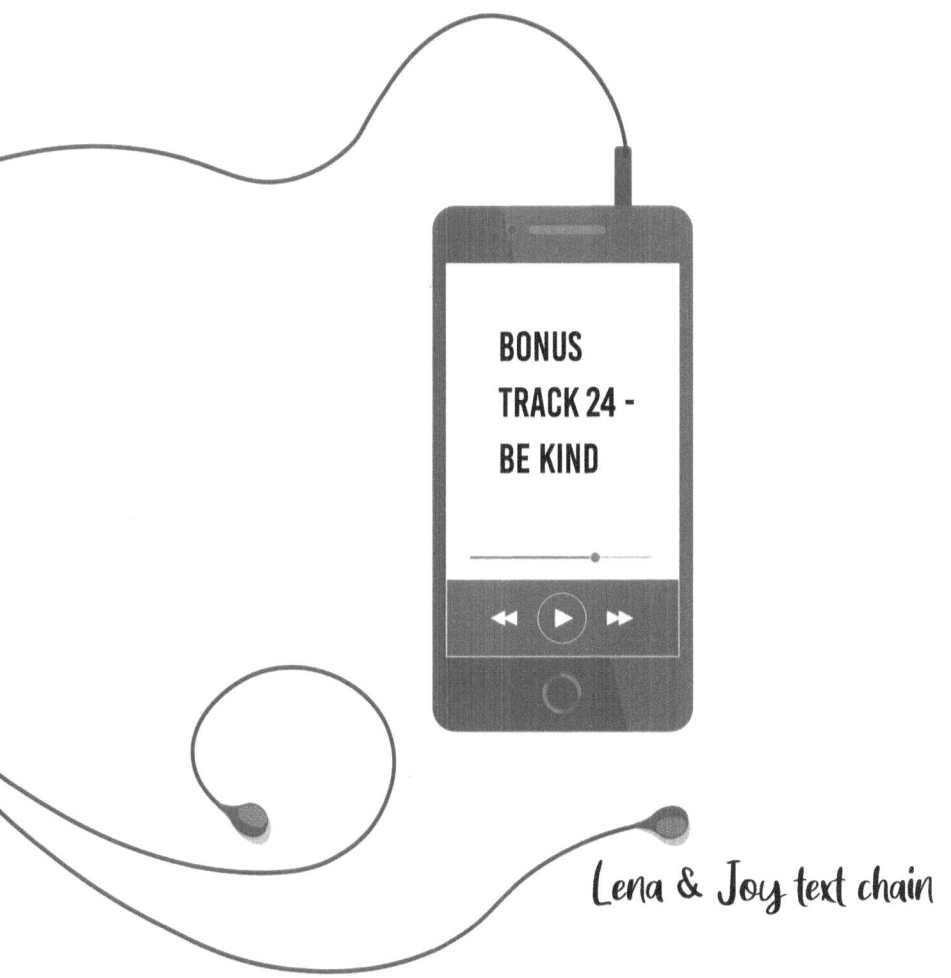

BONUS
TRACK 24 -
BE KIND

Lena & Joy text chain

September 8th, 2:27 PM

Lena: OK don't freak out

Joy: OMG I've been gone ONE DAY
Joy: Do I have to come back?

Lena: No it's not like that
Lena: It's just
Lena: Ugh, I didn't want to admit it before you and Jin took off yesterday

Joy: LENA

Lena: ...k I'll just come out
Lena: I kinda want to date your brother
Lena: I'm sorry

Joy: No
Joy: My answer is no

Lena: I wasn't asking permission

Joy: ...I know
Joy: gjlglkfgjkdfldk
Joy: You JUST said it was over

Lena: Yeah I didn't think it was a lie but it was
Lena: I promise I won't even kiss him
Lena: IF we date at all
Lena: I just didn't want secrets between us, because that sucks

Joy: Well, thanks for that I guess
Joy: You're lucky Jin's good at talking me off a ledge

Lena: You are both lucky

Joy: Me more than him

Lena: Nooooo way, other way around

Joy: You're just trying to get on my good side!

Lena: Always ;)

Joy: <3
Joy: Btw we both agree you're totally lying about the kissing thing
Joy: But honestly, if anyone can handle Carson, it's you

Joy: I can't believe I just said that

Lena: lol

BONUS
TRACK 25 –
BURN

Lena – October 12th

*N*o *kissing. This will be our first date.* Officially. Tonight, we're just talking and connecting. I made myself wait four weeks to pick a date after I told Joy. I had to see if I really, actually wanted to go out with Carson Becker.

I do.

After talking to Carson on the phone all week, he begged me to drive down to Willow Haven for the weekend.

Okay, he didn't *beg*, but still.

We will not end up kissing because that's not what matters. Kissing leads to things. Like feelings and screw-ups. We agreed. *No kissing.*

I blow out my hair so it's as silky as possible. It's nice to be back in my old room, back in my element. I lean over my sink and get up close to my mirror to do my eye makeup, but I pause. It doesn't feel right to do a full face of makeup.

Which is weird. I usually pull out all the stops for dates. Always, actually.

A few swipes with the mascara wand and I call it good.

I slip on my violet sheath dress that's not too short. Okay, it's a little short, and the back is exposed, and yeah, it's a little bit tight on my curves too, but I'm not bearing all. The neckline closes at my collar, so in that one way it's modest.

No kissing. Don't even think about kissing Carson.

I look myself over in the mirror and realize my inner mean streak is still intact. I clearly didn't plan on making the no-kissing thing easy for him.

I head downstairs at the proper time and open my front door to see Carson leaning against his grungy, red Dodge Dakota.

The car is one thing, but Carson... he's pretty sharp. Okay, *really* sharp.

He's in a crisp white button-down shirt and gray slacks that I think he might have even ironed. The shirt stretches against his upper arm muscles, which is nice to look at. I also love the way his hair bounces when he jogs up to me with a handsome, stupefied look.

"Oh wow, Lena. You look..."

I'm not sure what he's gonna say, but there are limited options.

"So hot," Carson finishes. Option one.

I squint at him, a hint of a smile on my face, but mostly my eyes are judgy.

"What?" he says, unable to read me. "I'm not lying."

I step down off my porch and walk past him toward his truck. "I don't think you're *lying*."

"Oh, so you *know* you look hot, then?"

There's a challenge in his words. I turn around. "Are you going to criticize me for agreeing with you?" I'm only a little playful, but I could become irritated depending on what he says.

"No way! I like that you know how sexy you are." Carson grins.

Huh. Even though we're on the subject of my looks and I'm usually not thrilled to keep hearing about them from thirsty boys like him... I like his answer.

I don't tell him. But I like it.

I enter his truck and now I'm in that awkward situation where the contrast between my dress and the quality of the vehicle are so starkly opposite, it's funny. My slinky plum dress against this peeling pleather bench seat is like a gourmet meal in styrofoam. I check my make-up in the mirror just to get a sense of the lighting, but the mirror is hazy with dust and fingerprints.

I like that you know how sexy you are.

Carson sure doesn't care about feeding my ego, does he?

When he gets in the driver's seat, his pants tighten around his legs and he looks really good. I savor how physically affected I am by it. I refuse to feed *his* ego, though. Better to have the upper hand.

"Alright," he sighs, looking me up and down before his eyes must belong on the road. "You ready?"

"Stop ogling and let's go," I say as I look away.

He laughs. "Yes ma'am."

He picked the sushi place I've raved about. Like, he *listened*. I'm impressed.

We look over the menus at the sleek table. It has a shoot of bamboo sticking up from some shiny black rocks in a vase. I kind of hate that such simple things can look so classy. Stupid bamboo doesn't have to try so hard.

"You'll have to tell me what's good here since they don't have regular sushi rolls," Carson tells me as his eyes travel the menu. I like how there are glints of gold in his hair because of the flickering candlelight. He doesn't have to try so hard, either. Ugh.

"You've never had sashimi? Or nigiri?" I don't try to sound judgmental, but sometimes I do anyway.

"I don't speak Japanese so I don't know what those are," he says.

What a dork. I grin at his lack of refinement, a little satisfied that I'm maintaining this upper hand. "You don't need to speak Japanese to know what those things mean."

"Sorry I'm not as fancy as you," he says, but I'm a little concerned he thinks I'm putting him down. Maybe I am, but I'm not trying to. I don't like how the air shifts and he isn't as stupidly happy to be with me anymore.

I should really rein in my upper-handedness. "Sashimi is just raw fish sliced by the chef. Usually high quality. Nigiri is a piece of fish with rice, but usually no *nori*." Carson's eyebrow goes up. "*Nori* is seaweed."

"Do you speak Japanese, Lena?" Carson asks, a grin returning.

"No, I just love sushi. And I've been to Japan."

"How does this place stack up?"

"The atmosphere is nice, but you can get sushi like this at a convenience store in Japan."

"Oh." Carson hides behind his menu. "Sorry it's not that great."

I shut my menu. "That's not what I meant, okay? The sushi in Japan is *so* good that you can get it anywhere. It's really hard to find good sushi like that in America. That's why I like this place. Because it's *good* here."

Carson's amber eyes float above the menu and meet mine. "So you're happy I brought you here?"

I open my menu again. "Yes, you doofus."

"Good. Well, get whatever you want. Just don't go too crazy. My funds are limited."

The word *omakase* jumps out at me from the menu. "What's your budget?"

"Isn't it weird if I tell you that?"

"Not to me. I'm only asking because I want to try *omakase* and you have to tell them your price," I tell him. And it's true, honestly. I don't care what he planned to spend on me.

"What's *omakase*?" he asks, scouring his menu for the word.

I tug on his menu and he lets me take it. "How about I show you? Is there anything you won't eat? Like an ingredient?"

"Not really. I'm not picky."

That makes me smile. Totally believable, brother of Joy.

When the waiter comes, I order *omakase* and the waiter asks what the budget is. I gesture to Carson, and he says $60 each, which is actually more than I expected. *Omakase*, I explain to Carson, means "I leave it up to you." Which is to say, the chef will create a menu especially for us. They fit it into the price and bring out the dishes as they're ready.

The first is an appetizer of silken tofu with a pepper and mushroom oil. Carson doesn't need to ask me what it is because the waiter explains everything to us both, and I really like watching Carson learn about this foreign cuisine. It's... adorable. I like how surprised he is by the explanations of the food. How welcoming he is to something new and undiscovered.

The look he gives me when he's convinced the food sounds delicious is heart-warming.

Yes, I said *heart-warming*. Me. This is what Carson Becker does to me.

And oh my goodness, the meal is divine. A salmon roll with an apple compote shouldn't be so good. Spicy calamari with avocado drizzle. Fatty tuna sashimi with ponzu sauce and green onions. I'm taken aback by how incredible a meal $60 can afford you if you let a chef show you what they can do. If I hadn't literally heard the dollar amount, I'd easily assume this meal was $100 each.

"So, what do you think?" I ask, before using chopsticks to stuff a piece of yellowtail nigiri in my mouth. It's too big of a bite, but I work with it anyway.

"I think I love watching you eat sushi," he says before using his fingers to eat his nigiri in one, much more graceful bite.

I can't talk because I'm still chewing, but that makes me smile. Once I'm done chewing, I say, "What about the *food*, Carson?"

"Oh yeah, it's all really good. I liked the fried squid."

"The calamari?"

"Yeah, whatever the Japanese word is. It was delicious."

"Calamari is Italian," I correct him.

"Oh, *come on!*" He pretends to be upset, but his dimple is showing. "How are you so much more mature than me? With all your food knowledge and grammar and world travels. You're making me feel like a chump, Lena."

I roll my eyes. "You are not! You just need to teach *me* something. Something I know nothing about. Like baseball."

"Really?" He sounds skeptical, but I can tell the idea excites him.

"Yeah. Why not?"

"Okay. Well, I could take you to the batting cages, I guess. Would you really like that?"

"Yes, let's do it. How late are they open?"

Carson lifts his brow. "You wanna go tonight?"

"What? You don't want to show off tonight?" I take a sip of water, and then add, "I did."

A full, giddy, irresistibly handsome smile unrolls on his face.

"Okay, first I'll have you watch and take note, so you can see what I'm doing," Carson tells me, swinging the bat low as he plants his feet a measured distance apart. We stand under the fluorescent light, both of us inside the chainlink cage. It's just us here because Carson has special privileges, which was a flex and I know it. "Just remember, I'm a little handicapped with these nice clothes," he tells me, positioning himself to teach a good swing.

I stand a fair distance away, trying to watch his form and *not* only his body... which is a challenge.

"Keep your hands close on the bat like this. And then pull them back while putting your foot out at the same time," he says, emphasizing with his voice each new point he makes. "Then you have to push your back hip towards the ball with your hands following the same movement, like this." He motions in time and I am *very* much taking note of him and his hips. "Then you have to push the knob toward the ball, swing, make contact, put some extension in your arms. And then..." He pulls the bat through the air so the end reaches his back shoulder. "Follow through. Got it?"

"I'd like to see it in practice," I tell him. "I'm a visual learner."

He nods. "You got it." Then he hits the switch with his foot, it whirs in response, and he gears up to hit.

I stifle a laugh. In any other context, Carson might pick up the hints I'm dropping. I'm fully checking him out, but his one-track mind is on coaching me through the perfect swing. It's kinda cute.

A ball hurtles toward him and his every instruction plays out in one swift motion. His hit is both beastly and precise. Truly something to behold, this guy.

He turns the machine off. His eager face finds me. "That help?"

"Yep." I bend down to take off my patent leather high heels because there's no way I can do that in these shoes. "I might still need some guidance."

"Yeah, sure."

I plant my feet and Carson nitpicks with instructions before he finally gets to touching me. The part I was looking forward to. His hands push mine around the end of the bat. He's talking, but I'm not really taking in anything other than his adorable excitement. With his strong grip adjusting my hips to show me the motion, I follow as well as I can.

But him touching me like this... I'm dying. *Dying.*

"You ready?" he asks.

"Yeah," I say, but I haven't really registered my answer.

He taps the machine on.

I drop the bat.

And I grab him by the neck with both hands so I can give up totally on our *no kissing* agreement. I have to kiss him. Carson grunts in surprise, but he caves right away, kissing me back. His strong arm curves around my low back and he pulls me up close.

I really am weak for him. I *never* had the upper hand. The way his lips press into mine, I'll remember forever. I'm not forgetting him for a *long* time.

If ever.

He forces himself away and startles me with a yell. "Lena!"

A ball slams in our direction, but Carson catches it bare-handed. It's so fast I had no idea it was coming until I hear the loud smack in his palm. He drops it immediately and shakes his hand out. He turns the machine off.

"Ow! Eye on the ball, Lena," he says, a smile trailing after his words.

"I thought it was 'eye on the prize.'" Oh God, what is he *doing* to me??

Carson grabs my arm and tugs me toward him. "You are something else." And he kisses me again. I could stay here, barefoot in a fluorescent lighted metal cage, forever. So long as his big, rough hands press me to him, and find the nape of my neck, and his fingers tangle in my hair. So long as it's my hands traveling him. So long as we could kiss just like this.

But I should probably give him a break. I pull away and just take him in.

"You weren't really paying attention, were you?" he says.

I twirl one of his spirally curls in my finger. "I was sufficiently distracted."

"I know the feeling."

How did I wind up in something that feels very mutual and still so undeserved? This is honestly the best date I've had in my life. It's a little scary.

I hope Joy will forgive me someday for falling for her brother. Actually, I doubt she's as resistant as she pretends to be. But I still have to be careful.

Up until now, I thought my caution was for her sake. But as I stare into Carson's really, actually beautiful eyes, I know I have to be careful for him, too. I can't afford to break him.

I step away a little further. "I did want to give it a try, actually. I just..."

"Couldn't resist?" That smug grin makes my eyes roll.

"Shut up."

His laugh is warm and I forgive his cockiness. "Okay, well, don't worry if you don't get it the first few times." Carson turns the machine on again. "For a first-timer, you can go a dozen balls without getting a hit."

He doesn't know who he's talking to.

I center myself. My feet find their place. I squeeze the end of the bat and test the edges of my reach. Limber up.

The first ball speeds at me and I don't even try to hit it. It thunks against the plastic sheet on the back wall.

"Just give it your best, Lena." What a cheerleader.

I smirk. That first ball was just to get the timing down.

When the next ball comes at me, I fall into each step he showed me. It's not like I wasn't paying attention, I just really enjoyed the view. I still made note of the details.

Crack! The metallic ring of the bat against the ball echoes in the chamber. The ball flies the other direction, up, stretching the netting taut before it crashes back down to the ground.

"Great hit, Lena! Try to copy that for the next one, but don't worry if you just got lucky."

Silly boy.

I watch the machine. Time it. I won't miss the next one.

The ball speeds my way and I do the same thing. *Crack!*

"Nice!" says Carson.

And three more times, I hit them with the same accuracy. Carson's tips really were good, I'll give him that. Usually, the first try is the only one I have to worry about. I catch on really fast. It's... my thing, I guess.

I tap the switch with my foot and the whirring fades. Carrying the bat to a completely awe-struck Carson, I shove it into his chest. His surprised eyes linger on me.

"I'm a quick learner," I tell him.

"You scare me."

I laugh. I think he's a little serious.

He shakes his head. "No, really. Did you hustle me? At least one of those was a home run."

"No, you're just a really good coach."

"Yeah, right. You're just a... a goddess or something."

I stand up on my tiptoes, putting both hands on his pecs and smiling. "Or something," I say before planting another kiss on him.

BONUS
TRACK 26 -
WISH YOU
WERE SOBER

Joy – October 31st

MAYBE I SHOULDN'T HAVE DRESSED UP LIKE WINNIE THE POOH, but it was really easy. I had an apple-red crew neck top and a cute a-line skirt in mustard yellow. Plus, I bought some yellow knit tights and put my hair half-up in two round bun-ears. A little brown eyeliner to color the tip of my nose. And honestly, I miss being called "Joy Bear" now that I don't live with my brother anymore.

But I kinda wish I didn't look like I was ten. Without the name on my shirt, I feel more like condiments than Winnie the Pooh. Maybe when I'm standing next to Jin in his Piglet costume, people will get it.

Fiona wasn't about the themed costumes this year. She always dresses as a witch, she says. And Krista is always a pirate lady. I learned early that my band/roommates are happy in their set ways, which actually made it easier for me when I moved in last month. They basically gave me a week of orientation and now I know how to stay out of the way. But they've been pestering me about when my boyfriend is going to stay overnight. Asking me if they should go spend the night at the studio so me and Jin can be alone.

Hasn't happened, which is totally fine, but I can't tell if my building nerves are because they keep asking or because I kinda want to take them up on it.

Jin and I have never talked about sleeping together. I mean, not on accident, like the time we crashed on the couch while binge-watching *The Walking Dead*.

I'm not thinking about that type of "sleeping."

There's a knock at my door. Fiona doesn't wait for me to respond before poking her magenta head of hair into my space. "Hey, your boy's here." She winks at me with her way-too-long fake lashes that sparkle. She looks sickly pale with all the dark make-up, but maybe that's part of the look.

"Send him in," I say, adjusting my left bun in the mirror so it matches the right one.

It takes him two seconds because our place is freakishly small. I have no idea what kind of party is going to happen when you can only physically manage ten people in the living room.

I burst into laughter when I see him.

"What?" he says, defensive.

"Jin, you look like someone steamrolled Piglet," I say, sputtering chuckles because it's true. His flat frame with the striped pink shirt and straight shorts betray the cute little creature that Piglet usually is. He has a rounded paper triangle stuck to his nose and those cute teardrop ears, but no one is going to guess what he is. There's just no hope.

"Well, you look good enough for both of us," he says, walking up close to me. His hands rest on my hips and I grin up at him before he leans down to kiss me.

It never gets old. I mean, maybe I'm used to it, but I still adore it when his lips are on mine.

I hum in happiness. Then I ask, "You sure? I kind of look like a Heinz ad."

"No, no. You look great." He pushes me away so he can check me out from top to bottom. "Ooh, yes. I'm glad you're taken." He laughs and pulls me in for another kiss, the paper stuck to his nose tickling mine.

"Can I *please* close the door?" says a familiar raspy and teasing voice. Krista, my other roommate and bandmate.

I peek past Jin. Krista's decked out in shimmery gold makeup that pops against her dark brown skin and bright emerald side-buzz. I can't tell if the lacy black bra she's in is part of her outfit or if she just hasn't located the rest of her costume yet.

"It's okay," I tell her.

"Yeah, Imma just close you two lovebirds off and escape the *nasty*."

I'd assume she was talking about something more illicit than just kissing, but knowing her extreme distaste for PDA, I'm sure that our googly eyes are enough to make her retch.

I weave past Jin. "Wait! What time is everyone getting here? I kinda wanted to run to the corner store."

She eyes me, or really, she eyes my get-up. "Rich'll eat you alive lookin' like that." Rich is the owner and most frequent clerk. He's no nonsense and kind of sexist, but there's a good heart in him somewhere, I'm sure.

"I'll go with her," Jin assures her.

Krista lets out a single laugh. "You even more, Jinglet."

I giggle.

She lands her gold-dusted eyes on me. "If you do go, I need tampons."

That's so like Krista. No shame. She's not shy, she just knows how she feels and she's very direct about it.

"No problem," I tell her. Then I look at Jin, amusement coloring my next question. "You still want to come?"

"You think some feminine items scare me? I survived a tiger mom. I can handle it."

"No way, Jan-di's not a tiger mom! Is she? I thought tiger moms were like dance moms but with, like, everything."

"Kinda," he says. "She's not like that anymore, but she had some tiger ways about her in the past. Why do you think I went for Piglet instead of Tigger?"

I can tell he's using the context for a joke. He already told me he played along to wear pink.

"Whatever you say, Jinglet," I say, the corner of my mouth turned up.

"You might want to slow up on the rum and coke, sister!" Fiona yells into my ear. Her wide-brimmed spiderweb hat tickles my hair. The music and the people are far too loud right now, but it's a lot more fun with a little alcohol. I look down at my red Solo cup and examine the wavering brown edges of my beverage.

"But it's so yummy!" I yell back, giggling and warm. "Where's Jin?"

"Be—ink—sta at ch—sin the co—er," she says.

"WHAT?"

"BEA-TING KRIH-STAH AT CHESS," she enunciates loudly, pointing to the corner of the living room. Sure enough, I see my bubblegum-pink pillar of boyfriend hunched over a chess board. I bob through the holiday-morphed bodies, a drop of my drink spilling on the back of my hand. I decide to take another drink so it's not so full.

I get to a decent space in front of people who are watching the chess game and talking to each other. Too much glittery skin and body odor mixed with over-sweet perfume. I take another drink because, really, this drink is super tasty.

"This seat taken?" I say, giggly and definitely without my normal amount of already low grace. I plop myself on Jin's lap and some of my drink splashes on the floor.

A girl dressed as a feathery white angel shoots me a glare. "What a slut," she says loud enough that I can hear her.

Angel girlfriend clearly doesn't know that I'm still a virgin. "You don't even know!" I say to her and sip more rum and coke.

Her jaw drops and Krista says, "Damn, Joy!" I might be mistaken since the edges of my judgment are kinda fuzzy, but she sounds impressed. I lift my drink to her because, why not? I feel kinda cool impressing Pirate Krista even though I don't know how I did.

And another big swig.

The girl bends down to me. "Are you sure that *he* wants *your* ass cheeks on him?"

Suddenly liquid spews from my mouth because I'm laughing at the way she emphasized "ass cheeks" and, like, who says that?

It takes me a second to realize I spit in her face. I laugh even harder.

Krista plucks my cup from my hands. "That's enough of this!"

I wipe my dripping mouth with my sleeve.

The angel girl's devil friend returns with some paper towels and the girl dabs her face. "Who the hell do you think you are?" she says as she removes my spit drink from her overdone face.

Oh, she's *mad*. How did I not realize that? "Oh my gosh, I'm so sorry! You just, the way you said 'ass cheeks' was so funny!"

Jin finally moves a pawn and turns to our conversation. Then his arm wraps around my waist and he talks loudly so the soda-coated girl can hear him. "Pooh Bear's ass is safe with me."

I erupt into a fit of giggles again. I CANNOT believe Jin just said "Pooh Bear's ass!" GOODNESS. I snort.

"Ava, did you ever meet our new lead singer?" Krista asks her as she gestures to me. I grin wide.

This Ava person is frozen and wordless. She rolls her eyes and leaves, her friend following.

"We dated a few months back," Krista informs us, her voice amplified but casual. "Decided she likes pretty boys more than tough girls, I guess."

"Clearly you deserve better," Jin says. "Your move."

Krista adjusts her captain's hat so she can see the board better. I nuzzle my head into the crook of Jin's neck. He smells like jasmine again. I smell like rum, probably. He's not drinking tonight. Besides that, he doesn't drink much anyway.

And neither do I, which is obvious to everyone who has spoken two words to me in the past two hours.

I'm buzzed and happy. Actually, I'm probably drunk and happy. Jin's hand on my stomach fills me with tingly warmth. Could be the booze. But as I sit on his bony legs and stare at the old popcorn ceiling, I'm doubting that my mood has much to do with inebriation.

I started drinking two hours ago because I was in a room full of mostly strangers who are all older than me. I feel like a little kid trying to impress the cool, older kids. Not an unfamiliar feeling given my brother was always kinda that figure in my life. I still hoped the alcohol could help it.

But right now, I know it's not the alcohol that eases my anxiety. It's Jin. I melt into him.

I love him more than anyone else I know.

My lips graze his ear. "When are you done with your game?"

"Won't be long," he says, eyeing Krista.

"Hey!" she responds defensively. "If you beat me in under ten moves, you owe me fifty bucks!"

"Since when does the loser get the prize?" he says.

"I want you to take me to your apartment, Jin," I say in his ear. I feel him tense. I realize after the words have left me just how sultry I sounded. There was no mistaking the alcohol-induced suggestiveness of it.

Krista stands up from the stool. "Okay, never mind. I'm out. Forfeit. Y'all get outta here with that mess."

"Is everything okay?" Jin asks me. I shift so I can see his face better.

"Yeah, of course," I tell him. I'm calmer than I should be in this pounding room. "I just don't really want to be here."

"You'd feel better at my place?"

I lay a kiss on his cheek and then smile at him. "Definitely."

He rubs my back, looking into my eyes for a long moment. I cock my head and watch the room sparkle in the reflection of his dark eyes. Eventually he says, "Okay."

I head to my room and pack a few things into my famous Justin Bieber bag. Some leggings and a sweater, my toothbrush, and then I kinda don't know what else I should grab, but I also don't really care right now. I take my wallet and phone out of my purse. That's enough, I'm sure.

I really want another drink before I go, though. I bought all that soda at the corner store, after all.

Jin told me he'd be waiting at his car out in the lot, so I hastily craft half a Solo cup of rum and coke and down it as a final farewell.

What am I doing?

Right. Walking down the concrete stairs. The cool October air feels pretty nice. The steps are pretty wobbly. I really have to focus so I don't skip any. 1-2, 1-2, 1-2, oh hey! I see Jin's white car right under the streetlamp. I giggle and walk over there.

I miss a step here and there, but I'm actually pretty good at remaining upright! Go me!

I crash my body into his car, hugging the roof and grinning up at him. He stands on the other side, staring at me. He's so pretty.

"Let's go!" I say, and fumble to open the door before I crash into the passenger seat. Click the buckle.

He's still just staring at me.

"What?" I say. "Are we going?"

"Yeah," he says, shaking his head. The radio blares some ethereal synths and hard beats and I love it. Halsey, her voice all cool and crystal clear. I know the words and sing them loud. I shake my hair and pound my palms against his dash to the beat.

Before I know it, the passing streetlights have led us to his tower. It's a brand new build, sleek like a sheet of metal. I know he has a roommate.

Zane. Nice guy.

I also know Zane is gone for tonight.

Jin drives into the underground garage, circling to the passenger door to offer to help me out. I'm still loopy, so I grip his hand more than usual just to steady myself. We walk into the building.

"Should I make you some tea when we get up there?" he asks, when the bronze mirrored elevator doors close.

"Oh yes! That sounds good," I say. I've gone to Jin's apartment many times, but never at night.

What am I doing? Jin's tugging on my arm. I'm leaving the elevator.

I follow him in the well-lit hall, super clean as always. He pushes his heavy brushed metal door open and we walk onto his super clean apartment. The biggest mess he and Zane make is a bunch of envelopes on the counter and whatever little pieces of junk end up in the key dish.

Jin walks over to his electric kettle, filling it with water and turning it on so the blue light fills the pot. It hisses immediately and he gets down the metal tea canister, identical to the one he has at his house in Willow Haven.

I stare out of his massive window, into the city lights and glittering Portage Bay. He's on the twelfth floor, so the view is impressive.

The sound of a tea cup settling in front of me grabs my attention. The aroma of jasmine rises with the steam.

"Feeling better?" he asks.

"I feel better because of you, Jin." I can sense that it's the kind of unfiltered truth that doesn't need me to be drunk in order to say it.

"Me too. I'm glad we're together. And that it's quiet," he says, sipping his tea. "I was missing you at the party."

"I don't want to go home tonight," I say. "I want to stay here."

That's the sort of unfiltered truth that kinda needs the alcohol.

"Okay, sure. If that's what you want," he says. He's so calm and accepting and not at all picking up what I thought I was hinting at.

So, I guess I'm getting off this barstool, leaving my steaming cup of tea on the granite counter and pulling him by his silly pink shirt to kiss me. Sometime in the night he lost that pink paper nose along with those ears. I wrap my arms around his neck and full-on make out with him. I pause to hoist myself onto the counter to sit and then I yank him back to me, nice and level with his height.

His mouth tastes like jasmine tea, still warm like a cozy fireplace. I love how welcoming he is to my kiss, and how every nerve in my body rises in bliss when he does something different. Stroking my hair. Thumbing my cheekbone. Grazing the small of my back.

I don't want it to stop. I hold his head in my hands and keep kissing him, over and over.

"Joy," he says, muffled by my lips.

"Yeah?" I answer, muffled by his.

"Can I—" Kiss. "—catch my—" Kiss. "—breath?" Slightly lingering kiss.

I pull back. "Yes. Sorry." I smile, knowing my face is flush, especially my lips. Just like his are.

He walks over to his phone, snatching another sip of tea while he thumbs through his screen. "I'm gonna ask Zane if I can just take his bed so I don't have to sleep on the couch."

"Why?" I blurt, barely registering that I've said it aloud.

"We can't stay in my bed together," he says, matter-of-factly.

I hop off the counter, but wobble a bit too hard and stumble. Jin dashes over and steadies me. I look up at him, wondering why he won't hold me a little closer. "I thought you'd stay with me in your room."

"I can't do that, Joy."

I don't know if I've sobered up or not, but I'm definitely not as dizzyingly happy as I was a few seconds ago.

"Why not?"

"First of all, you're drunk. When you were sober and we accidentally fell asleep on the couch, and nothing even happened, you were really upset. I won't take the chance that you won't be upset when you wake up tomorrow."

"So, what if I was sober?" I can hear it in my voice. The slurring. Then there's the long blinks. I wish the giddiness were still here.

"Then I could have an honest conversation with you about what this sort of thing should look like for us."

"This sort of thing? What does that even mean?"

"You know, boundaries, and what... what we want out of our relationship."

I blink at him. "What?"

"This is why we can't talk about this right now. You're foggy-headed."

"But you were cool with kissing me!" What am I doing? Why am I arguing?

"I know you're okay with kissing me, Joy. But we can stop that until you're sober, too."

"No! What? What the heck, Jin?" I giggle. Okay, some giddiness remains. "I don't want that, I'm just... you're right. I'm *drunk*. I've never been drunk before. I can just say things that are on my mind and they're out there. Bam! You know? I want to kiss you still. Sleep on the couch or whatever, but I want to keep kissing you."

Jin laughs at me. "Okay, deal."

He walks over to me and places his warm lips gently on mine. They're so smooth and perfect and floral. I'm getting sleepy.

My eyes peel open, looking at his gorgeous face. "You're so perfect, Jin. Your face and your-your heart and your super... good brain. I'm gonna have to marry you someday, like for real, for real."

Oh, look. More unfiltered truth.

"Oh, really?" He's obviously amused by my rambling.

But I'm not just rambling. I'm only sober enough to know I'm not.

I put my cheek against his chest. "I've thought about it from when we started dating. When you said you were all the way in love with me. I knew. You're the one. And all the time, you prove it." I look up at him.

"Really?" he asks. That amusement is gone now.

My unfiltered truth is escaping, and the more that comes out, the sleepier I get.

"So I try to prove it, too, you know? I try to be... try to be the one you need. But I don't know if you'll ever need me as much as I need you. So I have to marry you or you'll just... you know, you'll find some actually grown up woman who gives you more than I can."

He cups my head and steals my tired gaze.

"That will never happen," he tells me, his voice low and serious. "I need you way more than you know."

"Really?" I ask, sounding like a pitiful child.

"Joy, I don't know if you'll remember how much I mean it tonight, but yes. I need you. And I'll make sure to remind you when you're sober enough to fully understand how much I still mean it."

He kisses me, sweetly. Then he runs his hand down my arm and grabs my hand, pulling me to his room.

"Let's get you to bed, Winnie the Pooh," he says. "You need to sleep."

I giggle. "Whatever you say, Jinglet."

BONUS
TRACK 27 -
I'LL WAIT

Joy – November 1st

I PEEL MY EYES OPEN TO THE COOL WHITE WALLS OF JIN'S BEDROOM. He has floor to ceiling windows on either side of his bed, the soft morning light from the overcast sky filtering through. I'm toasty warm in his heavy white comforter and I scrunch my body up before stretching out and wondering how I got so lucky.

That's when the headache comes pounding in like a bass beat through a bad subwoofer.

Oh, God. Is this a hangover?

I rub my forehead and reach for my phone and tap the screen. 8:42 a.m. Do I still have my Winnie the Pooh makeup on? Last night's a little fuzzy.

But I remember why I'm here, so points for me!

And I recall that I totally came onto Jin with some strong, alcohol-encouraged force. I squish my face with both hands and try to remember how he reacted.

Oh, right. He was gorgeous and perfect, body, mind, and soul. As always. He didn't take advantage of my inebriation. Many, *many* points for him.

I sit up and realize I borrowed one of his T-shirts. It's jersey-knit and glorious. A small, lime-green pillar on his nightstand catches my eye.

A green juice. It reads *Cafe Charlotte* on it. Next to it, there's a note that reads, "In case of hangover." With a little heart. I picture Jin writing it and I'm enveloped in happiness, headache be damned.

I take a sip and am hit with such strong ginger, I almost spew it all over Jin's white blanket. It's a miracle that I don't. My cue to get out of bed, I think.

I stumble into the obtrusive brightness of Jin's living room. He's sitting on the couch, working on his laptop.

In his *glasses*. How I love him in glasses.

Jin looks over at me. "Hey, you're up. How are you feeling?"

"Well, the juice is necessary," I say, holding it up before I take another spicy drink.

"That bad?"

I swallow. "Nah. I'll be fine. What are you up to?"

Jin looks like a model in those dark, rounded frames. "I just sent my paper, so... I'm free for the rest of the day."

That's my boyfriend. Accomplishing life in the wee hours of the morning.

I plop onto the cloud gray couch next to him. "Awesome. I have a paper I'm procrastinating from, so I'm free too."

I grin at him, but my stomach flutters. Holy crap, we're both free. And alone. Jin sets his computer on the glass side table.

"When's Zane get back?" I ask.

Jin checks his watch and then says, "Sunday."

I burst out laughing. "Why did you check your watch?"

Jin spits out a laugh and shakes his head. "I don't know."

Then we sit, silent. Reading the air. Waiting to decide what this moment could mean.

Jin cuts the silence. "So, what should we do?"

I shrug. "Maybe make out or something."

"I was thinking Pike Place Market, but your idea's fine too."

I love how we tow the line between cheesy and suggestive. I reach up to take his glasses off so they aren't a casualty of the kissing I intend to do. Jin tenses a bit as my body crosses his to put them on the table beside him. We haven't even gotten started and he's super into it already.

Despite my pounding head, I'm so glad I'm sober.

I kiss him softly at first, my palm rubbing his jaw and neck. Ginger still tingles my lips, and as the kiss gets deeper, I'm struck by how thoughtful he is. How he doesn't force anything, but he's ever-present. I don't let him go, drinking up this delicious moment. His gentle hands run along my side and graze my shoulder. My whole body is twinkling stars. I can't get enough.

Jin's lips cure me. I'm entrenched in bursting affection for this man. I love the way he feels, but mostly who he is.

I don't want to stop. I climb on top of him without letting go of our kiss. He doesn't fight it as we press against each other in new ways. My heart lifts like a crescendo. I'm on the edge of getting carried away.

I want him so much.

"Joy," he whispers. "Hold up."

I pull back. "Yeah?"

Jin's eyes meet mine. There's sweet hesitation in them. Of course he would ask me first, before things went further. I'm ready to say *yes*.

"I can't do this," he says.

"Oh." I try to sound light, like I'm not... shocked. Or disappointed. Pretty sure I fail at both.

His fingers are feather-light as he pushes me away. I return to the seat beside him. Embarrassment floods me and the headache returns. Was I reading him wrong?

We're both tousled a bit from the encounter, my heart still pounding.

I bite my lip. "Is it because of what happened to me? Because I don't want—"

"No," he cuts in. "It's not that."

Oh, no. It's something else. My nerves take a hasty retreat from bliss to panic. "What's wrong?" I say in an exhale.

He looks at his lap, his brow tense. "I'm worried it's a dealbreaker."

Five million possibilities scatter into my brain, but none of them stick. I have no idea what could possibly be a dealbreaker.

Jin swallows hard and fiddles with his hands.

"What, Jin?" I prompt, running low on patience even though I shouldn't. But he's freaking me out.

His dark eyes snatch mine. "I'm not ready to have sex with you. Not yet."

I blink, nod, process. "Okay." Not a *dealbreaker.*

He frowns. "It's not..." He looks off, in search of the right words. "I *want* to, I just. I can't."

My stomach drops. "You *can't?*"

He sighs, frustrated. "I mean, I'm *capable.*" He winces. "I just can't, we have to wait."

"Okay. How long?"

He squeezes his eyes shut, like he's bracing for something. "This might be the... you know."

Dealbreaker.

"Until we're married," he breathes, almost wistful.

I wish my mouth wouldn't hang open and my eyes wouldn't blink so rapidly, but here we are.

Marriage. Not what I expected.

"I get that it's super old fashioned," he says, sounding small and worried. "But I can't risk it. Not again."

"Again?" I guess that answers the question of Jin's virginity status.

Even though I didn't *really* wonder, it never came up.

"Yeah," he says. His face is downcast, like he's in pain trying to talk. "I'm sorry I never brought it up. I understand if... if you don't—"

"You *seriously* thought that would be a dealbreaker?"

His eyes widen and he hesitates. "...Yes. Is it not?"

Goodness. After everything we've been through. After our intense fall and the perfection our relationship has been so far. I mean, just that overpowering ginger juice he bought me is enough proof that he's worth waiting for, even if it's hard.

I angle myself so I can face him. "Jin, I *love* you. I *want you*, too, don't get me wrong. But I'd do anything for you. Including wait." I scan his awesome body before making eye contact again. "Though it's a lot to ask."

A laugh shudders out of him. "Joy, you have *no* idea."

I slap his shoulder. "Shut up, you're not making it easy."

Jin leans in and kisses me hard for one long second. After, he gets off the couch and grabs his laptop and glasses from the side table. "So, there's a huge old tea shop at Pike Place, I thought we could go check it out. And maybe get donuts."

My heart warms at his words. And my stomach. Goodness, he's worth it.

Shouting fish throwers, check. Bronze pig selfie, check. Super sweet and juicy fruit samples, check. Delicious, headache-curing perogies, check.

I should say this was the best possible outcome for today. Food-hunting in the chilly humidity, wrapped in Jin's heavy wool coat. There are Thanksgiving and Christmas displays out in some corners of the market. Clove and cinnamon already dance in the air, uplifting my heart.

But...

Something has been haunting me like the Halloween decorations that are left up on this fruit kiosk.

I can't risk it. Not again.

Jin didn't elaborate. Is there a reason or am I overthinking it? Probably overthinking.

I traded Jin's t-shirt for my red turtleneck from last night's costume. I'm counting the minutes I have left with him because I cannot be late to rehearsal tonight. Not with the show at Metro Alley tomorrow.

I need the practice more than anyone. Metro Alley seats like five hundred.

"You look nervous," Jin says, squeezing my hand through our interlaced fingers. "Are you worried about the show?"

I shake my head, in awe. "How did you know that? How do you always read me so well?"

He shrugs. "Quick *noon-chi*, I guess."

"*Noon-chi?* What's that?"

He looks off trying to figure out how to explain it. "It's like... reading the room. Taking the time to sense how people are feeling and how to respond."

"A Korean thing, then?"

"Kind of. Everyone has some level of *noon-chi*. Try it. What kind of room are we in? Think feeling or what's unseen more than what's seen."

I look around, noting the bustling stands and bundled up shoppers. People carry paper bags and walk fast, others are stopped and eating some produce or looking at the displays more closely. The fish throwers hype up the energy when they yell out to one another. People grin wide, especially the little kids with their rosy cheeks and noses.

Feeling. Hmm. "I think most everyone in here is happy to be here. They're intrigued and having a nice time."

He nods. "Okay, then," he says, "Is there anyone who *isn't* matching that?"

I take a closer look, scanning the market, but all I can think about is how I kind of wish I were happy and carefree like everyone else. Then it registers.

"Me."

"Come on," he says, wrapping his arm around my shoulder, "Let's go talk."

We find a table in a quieter part of the indoor space. Still not super private, but it's not in the fray of people walking back and forth between the shops.

Sitting across from me, Jin scoots his chair in, the metal scraping against the floor. "So," he starts, "what's bothering you?"

I stare at his sparkly brown eyes and sigh. I can tell my nose is pink from the chilly air sneaking in from the outside.

"Do I have bad *noon-chi?*"

He smirks a little, and I'm guessing I used the word wrong. "Why do you ask?"

"Because... I don't know. It feels like I'm lacking."

"In *noon-chi* or in something else?"

My shoulders fall. He's onto me. "Something else. And it's not about the show tomorrow. I still have jitters, but we've performed four times already, so I feel fine about being on stage. It's that... even you mentioning *noon-chi* or whatever reminds me that we don't know each other that well. And this morning, you know, on the couch..."

He nods. "Right. I should've told you sooner."

"No, that's not what I'm saying. What I mean is... I didn't even know if you'd been with anyone else. I still don't really know why you want to wait." I hastily add, "Even though I respect it, totally."

"You want to know everything," he gathers.

"Of course I do."

Jin heaves a sigh and avoids looking at me. I hate that he doesn't want to tell me. I hate it because I don't know why he won't. Have I not proven myself?

"I really didn't want to do this in public, but I'll tell you now if you want me to."

I look around. The space around us is emptier than it was a minute ago, but there are people within earshot. I weigh my options. If he's willing to reveal whatever this dark secret is, should I ask him to?

"Why would you rather not be in public? Is it... like, graphic or something?"

"No." He gazes at the ground. His voice is small and shaky when he says, "It's just hard to talk about."

I can't do this to him. "Okay, then tell me later."

He makes eye contact again, chewing his lips, before breathing out a sigh of relief. "I will. Today."

I lean forward and decide to change the subject. "So, I have a question of an entirely different nature that I've been meaning to ask. Why does everyone call you 'Jin' and not 'Woo-Jin' like your mom does?"

Jin smiles, his mood completely altered. "When I started elementary school, I actually went as Woo-Jin Park. In second grade there was this kid who thought my name was *Eugene*, so he said it was the same as his dad's name. I thought it was weird that I had the same name as this kid's dad because he was a redhead, and, like, how could his dad have a Korean name? But he told me his dad went by *Gene* and asked if I wanted to go by that, too. And I was like 'sure,' so that's what my friends called me."

I squeeze my eyes shut and squeal a tiny bit. "I can't handle the idea of little Jin in elementary school!"

"Hey, Joy?" he says, rubbing his paper cup and looking down, a notable dip in the happy tone.

"Yeah?"

"Do you... *like* the Korean side of me?"

I'm suddenly very confused. "What?"

"I know that... interracial couples have it harder sometimes. I just want to know you really want *everything* that comes with it."

I try to imagine what he's thinking, like he showed me earlier.

Something remains unsaid, but I can't think of what would keep me from him. I have yet to figure out what *everything* actually is.

One thing I do know: *everything* means green juice when I have a hangover. *Everything* means respect and love in ways I never thought existed.

I lean in closer and squeeze his hand. "I still mean it, Jin."

His shoulders relax and he offers me a soft smile in acknowledgement. It fades and I notice a tremor in his bony hands. "I'll *always* mean it, Joy."

Whoa.

How do his words make me feel like I'm floating? Like I'm on top of the waves of a melody.

Always.

"Tea time?" he says, as if he didn't just flip my world on its head with that word.

I laugh and we leave the table to walk up the steps toward the second floor where our desired location is. A vast array of aromatic herbs and spices wafts over to us as we ascend. It's floral and decadent with seasons and nature and the essence of potent seeds. There's something like a rosy peach that hovers in front of all the smells.

Jin inhales deeply and excitement registers on his face. His tea nerd persona is not struggling to make an appearance and I am here for it.

We enter the scent-rich store and I'm impressed by the many walls of jars. There are teas galore, as well as spices and herbs and trinkets and tea sets painted with intricate scenes. The stuff of Jin's dreams. I turn to witness his reaction.

Frozen. Slack-jawed. An open smile unfolds. My best experience here is definitely to just watch him.

Jin examines the hand-written labels, sniffing and sighing. Grinning ear-to-ear. Then he gasps and reaches up much higher than I can.

"Assam! I've been looking for a good assam," he says, his eyes traveling the jar. He unscrews it and inhales. "I have to get some, right?"

"I would buy you a thousand pounds of assam if you'd always be this happy," I say.

"I am happy. I love this place. Why haven't I come here before?"

I laugh. "I'm glad you waited so I could witness Jin in Tealand."

Jin latches onto my face with both hands and kisses me hard on the forehead. "You're the sweetest girlfriend ever, Joy."

I blush. It doesn't happen often now that I'm used to all of Jin's amazing compliments, but this time I feel the heat in my cheeks.

I love him happy. His eyes are so bright and his smile is gorgeous. I never want it to end. Is it possible to love someone else's happiness this much? I want to build a tea shop with five thousand varieties just for him. For his *hobby*.

"What kind of tea do you think you'd like?" he asks, perusing the glistening wall of jars.

"I don't know... I like it whenever you make it."

"Strawberry white tea?" he asks.

I shrug. "Sure!"

"No, I need you to be pickier. It has to be the tea that reminds you of today."

"Okay..." I scan the room, but there is so much to choose from.

I don't want it to be too normal. My eyes wander along the colorful, mostly dark green or brown dried leaves. There's one that looks laced with shriveled orange petals, red flecks, and dried pale green leaves. *PEACH AMBROSIA.*

I reach my hands around it and I can already tell this is the one. The floral peach jumps out at me like a bouquet of fruits. My mouth waters when I unscrew the top.

"Smell it," I demand.

Jin leans over and sniffs. "Ooh, yes. It's you."

He spends the next fifteen minutes making a mental list of the teas he wants, from most to least. Not surprisingly, it's a formidable challenge.

"I can't take ten teas, can I?" he asks, half-joking.

I cock my head. "How many were you planning?"

"Three or four. But… I'll go with five."

"Make it seven. Two will be my treat," I say with a smile.

"Then it'll have to be eight with your peach one."

"Round it up. Why not?"

"God, you're the best. What's your ring size again?"

"Five and a half, I think?" I giggle, but my nerves flutter inside. It's not the first time Jin has hinted that he thinks I'm marriage material, like he's planting seeds. Maybe not deliberately. But I have to wonder… are they growing?

Is Jin the *one*?

The last thing I want is my primal urges telling me he is and jumping into marriage. But something about him, something beyond just the physical stuff, draws me closer to that *forever* conclusion every day.

I'd be lying if I said the very serious, non-primal part of me doesn't want Jin to be my husband someday.

I stand in the corner of the tea shop as Jin shows the clerk the teas that he wants to take home. One bag at a time, he makes this girl wish I didn't exist, I'm sure. She suggests a few teas to fill up every slot of those ten teas he wants. He likes loose leaf tea better than sachets, but he buys some tins anyway. And the whole time, I'm wondering if this is the moment where I decide that my full intention is to marry him.

I'm two weeks from being nineteen. This is crazy! I can't be this sure yet.

Right?

After we've checked out and headed back toward the market, Jin reaches down to grab my hand and I love it so much. "You look deep in thought."

Thump thump. "Yeah. I was thinking about my birthday."

"Oh yeah! I wanted to ask if that night was free. There's an opening for a *thing* I wanted to take you to."

"What is it?" I ask.

He pinches his lips in a smile. "A surprise."

"What if I say 'no'? Will you tell me what it is?"

"Nope, it'll be a mystery forever."

I snort. I know off the top of my head that it's open since the band has a show the next day and I'm heading back home for Carson's birthday on the 17th. "Fine, I guess I'll keep it open, then."

"Perfect. Can we go now?" He holds up his bursting bag of teas. "I've got plans."

I laugh out loud. There really is no arguing with that.

"It smells divine." Curls of steam lift off my robin-blue, daisy-dotted teacup, which I bought for moments like this. Jin just poured my tea, a deep orange color that smells like peach perfume.

"I bet it tastes even better," Jin says. "It's not quite ready yet, though."

His internal tea clock is impeccable. It's tuned precisely for each tea, and now he has ten more to figure out. This excites him because he's a dork.

He watches the tea steep, which *to me* is like watching paint dry, but to Jin, tea is like ballet. He looks up at me sometimes, and apparently he's "ruined" a good cup because I "distracted" him from this precious ritual.

He never actually complained about it, though. Can't say I have either.

When our infusers are out and the tea is drinkable, I take a sip. It's a burst of vibrant peach flavor with a hint of floral that keeps it from being strictly fruit. This is the tea that will bring me back to this day. Definitely.

I settle into this moment so I'll never forget it. Half-spinning in the barstool, I drop my cheek into my propped up hand and commit this day to memory.

Waking up in this sleek apartment, peach ambrosia tea filling the air, and Jin spending his free day with me. I love being here.

My eyes land on him, staring off into the city right outside.

He hasn't taken a sip yet.

"What's wrong, Jin?"

"I should stop procrastinating. The thing I couldn't talk about before."

I sit up straighter. "I'm listening."

"So, when I was with Sunny… things got pretty bad." He already told me bits and pieces about his very successful, beautiful, Korean ex-girlfriend. Things were great until she stopped finding his Americanisms cute. She criticized everything about him. Tore him apart. No matter what he did, and it was *a lot* from what he's told me, nothing was enough for Sunny.

"I wanted to break up with her, but… instead I proposed to her."

My heart constricts. Steam from our cups fills the thick air. He *proposed?!*

"You never…" My brow tenses. Engaged? *Really?* "Why?"

He slumps forward and traces the rim of his cup with his finger. "Because… she told me she was pregnant."

BONUS
TRACK 28 –
JANUARY
RAIN

Jin – January, last year

S HE WAS LIKE A REED, so thin like she'd blow away, yet she somehow still immovable. Her sharp beauty steamed like a cup of tea that steeped too long. Hot and bitter and strong, but I loved her.

And my mom loved her.

"Sunny is perfect," my mom always said. "Perfect, perfect, perfect."

Sophisticated and cultured and best of all, Korean. Her warm laugh caught my attention from the first day we met.

Sunny also had the instinct for balancing the elements of a room. Furniture, accents, and plants, of course, but also the atmosphere whenever a person walked in or left. Each room lived and breathed in Sunny's mind.

My house was her big American project. She and my mom would go hunting for pieces every Sunday. It was a privilege to join them, but I was useless. I never saw what they saw in chairs and fabrics and vases and hutches. My mom insisted on antique furniture, but Sunny convinced her to streamline the decor. They made a good team.

We went out in rain and sunshine, to flea markets and consignment shops all over the area. Sunny had a knack for getting the sellers to include delivery right up into the mountains where our house was, which was something to behold.

"When will you let me get to your room, Woo-Jin?" Sunny asked on one outing.

I remember when she asked me that, my mom was there, oblivious. My room was my space and I hadn't let Sunny there yet. I didn't think she'd bother with it. I kind of didn't want her to.

I couldn't look at her when I said it, so I examined a sculpture of a rabbit. "You can leave mine alone."

"Oh no. I'm not leaving it," she said, taking the rabbit out of my hand and putting it back. She snatched my eyes with her intensity. "I'm doing the whole house. Your room included."

Because I loved her, I said yes.

I didn't know that it was her way of getting close to me. I didn't know it would lead to dramatically increased privacy for the two of us with little question from my mom.

I didn't know we'd get closer than ever. And farther at the same time.

Sunny left her mark on me.

"Copper. That's what this wall needs," she said once as she intruded on my studying. I'd gotten used to the feeling at that point.

"No, I'm not doing that."

She ignored my protest. "I bet I can find metallic paint. Or we could do wall tiles. And some black velvet, too."

"I said I don't want to do that."

Her eyes scoured my room. "I don't care what you want. I'm doing it."

At the time, I didn't recognize it as the trajectory of our relationship. Up until the very end, it was always what Sunny wanted. She called the shots and, inch by inch, I became reclusive.

Of course, that didn't please her, either.

You are some excuse for a man, Woo-Jin.

Why don't you take more initiative?

You're not serious enough.

You think good grades impress me?

When Sunny first came to America, she was charmed by it all. Everything was new, pretty, and shiny. She loved how I fit with the culture, initially. We laughed a lot. We ate all kinds of food.

But then, she got tired of it. Our relationship became motions. She motioned, I reacted.

I hoped to become special again when her birthday came around. I wanted to surprise her with a meaningful gift and an unforgettable dinner. I asked Lena to join me in picking Sunny's present.

"She's a raging, manipulative nightmare, Jin," Lena told me on that trip. We sat at a bistro table near the boba shop.

"No, she's not," I argued weakly.

With boba still in her cheeks, she said, "Yes, she is. She's got you strung up like a puppet."

I didn't think it was true. More like a stuck section of wallpaper. I was peeling away.

We found a white gold necklace with an asymmetrical circle pendant. I wasn't sure if she'd like it, but I liked it for her. And I hoped that would be enough.

That night, I showed up at her apartment and texted her I was ready.

She wore a black velvet dress. I wonder now if it was because she was trying to fit the design of the room she made me.

"Your hair is too messy," Sunny said right as she got in my car. "Why couldn't you make it neat?"

"I wanted to be like Ahn Hyoseop," I admitted. I framed my face with my hands the way a lot of Korean celebrities have done, and grinned, trying to be cute.

Sunny's sense of humor faded to nothing when we were together.

"Really?" she said with no amusement. "You're nothing like Ahn Hyoseop. And you never will be if you try too hard."

Trying too hard. Not trying hard enough. Those were my only options.

"The food better be good," Sunny said.

I knew it would be. We drove to an upscale French restaurant, the kind with provincial furniture and Rococo art and a live classical band echoing on the domed walls.

We got seated, sipping water while we waited for the first course.

"This music is terrible," she said.

"I think it's nice." I knew it would upset her, and maybe that was why I said it.

"Why do you have such bad taste? Ugh. I don't know how someone could like that stupid violin. It's like a whining child."

"I like it."

"You need your brain adjusted."

"Why are you so combative? I can have a different opinion than you."

"Not when your opinion is objectively ridiculous, Woo-Jin."

The other couples smiled at each other, enjoying the music. Perhaps they didn't care about the music, just each other's company.

What a concept.

When the white-tie waiter brought out the hor d'oeuvres, Sunny complained about eating with her fingers. When he brought out the salad, Sunny complained about the oily dressing. When he brought out the roast duck, Sunny complained about having to share it and not having her own plate. When he brought out the cheese, Sunny complained that all the food was too rich.

I tuned her out and watched the candlelit evenings of happier people. I relished the violin and piano, trying to recall the name of the composition. I escaped however I could.

"Jin," she said, snapping her fingers at me. I took my eyes off of the city lights I came here to enjoy. "God, why are you so distracted? You need to listen better."

"I don't want to be with you anymore," I blurted. "I'm done. This is over."

I motioned to leave, but it was a terrible move, trying to break up with a manipulative woman. But I hadn't known that's what I'd come there to do. It wasn't planned.

She stabbed her plate. "Sit down, you idiot."

Pretty only goes so far. Sunny's shiny hair and winged eyeliner and full red lips did nothing for me. Nothing. She could've been a bulldog. I was done with her. Forever.

"We're not breaking up, Jin."

"Why not? You don't like me. What's the point?"

Sunny glared at me. "I can make you great."

"Why not find a guy who's already great, then? Seems easier."

"Because I *love* you. And our life is already planned out. Sure, I could find another successful Korean man with good looks like yours, but why would I waste the time? I have invested in you, Woo-Jin. And we are *not* breaking up."

"I don't love you anymore, Sunny."

She gripped me with cold eyes. "Well, that's too bad. Because I'm pregnant."

That was the first night of the most horrible season I've ever been through. But even when she threw the necklace away before we left the restaurant, I really thought I was happy.

All of that happiness turned out to be a lie.

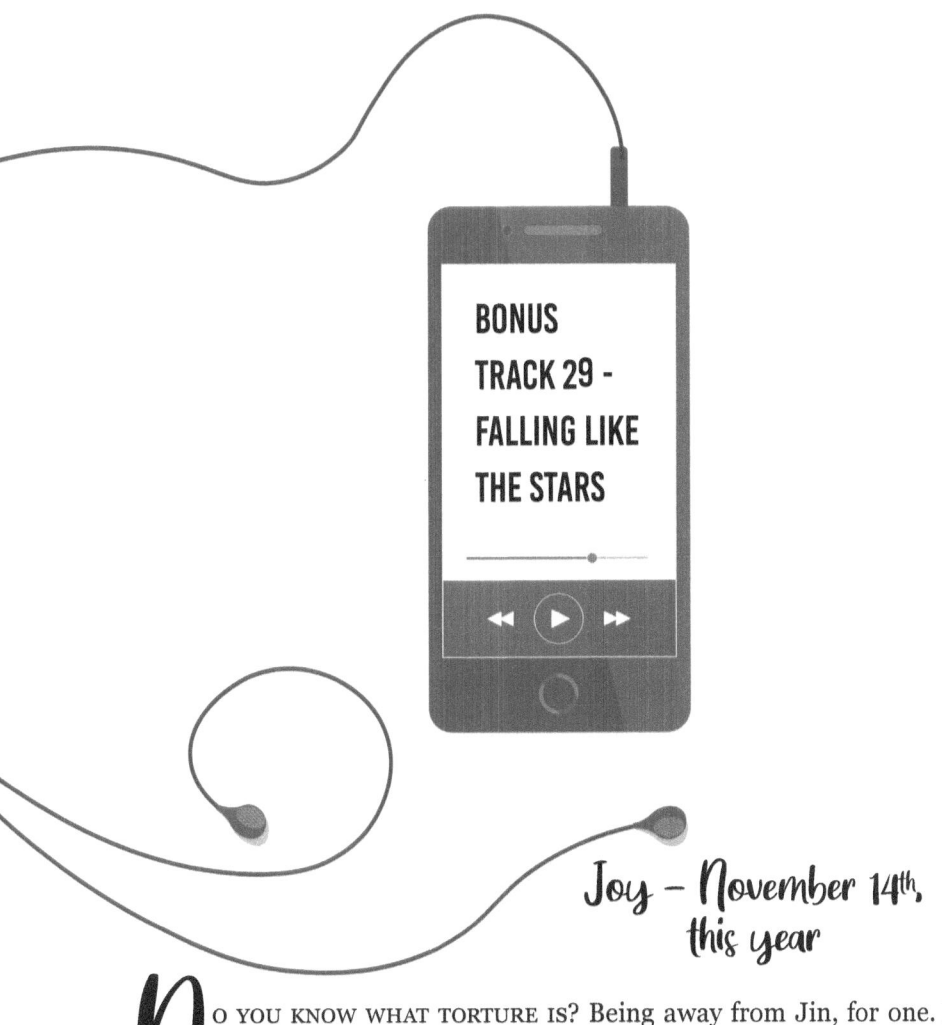

BONUS
TRACK 29 -
FALLING LIKE
THE STARS

*Joy – November 14th,
this year*

DO YOU KNOW WHAT TORTURE IS? Being away from Jin, for one. I haven't seen him for more than thirty minutes since that day at Pike Place.

Another form of torture: Fiona pinning my hair up, which is more like jabbing my skull.

"Ow! Can you lighten up?"

She ignores my request and sizes me up in the mirror. "You sure you don't want something tighter and shorter and blacker and more low-cut?"

I'm wearing my vintage maroon lace dress with the cinched waist and pleated knee-length skirt. I'm putting it with the cream cashmere shawl my mom gave me.

"It's cute, but it won't drive him wild." *Stab.*

I wince before slapping Fiona's hands away. "I'm not *trying* to drive him wild. I'm supposed to be fancy tonight and this is my special occasion dress."

"Okay, but even if you aren't going to do the deed, at least make it hard for him!"

I scoff and twirl around. "It's hard enough for *me!*"

"WOULD YOU BOTH SHUT UP!" The demand comes from Krista, who's playing video games in the living room. I've come to appreciate her distaste for mushy romance talk, especially since that's like eighty-three percent of what Fiona talks about with me.

I face my mirror again. My makeup is muted but still pretty, with a deep purple lip that fits the autumn mood.

I'm so eager to see him. I started working at a bank and then we had midterms and CruxCon shows on top of that. We've had almost no time together the last two weeks, besides when I was sweaty and tired post-show. Late-night phone conversations and long text chains, yes, but tonight, he's in proximity and all mine.

Something deepened when he opened up about his past the day after Halloween. I'd never seen him really cry before. He broke in front of me, folded over on his counter, sobbing into his arms.

The only thing I ever wanted was to be a dad.

Jin's heart is still broken from what happened, but when he shared it with me, I finally understood him.

"He's the one who wanted to wait, Fi," I say, smoothing my skirt. "And he would respect me if it were the other way around. No question."

"Well, I have to try," Fiona argues. "The sexual tension between you two is oppressive."

"Took the words right outta my mouth!" Krista yells, sounds from her first-person shooter game non-ceasing.

Mid-giggle, I hear a knock on the front door.

Jin!

I race out of my room, barely remembering to grab my sparkly clutch. I can't get to the door fast enough.

I open it and Jin stands before me in a sharp grey suit. Goodness, I can hardly stay upright. Probably should have opted for flat shoes.

"Hey," I squeak.

"Wow," he says to me. "You look gorgeous, Joy."

A potent floral scent hits me. I'd hardly noticed the bouquet of white roses in his hand.

"Happy Birthday," he says, handing them to me.

Fiona walks over to us and shouts to Krista, "He bought ROSES!"

There's a lot of playful shouting in this itty bitty apartment.

"You ready?" Jin asks me.

I nod and I shove the flowers in Fiona's direction. "Can you put these in water for me?"

Fiona takes them, laughing. "Okay, yeah. See you kids later."

I walk out of the apartment flooded with happiness. He takes my hand when we walk down the steps, which helps with these strappy high heels I wobble in. I feel like a princess entering a ball, but the ballroom is an asphalt parking lot with weeds growing in the cracks and the spotlight is an incandescent street light. My chariot is a freshly washed white Mazda.

Of course, Jin Park is my prince. My knight in pinstriped armor. He even holds my hand helping me into the car.

Best birthday EVER.

I watch the suburbs pass by as we drive into the big city. The anticipation is a thrill. Even though I don't know what we're doing, Jin said it's fancy, so I'm pretty sure it's *fancy*.

The lights pass through the windows like glowing spirits, guiding us into downtown. Jin's a very attentive driver, so I can stare at him for a while before he realizes.

Oh my god. She was pregnant?

I sigh. I thought that I loved him most when he was happy. That wasn't true. A potent love shows up when someone shatters in front of you and you help them pick up the pieces.

No. She lied.

Sunny manipulated him. She lied about being pregnant because she knew he'd do whatever she wanted.

"The worst part was that I was so stupidly happy. It was the only thing I thought about," he told me. Tears of regret and pain came forth. He had loved something that never existed. Sunny stole from him what even the best thieves can't steal: love.

When Jin learns he's a father for real someday, it'll be soured with that lie. He'll always remember what she did. You can't take expended love back, and Jin gave as much as he could.

He's serene as he drives now. I linger on the memory of our embrace in his kitchen, where our tea went cold. He leaned more weight onto me than he ever had before.

Jin never should've been hurt like that. Just like I shouldn't have been hurt by Tyler. But because of these things, both of us are together. We're here.

"I quit Harvard," he told me at one point. "I wanted the baby more than anything."

And that was when Sunny flipped. When she found out, she let him have the truth, served bitter and cold. There was no baby. She'd wanted a successful, subservient Korean lawyer husband to bend to her high expectations. The stupid thing is that she could've had him.

He would've stayed with her if she loved him back.

Jin's final words told me everything.

You let me go because you loved me. That's why I came back to you, Joy.

The car stops and Jin smiles at me. I look outside for the first time this whole, silent drive. We're at the bay.

The freezing wind crashes into me and I'm suddenly awake in the present. I always forget how windy it gets right by the water.

"You were quiet," Jin says as he helps me out of the car.

"So were you. What were you thinking about?"

"Boring stuff. Mock cases I have to analyze before Thanksgiving."

I shiver and curl up under Jin's arm. "We're not going to be outside, are we?"

He shakes his head. "No, don't worry."

There's no warm shelter in sight. "It sure doesn't look like we're going to a building."

"That's because we're not." He grins.

Jin leads me to a huge yacht and I gasp. The sign in front of the boarding dock reads Port Love Cruises. I'm officially dazzled. The city glitters on the water surface like Christmas lights. The staff are dressed in white ties and waistcoats, like we're walking into a posh gala. The boat is covered in floral garland and there's a live band out on the deck playing something romantic and classical.

I'm breathless.

Jin rubs the small of my back. "Do you like it?"

"I love it. I love it so much. It is a dinner cruise, right? I'm starving."

Jin laughs. "Of course! Three courses."

He knows me so well. And I adore it so much more than I thought possible.

Jin hands our tickets to the tuxedoed gentleman with a literal curly mustache. We walk up the ramp and onto the boat. Inside there are white tablecloths, a row of chandeliers, swirly carpet, champagne at every table, except for one. One of them has two white roses where the champagne would be.

"That's ours," Jin says, pointing to it. He whispers to me, "I said we didn't drink so they wouldn't check your ID. Technically, you're not allowed to be on board."

"Scandalous," I whisper back.

Jin turned 21 on September 25th, so he's a freer man than me. The rule-follower in me would normally be nervous, but I'm not. Even if there was an issue, Jin's lawyer persona would come out and he'd take care of it, like he does everything.

My heart is warm, even if the air is cold and I'm hungry. I don't feel worthy of a date like this. Jin has outdone himself.

The boat shifts and we're off on the cruise. The lights roll by, floating like shooting stars in slow motion. We head outside, where the other guests are enjoying the live music. Most of them are chatting, holding champagne flutes, but a few of them are dancing slow, embracing each other.

"Shall we?" Jin asks, gesturing to the open space.

I crack up. "*Shall we?* You dork."

He shrugs, his hand still open.

I take his hand. "Yes, *we shall*."

I flow into him, settling in against his chest and wrapping my arms around his back. When I look up, my neck is craned entirely because of our height difference, but I don't mind. I press my cheek to his chest and *feel* it all. The ice-cold wind and rocking boat. The vibrations of piano, violins, bass, and trumpets. His hands and heartbeat. When the music swells, I don't think a moment has been more perfect.

I want him to always hold me like this.

But my stomach rumbles.

As people shuffle inside to the dining room, we follow suit hand-in-hand. I've never been so content, which means a lot because I'm super hungry. I would give up food forever in exchange for *Jin* forever.

Physically impossible, but still.

When we sit, Jin looks like he's in a movie in the candlelight on this pretty yacht. Like he's the super slick spy, and I'm the unwitting love interest.

"What?" Jin asks with a grin.

I grab my cloth napkin and spread it across my lap. "I just like you, okay?"

Irresistible, the way he looks at me. Pleased with my fangirling.

A waiter brings out the first course: shrimp cocktail and Caesar salad.

There are only two foods in the whole world that I will not eat.

"Oh my god, this is weird. I hate shrimp cocktail," I say.

"Oh? I guess... I didn't imagine you not liking something."

I laugh. "It's the only thing. And I'm allergic to hazelnuts."

Jin waves down the waiter.

"Is everything all right?" the man asks. He has a napkin draped over his arm and everything.

"Can you take this? We don't want it." Jin hands him the shrimp cocktail. The waiter of course obliges.

I poke at my salad. "You didn't have to do that."

"It's fine. Is it just shrimp cocktail or is it shrimp in general?"

"Well, I don't mind seasoned shrimp in, like, a taco or something. But I hate cocktail sauce. I feel like I can never trust how horseradishy it will be."

"So you don't like horseradish?"

I scrunch my nose. "Not really. That's an ingredient, though, not really a food."

"True," he laughs.

And then we don't talk for a little bit, and Jin stares at me like he has stars in his eyes.

My turn to prompt him. "What?"

"I just like you too, okay?" he argues with a smirk. Then, suddenly, he's solemn. "Actually, I love you. More than I've loved anyone."

Holy... he's serious. My heart thumps deep into my soul. He loves me more than anyone?

The laugh I let out is far more nervous-sounding than I mean for it to be.

"Oh, god," he says, rubbing his knees. "I freaked you out. I'm sorry."

"No, you didn't," I say, but I am kind of freaking out in the best way.

I push my salad around.

Jin Park loves me more than he's loved anyone.

!!!

Jin turns his attention to the window beside us, looking cool even though I know he's freaking out too. His tell is much, much more subtle than mine. It's like an ultra-controlled Jin. Invisible unless you know him.

I want to put him at ease, but I can't tell him to not worry about it. I want to reciprocate, but it feels disingenuous to repeat it back.

Even though it's true. My god.

I take a sip of water and remember something I said to him. On Halloween, when I was nice and drunk and things were just flowing out of me. Before I stole one of his t-shirts and crashed to sleep in his bed.

I'm gonna have to marry you someday like for real, for real.

The waiter brings our dinner to the table, lifting away our salad plates. In their place, a crusted Halibut filet, buttery mashed red potatoes and roasted asparagus.

"Excuse me," Jin says, lifting up my plate to our waiter, "Is this a hazelnut crust?"

The man nods. "Is that a problem?"

"She's allergic. Can you prepare another with no nuts?"

"Certainly," the man says, taking my plate.

How is this all so easy for him? He just internalized what I said and acted on it like he's known me my whole life.

"I'm sorry for springing that on you," he says. "I don't need you to say it back."

I take a sip of water and clear my throat. "I already did, though. When I was drunk on Halloween."

The corners of his lips turn up and he narrows his eyes. "Is that how you really feel?"

"Well, if I had some alcohol, you might get the truth."

"So what you said on Halloween *was* the truth?" His cocky smile flashes before he takes a bite.

I roll my eyes, unable to contain my smirk. "You're insufferable, Jin Park."

His eyes travel me. "And you're beautiful, Joy Becker."

My word. My heart squeezes. I'm melting like the buttery sauce on his plate.

This is definitely not the first moment I've fantasized about marrying Jin.

"Joy Park," I try aloud right as Jin takes a drink. I wince. "Sounds like a nudist beach."

Jin spits water everywhere, dripping from his nose onto his hand. I burst into a full, obnoxious belly laugh. He's stuck there, hunched over and dripping wet, before he coughs and laughs. Finally he wipes his face with his napkin.

I'm still laughing somewhat when I say, "Hyphenating might be better."

"Joy Becker-Park. That sounds good."

Good gracious, hearing him say my potential married name does things to me.

My dinner comes back and we talk about normal subjects again, like how Carson and I call this week of the year "our birthday" since we're only one year and three days apart. And how awkward it'll be to see Lena with him when I go home this weekend, even though we both agree they make sense together. And how Cale landed the solo for the men's choir and earned some shade from a fourth-year who wanted it. Through dessert of fudge-layered chocolate cake, we talk about how I'm learning the finer points of writing cashier's checks at work. How Jin's professor recommended him for a paralegal position at a firm that specializes in the types of civil cases he wants to work in.

"You changed my life's direction," he says, matter-of-fact. "I didn't even know what I wanted. Now, I do."

I need you more than you know.

Our dessert plates are cleared and all that's left are candlelight, white roses, and Jin's steaming cup of green tea. I reach out and pinch one of the soft rose petals.

"Jin," I say, calm like the nighttime tide. "I'm so happy we're together. So happy."

He smiles, and though it shouldn't be a surprise, I know now why he still is taken aback when I say things like that. "So am I."

Everything about this night has been a magical wilderness of hidden wonders and secret ponds, normal conversation and life-altering declarations. I owe it all to him.

Once Jin finishes his tea, we wander the boat and eventually make our way outside. We find a darker part where we can watch the water pass underneath as the city floats by us.

It's almost over.

I shiver in the bay breeze and Jin takes off his jacket for me like the gentleman he is. It's warm from his body heat and way too big. I give him my cashmere shawl and tell him to wear it like a scarf, so he hangs it from his neck and looks no less exquisite than before.

He leans on the railing, gazing out with wind in his hair. I face the other way, leaning my back against it. *Deep breath.*

It's dim and lovely out here. My breath is a cloud and my nose is probably red (thank you, complexion), but even though the air is heavy with cold humidity, I'm as warm as ever.

"I don't know how this birthday could ever be beat."

"Good," he says, and then he leans in to kiss me, tender, soft, full of his love.

When we part, I reach my hands into his jacket pockets to warm my fingers.

And I feel something. Round, small, and metal.

I pull it out.

"Oh no," Jin says when he sees it. "You weren't supposed to—" His words turn into a defeated whisper— *"find that."*

It's a ring. A sparkling, beautiful, gold and diamond… ring.

Despite the fact that I'm well aware of what this tiny object is, I still ask, "Is this a ring?"

Jin sucks in a sharp breath, rubbing his forehead with one hand. "Well, yeah, but I wasn't going to… I hadn't planned to ask you *right now.*"

I gape at it.

He picked a ring.

"It's too fast," I say in an exhale, but not to him. To myself. Like I have to convince myself.

"Yeah, I know. I just," he fumbles his words, "I had this thing about picking a ring as soon as I knew. Having this whole story about how long I carried it around. God. I'm such an idiot."

My eyes are stuck on it. Vintage and understated and perfect. "It's too fast, right?"

Jin tries to shake off the residual panic. He blinks a few times before saying, "Isn't it?"

I saw Jin for the first time when I was lying on the floor, on full display as myself, and I thought he was gorgeous then.

But now... in the waiting, the *hope* for me to say something, I can't imagine him more insanely beautiful. It's so clear he loves me.

I look at the glimmering diamond again.

"Maybe," I murmur. I still can't believe what I have pinched in my red, frigid fingers.

"*Maybe?*" he repeats with an accent of hope, I think.

"How long have you been carrying it?"

He takes a second to answer. "Twelve days."

So he's had it since the second. Right after our day tea shopping at Pike Place. After he told me everything about himself.

Deep breath.

"Um, I know you weren't planning to ask me yet, so you can have it back." I hand it to him. Jin takes the ring in his palm but keeps his eyes locked on me.

"If I had asked you tonight, what would you have said?" His words carry that adorable wariness I fell in love with.

I smirk. "I'm pretty sure that's cheating, Jin."

He hangs his head and lifts his eyes to me. "You call *me* insufferable?"

I walk up close to him and he looks straight down at me. I'm sure to meet his eyes when I ask, "What do you think I'd say?"

Without answering me, Jin leans into a kiss, holding me close against him. I wish this night and this kiss didn't have to end.

Floating in the slow silence, with the stars above mirrored in the water below, Jin palms my face. As he searches for my answer, he sees me. "I think you'd say..."

I finish for him. "Yes."

Joy's Beach Mix

Playlist

TRACK 01 –
GROW

June 12ᵗʰ the summer after

I

F THERE'S ONE THING I'VE LEARNED from having a star pitcher for a
brother, it's that curveballs come out of nowhere. I thought I trained
hard for the game, anticipating the next thing life will throw at me. I
have hit a few home runs. They were a thrill.

But I wasn't ready for the curveballs at all.

I stare out the car window, mood music forcing me to the edge of an
existential crisis like I didn't grow out of them in middle school. I fiddle
with the watermelon pendant Lena gave me, my fingertips raw from
running them over the little gems.

My breath leaves condensation on the window when I sigh, blurring
the trees as they whip past my aimless gaze.

Melancholy is my friend now. At least the list has grown.

"Joy Bear?"

I roll my head in Carson's direction. "What?"

"Still got a couple hours until we're there."

"Yeah."

The road has been straight for a long time, fields and fields of various vegetation spreading out toward the hills on our way to Cannon Beach. It's the trip of my dreams—a beach house right by the sprawling, sandy coastline. Perfect sunset views. All my favorite people. And Cale's bringing his firecracker little sister, Jayla.

Ocean waves and nature and good coffee and fried seafood. Perfection.

It'd be nice if I weren't about to break.

"I *hoped* we could talk," Carson says. "Usually you like that sort of thing."

I peel my palm from my face and look at him. Wistful staring in silence won't fix anything.

"I'm sorry. It's hard to have a normal conversation."

He nods. "Anything to do with Jin and Lena driving down together?"

My heart constricts. "I don't want to talk about it."

I should be more appreciative of how great Carson is at being a self-controlled, engaging person now. But I'm tired. And I've learned that Carson needs me as I am and not as the codependent version of myself.

We sit in silence, my red cheek returning to my palm.

But when the longing tugs on my heart, I give in. "Probably."

"They said they just needed to talk about stuff," he says with a reassuring tone.

"I know."

They've been "talking" a lot lately. Lena's always at Jin's apartment when I stop by, cold tea sitting in front of her. He's always taking her calls in another room because Lena doesn't do well with group conversations. It's picked up this past week. And that's fine. I have to keep it together for them. I'm pushing the edges of my trust and letting him deal with life the way he needs to.

Been harder to steady myself, though.

"Are you weirded out by them being alone?" Carson asks, like a good brother.

"No," I say, lighter than I feel. "I guess I hoped I could have more time with Jin, though."

"You'll get plenty of time with your boyfriend." He raises his brow at me to drive the point home. "Don't worry about it so much! Leave all the baggage and junk back home for the weekend and have some fun."

I nod. Easy for him to say, a lot harder for me to execute. But I have to try, I guess.

"Sorry about the band, by the way," he says. "Wish I'd seen more shows."

"Yeah, it's kinda sad," I say. But it's more than kinda. "There are a few more shows, actually. I'll be fine, but the timing is…"

"Bad?" Carson finishes, "Or is it good?"

"It's both," I sigh. "I needed a break."

The Crux Constellation sort of disintegrated after our Christmas show. Fiona, the guitarist, and Geo, the drummer, were apparently hooking up, which came out when Geo got himself a girlfriend that wasn't Fiona. "Enemies with benefits" is what Krista called them. We pulled through, but then Javed said he was leaving to spend more time with his kids, and like, how could we blame him?

One of those curveballs.

This beach trip is supposed to shake me of the endless dance of altered plans. I sort of wish someone would ask me to change my life for a good reason, though. Even though I'm getting pretty good at rolling with the punches, I wish these curveballs would strike me out already. It'd be nice to be benched for a little while.

Classes are mercifully over and the performances to end our set don't start until next month. I also took the whole week off work, per Jin's persistent suggestion. Even though we're only here for the weekend, it'll be nice to breathe.

I look over at Carson in the driver's seat. At least my brother isn't a source of constant worry anymore.

I force a smile. "I promise, I'm gonna try to have fun."

Carson smiles back. "Good. You deserve it." He slaps the steering wheel. "So, anyway... since I need more collateral on you, tell me the most embarrassing thing that happened on stage."

That breaks my depressive state a bit. I half-chuckle, half-scoff. "Excuse me, I am very professional."

"You're trying to convince me you never tripped on stage?"

I roll my eyes, but... "Okay, yes, I have."

"I knew it." Carson grins in satisfaction, and that's the moment I decide to leave it all behind. All the stuff with the band. The demanding law degree Jin's pursuing. The extra time he needed with Lena. All the weekends he spent back home, missing what would be my last few shows.

And Jan-di's cancer.

TRACK 02 -
KEEP IT
TOGETHER

Still June 12th

MY SPIRITS LIFT WHEN THE GLITTERING WATER BLINDS ME. Chill synth plays on the stereo when I see the ocean, a harmony I didn't know I needed. Gray sand stretches out like a giant blanket under a pale blue sky. Seagulls ride the breeze with no effort.

"Hello, Pacific Ocean," I say, waving back to the waves.

I roll the window down as Carson drives at an easy cruise. The fresh, salty air fills me with hope. It's a beautiful day, I'm headed to a fancy beach house for the weekend, and I will absolutely have the chance to eat clam chowder in a sourdough bowl.

With lungs full of ocean air, I exhale my worries. Carson's curls dance in the breeze, shining like he slicked them with golden oil. He turns off the main stretch of road onto a grassy path with two compressed tire lines. The house with the brown shingle siding and the big baby blue seashell on the front is ours for the weekend.

I get out of the truck, relieved to see Jin's Mazda is already here. No more waiting.

Just have fun.

Carson unlocks the cover of his truck bed to get his stuff, and then I dig mine out. I retired the Justin Bieber bag a while back, replacing it with a duffle bag covered in watercolor pink peonies. The Barbie blanket's also gone since it had a giant hole in it, but the Lisa Frank pillow remains.

I step onto the bumper so I can reach in. Once I have my things, I emerge and wobble a bit.

Jin steadies me.

"Hey, Joy," he says as he helps me down. With no warning, because none is needed, he kisses me.

Jin's lips really help me feel better. So does the resurgence of his AMER-I-CAN, shoulder-flaunting tank that brings back so many good memories of last summer.

"It's good to see you," he whispers in my ear, an extra helping of happiness in his tone. He grabs my things out of my hands, and we go up the cement stairs to the house. "How was the drive?"

"Fine," I try to tap into that happiness. "It's a nice day for a drive. Yours?"

"Good!"

We enter the house in the living room. There's a homeyness to it. Big floral couches with glass top end tables, seashells decorating every surface, big windows that frame the beach horizon right beyond the deck, watercolor paintings of Oregon birds, and a distressed shiplap my mom would fawn over.

I take my shoes off before walking onto the pristine sand-colored carpet. I've gotten used to removing my shoes inside. I prefer it now, actually. It's hard to imagine why it took a Korean boyfriend to convince me to make it a habit.

With his arms still full of my stuff, Jin nudges me toward the stairs.

"Lena and I stopped at this weird Elvis Presley-themed diner for breakfast, and she got the most massive cinnamon roll."

"It was bigger than my face!"

I find Lena through the archway into the kitchen, wearing a denim romper with sunglasses on top of her head. Her arms are already around Carson's neck.

"There's still some left if you want," she tells me with a sweet smile.

Then she kisses my brother. I avert my eyes. I try not to fuss since it's weird for both of them when I'm lovey-dovey with Jin. Despite their intense fights that happen like clockwork every month (and might coincide with a hormone cycle), they're happy. They've never threatened to break up, which gives me hope.

I turn to follow Jin up the curved staircase, but first, I catch Carson's low voice.

"You doing okay?"

"I'm fine," Lena whispers back.

Their eyes are locked, full attention. Carson's hands are square on her shoulders, his brow lifted in concern. For some reason, it forms a small but noticeable pit in my stomach.

"Joy?"

I turn back to Jin, jolted by the sudden guilt of eavesdropping without meaning to.

I should shake it off. I know why Carson's asking her. The same reason she wanted to ride with Jin. They're trying to keep their grip while Jan-di goes through chemo. She's a mom to both of them. My job is to make sure he's okay.

"How are you doing?" I ask him as we traverse the halls, passing vintage maps and black-and-white pictures of girls in bikinis.

Jin looks over his shoulder. "Great, actually! Optimistic about the weekend."

I blink. After two months of bad news piled onto finals piled onto full schedules, optimism has been evasive, especially for Jin.

"That's good to hear," I say, and I mean it.

I follow him into the bedroom designated for the females.

Jayla Thomas has already laid claim to a bed by perching her twelve-year-old self onto the edge of it.

She looks up. "Lisa Frank? Aren't you supposed to be in college?"

Jayla flips through a Cosmo magazine, her neon-pink fingernails catching the light. She's covered in leopard print, which I find pretty rich since she just insulted my leopard pillowcase.

"This pillow is nostalgic," Jin defends. "I hope she keeps it."

"Move on, lover boy! Girls change, and that's a good thing."

I laugh at Jayla's scolding. Jin takes it exactly like I expect him to: with grace and without backing down.

He puts my stuff on one of the three full-sized beds. "I appreciate it when people like what they like, even if they change someday."

"Jayla! WHAT THE FLUFF IS IN YOUR SLIMY HANDS!" Cale does not have the intonation of a question at all. Pure accusation.

"Come on! I never get to read stuff like--"

"NOPE!" Cale marches to her and snatches it, then turns to me with a big, friendly smile. "Hi, Joy! Let's do a duet later!" His big brother glare is back on Jayla. "Do you have any idea what Mama would do to me if she found out you read this?"

Jayla folds her arms. "No, but I was looking forward to finding out."

"Jayla, kill time with something else," he begs. Then, he shakes the magazine, and the glossy paper flops around. "*This* is going on the highest shelf in the whole house!"

Jayla's unamused face is more savage than Lena's. He storms off to find that shelf in another room, and all I can think is how easily thwarted Cale's plan will be.

"He's such a goober." I'm reminded that she's twelve by her word choice.

She leaves the room, so it's just me and Jin. He runs his hands down my arms and pulls me up close to him.

"So," Jin says, "How are *you*?"

"I'm optimistic, too."

I say it, but it's still in the *wishing* phase as far as feelings go. I have to settle for true enough. For his sake.

I won't lie. This cinnamon roll isn't great.

It's more of a multi-layered cake. As I dig into it, I try to enjoy the overly sweet icing. But it's too much, even for me.

Resisting the toothache of a dessert, I consider which duet I want to sing with Cale. We've done a few on his TikTok, which has been fun, trying to get them just right. We got over a million views on one of them. So did my Rainbow Connection song before the views dropped off. Cale's got internet fame now. It's crazy what a ring light and good timing can do on the internet.

"It's too sweet, right?" Jin asks me, noticing my full dessert plate.

I poke the pastry with my fork. "Yeah."

"You *said* I should find something else to do!" I overhear from the living room. I peek over my shoulder to see Jayla staring Cale down. He looks like he's begging God to intervene with the way his eyes are stuck to the ceiling.

"Lighten up, Cale. It'll be fun," Lena says as she takes a seat on the couch.

"Can't we just go to the arcade! PLEASE, FOR THE LOVE OF DDR!"

Jin sips the last drops of his tea, then eyes me. "Should we go see what the fuss is about?"

I nod, and we get up from the table, leaving the beast of a pastry behind.

Lena is nestled under Carson's arm on the couch while Cale's as worried as can be.

"What are we doing?" I ask.

"Truth or Dare! But with stakes," Jayla replies, and there's a fire in her eyes coupled with a wicked grin. "Wanna join?"

I can't resist smiling. I feed off of Jayla's eager energy. Jin turns to me with his brow up like he's leaving it up to me.

I nod.

Cale gives in with a groan. "FINE! But I'm only picking dare. I shall reveal NO dark secrets!"

"Psh, like you have any dark secrets," Jayla bites back. She smirks with her plump, sparkle-glossed lips, paying no mind to Cale's dropped jaw. She flops onto the tan couch and grabs the throw pillow with the sand dollar printed on it, hugging it while beckoning Jin and me to join the circle.

"Okay, rules," she begins. "The asker gets to pick whoever they want to answer, but they can only pick each person once. No changing your choice after you get the deed or question, ever! No repeat questions or dares. And if you can't do it, you owe me five bucks."

"You mean they owe the *asker*," Cale clarifies with a pointed finger. "Caveats!"

Jayla glares at him. "Fine. But I'm determined to make..." Her eyes count the bodies. "Twenty-five bucks. And no less!"

Jayla puts me on guard and at ease at the same time.

"Ah-ah! I'd like to add a rule!" Cale says. "No truths or dares of a romantic nature."

"Boo!" Carson says, jerking Lena toward him and planting a kiss on her head. She yanks back and slaps his chest, giving him a stern look before she announces, "I agree with said rule."

"Fine," Jayla says confidently. "I'll still slaughter you all."

Cale's head flops back, and he groans. "Here we go."

"Cale!" Jayla starts, angling herself toward her brother. "Truth or dare?"

"DARE!" His answer is so fast, my nerves jolt.

"Slap that guy's butt," she says, pointing to Carson. Carson sputters a laugh.

"JAYLA!" Cale squeals. Through his teeth, he says, "That doesn't count."

"What do you think, Lena? Is that romantic nature or whatever?" Jayla asks. She sure knows her way around the room, asking Lena's permission.

"I'll allow it," Lena says, scooting away from Carson. His eyes widen, but his open grin says he's eating up the attention.

Worry settles deep in the lines of Cale's face. "I cannot just slap a man's behind without his consent!"

"Oh, no." Jayla shakes her head. "You gotta ask him first."

Confusion dresses Cale's face. "What if he says 'no'?"

"Then you owe me five bucks." She shrugs, smiling innocently. "I wanna see if you can convince him to save you some money."

Cale shuts his eyes and draws a slow breath, steeling himself. "Carson--"

"Nope!" Carson says with no attempt to hide his amusement.

"Please, man. I'm too broke!"

Carson winces, his white teeth shining as he says, "Not my problem."

Cale stews for a moment. But he still pulls his wallet out and forks over the cash. Jayla snaps the bill with glee.

"All right. Since I won, I get to ask again. So... Jin. Truth or dare?"

Jin thinks about it a moment. I'm almost positive he's about to say "truth" because he never has anything to hide. But to my surprise, he says, "Dare."

"Ooh, okay," the game master says, rubbing her hands together. "You gotta lick Cale's naked foot."

I spit out a laugh.

Jin's eyes open a bit, which tells me he's shocked at the prospect and trying not to show it. He's holding his breath, too. Finally, he says, in his most gentlemanly voice, "Cale, might I lick your foot?"

I'm ready for Cale to give Jin the relief he clearly wants by rejecting him, but he eagerly pulls his foot right out of his shoe. "Sure, yeah! Just the bottom, though."

Jin's disgust cracks through. The rest of us snicker. Jayla is proving herself quite formidable.

Cale slides his sock off, wiggling his toes once they're exposed. He makes a show of it. "I just washed it!"

"Really?" Jin asks, not sounding hopeful.

Cale nods. "Last week. I even used that cheese grater thing for my callouses!"

Lena covers her mouth, muffling her laugh.

Jin looks at Jayla. "Do you take Venmo?"

"Sure do!" She grins like an angel.

"I think you just got hustled," Carson gathers.

"Oh, come on, Jin!" Lena interjects. She slaps her hands together. "You gave me a foot rub like two days ago."

The revelation hits me like a wave I wasn't watching out for. A foot rub? My chest heats up. I turn to the wide window to watch the slow-moving clouds outside.

Have I gotten a foot rub from Jin before? I mean, I haven't asked much of him lately. Maybe Lena *needed* one. It's not a big deal.

Don't be bothered.

"Your feet are frequently pedicured," Jin argues.

"Babe, who cares about a foot rub?" Carson says. "Licking and rubbing are not the same thing." He smirks, and Lena immediately frowns.

"Ew. Obviously. I was just saying Jin could have done it if he really wanted. It's truth or dare, people! It's gonna get uncomfortable."

Don't let it bother you. Don't let anything bother you.

I swallow my pride. Even if it's slightly intimate, very slightly, it's not like a foot rub threatens Jin's love for me.

"Joy," says Jayla. I turn to her.

It certainly doesn't threaten my love for him.

"Truth or dare?"

Keep it together.

"Truth."

Jayla taps her chin, squinting at me. But I'm distracted by the image of Jin rubbing Lena's foot, and I miss her question.

"And you can't choose me! Since I'm torturing you all."

"What?" I ask, refocusing.

Jayla leans forward. "What bothers you about someone here that you never told them?"

"Oh gosh," I say, wincing as I come up with my answer. I keep them waiting a moment too long, so I just pick. "Um... the foot rub thing?"

Jin strikes me with a worried look. "It does?"

Oh no.

My gut tells me to pull back. "Actually, no! No, that was a cop-out. Sorry. That doesn't bother me." I give him and Lena a small smile. "I'm bad at this. I can't think of anything."

With that, I pluck a crumpled five-dollar bill from my front jeans pocket and hand it to her.

Cale scoffs. "You can't take that! She answered!"

Jayla smooths it out. "She said it was a cop-out answer."

My heart races a bit. I should have picked dare. Might've rather licked a foot than have Jin look at me like that.

Stay strong for him.

"Lena," Jayla calls out.

Lena sits up straight, ready for her assignment. I'm still trying to move on.

"Should we talk?" Jin asks me in a quiet tone.

"Truth or dare?" Jayla says to Lena.

I shake my head and whisper to Jin, "It's fine."

"Dare." Lena's eyes challenge Jayla.

"I wanna hear the dare," I insist to quell Jin's unrest.

Jayla leans back. "Give yourself a mustard facial."

Lena gapes at her. "Okay, look. Don't ask me why, but I know my skin will have a reaction."

"Oh, so you'd prefer to pay me?"

Lena's mouth drops open. "You little--"

Carson leans over and hands Jayla a ten. "I'm covering us both, babe. Not taking any chances."

Jin leans in front of me. The concern hasn't left him. Everyone else keeps talking or arguing on Cale's part, but I don't hear them.

He's disappointed. Why did I have to disappoint him?

"Can we go for a walk on the beach?" he asks.

Deep breath. I nod. "Sure."

TRACK 03 - LIGHTHOUSE

Still June 12ᵗʰ

I LIKE DRIFTWOOD IN A MORBID SORT OF WAY. It was once a green sprout, planning to stay put forever. Then a tree, broken into pieces after some tragic event. The ocean had its way, washing life and color off of it, yet smoothed it out. Softened the sharp edges.

And then it took a new life. Lounging at the beach, giving shelter to animals, or picked up by passersby. More than just a shell of the former; something different altogether.

It's a reminder that things can seem over when they're really just changing. But I guess there is death in that, no matter what.

Deep breath.

"You're quiet," Jin tells me, with all the gentleness I need. He holds my hand, his tank flickering in the beach breeze.

"So are you," I say back.

He looks down at our bare, sand-covered feet. "Fair enough."

"Don't worry, I was just thinking about driftwood."

"I was trying to think of a way to ask if you're okay." Jin's wary eyes linger on me.

"I'm good." I try to sound reassuring.

"The foot rub thing bothered you, though."

I stop our walk and square myself in front of him, pushing my windy hair behind my ears. "I guess so. But not for the reason you think. It was just Lena. I..."

I look out to the gray ocean for help expressing myself. Water is always so good at that. Reflecting back the things I don't normally see inside.

"I cared that it wasn't me," I tell him.

Jin looks deeply into my eyes, his finger on my chin. It's what he does when he's trying to get to the truth. He seeks what's buried in the sand of my heart.

"It's been hard for me, too." Tears rush to my eyes and I have no handle on them. "I know she's your mom. Lena's—" My breath hitches. "—other mom. I love you both so much. I'm doing everything I can to make it easier."

"Oh, Joy..."

I swallow a sob. My lips tremble, and anguish fills my stomach, but I keep my eyes on his. I'm not blown around by the winds of life. For the first time in a long while, Jin's concern steadies me.

I don't have to hold it in anymore...

Say it.

"You know I love her too, right?"

Out in the open, I finally bleed. The pain cascades from my heart in full force. The uncertainty, the worry, the grief... it was all restrained. The band falling apart didn't matter. The time he spent away couldn't matter. I had to hold it together. For him. For everyone. But...

I love Jan-di, too.

Jin pulls me into an embrace, gripping me so there's no way I'll fall apart. I sob into him louder than I would if I could hold it back.

I had fully accepted her into my life when it happened. The diagnosis. *My* Jan-di, who, three days earlier, demanded that I marry her son with a gleam in her eyes. She's supposed to dance at our wedding. She's supposed to hold my children as soon as they're born. Every holiday and history that were meant to come from her vibrant life... they dangle from the thread constantly frayed by *liver cancer*.

A few bright spots on a dark image and the future became a broken promise.

"I'm so sorry, Joy," Jin says, pained. "I'm so sorry I didn't think of it that way."

I grip his shirt in my hands, unsure if I'll stay upright if he lets go. But he doesn't. He lets me be here. Long and drawn out because it's overdue.

When my breathing is steady enough, I say, "I know Lena's struggling too. I didn't want to care about the foot rub or all the time you guys needed. Or any of it. I'm sorry."

Jin wipes my tears away with his gentle fingers. "Don't say that. You matter so much more than a dumb foot rub." He laughs sadly like he's struggling to keep our happiness alive.

But it still lives.

A smile cracks through my residual crying. "Okay."

"You are the most important person in my life. You know that, don't you?"

My heart quiets. All the ocean spray and wind, all the sand tickling my legs, all the gray clouds and waves crashing onto the shore, all of them frame him and his words.

Me.

I'd forgotten, but now I remember.

I hold him closer. "I do."

Jin still loves me with a heart that's broken. We can be weather-worn driftwood, together. We're still the same tree deep down.

We've been surrounded like this before. By forests of pond-watered evergreens and decaying nurse logs and starry skyscrapers and saltwater-brushed splinters. No matter where the currents of life take us, no matter how much we feel like we're drowning, if we endure for the sake of love, we'll find home on dry land.

TRACK 04 - GOLDEN HOUR

Still June 12th

"WHY CAN'T I GET THE BAG? IT HAS ALL THE FLAVORS." Carson holds up the cellophane bag with the 100 TAFFYS label and a huge red VALUE sticker on the front.

"That's cheating!" I argue as I scan the jars of pastel-colored taffy, "You have to choose the right ratio. It's highly personal."

After my beach walk with Jin, I felt far more capable of enjoying myself. It wasn't just cathartic. I needed to hear him say that I'm still who he chooses through all this. And to know that he wants to take care of me too, even when I'm too blind to see that I need it.

After lunch, Jin and Carson agreed to hit the candy shop with me before heading to the arcade. The other half of our group couldn't wait for the overpriced, flashy thrills.

Carson frowns at me from across the taffy jars. "Well, I want a few of everything. Same bag, more money."

"That's just how it's done," I insist as I pluck some watermelon taffy and toss it into my paper bag.

Carson flashes me a skeptical look but starts dropping salt water taffy into his bag by threes. "When were these rules established anyway? I don't remember doing this when we were kids."

"Because Mom always bought you the variety bag. Me and Dad did it this way," I tell him. "It's a beach ritual now."

"I like this ritual," Jin garbles, one side of his mouth full of taffy. "Half my bag is caramel banana."

He's so happy with little things. I like it. That, and the slow way he chews taffy while smiling at me.

Jin buys our taffy bags, and Carson grabs some chocolate for Lena. The bell twinkles as we head out and walk in the direction of the arcade sounds. Jin slips his palm in mine.

Even though every shop at the beach is subpar, with tacky neon t-shirts, cheap knick-knacks, overpriced candy and greasy seafood, somehow it's exactly as it should be. That dreamy feeling I wanted last summer finally reaches me. Breeze and sand and seagulls have found their way to us.

Jin should really bring a breeze with him everywhere. Breezes do good things to him.

I pull out my phone, and he smiles dutifully. It's mostly the two of us in those social media squares now. Sometimes I scroll all the way back to lone selfies with vague captions like "can't focus" or "think of happy things" to reminisce knowing he was on my mind.

It feels like it was so long ago, but it wasn't. Crazy how one year can be like that.

Arriving at the arcade, it's not hard to find the DDR setup where Cale and Lena compete. The music is extra-loud, as are Cale's triumphant shouts.

"HOO BOY! Another one for me!" Cale taunts Lena as he jumps on the flashing arrows. She glares at him, but I can tell their competition isn't over yet.

"Who's winning?" Carson asks. He strokes Lena's arm, but her eyes don't leave the screen as she swats him away. He's never offended when she does stuff like that. I think it's her way of being playful.

"I am," she says with some bitterness. She taps her foot to flip through the songs. "By one point."

Cale leans his hips against the back bar. The neon screen paints them both with a colorful glow. He glistens with a bit of sweat and flashes a grin. "But we have four songs to go, so it's anyone's game."

"I *will* crush you, Thomas!"

"Oh hey, Carson! Jayla was looking for you," Cale says, completely ignoring Lena's threat.

Carson gets wary. "For me?"

"Yeah, she wants you to get a perfect score in skee ball. For the tickets."

Carson shakes his head, but I know he likes showing off. Even for a twelve-year-old.

"Fine. For the tickets," he says, then turns to Lena. "Be right back, babe. Don't do the last song without me."

Lena finally acknowledges him. "Okay, then be quick." Then she gives him a kiss.

Cale turns around and rests his arms on the bar. "What are you two gonna do?"

Jin's arm ropes around my shoulders. "I'm going to steal Joy to myself for a little bit."

Cale spreads a sly grin. "You do that."

I raise a brow, and my heart races at his suggestive tone. Jin pulls me back outside before I can object, so I yell over my shoulder, "I'm rooting for you, Cale Salad!"

The last thing I hear is Lena's offended callback before we're cloaked in daylight again.

I look up at him. "So, what's going on?"

Jin feigns obliviousness. "I just wanted some time alone."

I frown. "Why was Cale acting weird?"

"Was he?"

We get back to the Mazda, parallel parked by the shops. He opens the passenger door for me, but I refuse to get in.

"What?" he says, his eyes round. Still pretending.

"Are you planning something?"

The corners of his lips turn up. "Maybe."

Oh. I didn't think he'd say it. Is that why my heart is racing? Is Jin going to...

No. I'm way ahead of myself.

I get into the car. "What is it?"

I have to wait a second for him to get into the driver's seat, but he fiddles with the keys when he sits. "I might have planned more one-on-one time than I let you believe."

That sounds more like it. "What did you have planned?"

"Well, right now, whatever you want. We could go swimming at the beach or watch a movie at the beach house. Maybe get ice cream. Or we can go back to the arcade if you want."

I love the special treatment, but we've avoided one very important thing.

I swat him with my candy bag. "Why was Cale acting funny? Tell me! I know you know."

"Maybe because he knows I was going to ask you something."

My heart thrums hard. *Maybe.* "Ask me what?"

He chews his lips, but I can't tell if he's nervous or excited. "I was wondering if you'll ditch everyone tomorrow and go on a hike with me. They're all fine with it."

I'm kind of in awe. He thought to ask the group first so I wouldn't feel bad leaving them. It's such a small but very personal gesture.

Wow, I'm so stupidly in love. "Absolutely."

He grins. "And where to now?"

His eagerness fills me with bubbly happiness. I love him.

"Let's go swim in the ocean."

Our phones. Our regular clothes. Our cares. Our everythings. They're left back at the beach house. We bring ourselves to the soft sand, wearing bathing suits and a couple of towels. The clouds roll in and block the sun, providing one more reason for Jin to hold me close.

The other people on this beach don't exist to us. The sky is vast, mixed gray and blue, the wind fills the sails of our striped towels, the waves crash into the earth we claim as ours for right now.

I open my heart and soul, splayed out on the sand like a starfish. Just like when I met him.

I like that Jin's emerald green trunks are a little too bulky for him. That he's pale and lanky, and that, when he kisses me, I have the chance to feel more parts of his skin because the context allows it.

We lay our towels down next to each other, plopping onto the cushy patch of sand as the sun briefly breaks through the clouds. Jin beams at me, all handsome.

It's never been easy to hold back when my love begs for more. But it is easy to belong to him. To know he still means it.

He stopped carrying the ring after I found it. I didn't want him to lose it, and I already knew what the gesture meant. Sometimes I wonder if I'll find the ring and ruin the surprise again.

But getting married won't come as a surprise. It's not if, but when.

We often talk about our future, but I still don't know when he'll ask to make it official. Knowing he's a sure thing makes it a little easier to wait.

And a little harder.

Him spread out on a beach towel really makes me wish we had a wedding date nailed down for yesterday. Especially when I catch him staring.

"I love that swimsuit on you," he says, propped up on his elbows.

I look down at my high-waisted bikini with the ruched top. It's a bright coral, vintage in feel but still modern. Very me.

I sit up and glance over my shoulder at him. "But you're imagining it *off* me."

I smirk. Teasing Jin is one of life's most satisfying pastimes.

He flops flat on his back, covering his likely hard blushing with both hands. He groans and not like it was a bad joke.

I crack up. I totally caught him.

When I feel like I'm about to burst and throw caution to the wind because I can't take being not-quite-close enough, laughter is a good release. It helps. The exhaustion and busyness have helped too, in a different way. Holding back has an edge, but it's dull in the presence of a deeper love.

He carved out just what I needed without being asked.

His thoughtfulness amazes me. My heart hums thinking about it.

Jin sighs and looks at the ocean. "Let's go in."

"Need to cool off?" I jest.

He gets up, then holds his hand down for me. Nodding, he says, "I do. Yeah."

We abandon our towels and dip our feet into the foamy surf. I spread my toes under the salty, clear water. Then a wave crashes into my legs and gives me a chill.

"It's cold," I warn Jin before he steps foot in.

"I'm just gonna go for it," he says with a giddy grin. Then he races into the water as promised, white foam encircling him before he stops, shocked by the chill. He turns and yells, "It's cold!"

"It's an Oregon beach, Jin!" I laugh, pulling my feet out from the silky sand that suctions them.

The water forces the chill higher and higher as each wave hits me. Being much shorter than Jin, my entire body is sprayed as I make my way to him. My stomach shrinks back into my body and a shiver runs through me.

Staying above this is pointless.

I dive completely under.

In one second, I'm back up and awash with the glorious cool ocean. I scream out from the cold and laugh. It's refreshing right down to my soul.

Jin shakes his head, but I got him smiling. "You're crazy!"

"Am I?"

I swim over, the water up to my shoulders, until I'm next to him. Then I leap up, securing Jin's shoulders with my arms and wrapping my legs around his waist. I expect him to catch me, but he loses balance right away.

We both go under. Our bodies tangle, slowing to a submerged dance. His arms slide around me and he takes us both up for air.

And he keeps hold of me.

Jin wipes his dark, wet hair from his eyes and smiles.

"I love you," he says, dripping and gorgeous.

And then he kisses me. His lips are slick and cold, but my soul lights up. I kiss him back, my palms on each side of his face. We rise and fall with the waves.

Floating.

I giggle. "This is what I was wishing you'd do when we were swimming in the pond."

"It's what I *wanted* to do," he says. "You were all I wanted."

My heart is fuller than this ocean. I'm so in love with him.

"Wait," I say, "Tomorrow is one year since we first met."

His lips form a knowing grin. "Yes it is."

That's why he wants to be alone. Why he planned this special trip. It's the end of our first year. A full cycle of us, starting with me spread out on the floor and leading...

Here.

"I love you, Jin."

We celebrate this last little bit of our roller-coaster year. Kiss in the ocean, flowing together more than we ever have. Indulge in the sight of each other under the cloudy light. It's insane that he sees me like I see him. Sometimes I feel so human and undeserving and flawed. But sometimes I feel more precious than all the gems in the world, worth every challenge we've ever faced.

I wouldn't trade him for anything. No amount of money, no thrilling career, no other person I can dream up, not even an easier life without a need for hospitals and doctors.

Jin is it. I take it all.

I trace the naked line of his neck and collarbone. The droplets make a path on his skin as I draw my finger to the edge of the shoulder that I love so much. I press my lips there. And again on his collarbone, and on his neck, his jawline. I close my eyes, soaking up the warmth under the saltwater on Jin's skin. He strokes my hair.

It feels like heaven.

My face buried in his neck, I feel him swallow. "Say it again," he tells me.

"Say what?"

"What you said before."

He's never asked me to say it again, but I think I know why he is now. Filling the end of our first year with as much good as it will allow us.

Slow and with purpose, I say the words again.

"I love you, Jin."

TRACK 05 -
CLOSURE

Still June 12th

MY SAND-DUSTED FEET ITCH ascending the wood stairs back up to the beach house. It feels like we've been gone a thousand years and it wasn't long enough.

It's good we have our hike tomorrow.

My inner explorer is excited for the tall evergreens, the fresh air, the misty green hills stretching to the ocean, and the moment nature settles in me and makes me part of its beauty. That unrivaled peace can't be manufactured.

I stare up at the back of Jin's head, following behind him on the steps up to the beach house deck. The best part by far will be that it's just us. That he went out of his way to make it happen means the world to me. We'll be able to talk about what matters to us without making everyone feel so awkward. We talk about kids now. *Kids.*

And we can make out a lot. Super bonus.

I'm sort of dreamily imagining tomorrow's hike when we walk into the house, certain that my bliss won't be bothered.

But then I see Lena. Nuzzled against Carson's chest. Crying.

She looks up shocked, and wipes her face with a swipe of her palm. Rapidly blinking with wet lashes, she smiles at me and Jin and shoves Carson away. "Oh hey, you're back!"

Carson drops his arms, unoffended. He turns to us, faking a smile too. "How's the water? Bet it's still super cold."

I don't think about it. I just walk over to Lena, ignoring the cover they're poorly crafting. "Are you okay? What happened?"

Even as her face is swollen, she rolls her eyes and smiles. "I'm fine. I promise. Except Cale beat me at Dance Dance Revolution." She laughs like it's a dumb joke.

"Lena." It's Jin's stern voice from behind.

I turn around. He's not harsh. His eyes tell me he knows. "It's okay. Tell her."

When I look back, her eyes shine with fresh tears. She nods, then clears her throat. "Get changed first, then meet me on the deck."

I want to ask what it is. Why everyone knows but me. But, with a shiver, I go to the bedroom to get some clothes.

My racing mind occupies so much of me that everything takes twice as long, from peeling my swimsuit off to tugging my sweatshirt over my head.

What is going on with my best friend?

Did I miss it because of Jan-di's cancer? I figured nothing else could upset her that much. What's worse than that?

I don't know if it needs to be worse. Jan-di takes precedence, but some pretty awful things could take second place.

I find Carson alone in the kitchen, snacking on some grapes and scrolling his phone. He's not engrossed, though. Looks like he was waiting for me.

Carson swallows. "She's out there."

"Should I be worried?"

He sighs. "Just talk to her."

No reassuring smile. No clarification.

I head outside.

Lena's leaning on the rail, staring at the newly orange sky painted with powder blue clouds and a stream of pale pink on the horizon. She's somber and beautiful, and somehow the looks are synonymous. Maybe that's just what happens when tragedy's fixed on someone.

"What's wrong, Lena?" I ask, settling beside her.

Her bright green eyes stay fixed on the sunset. "My parents are splitting." There's no fight in her. She sighs. "But it's fine."

God, she sounds like me.

"That's not fine, Lena."

"I should've seen it coming," she argues. "And I'm fine. I will be."

"Why didn't you tell me?"

"I wasn't, like, keeping it from you. I just found out on Tuesday." She rests her head in her hand. "And I didn't want to ruin the trip and make it all about me."

"I'm so sorry," I say. I pull her close to me, squeezing as much as I dare.

She caves. She always caves to my hugs. Tough exterior, fluffy inside. It's a long time before we part.

"Thanks, Joy." The hurt in her eyes wounds me. "It wasn't getting to me until I found out, like, an hour ago, that my dad's moving to Puerto Rico." She shakes her head and sniffles. "I shouldn't be surprised. He's always wanted to live near his dad. And I don't need him to be here, so..."

"Lena. That sucks."

She puffs out a laugh. "Yeah, now I'll be stuck here with my mom. But, please, don't worry about me. Jin only knew because his dad told him, and I tell Carson everything now, so it's not like you were left out on purpose."

I meet her eyes. "What can I do?"

She smirks, squaring herself to me like she's ready to give me a command. "Just have fun."

I grin. I don't deserve all these people interested in my happiness.

The sky above falls into a deeper purple as the sun dips lower behind the ocean, leaving some warm amber light. The waves are our soundtrack, lulling us to the inevitable end of the day.

So that's what all the extra time with Jin was about. The ride up here. The notorious foot rub, too, probably. Lena's broken heart was rattled all over again.

And I didn't know because she wanted to spare me.

The door behind us opens, and we both turn to see Cale standing there, wide-eyed and frozen. "Oh. Uh... am I interrupting something? Cuz I can mosey back inside!"

Lena laughs. "You're fine, Cale."

He fake wipes his brow. "Good, good. I wanted to know if either of you are up for some *some-mores*."

I keep an even tone when I say, "Did you say *s'mores*?"

He flashes a cheesy grin. "I also got a BUTTLOAD of rubber bands and a couple of watermelons to obliterate."

Lena straightens her spine and faces me. "Well? Are we in?"

I smile at them both. "Definitely."

TRACK 06 -
WHEREVER
YOU ARE

June 13ᵗʰ

L AST NIGHT, AS I STARED AT THE SPARKLING STARS over the dark ocean, I felt something I hadn't expected last night: contentment. Even as watermelons caved to the excess pressure of many rubber bands and splattered us with pink guts, it was like a dream to have so much happiness. It's been elusive lately.

Stuffed full of s'mores from our sandy bonfire, everyone in our party crashed hard way later than we should have. Jin made me promise I'd be ready right at 7:30 A.M. for our hike, so I obliged him.

My delicious anticipation for alone time didn't hurt. It's still early, and I don't feel the lack of sleep at all.

Contentment follows me into the cab of Jin's car, with his hand on mine. The drive is short, but we're not the first ones at the trailhead this morning. There's a veil of fog over the ocean vista, just enough to add to its beauty without obscuring it. Thick, misty clouds intertwine with the evergreens on the stark hillside.

Once we get hiking, it's quiet solitude. Just me and Jin. As the morning warms, the fog burns off, and the water turns blue with the sky.

We pause and I take it in. "It's beautiful here." *Deep breath.* "Would you ever live on the beach?"

The breeze dresses Jin well today. "The beach is nice, but I'm not crazy about the wet-cold."

"We could open a tea shop and warm this town up a bit." I flash a hopeful, ambitious smile.

He nods. "Okay. I'm convinced."

I leap up and kiss his cheek. "See? Give us a tea shop, and we're good."

Jin's adoration lays onto me as he traces my jaw with his finger. "I'll go anywhere with you."

I snag his hand and summon him for another kiss. And I let it linger.

This is the paradise I'd hoped for. *Anywhere with Jin.* The wonder of nature doesn't touch my soul nearly as much as this man's love.

We continue walking the dark dirt path until we see the majestic Haystack Rock. It sits among other rocks in the Pacific like a child set them down and forgot to pick them up. The scene captures me, just thinking about how this section of the Earth was laid down so long ago. So many eras of people have marveled at it. I'm the one chosen to be here now to witness it.

I'm so captured, in fact, that I trip on an exposed root and slam my knee into a rock on the ground.

"Ow!" It stings like crazy in half a second. I roll over to sit in the dirt.

"Are you okay?" Jin asks, turning back.

I lift my knee and find a sizable slice in my skin. Blood rises from the cut, gathering quickly and dripping down my leg.

I peer at his backpack. "Do you have first aid?"

"On a hike with you?" Jin says, already rifling through his bag.

I'd scoff, but it's the truth. I should bring first aid everywhere, including to the bathroom.

Kneeling next to me, Jin bandages me up. I love watching him do it, despite the throbbing pain. I love that his eyes flip up to my face for a moment to gauge how I'm feeling. And that he's also concentrating on doing it right.

When he's done, his hands stay on my skin.

I meet his eyes. "You done?"

"Do I have to be?"

I grin. "You like taking care of me?"

"I like *touching* you."

"I like you touching me."

Jin smirks. "Good."

"Good."

The fresh air fills with silent flirtation, his hands still warm on my thigh. I break first. "Should we call it a day?"

He gets up from the dirt floor and hoists me up. "No. We're finishing."

I crash into him from the momentum. The klutziness doesn't phase either of us now.

"But I'm injured," I say. I'm not arguing so much as petitioning for consideration.

"I can carry you. Like old times."

His hair falls over his eyes. It's longer now, but I still see the Jin that followed me to the pond last year. I think I always will.

"Okay," I cave. "For a little bit."

He turns his large backpack around so I can claim its spot on his back. It's always a thrill to have his arms around me, especially in a rare way, like when he holds my thighs to his hips. I squeeze his shoulders and lay my head down.

Like old times.

It's not that old, but it feels like it.

The sun peeks through the clouds, casting rays through the pine needles. Fresh air fills my lungs. My mind dances backward through our history. So many times he carried me. A few times I carried him. The smiles, the tears, the heartbreak, the longing. So much longing, even now.

I hum the song that pulled him close and carried us off together. *Rainbow Connection.*

But instead of pining after that someday when I'll figure it out, I've found it. He's here, in my arms and in my memory and in all of my possibilities.

He just listens. I get goosebumps remembering it all.

"Thank you, Jin. I needed this."

"So did I," he says, and I feel it. Every nerve of ours, harmonizing like a climbing symphony. It's not the atmosphere, no pin on a map, no empty space, no physical thing at all that tells me I belong here.

Jin lets me down and shifts his backpack. He looks ahead but doesn't go forward. I'm overcome by peace and thrill when he looks at me and says, "Almost there."

"Where?"

He doesn't answer. He just smiles.

I follow him, my heart racing. It dawns on me.

This is it.

We turn a corner, and there's a wooden carved sign with an intentionally paved stone path leading up.

Lover's View.

Reserved.

Calm down, calm doWNCALMDOWN!

This could just be an anniversary thing. That would be so much more than enough.

It takes everything in me to stop premature tears from forming. *Calm down, Joy!*

Jin takes my hand to traverse the path to a private little spot. It's a natural flat space with a small waterfall rushing down the hillside and an unrivaled ocean view. Red rose petals pepper the ground and table with a gingham tablecloth.

I finally look at Jin. *Freaking gorgeous.* Every part is amplified by his planning.

I sense he was watching my reaction. I sure hope my complete elation is satisfying.

He sets down his backpack and pulls out a few things, none of which I expected. A brown paper bag with bread in it. White cloth napkins. A covered, round container with chocolate chip cookies inside. He lays two sourdough rounds on the napkins.

"What is this?" I ask.

He smirks. "Lunch."

Following that is a metal thermos and a glass container with watermelon slices. The way he lays it all out makes me love him more. Steam rises from the white soup he pours into the bowls. The scent of cream and clams drifts toward me.

"I don't deserve you," I say, and it's not because of the food or the fact that he's such a gentleman with everything he does. I'm so overwhelmed by every intention he put into this day, and he still *asked* me if this is what I wanted.

He sets the thermos down, his hand quivering.

My nerves are set ablaze. *Holy rolling-up-on-a-motorcycle-when-I-wasn't-expecting-it.*

Jin walks up to me.

"You deserve so much more than just me, Joy." The stars in his eyes tell a story so full of love, it would fill a library of books. "Which is why..." He gathers a breath.

My heart soars right from my overjoyed soul before he says another word. He doesn't speak until he pulls it out.

The ring. The vintage gold diamond Joy ring.

I can't fight the tears. I really thought I was prepared for this. I didn't know it would strike me so hard and pull me into waves of bliss so fast.

I lose my breath when he does it. The thing!

Jin bends down on one knee.

"I would be honored if you would marry me, Joy Becker."

Sob. Laugh. I manage both at once. Why did I think I wouldn't be moved to tears?

I try to steady my breath enough to give my answer with an even tone. It takes a second, which I'm sure is torture but is also an answer on it's own.

I straighten my spine, but I'm so not steady. "Of course, I will!"

"Can I finally give this to you?" he says, his voice more wobbly than I expected.

I giggle. "Yes! Right now, please." It slides on like it belongs. Because it does.

Then Jin stands up and draws me into the sweetest kiss I can imagine. His lips are warm on mine, like a summer breeze that hits just right. Just like our first kiss, this one was worth waiting for. The promise is real. It's right now.

Neither of us want to let go of it, but we do.

And as soon as we do, I jump repeatedly from the sheer thrill of it, like a Cale-style burst of excitement.

"We're engaged!" We laugh at the thrill together. Or maybe he laughs at me. It doesn't matter. We're cascading joy like the rushing waterfall beside us.

With a peck on the cheek, Jin invites me to the table to eat. When I sit down, I realize my stomach, for once, doesn't dictate my attention. I'm not even a little hungry.

I nibble away at the food. Mostly I watch him.

"This whole trip was about this, wasn't it?" I ask with a bite of watermelon in my mouth. When I set the rind down, I notice the ring on my finger, and I can't get over it.

Jin raises his brow. "Huh?"

His confusion centers me on him. He must be beside himself since he can't even hear what I'm saying while staring at me.

"Inviting everyone. Planning this hike. Putting it on the day we met."

He grins. "Yeah. And my mom being cleared this weekend. It all worked out."

Past his smile, he swallows hard. He hasn't eaten a thing.

"Your mom was cleared? Even though she's at home?"

Jin gapes at me. Blinks. "About that. Um..."

I lift my brow. There's something beneath this. Jin blows air through his lips like he has something big to say.

"After everything you've done for me this year," he says, and it's hard for him to say it, which makes my heart beat fast. "I can't repay you, but I wanted to give you something."

"What are you talking about? Repay me for what?"

"Giving me time with my mom. For one."

I shake my head. "I didn't do that."

"Yeah, you did. And you've been patient with me." Jin's gaze falls to his shaking hands in his lap. He fidgets. "So I thought, 'why wait one more day?'"

Oh my god. Did he just say that?

Our eyes meet. It's real.

"Lena's waiting for a text about whether we'll have an engagement party or a--"

"Are you serious right now?"

He's stiff when he says, "Yeah." And less so, "Very."

I squeeze my eyes shut. "Wait, hold on." I gape at him. "Do you mean *get married*, like, tomorrow?"

He looks off like he's worried. "Well, actually, I had it planned for, like, a few hours from now."

Jin holds his breath when he meets my eyes.

I can't describe the pureness of this shock. I can't. I'm stuck.

"Joy?"

I blink away the shock as much as I can. "Your parents are here?"

"Everyone's here."

"Do they know?"

"I told them to reserve assumptions. It can be an engagement party if you want."

Oh my god.

Jin planned a wedding. *For today.* I am as dense as I've ever been.

I have to look out at the ocean again, just to get a handle on this feeling. This freaking incredible, best feeling I've ever had in my life.

I latch my gaze onto him. The word leaps from me, the most sure thing I've spoken. "Yes."

Jin's utter surprise comes on strong. "Really?"

"Why are you shocked?" I laugh. "Didn't you plan this?"

Jin leaps from his seat. "I didn't know if you'd say 'yes'!"

I can't help smiling. "Are you crazy?"

He locks me into a passionate kiss so suddenly, I crack up in the middle of it. He feverishly kisses my neck and shoulder and hands. I've never seen him--or felt his lips--this way. If I could bottle it up and open it whenever I wanted, I would.

But it would never be sweeter than this.

I have to push him away after a minute. "Okay, Jin! Save some for later."

He rubs my shoulders, adoration in his eyes. "Right."

And that's when it hits me.

Tonight is our wedding night.

TRACK 07 -
HOLD IT ALL
TOGETHER

Still June 13th

THIS IS WHO HE'LL SEE—this freckled, blushing, completely unprepared bride.

"I can't believe you knew," I say to Lena's reflection in the mirror.

She smirks as she tugs my hair into place.

I'm almost there. In my lacy white dress, hiding away in one of the beach house bedrooms, waiting to marry the only person I've ever wanted this much. It almost hurts.

My knee throbs. Of course, I'm going into my wedding injured.

Wedding. Oh, Lord.

I turn around to face Lena. "I'm not ready. Am I ready?"

She frowns and cocks her head. "What is it that Cale always says?"

I sigh. "There's no such thing as *ready*."

"There," she says with a small smile on her plum lips. She forces me to turn back to face the mirror. "You don't need to be ready. You need to be *committed.*"

She says it with a firmness that would sound rude to anyone else. But I hear all the pain that settled the belief in her. The twenty-two years her parents were together. The beat-down, drag-out fights she has with Carson that never break them up. The reason she came back to me that day in Seattle, even after our friendship seemed dead.

What helps relationships endure isn't readiness, or sense, or anything like that. It's commitment.

I cast my gaze down. "I'm nervous."

"About being married?"

I meet her eyes in the reflection and bite my lip. "About... tonight."

Lena smirks. "You don't need to worry about that."

"I don't want to worry," I start, fiddling with the gems on my watermelon necklace that matches hers, "But with trauma, it's not that simple."

"Joy." Lena's stern look startles me. "Seriously. Do you think he hasn't thought about that? Because he has."

She continues securing buttons on my vintage dress from behind.

He has?

"We planned all this on the drive up." She grunts with a particularly hard button, but then giggles. "Jin was more flustered than ever in his life, putting everything together. But more than anything, he wouldn't shut up about you. Shocker. You know what he said?" She stands up and looks me right in my nerve-rattled, hazel eyes. "He said he'd wait as long as you need him to, even after you tie the knot. He loves you, Joy."

Flustered. Dedicated. Gentle. That's Jin.

Lena pats my cheeks. "And you're the only person I'll give him to."

"Lena," I say, full of affection. I embrace her. She caves again, like always.

She forces distance between us and looks me up and down. "And look at you! You are ready."

I assess myself in the mirror one last time.

Deep breath.

My hair is braided into an up-do, make-up natural but elevated. I'm glowing. My feet are bare because it'll be better on the sand. My dress, procured by Lena and fitted by my mom, is white floral lace with long sleeves, a straight, off-shoulder neckline, and a tea-length skirt. It fits to perfection. Mom said she had my measurements from all the times I asked her to fix my vintage pieces.

That, and it's meant to be.

There's a knock at the door, and since I'm not allowed to answer, Lena does. She whispers a few things before she turns to me with a gleam in her eye. "It's your mom."

I nod, but it strikes me as odd. I just saw my family. They're supposed to be setting up. Lena tells me she's going to go help outside, leaving the door open, obscuring my mom.

But it's not my mom who emerges.

It's Jan-di.

A wave of emotion washes over me.

Her lavender sheath dress hangs on her too loosely. She's aged more than she should have, but her smile is the brightest I've seen in a while. In it, I see Jin. She's too thin and fatigued. Liver cancer can do that. Chemo and radiation can do that.

It's not over yet.

But today, I'm grateful that every uttered word of prayer brought her this far. She's worth every syllable of pleading I can offer.

"Look at you, Joey," she says with all the energy and adoration she has. "So beautiful."

My love pours out in tears. I'm so honored she came here before I marry her son.

"Thanks, Umma," I say through my overwhelm, using Jin's name for her because it feels right.

She sucks in her breath and covers her heart, blinking away her own tears.

Gingerly, she closes the space between us and palms my face, catching the streams flowing from my heart with her wrinkled fingers. "You so perfect for Woo-Jin. You take care of him, I know you will."

"Yes, I will. I promise."

She narrows her eyes at me. "Take care yourself, too, Joey. Let Woo-Jin help you."

I nod, but I can't say a word. I'm too overcome with jumbled admiration and sorrow and joy.

Her eyes sparkle when she looks at me. "Love be so hard sometimes. Is okay. Let be hard. Let be..." She shuts her eyes. "...*beautiful*, too." Jan-di takes my hand, lacing our fingers together and holding them between us. "Beautiful and hard. You can't take apart."

I gape at our intertwined hands, her soft, wrinkled skin and mine barely touched by difficulty. I've never seen our love or heard it spoken like this.

Beautiful and hard.

The most beautiful love in the world has the highest stakes. The hardest fall comes from the highest peak. The most brutal strikeouts make for the best comebacks. We don't get to choose when the pain comes, but we can choose the love it's matched with.

I look into Jan-di's dark, starry eyes.

Great love and difficulty are inseparable. They arrive together.

I enclose her interlaced hand with both of mine. "Thank you, Jan-di."

She nods, and with a shaky breath, demands, "Now marry my boy."

TRACK 08 -
I LOVE YOU
ALWAYS
FOREVER

Still June 13th

JIN IS SO ENRAPTURING WITH THE LOOK HE GIVES ME that I almost miss my own gorgeous wedding.

Driftwood lines. A sandy aisle. Bare feet. A canopy of bright ocean sky. A symphony of waves.

A beach wedding seems so obvious now. Fresh and wild and beautiful and easy. And it has the breeze that makes Jin look so handsome, especially in that sharp beige tux.

Good Lord, he is fine in a tux.

The set-up isn't the usual two-sided arrangement. Dad and I walk toward the driftwood arch covered in flowers and white gauze drapes, where Jin and the officiant stand. Beside them stand Cale, Carson, and Lena, dressed to the nines. Carson in a muted brown, Cale in forest green, and Lena in dark coral pink. Not exactly a cohesive concept.

And I don't care at all.

The seats are all together. Mom's beaming like crazy. I hear the onslaught of her "I'm so proud of you"s on repeat in my head. Now that I'm a proper woman, moved out *and apparently getting married*, she doesn't put so much pressure on me. I'm still her baby girl, if her shining eyes tell me anything.

Next to her sit Jan-di and Yuno, with warm smiles. Behind them, Jayla and Mr. and Mrs. Thomas, and Angela and Fernando, who have Diamond and Zany in white floral collars between them. Zane, Jin's blond, blue-eyed roommate, sits near Krista and Fiona. The two of them wave at me and whistle as soon as I'm in sight. Zane's consistent flinching at their wild behavior makes me laugh.

But my eyes find Jin's, time and time again. He stands up tall, pure love and quite a bit of awe in his eyes. My heart races with the knowledge of our imminent devotion.

It's hard to believe we were so normal at lunch.

And now, here I am, walking down the aisle on my unforeseen wedding day with my Dad, who knew more about this than I did.

"Daddy," I whisper, squeezing his arm. "Can I run to him?"

He slows the pace, eyeing me past his big, round glasses. I always told him I wanted to run down the aisle. And he always said he'd let me if he liked the man I chose. I don't know if he thought I was serious, but right now, I am.

He gives me a forehead kiss, because it's a special occasion, and smiles, because it's a very special occasion.

"Go."

Detaching from his arm, I hand him my seashell and rose bouquet. I go for it, racing like a wave unable to resist the crash to shore. My knee stings and I'm encumbered by a thick, white skirt, but they don't slow me down.

Cale's cheers are the first I hear, and then Fiona's. They're kindred spirits when it comes to egging things on. Everyone else laughs or claps or gasps, but it's just white noise.

Only one matters.

I jump into Jin's arms, my feet off the ground. I don't dare kiss him yet. I squeeze him with everything I've got before he sets me down with tenderness. I think I took him by surprise. By the way he looks at me, it's the kind that pummels you with gratefulness.

This is perfect.

I suddenly realize how ready I am. Maybe not for every curveball life will throw at us. But for commitment to this man I so desperately love? Yes. I'm ready.

Sunset.

Vows.

Summer.

I will take care of him, and he will take care of me.

I do. I really, really do.

Someday it'll be hard to endure the always we promise, but today it's the easiest thing I've ever done.

The ring slides on my finger.

He says it, too. "I do."

Hearing it spoken in his voice is otherworldly. My soul soars when I put a simple, golden circle on his finger, too.

Breeze.

Kiss.

I meet the eyes of my honest-to-goodness husband, Jin Park. This snapshot memory will never fade. It's sweeter and more perfect than anything I would have chosen for myself. It's crazy that I owe it to some of the roughest things I've ever been through. Crazy how worth it this is.

Beautiful and hard.

Just like that, I love him as something more. We take that first, literal step into the sand. Married.

"So, Jin told us this was an ENGAGEMENT PARTY, JOY!!" Fiona literally shakes me when she gets her first chance to talk to me. "Now you're freakin' hitched!"

"That mean you're bailing on rent?" Krista asks, lacking excitement.

Fiona gasps. "I didn't even think about that!"

"We'll figure it out," I tell them, my gaze drifting.

Our eyes find each other from across the beach bonfire, where he talks to Cale's parents. It's automatic.

Fiona snaps her fingers in front of my face. "I know your new husband is distracting you, but come on! I want you for a few minutes!"

"I said we should stay home," Krista tells me, almost complaining. "But I knew you'd say yes, so here we are."

Fiona gasps again. It means she's very happy for me. "Oh my god, tonight's the night! Right?"

My eyes go wide, but I can't hold back a knowing grin.

Krista groans. "Oh lord, someone deliver me."

"I should go," I tell them. "I don't know when we're supposed to leave."

"No, wait!" Fiona grips my arm. "As much as I want to kick you right into bed, you have to wait. We have a surprise!"

I blink at her. "You do?"

"Yes! Find your man and wait for us."

Fiona dashes off. Krista follows at a much less excited pace, headed up the steps to the beach house. They make me laugh.

I'll miss living with them. It was fun while it lasted.

But I'm also really glad it's over.

"Joy Bear."

Carson cuts off my path to Jin, but I don't mind. Not when I get to see him happy like this.

Beautiful and hard. Inseparable. Carson fits that description.

"I'm real happy for you," he tells me, and it's the most genuine and unselfish words I think I've ever heard from him.

"Thanks, Racecar," I say, ruffling his curls like I used to when we were kids. "Glad I get to have you as a brother."

There's the really great brother smile, gleaming by firelight. He clears his throat. "You know, I'm cool with Jin." He looks over at him, waving once. Jin smiles at my brother. Something in it settles all the shaken-up sediment between them. Like they're not just playing nice for my sake.

They're family now.

"MIC CHECK." Cale's voice is amplified by a mic and speaker, which were easy to miss in the dark. "BOOP BOOP-A-DOOP."

Cale stands at the base of the beach house steps next to Fiona with her sparkly magenta guitar that matches her hair and Krista on a keyboard. I love how the orange bonfire hugs their happy faces.

Just as a light wind chills me, Jin's arm slides about my shoulders. The fabric of his tuxedo jacket scratches my skin. I'll remember it forever.

"Hey," he says into my ear. "I was missing my wife."

Wife.

"Well, guys. WE DID IT! We got 'em married!" Cale says with a kilowatt grin.

Everyone cheers and claps a bit. Fiona strums a few times and whoops.

Cale puts his hand on his chest. "Now, I just want this for the record that without *my* shenanigans, they probably wouldn't be together." Cale looks right at us. At me. "And for the record, they deserve each other."

"Thank you," I mouth to him. Jin's fingers grazing my shoulder give me a good tingle.

Cale points behind him at Krista and Fiona. "So I struck up a conversation with these two alternative hair colors, and we decided to give them a special gift. A send-off song. So, you know, you both feel free to take your cute selves outta here when we get to the bridge, okay?"

We nod, baited to Cale's unexpected gift of song.

Fiona strums the build-up. My heart bursts.

Cale sings the words to *Rainbow Connection*, slow and dreamy in a way I've never heard before. Then Krista hits the keys, and I feel like I really am dreaming.

But the magic doesn't even start until Jin angles himself and tugs me into a dance. His hands find the small of my back. His eyes latch onto mine. It's just us again, despite the friends and family all around us.

"This is our song, isn't it?" I ask him.

Jin smiles. "Of course it is."

I grab him by the neck and pull him down to kiss him right at the moment in this song where we first kissed. The full cycle of us.

"Let's go," he whispers before I've even opened my eyes. I nod, rubbing my nose with his.

We hug them all. Every last one. Lena extra tight.

It doesn't take long until we get to Jan-di.

She hugs the two of us together, three times longer than anyone else. Umma.

Lena took care of so many details, so leaving is a breeze. She packed my bags and put them in Jin's car when I wasn't paying attention. Her thoughtfulness is in every detail, from the seashell bouquets to the watermelon skewers to the floral collars on Diamond and Zany. We head a line of our family and friends down the sandy path through tall grass to get to the street.

As much love is gathered behind us now, there's so much more ahead of me. I meet eyes with my *husband* from across the car before we get in. We wave goodbye to everyone. I note each of their smiles before getting in the car.

Then it's just us. As it will be from now on.

My eyes go wide. "Jin. No more nights apart."

He shifts the car into gear. "That's what I was hoping for."

I laugh. "You're really good at interrupting what I think my life's gonna be and making it a thousand times better. Did you know that?"

He responds with a very super handsome smile that proves my point. "You really feel that way?" he says.

"I just proved it, didn't I?"

He nods.

And we're off. I didn't know I was waiting for this moment. The car journey into marriage.

Jin drives us to a different beach house he booked for us up in the hillside. It's sleeker than the other one, with expansive windows facing the water. A starry sky welcomes us when we walk in. The ocean is like black ink, ready to write the book of our life together.

The house practically glitters. Everything is clean lines and luxury, like the white leather couch and the black fur rug and the modern lamps that look like sculptures.

I probably spend too much time soaking it in. I hardly notice Jin has taken our stuff to the bedroom.

I walk in, not expecting to be more impressed, but I'm proven wrong. One wall is just mahogany, stretching high next to the tall windows. The low track lights line the bed, with a gray satin bedspread and way too many pillows. There's a fireplace on the other side of the room, oozing romance and sophistication.

Jin sets our bags down by the dresser and immediately rips his tan bowtie off. "Tuxes are so stiff," he says.

And then he starts unbuttoning his vest.

Deep breath.

I walk over to the mirror and start pulling out bobby pins. My hair falls over my bare shoulders. I look at my bride self in the mirror. Bite my lip. Look over at him. Let myself watch.

We're *married* now.

I walk over to Jin to help with his buttons. It stops him in his tracks. He swallows.

"I love you," he says, so serious it makes me giggle.

My fingers keep working until I see his skin. "I love you, too. You'll have to help me next."

"Joy, no matter what happens tonight, I will always be here in the morning. Even if--"

I press my finger to his lips and secure his wary, adorable eyes. "Jin. It's just like you said."

Against my finger, he speaks. "What did I say?"

I smirk. "Why wait one more day?"

Later

THERE ARE A THOUSAND THINGS the people of the world never told me.

They never told me that all the love songs I belted out when falling in love would take on new meaning someday. They never told me how little I knew of adoration or marveling before I stepped into this stage of life. They never told me how insanely fast a human being can become your whole world. On the day I married Jin, though, one person told me it would be beautiful and hard.

It's true. Motherhood is steeped in that harmony.

Beautiful comes on a lot stronger when I stare at her snoozing in my arms. This little girl sure looks like her daddy.

I'm in awe of the small things. The little curve of her nose and curl of her eyelashes and the adorable squeak she does when she adjusts in her sleep. Every lyric I sing from old love songs means something new to me now. I quiet my humming and rock her slowly since she's on the edge of slumber.

I thought I had all the love in the world when I married Jin. I had so much more than I imagined having. I knew it would change when we had kids, but now I know why no one ever told me what having a kid is really like.

You can't explain it.

I shush Jin when he walks in, still in his paralegal suit. End-of-day relief hits us both when our eyes meet, and he leans against the doorframe to our bedroom. It's the same one he grew up in, with a couple frilly additions. The only home our baby girl has known her whole, short, lovely little life.

Next week, we'll move into our own house. No need to stay in this mountain mansion when our daughter's *Halmi* is as energetic as ever, in remission and ready to take on the world again.

"How are my girls?" Jin whispers, lawyer-specific exhaustion in his eyes, but love blooming brightly anyway.

I only look up for a second before my gaze settles on my baby again. "One of them is fed and sleepy. The other one is hungry, as usual."

Jin chuckles. "All right. I'll go make you something."

"No, wait," I stop him. My arm is going numb. "Can you hold her?"

His answer never fails to be the same. For me or for Hope Becker-Park. And I'm taken with it every time.

"Always."

Playlists

JOY'S SUMMER PLAYLIST

1. Can't Blame A Girl For Trying - *Sabrina Carpenter*
2. The Middle - *Zedd, Maren Morris, Grey*
3. Starving - *Hailee Steinfeld, Grey, Zedd*
4. One Call Away - *Charlie Puth*
5. Never Been In Love - *Will Jay*
6. Hold My Hand - *Jess Glynne*
7. Just A Friend To You - *Meghan Trainor*
8. Better Now - *Post Malone*
9. Woke Up Late - *Drax Project, Hailee Steinfeld*
10. Take on Me - *Weezer*
11. Catching Feelings - *Drax Project, SIX60*
12. Space Age Love Song - *A Flock of Seagulls*
13. Style - *Taylor Swift*
14. Bad Liar - *Imagine Dragons*
15. Forever Young - *UNDRESSD*
16. Rainbow Connection - *Gwen Stefani*
17. I'M DOWN - *Meghan Trainor*
18. Sucker - *Jonas Brothers*
19. Rewrite the Stars - *Zac Efron, Zendaya*
20. Feel It Twice - *Camila Cabello*
21. Somebody That I Used To Know - *Gotye*
22. Say Something - *A Great Big World*
23. Grip - *Seeb, Bastille*
24. Heartless - *Diplo, Julia Michaels, Morgan Wallen*
25. Bluffin'- *Khalid*
26. This Is On You - *Maisie Peters*
27. Make It Without You - *Andrew Belle*
28. Clearly - *Grace VanderWaal*

29. homecoming queen? - *Kelsea Ballerini*
30. Handmade Heaven - *MARINA*
30. Out of the Woods - *Taylor Swift*
31. Young and In Love - *Ingrid Michaelson*

B-SIDES PLAYLIST

1. Real Friends - *Camila Cabello*
2. Sing It With Me - *JP Cooper, Astrid S*
3. Girls Like You - *Maroon 5*
4. Rooting for You - *Alessia Cara*
5. Boy With Luv - *BTS, Halsey*
6. It's Nice To Have A Friend - *Taylor Swift*
7. Cool - *Dua Lipa*
8. Ice Cream - *BLACKPINK, Selena Gomez*
9. Dynamite - *Westlife*
10. Drive - *The Cars*
11. Win You Over - *Whethan, Bearson, SOAK*
12. Slow Dance - *AJ Mitchell, Ava Max*
13. Can I Kiss You? - *Dahl*
14. All In - *Bearson, Georgia Ku, JRM*
15. I Don't Know Why - *NOTD, Astrid S*
16. Getting Closer - *Justin Jesso*
17. Save Us - *Lennon Stella*
18. Thinkin Bout You - *Ciara*
19. Wrong Direction - *Hailee Steinfeld*
20. Don't Cry For Me - *Alok, Martin Jensen, Jason Derulo*
21. Falling For Boys - *Julia Michaels*
22. Someone To You - *BANNERS*
23. Wonder - *Shawn Mendes*
24. Be Kind - *Marshmello, Halsey*
25. Burn - *AJ Mitchell*
26. Wish You Were Sober - *Conan Grey*
27. I'll Wait - *Kygo, Sasha Sloan*

28. January Rain - *PVRIS*

29. Falling like the Stars - *James Arthur*

JOY'S BEACH MIX

1. Grow - *Josie Mann*

2. Keep It Together - *Matthew Mole*

3. Lighthouse (Demo Version) - *Georgia Ku*

4. Golden Hour - *Kacey Musgraves*

5. Closure - *Falcon*

6. Wherever You Are - *Kodaline*

7. hold it all together - *Sody*

8. I Love You Always Forever - *Betty Who*

9. i love you baby - *Emilee*

BONUS SONGS

Love - *Lana Del Rey*

Young & Alive - *Bazzi*

Crashing - *Illenium, Bahari*

Dream of You - *Camila Cabello*

Want to Want Me - *Jason Derulo*

GIRL - *Maren Morris*

Daydream - *The Aces*

Intentions - *Justin Bieber, Quavo*

as long as you care - *Ruel*

Dynamite - *BTS*

To Be Young - *Anne-Marie, Doja Cat*

Whenever You Call - *ARASHI*

Put Your Records On - *Ritt Momney*

Love Songs - *Sarah Barrios*

Nobody Compares To You - *Gryffin, Katie Pearlman*

Rainbow Connection - *Joseph Vincent*

Love Is A Compass - *Griff*

Acknowledgments

We're doing this Award Show style. Let's get right to it, shall we?

I thank the Lord God Almighty, Jesus Christ, for his love and sacrifice every day of my life. Victory goes to God, always and forever, and this sweet book is His domain. He used it to carry me through the massively difficult season of Coronavirus and inspired me to finish despite all the madness. So, He's **MVP**, and that's that.

The award for **MOST SUPPORTIVE AND ALL-AROUND GOOD GUY** goes to my husband, Jimmy. You powered through this with unprecedented enthusiasm for someone who never reads young adult romance books. I know that it was all because you love me.

The triple-threat award for **BUBBLIEST HUMANS AND MOST EFFICIENT HAVOC-WREAKERS** go to my three children. EV, Sammy, and Gideon, you are and always will be the reason I was brave enough to do anything. Also, the reasons I am certain of how much the world needs buckets of hope and cuteness.

The award for **BIGGEST JAN-DI PARK FAN** goes to Alicia Groff. You get bonus stars for being so cute and arting really well all the time. If not for you, we wouldn't have the adorablest member of the JSLP cast, who is clearly Jan-di.

The award for **EARLIEST MEMBER OF TEAM CALE** goes to Givens Lam. You also get bonus stars for being so cute and arting really well all the time. Your Jin-chokes-on-a-donut sketch will warm my heart forever. Also, to Givens and Alicia: my love life is a lot like Cale... ;)

The award for **MOST HELPFUL AND GUSHIEST REACTIONS** goes to Cait-Elise Vandiver. I seriously don't know how I snagged you as a beta reader AND friend, but just know, I cannot function without you now. I feel like that should read as a warning. (Update: We have now become best friends so we're on this roller coaster forever.)

The award for **BEST EYEBALLS AND SOFTEST HEART** goes to my editor, Elsie Bryan. I am so abundantly blessed to have you on my team, and to know you, and to be in awe of your creations that are separate from this project but not from my heart. You're wonderful.

The award for **MOST PRECIOUS CHEERLEADER** goes to Zar Foster. Your praise was wildly undeserved and eternally appreciated. You are a beautiful soul, and I'm the luckiest person alive to have you as my partner-in-crime. (Bonus stars for arting greatly to you as well.)

The award for **ABSOLUTE MOST FANTABULOUS COVER DESIGNER** goes to Amelia Buff, who made the cover of this book. You were FAR, FAR more incredible to work with than I dared hoped for, and the results are excessively amazing! I'll be real, I constantly STARE.

And the award for **BEST LISTENER AND BEAUTIFULLEST SISTER** goes to my sister, Sophie Aston. Your insight and love and friendship gave me lots of energy and hope while I was worrying about the aspects of this project and life in general. There is no one more perfect I could wake up and call every morning. No one can replace you.

Now, I'd love to give awards to everyone, but there are only so many (read: I've reached my capacity to come up with clever award titles). **HONORABLE MENTIONS** go to my mom, Tanja Newby and my dad, Jeff Lemire, for being supportive MY WHOLE LIFE and loving me the way I needed. To my brothers, Lucas Lemire and Travis Lemire, for giving me lots of sibling material, showing me how beautiful sacrifices can be, and filling my heart and soul with familial love. To Noliecha Reid, for loving my kids while I developed my writing skills and attempted to learn Japanese. To my Grammie, Susan Dorr, for faithfully liking, commenting, and following my author journey posts, and also faithfully liking and loving me my whole life. To all my other family members, all of whom are genuinely wonderful, unique, and precious to me. To my friends Haley Sharp and Michelle Walburn for supplying me with the most incredible friendships of my youth. Without you two, this book would never have existed. And finally, to all of the inspiring individuals on the Instagram writing community I somehow stumbled upon. Seriously, you all leave me in constant awe.

Wow, I didn't think my acknowledgments section would be so big, but I owe this debut novel of mine to a lot of people. More than I've named. Thank you, everyone.

ADDITIONAL ACKNOWLEDGEMENTS FOR THIS DELUXE EDITION

I never understood how there could be so many names in the acknowledgements until I gave authoring a real chance and discovered how many people add unique, irreplaceable magic to a book. So I've got more names!

As it was with B-Sides, I have to thank **Benét Stoen** and **Renee Dugan** for their love and feedback with the deluxe edition. I admire you both so much as writers and friends (and seriously, everyone who likes my work, go look at theirs!). Also, big thank you to my other beta readers, **Stephanie**, **Sania** and **Angelina**, who all jumped right in to B-Sides and Joy's Beach Mix to give me their invaluable opinions and reactions.

To my artists and formatters, **Amelia Buff**, **R.A. Rambones**, **Givens Lam**, **J.M. Ivie**, my original formatter, and **Julia Scott**, my deluxe formatter, thank you all so much for your wonderful hands and expertise.

Thank you to **Nix Damon** for existing.

Also to my new au pair, **Akie**, thank you for joining the family right when I needed you.

And thank you to every reader, potential reader, all the shameless dancers who joined #shamelessdancefriday, and to everyone who uttered a word of support, love, encouragement, and/or giddiness. You've made this very special and worthwhile to me. This writing thing doesn't feel like it means much to anyone else until y'all go out of your way to share your excitement for these fictional kids. Thank you, from the bottom of my heart.

About the Author

PIPER BEE was born and raised in the Pacific Northwest. For three years, she also lived in Charleston, South Carolina, where her love of air conditioning and fried food fully blossomed, and currently resides in South Texas, where queso is the new apple of her eye. She was married as a teenager and now has three kids who are pretty good at Japanese. She loves singing, learning about other cultures, watching cheesy romantic and undeniably epic TV shows, and eating, like, in general. Her current projects include a historical fantasy inspired by Lady and the Tramp, a princess fantasy many years in the making, and a science fiction thriller that will see the light of day eventually because it's that fantastic.

You can contact her at piper@piperbeeauthor.com and follow her on Goodreads, Amazon, her website, or Instagram (@piper.bee)

PIPERBEEAUTHOR.COM

Piper is *dying* to know what you're thinking!
Did the stories give you any FEELS?
Do you want to join the running list of people
who'd like to marry Jin Park?

Please tell the world about it (for science) by leaving a review on Amazon, Goodreads, or any other book-related website!

Updates and merch available at

PIPERBEEAUTHOR.COM

www.ingramcontent.com/pod-product-compliance
Lightning Source LLC
Chambersburg PA
CBHW031958120726
47898CB00004BA/1179